Dawn of the Tiger
By Gus Frazer

ISBN 978-0-9873295-2-3
Published April, 2012

JOIN THE CONVERSATION ON FACEBOOK

Go to www.facebook.com/dawnofthetiger

To my wife Kate and our daughter Mia

ACKNOWLEDGEMENTS

A pivotal element of my research involved interviewing Professor Hugh White, a Strategic Defence Advisor with the Australian National University in Canberra. His theories and scenarios have helped to form the (highly) speculative political and military principles in *Dawn of the Tiger*.

"In peace there's nothing so becomes a man
As modest stillness and humility;
But when the blast of war blows in our ears,
Then imitate the action of the tiger."

William Shakespeare

Chapter 1

Sydney, 4:56 am, 19 February 2034

He broke through the peaceful air of the wide corridor like a ship through still water. Dressed in a black suit and white shirt, Matt Lang was dishevelled and unshaven, the skin on his face drawn and creased despite his mere 34 years of age. Striding past opulent antique furniture and artworks, his footsteps were muffled by the plush wool carpet. Two burly security guards who were similarly suited flanked Matt. Both guards struggled to keep pace without breaking into a jog. Breathing heavily and muttering to himself, Matt stretched out his hand for the door to the bedroom, knocked once and opened it.

Prime Minister James Hudson was asleep, alone in the enormous dark bedroom. The light from the corridor shone through the open door onto his bed.

'Sir, you need to get up,' Matt Lang said with authority as the bedroom lights automatically illuminated the room with a soft yellow glow.

Hudson sat up quickly, confused by the impromptu awakening. 'What is it, Matt, what's going on?' he demanded, rubbing his tanned face, his eyes struggling to open.

Matt, who had walked directly to the chest of drawers containing Hudson's clothes, stopped and stared at the wall.

'The Chinese fleet. It's here …'

'What?'

'It's here.'

Hudson blinked. 'What the hell are you talking about, Matt?'

'Sir, we got it wrong. The Chinese are now stationed just off our coast.'

'Jesus, where exactly off our coast?' asked Hudson huskily.

'They're currently anchored in the Gulf of Carpentaria. Our surveillance picked them up a few hours ago — we thought they were just passing through the Coral Sea ...'

'Well, we predicted they would.'

'Yes, but as they passed Thursday Island they turned and headed south, right into the Gulf. The entire fleet is there now.'

Hudson moved more quickly now, throwing the sheets off and swinging his feet onto the carpeted floor. 'Pass me those,' he motioned to the clothes Matt had assembled.

'Have we made contact yet?'

'No, nothing, they're not responding on any channel.'

'Has the media got hold of it yet?'

'Not yet but in about 30 minutes, at sunrise, the locals will wake to see an armada of Chinese warships moored a stone's throw away.'

'All right, get the Minister of Defence and the Armed Forces chiefs assembled in Canberra immediately,' said Hudson, hands trembling slightly as he wrestled with the buttons of his shirt.

'Yes, sir, will arrange it now. Your helicopter is en route and will be here in less than five minutes. The security detail outside will escort you. I'll join you at the helipad.'

'Very good, see you at the chopper,' replied Hudson, sitting to put his shoes on as Matt left the room.

Five minutes later the sleek Sikorsky S-86D helicopter flew in from the east, with the blood-red horizon behind it. The flight path took it low, over the Botanical Gardens, past the Opera House and down onto the lawn at Kirribilli House. Landing softly, the pilot kept the engine speed high to ensure a quick lift-off once the prime minister was on board.

Hudson, Matt Lang and several other aides were walked out to the waiting helicopter by four armed guards. Looking up, Hudson saw two heavily armed Apache Tomahawk helicopters circling low overhead, waiting to escort them to Canberra. Their role was to protect the prime minister from a ground-based attack. High above them were two F-35 Joint Strike Fighters monitoring the airspace and protecting Hudson from airborne attack. Above them all was a surveillance satellite monitoring every move Hudson, not to mention everyone else within a five-kilometre radius of him, made.

When everyone was on board the pilot quickly lifted off, gracefully dropping the nose of the Sikorsky and, as it started to gain forward momentum, the pilot banked it steeply, turning to the west.

'General Draven is preparing a full briefing to be ready as soon as you arrive in Canberra, sir,' said Lang.

'Good, we need to get to the bottom of this quickly before there's widespread panic,' replied Hudson.

'Absolutely. I've spoken to Susan Curry in the Press Department and briefed her on writing a statement.'

'Good. Christ knows how we're going to spin this to the public,' said Hudson, turning to stare out the window as Sydney passed by below. He glanced back, briefly scanning the faces of the other men in the cabin, and then returned his gaze to the window. He wondered what they were thinking — whether they were questioning his ability to cope with an incident of these proportions. With his portfolio, heavy on the finance credentials but feather-light on national defence, he wouldn't blame them if they were.

Fifteen minutes later the Sikorsky landed in Canberra outside the Government's top-secret Strategic Operations Facility (SOF). Hudson and Lang were chaperoned from the Sikorsky to inside the austere concrete building, where they immediately stepped into a polished, stainless steel elevator. The doors shut swiftly, instantly cutting off the helicopter noise from outside. As they began to descend, not a word was spoken. The guards stared ahead while Hudson took a moment to gather himself, watching as the numbers above the door lit up. On the eleventh and last subterranean level of the complex, the elevator came to a stop.

The doors opened onto a stark white foyer. The guards walked out first, followed by Hudson and Lang. The moment they stepped out, thousands of biometric readings were silently taken from concealed monitors within the walls. At the other end of the foyer, where there looked to be nothing but a white wall, a door silently slid open to reveal a long, sterile corridor.

'This place still gives me the creeps,' said Hudson.

'Times like this and I'm glad we've got this facility,' replied Lang.

Walking through the door and down the narrow corridor, more security scans were being invisibly conducted. They reached the end of the corridor, where they stepped in front of a silver door that opened automatically. Without saying a word, the guards turned and walked back the way they had come while Hudson and Lang stepped into the smaller anti-microbacteria airlock. A hushed sound filled the air as the chemicals entered the chamber and a vacuum removed any unwanted microbes to ensure nothing foreign was brought into the inner sanctum of the SOF. Finally, the door opened to an expansive room. Here, rows of computer terminals, all manned by experienced operators, could monitor and control the entire country's armed forces and infrastructure. At this hour of the day, however, all was empty and still. In the centre of the room was a large, glass-walled boardroom, to which Hudson and Lang headed.

Upon their entry to the crowded and tense room, the glass walls frosted over so that no one could see in or out. Hudson immediately noticed the dead feel of the air, due to the sound insulation and the completely separate and independent oxygen supply from the rest of the facility. The boardroom was designed so that, even if the entire SOF complex was engulfed in a raging inferno, the occupants of the boardroom could survive for days.

Surrounded by military advisors, key political heads and various aides, Hudson levelled his eyes on General Paul Draven, his Chief Military Officer. Draven was a big man in his fifties — dour and grey, he looked, as usual, uncomfortable and grim. This morning his customary expression was particularly appropriate.

'So, how the hell did we not see this coming, Draven?' started Hudson.

'Well Prime Minister, as you know, the Chinese have been amassing a large-scale seaborne army for the past 18 months and —'

'And you said the most likely target was India,' interrupted Hudson.

'Yes, sir, based on our intelligence and that of the CIA, we concluded that China had aggressive intentions towards India,' replied Draven calmly, masking his irritation. He had endured Hudson's lack of understanding when it came to military practice for the last two years, after Hudson had cruised to power on nothing more than good looks and promises of more positive economic times ahead. Now, even when the prime minister needed the full support of the military, Hudson was still talking down to him.

'So now we have a mobile Chinese army anchored in the Gulf of Carpentaria numbering over 100,000?' demanded Hudson, glancing down in disgust to check the number on his screen, 'Supported by naval and air forces?'

'That is correct, sir.'

A murmur erupted as the others in the room grasped the full extent of the Chinese force.

'Also,' Draven continued, 'our military communications appear to have been taken out by the Chinese — we expect to have this solved by our tech department within 24 hours. But at the moment our communications are down.'

'Matt,' the prime minister leaned over to whisper quietly, 'is Ambassador Xian here yet? We need some answers now.'

'Let me go and check,' said Lang, standing and striding to the door.

Turning his attention back to General Draven, Hudson continued. 'So, what are the Chinese up to then? Can't imagine they're just stopping in for a bit of R&R in the Gulf before they head off to India. I expect a briefing on possible scenarios and our reactive options in one hour. That is all.' With that, Hudson was up and walking away from the table, leaving everyone else in stunned silence.

On Level 4 of the SOF, Ambassador Xian waited in the prime minister's office. The room, with its wood and leather, looked incongruous with the rest of the white-and-silver complex. Xian was perched on the edge of the old leather couch, opposite a large fireplace. He had his hands on his lap and sat bolt upright, staring straight ahead. Xian was a slim man, always properly suited and groomed to within an inch of his life. He was a staunch Communist Party member and though educated in the West, he embraced the communist ethos wholeheartedly. This made him a valuable asset to the Chinese Government. He knew how the West worked and yet his loyalty to the Party was unwavering, which accounted for his rapid ascent in communist politics and why he was now sitting in Hudson's office.

Xian looked the picture of calm, but inside his guts were churning at the thought of giving Hudson the news — news he himself had only learnt at 1 am that morning from his superiors in Beijing.

Hudson walked into the room and saw him seated on the couch.

'Ambassador, if you please,' Hudson beckoned to the chair opposite his desk. 'This is not a casual chat.'

The ambassador stood a bit too quickly, giving away his nervousness. It was not missed by Hudson, and it was a relief for him to see that Ambassador Xian was not comfortable in this situation.

'Prime Minister, out of respect, I shall dispense with the pleasantries and get straight to the point,' Xian began in his virtually unaccented English. Any of his feelings of nervousness or fear faded once he began to speak. 'Chairman Yun has deemed the current economic sanctions, in the form of highly restrictive quotas on the export of natural resources to China, to be tolerable no longer. He understands that Australia is acting upon the direction of the United States of America and is doing as their foreign policy has asked you to do.' Here Xian paused, making sure Hudson was grasping the implications of what he was saying.

Hudson, speechless, nodded for Xian to continue.

'China's future is dependent on raw materials for building a better society and securing the future of our people. This means we must have access to an affordable, reliable source of natural resources — something your country has in abundance — so China is taking steps to secure its supply chain of natural resources, to ensure we are not beholden to Australia — and therefore the United States.'

Hudson moved uncomfortably in his chair, his jaw clenched and eyes narrowing.

Xian did not stop. 'The intention of the Chinese Government is no secret, Prime Minister. China wishes to take control of your mines and establish a transportation link back to China. I must stress, we are not interested in controlling your cities or way of life. Our intention is to take control of the mines peacefully —'

'By sending an armada with 100,000 troops? This is an outrage!' Hudson burst out.

'Peace through power. You must see that to fight is pointless — you will only be needlessly killing your own people.'

Hudson was overcome with dizziness as the implications sunk in. He had to steady himself at his desk while the feeling of vertigo receded, trying to maintain an outward appearance of calm.

'Xian, this is the 2030s. Surely we could have come to, and I pray can still come to, a diplomatic resolution that ensures China gets her resources without resorting to all-out war?'

Xian looked incredulous. 'Prime Minister, you forget, China has being trying to establish a higher quota for Australian imports of iron ore, copper and uranium for the last five years.'

'But Xian ...'

'No "buts", Mr Hudson!' Xian interrupted. 'China has set in motion a military operation that will ensure the mines are secured under Chinese control. The Americans cannot help you. I think you will find they are somewhat preoccupied with their current commitments in the Middle East and in their own backyard,' said Xian before continuing more calmly. 'For too long you have simply done as the US has ordered. We know the US is trying to slow down China's development and we know that you are more than willing to do exactly as it demands. We have tried diplomacy, Prime Minister. It didn't work.'

'If that is your feeling Xian — and the position of your government — then there is nothing more to say. The Australian people will never lie down and let you come in and take what is ours. You underestimate us. Now please leave,' Hudson shot back.

Xian stared at Hudson, the corners of his mouth dropping slightly. Without another word, he stood, buttoned his jacket, turned and walked away.

Hudson put his fist to his mouth, staring at a pile of papers on the corner of his desk. He listened as the sound of Xian's footsteps faded as he walked down the corridor. The silence that settled after his departure was torture. Unable to move, Hudson sat for what must have been 20 minutes — an eternity for the leader of a country.

'Christ,' he whispered, his mind racing.

Eventually, Lang knocked on the door and entered. 'Sir, what did he have to say?'

Hudson looked up, his mouth dropping open but no words were coming out.

'Sir, what did Xian say?'

'We misplayed it. The Chinese, Matt. We got it wrong. We should have sided with them back in the twenties when we reviewed our foreign alliance strategy.'

'What do you mean, sir?'

'Reconvene the chiefs — I need to address them now,' said Hudson, more focussed now.

By the time Hudson had made it back to the boardroom he had regained outward control. 'Ladies and gentlemen, if you hadn't already worked it out, we are now officially at war with China,' announced Hudson. 'Ambassador Xian has advised me of China's intentions to forcibly procure our resource mining industry. He has assured me that they are not interested in our cities or way of life, only the mines. So our civilian population is not directly in harm's way. But I will not allow this to happen without a fight. We must coordinate our defences immediately. General Draven, you will lead the development of our military defence plan. I expect a full report ready to be implemented by tonight.'

Hudson reached over and took hold of Lang's arm. 'Get me President Allen on the Virtucon. He's got us into this mess and he can damn well help get us out.'

Once again Lang stood up and left the room to arrange the meeting with the US president.

General Draven began. 'Sir, we've already been working on an immediate response plan. Now, based on our intel, the Chinese navy has approximately 100 ships in a holding pattern off the Gulf of Carpentaria. We could send in the air force to slow them down, but their anti-aircraft technology will see our airborne attacks fairly well neutralised.'

'So why bother?' snapped the prime minister, a little too aggressively.

'Well, it may slow down their landing, allowing time for the army to mobilise and congregate near the Gulf,' replied General Draven, keeping an even tone. 'So, if we can buy some time, we can get our troops there in numbers and have a shot at pushing them back.'

Hudson stared at the table. 'What about the navy? What sort of response capabilities do they have?'

'Well, sir, since we decided a decade ago to reduce our fleet and focus on the task of managing immigration, we don't really have any naval response capabilities. We need a sizable submarine fleet, but we just don't have that at our disposal. Of the 12 subs we do have, only a few are capable of actually doing any damage to the Chinese fleet.'

Hudson stared at Draven in disgust.

General Draven continued. 'Though it would be far easier to take out the Chinese forces while they're seabound, the reality is we simply cannot. So we must plan for a land-based confrontation. Now, we could have 25,000 troops near the Gulf in less than four days. They can go head-to-head with the Chinese and stop them in their tracks.'

'One hundred thousand Chinese troops, stopped in their tracks?' repeated Hudson, his eyes narrowing. 'I'm a politician, not a soldier, but even I know the numbers don't stack up.'

'Sir, that figure is closer to 150,000, we think,' said General Martin Stephens, one of the country's most decorated senior military officials. The physically imposing man had been silent up until this point, his blue-grey eyes observing the room carefully.

'When we are outnumbered four to one, what's an extra 50,000?' Hudson seethed at General Stephens, directing a splintering look at him.

General Stephens was unperturbed by Hudson's display. Although Stephens, at only 47, was relatively young compared to his fellow generals , what he lacked in years he made up for in combat experience and smarts. His time fighting in Africa and Afghanistan had toughened him up enough not to be affected by the prime minister's disdain. 'Mr Prime Minister, I have an alternative strategy.'

'Well, let's hear it,' said Hudson as the others around the table shuffled uncomfortably in their seats.

'We do nothing,' said Stephens.

'Nothing?' repeated the prime minster incredulously.

'Yes, nothing. Let them land safely, then mobilise and begin their journey to South Australia.'

'Quit being a smart arse, Stephens. Why the hell would we just let them start Waltzing Matilda down the centre of Australia?' guffawed Hudson.

General Stephens remained calm and even. 'Sir, it's not as ridiculous as it first sounds. Five years ago we conducted extensive simulations and modelled a number of potential invasion scenarios. The analysis clearly showed that, based on a northern landing, there was only one defensive strategy deemed to have a significant probability for success — we called it the Cosgrove Response. It basically entails waiting for them to come to us. It's nearly 2000 kilometres from the lowest point of the Gulf to Woomera in South Australia. That's a lot of hard outback land to cover during summer, regardless of their technology. Let's draw them into the centre of the country, let nature soften them up, and when they think they're close, then we engage.'

General Draven had heard enough. 'Mr Prime Minister, the Cosgrove Response is flawed for one very simple reason. The Australian public will not accept a government that simply allows an invading army to walk down the middle of the country!'

Hudson looked at both men. 'So General Stephens, what happens if our military forces are overwhelmed once China has a foothold here in the Gulf? The Chinese will be in our backyard and there will be no room for a Plan B.'

General Stephens intensified his stare at Hudson. 'Sir, if our armed forces are overwhelmed at any point now, it really doesn't matter. The Chinese will take control of the mines and whatever else pleases them and we will be powerless to stop them.'

Chapter 2

On the same day President Hudson received the news that would change Australia forever, Finn Hunt was going about his usual Tuesday pre-work ritual.

It was 6:45 am and he was walking down the steps to the Boy Charlton Pool at Woolloomooloo. The air was crisp and cool, laced with salt from the harbour. The sun was rising over the imposing old cranes at the naval base across the bay. Berthed along the wharf were nearly a dozen warships, permanently docked in the harbour — decaying, rusting hulks going largely unnoticed by the populace. Finn had often thought of the irony of the forgotten ships — rotting away in clear view of the modern, thriving city.

Still, even the rusting ships couldn't put a damper on the pleasure of an early morning swim — for Finn there was no better way to start the day. He met his mates Sam, Jack, Zak and Jacob there every Tuesday and Thursday for swimming training before work.

Walking from the changing room to the pool, Finn felt the chill of the early morning southerly breeze on his skin.

Seeing Jack at the end of the pool, Finn smiled. 'What've you done, mate?'

'Five hundred, you've got some catching-up to do, fella,' replied Jack.

'Yeah, I better get cracking. You seen the others?'

'Yeah, everyone's here except Zak, he's training for some ridiculous bike race.'

'Shit, right, wait for me before you do the sprints,' said Finn, jumping into the water. Diving in, there was an immediate chill as his nerve endings registered the cool water, but it was relatively mild and he told himself to harden up.

The usual routine was a one-kilometre warm-up, followed by a lengthy chat with the guys, then a series of sprints to finish up. Finn was fast and had picked up the pace a lot since starting with the guys nearly two years ago, but it was Jack, 42 and as strong as an ox, who dominated the pool.

After Finn had powered through his kilometre, he spotted the guys in another lane, standing waist deep in water, bantering. As he breathlessly ducked under the lane ropes to join the pack, Jack slapped him on the back. 'Right Finn, ready for the fifties?'

'Gimme a second,' gasped Finn.

'No chance, that'll teach you for being late,' said Sam, an ex-rugby-player from England. 'Besides, a 26-year-old like you shouldn't have a hard time keeping up with an old bugger like Jack, right?'

'Come on, two minutes guys. Hey did you see the cricket last night?' Finn asked, trying desperately to buy himself a few minutes of rest.

'Yeah, how bad was Australia?' said Sam, who relished the opportunity to pay out on an Australian sports team.

'You have no idea, Sam. Australia was sandbagging. They were so good for so long that they've had to lower their standards in order to make the rest of the world competitive,' fired back Jacob, trying to justify Australia's miserable loss to the West Indies in a recent one-day test series.

'Australia's been sandbagging for years then, if that's the case,' replied Sam smugly.

'Whatever mate, no other team has won as many world cups as us.'

'No other team has had a losing streak last for fifteen T20's,' said Sam, with a smirk.

'Mate, you need to pull your head in. It's not like England has done anything in the last five years,' said Jacob, not letting-up.

'There is honour in our consistency,' replied Sam.

'Not when it's consistently shit,' said Finn, joining in.

'Alright, come on, let's get on with it girls,' Sam shot back.

'Yeah, come on, I'm getting cold,' said Jacob.

Jack looked disgusted. 'I'm getting cold, it's so chilly,' he said in his best girlie voice, mocking Jacob.

'Right, come on boys, what are we going to do?' said Finn, keen to get moving now.

'Ten 50s to start with,' said Jack, who usually set the agenda for the swims.

'Let's do it,' said Finn.

'On the zero,' said Jack referring to the clock.

Jack pushed off at the zero mark, Finn followed 5 seconds later. Stretching each arm forward in turn and dragging it back until his hand brushed the side of his thigh. Straining to drag his body through the water, Finn focused his mind on catching Jack. By the fifth sprint, they were all beginning to tire and Finn finally caught Jack.

After the sprints they were all breathless but in good spirits. Wearily hauling themselves out of the water, sleek as seals, they headed for the showers, talking and joking. Once changed into his 'trader's uniform', a $5000 Ermenegildo Zegna suit that fitted his athletic 6'5" frame immaculately, Finn walked up to his black 4x4 Jeep Hybrid.

'Office, please,' he said clearly as he settled into his seat. The Jeep's sophisticated radar and mapping software meant that Finn could catch up on the stock market as he drove to the city. He was aiming to be at the office by 8 am. The Jeep navigated itself smoothly through the congested CBD, to the carpark beneath the sleek glass-and-metal skyscraper where Finn worked. Pulling into his car park right by the elevator, Finn always got a bit of satisfaction from how his Jeep stood out compared to all the electric Porsches and Jags. As he stepped out of his car, he ran into a colleague walking towards the elevator. He could never remember this guy's name — was it Tim or Tom?

'How's the wunderkind doing this morning, eh?' Tim or Tom asked Finn, punching him in the arm with forced jocularity.

Finn smiled politely and nodded, keeping his responses to a minimum throughout the elevator ride, breathing a sigh of relief when they finally arrived at their floor. Tim or Tom was exactly the stereotypical 'trader' that he despised and avoided at all costs. Except for Chris, one of his best friends he'd known since school, he didn't spend any social time with his work colleagues. Though Chris did come from the finance world, they had a history and, for Finn, having a history meant he could look beyond the superficial — though it didn't stop him from regularly taunting Chris about his image-driven consumer tendencies.

Finn strode into his office, past the bullpen where most of the other traders sat. His office had floor-to-ceiling windows and a view of the harbour, but one detail distracted from its executive finishes: a framed poster that hung behind his desk with 'Gamer of the Century' emblazoned on it in retro characters. Chris had given it to him a few years back, when Finn's ascent had become complete and he'd moved into this office. It was their in-joke — privately, Finn had confessed to Chris that trading seemed like nothing more to him than a video game — one he'd mastered with disturbing ease. It had all been so easy for him that he had a hard time taking it seriously. But he wasn't going to turn down the wads of money that his employers were eager to throw at him for his 'skills'.

Later that day, Finn took a break and went downstairs to see Chris. Coming out of the stairwell, Finn looked across the cavernous floor with row upon row of long white desks seating hundreds of people. Spotting Chris leaning back repeatedly throwing a small stress ball in the air, Finn called out, 'Hard at work?' as he wandered up to his friend's desk.

'Mate, this is the engine room of the company down here, we analysts keep this place humming,' said Chris, defending himself.

'Uh huh,' said Finn, sitting on Chris's desk. 'You girls just keep doing those pretty reports and let the real men make the tough calls upstairs.'

'Whatever. Now, what's happening this Thursday? We hitting the clubs?'

'Damn right, mate, I'm ready to unleash,' replied Finn.

'Nice, I'll make sure the others are ...'

A loud cry interrupted Chris. It came from somewhere on the floor and abruptly stopped all conversations, people turning to see what was going on. There was a commotion at the other end of the office. A man stood up and yelled out to the rest of the floor, 'China's invading Australia!'

Finn looked at Chris quizzically. 'What the fuck?'

'I'll get online, let's see what's going on,' said Chris, hitting his keyboard. 'Chinese Invade Australia,' mumbled Chris as he typed the words into the Newsbot window. Instantly a front page of news appeared on the screen, all to do with the invasion. Live international commercial news feeds, social media feeds and government feeds filled the screen.

Finn's mouth dropped as he leant into the screen. 'Look at the volume of traffic, click on that article there,' he instructed Chris.

It seemed to take an eternity for the page to load.

'Come fucking on,' said Chris, impatiently staring at the screen.

Finally the page loaded and Finn read aloud from the screen. 'At this stage the government is not releasing any further details of the Chinese flotilla in the Gulf except to say that the military has been placed on full alert and diplomats are in communication with the Chinese Government, trying to resolve the situation.'

'We're going to war with China?' said Chris incredulously.

'Mate, I think China is bringing a war to us,' replied Finn, still staring at the screen. 'Oh fuck,' said Finn, his eyes widening. Turning from Chris's desk he began quickly walking back to the stairs. As the enormity of what he just read sunk in, he began to run. Reaching his office he was in full sprint. Pulling up at his terminal he accessed his trading program. The buzz on the trading floor outside his office seemed no different to how he had left it. Had no one heard yet?

'Sell everything now. Sell, sell!' he screamed to the floor as he started hitting his keyboard.

People stood up to see the maniac who had clearly lost his mind.

'Australia is being invaded by the Chinese. Off-load as much as you can!'

Frantically, Finn smashed at his computer, selling everything he had in his portfolios. If he was lucky, he might get rid of some of the stocks before the market collapsed, which he knew with certainty that it would upon everyone hearing the news.

His heart pounding, all he could think about was beating the market and minimising his losses. With three screens surrounding him, he looked at the one displaying the key market indicators. 'Fuck!' he cursed as he saw the real-time numbers and charts all head south.

'Too late, it's already happening,' he muttered as he looked up to see that the rest of the floor had caught on. There was yelling and cursing in all directions.

All night Finn and everyone in the company worked on strategies to minimise their exposure. It was virtually pointless though — the market collapsed before anyone could save any real value. Billions of dollars were wiped out in a matter of hours. By 7 am the next day an announcement was made that the markets would be closed, which meant there was no trading — and there was nothing more Finn could do. Exhausted from the last 24 hours, Finn left the office.

Rather than go home, Finn decided to go to his parents' house on Sydney's Northern Beaches for a week or two. Driving out of the city Finn considered how perverse it was that it was such a beautiful morning, the sun already hot and the sky cloudless. The drive up on the empty roads took him only 30 minutes, but he napped through most of it.

Pulling into the drive, he groggily got out of his Jeep and walked in the unlocked front door. Surprised his parents hadn't heard his car in the drive and come out to greet him, he hesitantly entered the bright and airy home and walked down the hall towards the kitchen. The walls of the hallway were studded with family paraphernalia: photos of Tom, Finn's dad, from his days as CEO of the Nine Network, photos of Sonia, Finn's mum, in various yoga and meditation poses and, most embarrassingly for Finn, the usual gallery of naked baby pictures and formal portraits of him when he was young, in his Army Reserves uniform.

He found both parents in the kitchen, glued to their screens which were flashing up news about the invasion. Finn's parents started when they finally noticed him. Sonia immediately jumped up and gave her son a hug and a kiss.

'Finn, you look terrible, poor thing. I'll make you some brekkie'. She immediately started bustling in the kitchen, her customary flowing sarong rustling with her movements. Finn noticed some new streaks of silver through her black hair. It seemed more peppered with white every time he saw her.

Tom stood and stretched, taking his attention away from his screen to grab his son in a rough hug. Although Finn had almost 40 years and four inches on his dad, he was always impressed with the vitality and strength of the old man. Tom chalked it all up to the miracles of his daily surf.

'Dad, hey, what's the latest?' asked Finn.

'Hey kiddo. I don't think anyone knows what's going on.' He rubbed his tanned, bald head in a weary gesture. 'I've been watching the news all morning and they just keep repeating the same thing. The Chinese have amassed a fleet of a hundred ships up in the Gulf of Carpentaria.'

'But why? What do they want up there?' asked Finn.

'I have no idea, son, but whatever it is, I don't think it's good.'

Back in his office and 24 hours after his rude awakening, James Hudson was a man in torment. He knew what he had to do and he knew that outwardly he was doing his job. Inside, however, his mind was tied in knots. He kept rolling the same questions through his mind: 'Why now? Why me?' He was paralysed by the questions and desperately fought against his obsessing, knowing it would get him nowhere. Still, he couldn't help but feel cheated. He'd come to power at a time of unprecedented peace and prosperity for the region. How could anyone expect him to be capable of handling this?

General Stephens knocked and entered the room. 'Sir, you wanted to see me?'

'General, come in. Sit down.' Hudson beckoned him to the couches near the fireplace in the corner of his office. Stephens strode briskly towards the couches and sat down. Whenever Stephens was in Hudson's office, he had to marvel at the man's image-consciousness. He'd had this statesmanlike office created in the underground complex at great taxpayer expense — Stephens couldn't even venture a guess at how much the installation of the real fireplace would have cost, considering the logistical problems in piping the smoke out of such a high-security subterranean structure.

'What an unbelievable situation we seem to have found ourselves in, General — the Chinese are going to invade our country and try to take over our bloody mines. The only good news is it sounds like they're not interested in our cities or infrastructure … for now. And it seems, from what you and Draven are saying, our military is powerless to do anything to stop them,' said Hudson wearily.

General Stephens looked down at his hands, which were clasped in front of him. He paused for a moment, then seemed to make a decision. He raised his head and, looking directly into Hudson's eyes, began to speak with controlled urgency. 'Sir, our initial military response is critical to the future of this country. May I be very clear in saying that our forces will not survive a head-on assault against the Chinese.' Leaning forward he continued, 'The Chinese think they can sweep down the centre of Australia and take over the mines with minimal fuss — and they're right. If we try to scramble our forces into a forward line of defence, we will be crushed.' He paused, praying that this was sinking in with Hudson.

Hudson listened, nodding calmly. He appeared to be absorbing what General Stephens had to say.

'Prime Minister, Australia's greatest and most potent line of defence is not our military, it is our environment and our geography. Let China in. Open the door and welcome them! Let the desert sort them out and make them realise that this is not an easy country to invade. Let's use nature to our advantage. Then when they have been exhausted by the journey to our mines, we attack in a planned and organised fashion.' General Stephens' big frame was perched on the edge of the couch now, talking with more enthusiasm than he had intended so early in their meeting. He sat back to mirror the prime minister's body language.

'I see your point, General Stephens, and, if we didn't have the Australian public to answer to, I would be inclined to implement this Cosgrove Response.' Hudson now looked weary. Given the day he had been through, a man half his age would be feeling jaded.

'But, sir, the Australian public cannot dictate military strategy. We have only one chance of defeating the Chinese. If we send our forces to the Gulf they will be annihilated. If we are smart and hold back, we have a chance of pushing them back to sea.' Stephens could no longer hide his emotion. 'Mr Prime Minister, I implore you not to send our forces to the Gulf. It will be the greatest mistake this country has ever seen.'

Hudson raised his eyebrows, frowned and sat back. Immediately, General Stephens knew he had gone too far. He wanted desperately to convince the prime minister not to cobble together a head-on military defence, but this was not the way to do it.

Hudson was eerily calm. 'I know what you're saying, General, but what's right or wrong for this country will be determined by me and me alone. Thank you for your counsel, but I will be instructing General Draven to deploy our forces to the Gulf. I will not go down in history as the prime minister that let an invading army in the back door without putting up a fight. That will be all, General Stephens.' he added brusquely.

Excusing himself, General Stephens stood and walked to the door, his face flushed, hands shaking and body prickling from the sweat on his back.

Opening the door he turned to Hudson. 'You may be known as the prime minister who put up a fight, but you'll also be known as the leader who signed the death warrant of thousands of young Australians.'

Hudson just stared into the fireplace as General Stephens closed the door behind him.

Seeing General Stephens coming out of the office, Lieutenant Sarah Dempsey strode over to him. 'General, how did it go?' she inquired, walking quickly to catch up with him as he strode down the hall.

'Not well,' replied General Stephens, not slowing his pace one bit.

'So what's his plan?'

'He's going to send our forces to certain death in a pointless and doomed exhibition of defence,' said General Stephens.

'Jesus, what are you going to do?' asked Dempsey.

'Get me Fletch, Colonel Main and Connor Adams. I want to see them at my house tonight. They need to be briefed on what's happening.'

'Right away, sir.'

At that same moment in Beijing, Chairman Yun was on the Virtucon to Ambassador Xian.

'Yes, Mr Chairman, my family is safely out of the country and, of course, I will stay and do my duty. It is the Chinese-Australians that I am concerned for right now. They are likely to be targeted by racist groups within Australia.'

'Yes, I know. It is regrettable, but there is little we can do for them. They are, after all, not our citizens. We must rely on Australian law enforcement to protect them,' replied Chairman Yun.

'Sir, the Australian law enforcers are the ones Chinese-Australians should fear the most. Corruption and violence in the state police services is rampant.'

'Regardless, they are not our concern. And anyway, any brutality on the part of Australian authorities will only reinforce our stance that China has no intention to cause harm to any civilians.'

'Yes, Mr Chairman.'

'And how has Hudson taken the news of our plan?'

'He has reacted exactly as we expected, Mr Chairman. He is utterly unprepared for this. In all likelihood, he will try to pit his army against ours in a reactive show of might. He will lose. He is not a concern.'

'Good. These next three weeks will be the toughest of your career, Xian, but you will be rewarded greatly for your service,' said Chairman Yun.

'Thank you, Mr Chairman. To serve is enough,' replied Xian.

After the holographic image of Xian disappeared, Chairman Yun turned to his war cabinet, seated around a large oval table.

'This morning, Australia woke to a new dawn, the dawn of the tiger. Our ascension to primacy of the Pacific region is nearly complete. The future of our great nation is secured and our people will prosper for the next hundred years. This is a truly great day in our long history.'

With that, he ordered them to leave the room. He was overcome with a feeling of exhausted triumph and wanted to be alone. If he were ever to feel his 72 years, it would be on a day like this. The stress of the last two years had worn him deep to the bone. He had presided over China for 10 long years and he knew he did not have the energy to continue for much longer.

Wrestling the top button on his shirt loose, he let out an audible sigh, slumping back in his chair. The invasion of Australia had been in planning for over two years. When the Australian people elected James Hudson, a man who knew nothing of the military realities of the world, it was a stroke of unbelievable luck. The carefully orchestrated tensions between India and China had all been part of the ruse to keep Australia at ease, unsuspecting of any threat. The building of enormous troop carriers had been carried out 10 years ago when China was ready to go to war with Korea over manufacturing and production infrastructure. The war had been averted when the Korean Government capitulated to China's demands, enabling Chinese corporations to create enormous factories in Korea, using cheap local labour. After decades of Chinese people being exploited for cheap labour, China was now exploiting others.

While the world looked on as China antagonised India and threatened invasion, China was creating a massive army and navy force that would set out from China under the guise of an Indian invasion. The reality was that India and China were working together. India, under the nuclear non-proliferation treaty, was finding it difficult to secure uranium for its defences and energy program. They were happy to play along with China and create a guise of fictional tension. China was happy to agree to generous terms of sale for uranium once they had control of the mining industry. The ruse worked. By the time Australia realised what was happening, it was too late.

The Chinese military strategists had planned for almost every conceivable response to the invasion. They knew that the Australian military was in no position to mount a serious defence. They knew that there was little Australia or her allies could do. Their closest and oldest ally, New Zealand, had long ago given up the idea of a serious defence force. America, the strongest ally, had committed the vast bulk of her military resources to the Middle East. What forces remained were preoccupied by the growing tensions in the Arctic Circle around Alaska and Northern Canada.

The recent polar ice melts due to global warming had made it possible to survey more of the Arctic region and vast oil reserves had been discovered between the Baffin and Beaufort Seas. This, and the fact that the waterways were now clear of ice, made the area a geopolitical minefield. America, Canada, Russia, Greenland, Norway and the UK were embroiled in a legal and military battle, the likes of which had never been seen before. And, once again, the cause of the conflict was natural resources. With the world in such a state, Australia could hardly rely on help from an international group, like the now-defunct UN — it was a perfect sitting duck.

China's strategists had considered all these factors and it was deemed that an invasion of Australia had an extremely high probability of success. Naturally, they had considered simply purchasing natural resources in other countries such as in West Africa. Iron ore was not a scarce resource, but China was after a large supply they could control. Economically, it was calculated to be more efficient for China to invade Australia and, strategically, it was an adroit move.

Control of resources was a key component in their strategy to control the Asia-Pacific region. Before China could effectively challenge the US to primacy in the region, they had to control the flow of natural resources back to the mainland.

For Chairman Yun it was as if the stars had aligned and he was given a blessing to invade Australia and thus secure his country's future growth. Taking control of Australia's key mines would be his swansong, a memorial to his years in power that would resonate throughout China, and the world, for decades if not centuries. Chairman Yun's plan was to publicly retire from politics after the Chinese controlled transportation of Australia's iron ore. Right now, sitting in the darkened situation room, heavy with exhaustion, Yun prayed that it would be over sooner rather than later.

It was nearly 1 am in Canberra. The lights of General Stephens' house were all on. Inside, he was sitting in his old brown Chesterfield chair. It was deep, soft and the leather was worn by time. Like the rings inside a tree trunk, every mark indicated a different time in his family's history, for this chair had been his father's and his father's before him. Normally, he felt comfortable and relaxed in the chair. But not tonight. Tonight he was tense and apprehensive. He felt uncomfortable in every position, agitated by the recent events and what was weighing on his mind.

He was remembering the Mineral Wars in Africa, which had started 14 years before. A much more complicated situation than the one he was currently dealing with, Russia, the UK and India had all been involved. The UK supported the African countries, while Russia and India aggressively sought to control the gold mines of Ghana and the uranium mines in Namibia. He'd been sent out to fight with the British soldiers and aid in the defence of the Namibian mining region called the Uranium Corridor. He'd been based at a city called Swakopmund on the coast, which was completely destroyed by the Indian invasion, forcing all the civilians to flee. British and Australian forces had to regain control of Swakopmund as it was the gateway to the uranium corridor. Lost in thought, Stephens tried to summon experiences that could help him now.

Sitting beside him was his Chief of Staff and closest friend, General Simon Fletcher. They had known each other for over 20 years. Fletch had served with him in Afghanistan and Iraq when the Americans went in to secure their oil early in the century, and through the Mineral Wars. If there was one man General Stephens could trust, it was Fletch. He had proven his worth on the battlefield more than once.

A car pulled up on the gravel driveway. 'I think that's Sarah now,' said General Stephens, standing to look out the window. Sure enough, he recognised her trim figure striding towards the house, long dark-brown hair flying in the cool night air.

Sarah Dempsey opened the front door without knocking, followed by Colonel Main and Connor Adams.

'Good evening. Thanks for coming at such short notice and at this hour,' said Stephens, greeting his visitors.

'Don't mention it,' said Colonel Main, shaking Stephens' hand. 'I assume it's of the utmost urgency.'

'It absolutely is,' replied the general. 'It's good to see you, Connor,' said Stephens as he reached for his hand. Having retired from politics a year ago, Connor Adams was enjoying life outside the machinations of parliament. He had been Minister of Defence for a number of years and understood military strategy, but also had a head for politics. His connections in Canberra were vast. There were few people in government circles who didn't know of Connor Adams, and even fewer that Connor didn't know of or have dirt on.

Once seated in the lounge, General Stephens began, 'Gentlemen, you all know Lieutenant Sarah Dempsey'. He gestured to her, sitting in the corner of the room. 'She is my aide and I trust her implicitly, so feel free to speak your minds. What is said in this room stays in this room. I have called you all here today because I trust you and I need your help.

'At this very moment China is beginning the deployment of some 150,000 troops from a naval fleet positioned in the Gulf of Carpentaria. The prime minister has been in diplomatic discussions with Ambassador Xian, trying to work out a peaceful resolution, but it is clear China has no intention of compromising.' General Stephens took a deep breath. 'The Chinese have stated their intentions very clearly. They wish to take control of our mining infrastructure in South Australia to procure the natural resources that will feed their growing economy. They are not interested in our cities, culture, workforce or way of life. In fact, they are imploring Australians not to fight, but to remain in the cities and towns living their life like nothing was wrong.'

'Jesus, who do they think they are? Or, more to the point, who do they think *we* are?' interjected Fletch.

'Indeed,' said Adams, 'but they're smart the Chinese. They know that both America and the United Kingdom are embroiled in their own problems much closer to home that are sapping their military resources. They know that our military forces have been scaled back severely and are not optimised for defence, not of this size. We have automated most of the defence practices; unmanned drones patrolling the coast and fishing waters; satellite surveillance of our region, and now the defence force has nearly as many people in office buildings as there are in combat-ready bases. We thought we were being smart about defence. Turns out we were extremely naive.' His face was ashen.

General Stephens caught and held his stare. 'Adams, don't for a minute think this is your fault. No one saw this coming and given the budget cuts back in the twenties, the protocols you developed are absolutely first-rate. You did the best you could with what you had.'

The look on Connor's face said it all. 'I should have pushed back harder. We made the wrong call on defence spending. Once we spent two per cent of GDP, then we dropped it to one per cent — when we should have been at five or six per cent.'

'At the time it seemed like the right thing to do,' said Stephens.

'I knew in my gut that it wasn't right, but how do you argue against better hospitals and schools in favour of submarines and planes?'

'You don't, and we didn't. So here we are, and we need to do something,' replied Stephens calmly.

'So General, what's Hudson's plan to address the situation in the Gulf?' asked Main, trying to move the conversation on for Adams' sake.

'Hudson, in all his wisdom, is planning to send the bulk of our military forces to the Gulf immediately,' responded Stephens. 'He and Draven have developed a plan to mobilise our naval, air and infantry forces in a combined attack on the Chinese in the Gulf. It's my view that this is tantamount to military suicide.' The general surveyed the room and continued. 'He is planning to send our men and women into a battle they are not prepared for, either strategically, physically or psychologically. Our forces have never been trained for this sort of attack. The Chinese have obviously planned this for some time. They will massacre our forces. And for what? For a public display of defence by our nation's esteemed leader. It's criminal.'

'More like a public display of stupidity,' said Fletch.

'This is beyond stupidity,' said Adams. 'He is sealing our fate. Once the initial defensive action is overcome, there will be nothing to stop the Chinese from marching down to South Australia and taking control of our mines. Once they have established themselves and their defensive lines, with our military destroyed, it will be extremely difficult, if not impossible to get them back out.'

'And this is precisely why I have asked you all here tonight,' said General Stephens. 'I cannot sit by and watch a mistake of these proportions be made. Hudson is simply not capable of leading Australia through this mess. I propose a coup. Oust Hudson — and I will take control of the country until we get the Chinese out.'

The words hung in the air as the others absorbed what he was suggesting. Fletch and Colonel Main both leaned back as if recoiling from what Stephens had just said. Adams was noticeably unsettled, putting his hand to his mouth. Everyone in the room stared at General Stephens.

'I suggest you never repeat what you just said ever again, Martin,' said Adams, staring directly into General Stephens' eyes. 'What you are suggesting is not only treasonable — it's morally reprehensible. Furthermore, by telling us you have put us all in a highly compromised position. It is only that I am now retired that I'm not bound to report you to the federal police.'

Main spoke slowly. 'You're saying you want to usurp the prime minister? At a time when the nation is being invaded by an aggressive and mobile Chinese army?'

General Stephens was calm but certain of what needed to happen. It was as if hearing his own words out loud helped confirm his belief. 'I'm saying we're going to war being led by a prime minister who is not capable of making the decisions that will see this country guided to safety.'

'I can see where you're coming from Marty, but don't you think it's too soon to be considering this sort of action?' said Fletch diplomatically, still trying to work through the implications of what Stephens had just suggested.

'No, I don't. Time is one commodity we don't have in abundance. Once the Chinese destroy our army we won't be able to do anything to expel them,' replied General Stephens.

'Yes, but perhaps Hudson's defensive strategy will work and it will push the Chinese back out to sea,' said Main somewhat desperately.

The five faces staring back in disbelief said everything.

'Okay, I guess not then,' said Main.

Connor stood, walking to the centre of the room. 'Look Martin, I think we can all see that you have the nation's best interests at heart, but now is not the time to be challenging leadership. The public won't stand for it and neither will the government. The only way a coup can be successful is when the prime minister has lost the confidence of the public and of the government. He needs to be given the chance to defend the country, whether we believe in his capabilities or not. Let's not talk of this again until the time is right — and let's pray that time never comes.'

'I agree,' said Colonel Main.

'Fletch, what do you think?' asked Stephens.

'I agree with Adams, it's too early for this sort of thing. We should be putting our energy into helping with the defensive operation at hand, whether it's right or not,' said Fletch, alternating his gaze between Stephens and the carpet in front of him.

'Right then, well without your support, I can do nothing. But mark my words, the Chinese will not be stopped. Australia is soon to be a nation occupied by a hostile military for the first time in history,' said General Stephens.

As each of them left General Stephens' house, the conversation they just had weighed heavily on their minds. They knew that General Stephens was right, but they also knew that to attempt such a thing would result in their imprisonment. For now, they had to remain under the leadership of Hudson — for better or for worse.

Chapter 3

The defensive operation mounted by Australia's naval, air and ground forces was predictable. The Chinese had estimated the response and were ruthlessly efficient in their onslaught. China's fleet of submarines, aircraft carriers and other warships quickly and effortlessly disabled the Australian navy. The prized *HMAS John Howard*, the newest and biggest of the nation's destroyers, was unceremoniously sunk off the coast of Far North Queensland without even firing a round. Over 200 men and women were on board the ship when it was hit broadside by a torpedo that turned the vessel into a floating fireball. Fewer than 50 survived.

The navy's submarines were embarrassingly inept in the face of the Chinese sub-hunting ships, which employed stealth technology to operate silently, making them virtually undetectable. This, coupled with the state-of-the-art underwater sonar equipment and a deadly arsenal of mines and noise-seeking torpedoes, made the sub-hunters a deadly weapon. Australia's dated submarines were never going to pose a threat to China's technological might. They were old, loud by modern standards, and completely useless against such an adversary.

The Australian sailors who went to do battle against the Chinese in the submarines went in knowing what they were up against. Each person on board had to have known that it was futile to pit themselves against a modern, aggressive navy. And yet they followed their orders like the dutiful troops they were, sailing off to their inevitable death. Had the Australian public understood how vastly inferior the Australian navy was to the Chinese, they would never have allowed their loved ones to go to sea.

Australia's two newest German-built submarines, the U215s, which the navy had purchased five years ago, fared much better. Powered by nine hydrogen-oxygen fuel cells, they were silent and had no heat signature. Their composite structure meant they left no magnetic trace and were ideal for patrolling and defending Australia's vast coast. Nimble and fast, they could dive in just 20 metres of water — allowing them to navigate the tight reefs and waterways common around Australia. But with only two of them in service, their efficacy at neutralising the Chinese navy was limited. Both submarines managed to inflict losses on the Chinese navy, however, after they had delivered their deadly load of missiles and torpedoes, they then had to sail all the way back to Perth in order to reload. Despite their stealth and usefulness in Australian waters, the Chinese considered them a nuisance rather than a genuine threat. The Chinese navy, not even feeling its resources stretched by its engagement with Australia, was expanding its aggression and had also taken control of the offshore oil and gas rigs in the Timor Sea and Indian Ocean.

The RAAF, like the navy, was out-gunned and outnumbered. With three Chinese aircraft carriers stationed around the Gulf of Carpentaria, they quickly created an air defence perimeter — turning the Gulf into a safe-harbour for their carriers, tankers, supply vessels and troopships. From the aircraft carriers, China launched their J-35 fighter jets, which easily took care of the RAAF's ageing Joint Strike Fighters, the F-35s. Though 20 years old, the F-35s were a phenomenal air-to-air and tactical fighter jet, yet China's combination of superior hardware and fighter training made the Australian F-35s easy targets.

The fight for air supremacy over the Gulf was over before it began. In the space of a few days the main thrust of Australia's air force was all but destroyed. The RAAF was forced to hold back its remaining planes for fear that they would be without any air force. As it was, the air force had been reduced to 'air support' as opposed to 'force'.

With air protection assured, the Chinese troopships unloaded their infantry at a small port called Karumba. This was the launching pad for the Chinese army's sweep down to South Australia.

And so it was that the defence of Australia was left to the infantry. Never before had Australians been forced to fight for their land so literally. The infantry was outnumbered, with little or no air support; they were ill-equipped and poorly trained for this sort of operation, and disillusioned by the staggering might of the Chinese army. Every form of transportation was used to get as many of the country's fighting men and women to the frontline. By air, by road, by rail, the military descended on the small town of Cloncurry in Queensland, not far from Mount Isa. Over 20,000 Australian troops were gathered in less than seven days. Reports had made it back to the troops of the sinking of *HMAS John Howard* and the huge losses suffered by the navy and air forces. This further enraged the troops and it was the topic of many conversations around the camp.

The battle lines had been drawn. Australia's defence would be decided in the desert areas north of Cloncurry. This would be the first push by the Australian army in an attempt to force the Chinese back to Karumba. It would be a joint strike at the mobilised Chinese army with support from the RAAF. While outwardly everyone was full of bravado, the dire reality of the situation could not be mistaken. They were up against insurmountable odds. The only hope, they knew, was to inflict immediate and heavy losses on the Chinese and force them to reconsider their initial plan, perhaps even provoking them to retreat and re-evaluate their options. This would give the Australian army time to manoeuvre and surround the Chinese in an attempt to curb their advance.

The fighting was fierce. Day and night the artillery and air strikes bombarded the battleground. Heavy losses were incurred on both sides. China could afford them, but Australia could not. In the three days of fighting, the Australian forces did not push the Chinese back one millimetre. At the very pointy end of Australia's defence was the 5th Battalion Infantry Regiment, a proud and distinguished unit whose history went back to the Second World War. In the Vietnam conflict of the 1960s, the battalion earned the name 'Tiger Battalion' for its ferocious and highly efficient fighting ability in the jungle.

Major Pete Cowell commanded C Company of the Tiger Battalion. He had barely slept in the last three days of conflict and now, sitting in his foxhole surrounded by a rag-tag bunch of men whose rank meant nothing at this stage of fighting, his eyes became uncontrollably heavy. There was a respite in the fighting, a lull that had a distinct feeling of being the eye of the storm. With the almost rhythmic sound of heavy artillery landing on the Chinese forces nearby, his world was fast turning black and he was slipping into unconsciousness. It was night, and even this far north it was cool in the desert. The air was filled with a myriad of constantly changing smells. One second it was crisp, clean and earthy, as the desert should smell, then the breeze would change and the smell of death, violence and pain would fill the air. At times, the air was so thick with the stench of death that Major Cowell felt he was choking.

Most of the men had never seen real combat — the training camps and joint exercises could never compare to the fighting they had just been through. At times the men were fighting hand-to-hand with knives and their bare hands. This sort of fighting hadn't been seen since Vietnam, a war that was ancient history to most of them. Over the course of these few days, the morale of the men had gone from gung-ho bravado to resolute doggedness to desperation and, finally, to pure survival. The kind of survival instinct that none of them had even known they had. It couldn't be described as a sense or knowing, more of a deep vibration at each person's core. Though their bodies were spent and their minds numb with depletion, there was still this vibration. None of them spoke of it. There was no time to dwell on introspection, but each recognised it as their will to survive.

Cowell tried to think of his wife and two daughters but he couldn't. His mind refused to bring up their images. It was as though his mind was protecting him, not wanting their memory in any way associated with this hell. He was happy to let sleep take over and relieve him of the moment.

'Major,' he heard faintly. 'Major!' louder this time. Layers of noise came to him — the sounds of artillery, the commotion of men with gear. Opening his eyes he could see Corporal Higgins' battle-scarred face close to his own, yelling his name. It was night, but flashes of artillery constantly broke the darkness. Suddenly he was starkly aware of where he was and his ears registered the exploding sounds even faster. His vision sharpened and he was suddenly very much in the present.

'Major! We've got orders to move out!' yelled Corporal Higgins above the artillery.

'What's going on, Corporal?' Cowell rubbed his dirty face.

'Sir, HQ've posted new orders.'

'Christ,' said Cowell tapping on his wrist mounted screen reading the orders, 'this has to be a last-ditch effort,'

'Sir, the men are ready to move out —'

An artillery round exploded nearby, showering them with dirt and making them curl their bodies into a ball, protecting as much of their flesh as possible.

'—but they don't have a lot left in the tank,' yelled Higgins, resuming the conversation as he straightened up.

'Corporal, this is it. This is our last chance to push the enemy back,' yelled Cowell above the artillery.

'Yes, sir! So what's the plan?' replied Higgins.

'Men,' Cowell yelled to the others in the foxhole, 'huddle! We have an objective and it is imperative we achieve it. We are to advance on the Chinese forward post, here.' He pointed to the digital mapscreen unfurled on the ground in front of them. 'We will have artillery support and B Company will be flanking the post to our left, so watch your friendly fire and remember that our guys are out there, too.

'Okay, Corporal Higgins, I want you to take your section out to the right 200 metres before flanking the Chinese post. Be careful, we don't know if the Chinese have moved into position out there. You may stumble upon enemy fire. If you do, retreat and come up behind us. Our objective is this forward post. Nothing else. Understood?'

'Yes, sir,' replied Higgins.

'Right. The rest of you are with me. We move quickly and silently up to this point. Here we wait while our artillery boys hammer the hell out of them. When they've had a good dose of Aussie fireworks we go in and clean up while Higgins' team causes confusion on the right and B Company sweeps through on the left. Any questions?'

The men were stoic and silent. They were experienced enough to know that what the major had just explained to them was going to be difficult, if not impossible even though he described it like it was a straightforward operation. But they had been conducting similar operations in the last three days, all of which had ravaged their battalion.

Higgins knew that this was another insane operation that the commanders deemed necessary. He knew it was all pointless — he knew it right from the start of the defence, when he'd been sent from the Darwin US Military Base, where he'd been enjoying the cushy posting after some tough tours of duty in the Middle East and Africa to help out the Aussie forces. But soldiers simply do, they don't question, postulate or consider, even if it's someone else's country they're fighting for. Ruthless execution of orders and fulfilment of your mission at all costs was what his sergeant always said during his training. Here he was and he would do exactly that, no matter what the cost.

'Set Higgins?' called Major Cowell.

'Yessir,' replied Higgins through gritted teeth.

'Then let's have some hustle. C'mon — move out!' said Major Cowell through his clenched jaw.

Corporal Higgins looked into the faces of his four remaining men, Jones, Jameson, Cahill and Davis, nodded grimly and moved them out silently over the top of the foxhole with no dramatics. The Chinese either didn't see them or were waiting to see what they were up to, as there was no hail of bullets. 'All right men, follow me, heads down, eyes up. Let's go!'

Higgins crawled along the dirt and sand. There was little cover in the desert and the Chinese used sophisticated night vision and thermal-imaging head-gear that meant they could spot the enemy over a hundred metres away. There was nowhere to hide in the desert, nowhere except the odd shrub or occasional rock — and the shrubs couldn't stop a well-thrown pebble.

What the fuck have we got going on here? thought Higgins. The going was slow and painful, crawling over rocks and hard-packed dirt. After about one hundred metres he checked his wrist-mounted GPS for their position on the attack map. Another hundred metres and he would make a 70-degree turn to the left and start heading directly towards the objective. Their artillery was pounding around them. The Chinese were certainly taking a hammering. It would stop soon though, and that would signal their turn.

After another hundred metres on their chests, Higgins stopped, rechecked his GPS and made the turn. Crouched low, he moved as quickly as possible — eyes straining to stay at the top of their sockets, ears aching with concentration, skin raw and prickly as a cold sweat layered his filthy skin.

Just another 20 metres then we're in position, he thought to himself.

Come on! Ten more now, little bit further …

Finally in position, he tapped his GPS screen, sending a coded signal to the major and B Company announcing that they were in position and ready. The artillery had stopped now. Over his earpiece the major's voice came through with crystal clarity, 'Okay, we're moving in. Higgins, give it 60 seconds then commence your assault.'

'Copy that,' responded Higgins.

He heard the crackle of the machine guns and the muzzle flashes from what looked like hundreds of rifles from the Aussie side.

Sixty seconds. Forty-five seconds. Thirty seconds, he counted down to himself, watching the firefight just a few hundred metres away from his men.

'Fuck this, let's go!' he yelled as he lifted himself, heaving his body armour. Raising his fully automatic RP-12 assault rifle to his shoulder, he moved forward at a slow but methodical pace. The sound of his men behind him doing the same comforted him.

Moving more quickly now, Higgins and his men were almost running when he saw out of the corner of his eye the flashes from rifles and heard the distinct whine of Chinese bullets passing within centimetres of his head.

'Down!' he yelled, falling straight to his chest and turning to the right, the direction of the fire. Taking aim, he cleared a few rounds in the direction of the muzzle flashes.

They snake-crawled as quickly as possible toward a large rock, bullets smashing into the ground centimetres from their bodies. Scuttling behind the rock in a cloud of dust and heavy breathing, Higgins and three others huddled. Not far away Jones, a young guy from Lennox Head, lay face down and still — no time to worry about him now.

'Fuck, we have to get over there and flank the objective or the major will be cut down,' Higgins shouted to the others.

Higgins tapped his throat mic to connect to Major Cowell. 'Major, we are under enemy fire, pinned down, cannot get to you!' he yelled above the sound of the firing.

'Affirmative, Corporal, do your best to get over here. We're pressing forward!' came the major's voice through the earpiece.

'Corporal, what about Jonesie?' asked Davis.

'No time, he's gone, and we will be too if we don't get over to the major,' replied Higgins. 'Grenades? How many grenades do you have?'

'Three,' 'None,' 'Three,' came the replies.

'Davis, you and me split the grenades. Jameson, Cahill, you cover us.'

Turning to Davis, Higgins continued. 'You break left — I'm going right. At the count of five, we throw. And make them count.'

'Let's do it!' said Davis, composing himself.

Higgins and Davis took two grenades each and pulled the pins, clasping them tightly in each hand, ready to throw.

'Ready?' asked Higgins, and without waiting for a reply, barked 'Now!'

Running out from behind the rock and into the enemy fire, Higgins ducked and weaved his way through the hail of bullets. He counted to five before hurling both grenades.

Two successive explosions rang out as his grenades hit their targets, plumb in the middle of the Chinese dugout, followed closely by a huge explosion to his left where Davis had run. Davis had been mowed down by enemy fire and the grenades had gone off beside him, very nearly taking out the others behind the rock.

Running back to the others and collecting his rifle, Higgins told the men to move out. The three of them now moved quickly and silently toward the ensuing battle, rifles at their shoulders, eyes scanning for movement in the darkness which was constantly illuminated by bright bursts of light.

'Major,' he yelled with his finger on his throat mic, 'Major, we're flanking to the right, I repeat we are flanking to the right.'

'Copy that, Corporal, we are under heavy machine gunfire. Attack the position I'm highlighting on the attack map.'

'Yessir,' responded Higgins, looking down at the screen on his wrist.

Beckoning his remaining two men forward, he asked, 'You guys copy that?'

The men nodded feverishly.

'Right, spread out, keep low. Jameson, here, you take this,' handing him one of the two remaining grenades. 'These are the last two, let's make 'em count.'

'You bet,' replied Jameson.

Spreading out in a line, they crept forward slowly, every nerve ending screaming information to their brain. The men could see the dugout and the machine gun that was ripping into the major's team. Higgins could see the silhouette of the Chinese soldiers in the dugout.

Calmly dropping to one knee, Higgins pulled out his last grenade, unpinned it and threw it in one fluid motion as he dropped for cover. The grenade sailed through the air and into the dugout. The Chinese stopped firing momentarily as they realised what had just joined them. A split second later and the grenade exploded, sending pieces of flesh and metal flying.

Without hesitation, Higgins and his men leapt into the destroyed dugout for shelter. Holding the button on his throat mic Higgins yelled, 'Major, dugout secured, I repeat, dugout secured.'

'Copy that Corporal. Now focus your attention on the main Chinese line. I'm highlighting them now, do you see?'

'Yessir, I have it.'

'B Company is under heavy fire but is pushing through. I'm not waiting for them though. Let's keep the momentum,' continued the major. His team had sustained heavy losses, but he'd be damned if he was slowing down now that they had the advantage.

'Do you want us to move down to your position, sir?' asked Higgins.

'No, you keep out to our right and come in on a pincer movement.'

'Yessir. Say the word, we're ready to move out,' replied Higgins, turning to look at the others. He knew the next stage was the most difficult and would in all likelihood result in their deaths.

'Move out,' came the order from Major Cowell through their earpieces.

Heaving his body up, Higgins readied himself to face the enemy fire once again. He looked over to his left and made out the silhouettes of the major's team with their muzzle flashes moving quickly forward. Raising his rifle he fired at the Chinese line, aiming only at the white flashes coming from the enemy guns.

Moving forward as quickly as possible, they were soon running. Mouth open, Higgins wasn't thinking anymore. He just ran and fired his weapon as accurately as possible — which wasn't very precise given the terrain, darkness and speed they were moving. Higgins didn't notice that the further forward they ran, the less the enemy fired back.

Still running forward and firing sporadically, Higgins finally noticed that there were no more muzzle flashes coming from the Chinese side. It was quieter, there was less movement around them and no bullets in the air.

Confused, he kept moving. Reaching the enemy trench, they dived in, the dirt sticking to their sweat-covered skin and soaked clothing. Jameson was beside him breathing heavily. Cahill was nowhere to be seen. 'What the fuck?!' said Jameson, 'Where are they?'

No time to answer. They could see movement out of the corners of their eyes. Someone was running toward them down the trench. Lifting their weapons, they took aim. Higgins recognised the loping gait more than anything — it was the major.

'Major!' he yelled, lowering his rifle.

'They fucking ran, Corporal,' panted the major, struggling to catch his breath. 'Soon as they saw that we'd busted through their first line, the little cunts turned and ran!'

'We got 'em on the back foot now,' replied Higgins.

'Yep, we can have these bastards, we can push 'em back to where they came from,' said the major with a fierce look in his eyes. He was high on adrenalin and the chemicals the army gave them to stay awake. This was the first taste of victory, however small, that the Australian infantry had achieved since the fighting began.

'We need to set up a defensive position here — we can't risk losing this ground to a counterattack,' said the major rapidly. 'Higgins, I want you to take your men back to base camp and bring up as much ammunition and supplies as possible.'

'But sir, can't the support company bring that forward? Like you said, we can't lose this ground to a counterattack.'

'Support company? They could take hours just to get themselves organised. No, I want you to go back immediately, is that understood?' said Major Cowell.

'Yessir, understood.'

'Good man, Corporal. You did a bloody good job out there tonight. I'll be recommending you for a promotion.'

'Thank you Major,' replied Higgins brusquely.

With that, the major turned and in a low crouch he jogged back down the trench line. 'Jameson, let's get the ammo and get back here,' ordered Higgins. The adrenalin was quickly wearing off and being replaced by a heavy tiredness. Higgins knew they had to keep moving or they would collapse with exhaustion.

Higgins checked his bearings and led Jameson out of the trench, back the way they had come. They moved quickly and silently through the cool night air. A 30-minute jog later and they were at the base camp they had left earlier that night. In an hour or so it would be light — and they did not want to be out of the trenches in the light of day.

'Help me with the PAL,' said Higgins, opening a large alloy crate containing the PAL, an exoskeleton Power Assisted Limb suit worn by the operator to aid in carrying substantial loads.

Suited up, Higgins and Jameson looked like alien cyborgs.

They loaded one another's backs with munitions. Each was able to carry nearly 300 kilograms with the PALs.

'Remember, take it easy for the first few minutes,' said Higgins, 'PAL will mess with your coordination with these loads.'

'I'm good,' replied Jameson, moving forward — slowly at first.

They were able to walk at a good pace despite the difficult terrain. The PAL sensors could maintain perfect balance for the operator at up to 45-degree angles.

Shortly after starting out, they saw and heard the enemy counterattack. The night turned to day as mortars and artillery lit up the sky, the ground shaking beneath their feet. Unmanned jet-powered drones swooped down low and fast over the ground, unleashing thousands of rounds on the Australians with each pass.

'Come on! Eject the loads. Let's get into it!' yelled Higgins to Jameson.

Hitting the emergency release button on his suit, the munitions dropped instantly to the ground.

'Switch your PAL to combat setting,' yelled Higgins, checking the ammunition count on his RP-12. 'No time to eject!'

None of the soldiers liked using the PAL in live combat. The armour couldn't stop a direct hit and there had been cases of PALs jamming up completely. When hit effectively, they seized up, leaving the operator a sitting duck. Because of all this, they were generally considered too risky for combat. But at least in combat setting the PAL suits became faster and more responsive than in their load-bearing setting.

Higgins and Jameson sprinted to the forward line. The closer they got, the more carnage they could make out. Then people began to appear, running towards them. Higgins spotted the major, injured but still barking orders.

'Turn around! Get back to the base camp and set up a defensive line!' yelled the major, tracer rounds framing him as he ran toward Higgins.

The unmanned Chinese tanks were unleashing a hail of bullets and munitions on the retreating soldiers — no mercy from the enemy. Not that Australia had shown any mercy earlier when the Chinese had retreated.

In the PAL suit Higgins was faster than the others, so he dropped to a knee and started to lay down suppression fire on the Chinese, hoping to buy the others some time to retreat.

As the major ran toward Higgins, a plume of blood vapour exploded in front of his torso. Half a second later he went down, face-first into the ground.

Higgins was up, running towards him. A bullet smashed into the shoulder armour of the PAL, twisting Higgins wildly. Regaining control, he ran forward to where the major lay.

Reaching him, Higgins kneeled down. 'Sir, get up!' he yelled over the carnage around them.

The major mumbled something Higgins couldn't make out.

Higgins, looking down at the major's back, could see a small smouldering hole in his armour. Higgins realised that he must have been hit.

'Major, come on. We have to move!' screamed Higgins, teeth grinding as he leaned down and hauled the major up to sitting so that he could get him onto his shoulder.

Higgins saw the blank look on the major's face as another volley of rounds punctured the air close by. He looked incredulous, not in any pain, just sitting there confused. At that moment, a small-calibre, hyper-velocity round entered the major's back plate of his armour, shredding through the kevlar composite with ease. The round ripped through his sternum, exiting with a spray of blood, flesh and shards of bone, much of it ended up on Higgins.

In shock, he let go of the major's limp body and stumbled backwards, falling. The major's blood covered virtually every part of Higgins and the PAL unit above the waist. His eyes were the only bits of his face that were not covered in gore.

He sat frozen, legs spread, arms propping him up, staring at the major's ruined body. He fell back, lying in the dirt, paralysed. An intense ringing in his ears drowned out everything. The flashes of explosions were all in the background now, and the strobe effect of the light seemed to draw him further into a state of shock.

Higgins' fuzzy mind slowly came back to him. An intense feeling of vertigo overcame him, and he was overcome by nausea. He leant over to his right to vomit the contents of his stomach up. Picking himself up groggily, he focussed hard on willing his limbs to move. As soon as he did, the PAL took over and he began to run quickly back to the trench.

Crashing into the safety of the trench, he saw Jameson firing furiously at the enemy. Higgins wiped his mouth and noticed the blood and bone on his hand. It took a second for him to realise it was the remains of the major on his face. Scrubbing furiously at his face with his gloved hands, he rubbed so hard his face was scratched and red and sore.

Jameson, still firing, looked down at Higgins rubbing his face. 'Get the fuck up here! Shoot! Shoot!' he yelled.

Higgins ignored him, so Jameson paused shooting long enough to kick him. It was enough to give Higgins a physical sensation to grab onto and focus on.

Slowly Higgins stood and lifted his rifle. Taking position beside Jameson, he unleashed his weapon on anything that moved.

With every burst of fire he became more and more focussed on the present, on what was going on around him and on his uncontrollable fury. Half-man, half-machine, flesh, blood and bone adorning his body, he was a terrifying sight. The enemy would receive no mercy from Corporal James Higgins.

The order came after another two hours of intense fighting: 'RETREAT IMMEDIATELY.'

For most of those on the frontline it was a welcome order. They were beyond exhausted mentally and physically. Many of them were collapsing unconscious, their bodies unable to continue after the fierce fighting. But the order was a bitter pill to swallow for Higgins. He knew there was little hope of holding back the Chinese forces, but he couldn't stand the thought of being beaten. The pain he felt to his pride far outweighed any physical pain. He felt embarrassed that they had not been able to succeed in their mission. He could barely look Jameson in the eye.

Even though the order was simply to retreat as opposed to surrender, he knew that Australia was screwed. They had suffered too many losses and the Chinese were too strong. The walls of Fortress Australia had been breached and now the enemy had the chance to build a foothold. They now had a platform from which to launch the second phase of their plan — securing the mines of South Australia.

At the end of the fighting, over 10,000 Australians, and a good percentage of the US soldiers who were assigned to the battle from their base in Darwin, were either dead or seriously wounded. Nearly 30,000 Chinese were dead or wounded — acceptable losses by Chinese standards. Their military still vastly outnumbered the Australians, who were now half the fighting contingent they were at the outset. After just over a week of bloody fighting, it was clear that Australia had no chance of stopping the Chinese.

The Australian public could take no more either, as people were bombarded with high-definition graphic images from Sky World and BBCNN. The channels broadcast 24-hour live coverage, with military analysts providing commentary and speculation. The charts, the maps, the statistics were overwhelming. Every Australian with a digital media device could see the same sorts of reports Australia's military leaders were seeing.

This was one reality show that the public could not stomach. The media's no-holds-barred coverage made watching almost unbearable for many. However, in the vain belief that watching the massacre was akin to a show of support for the soldiers, many of the people thought it was the public's duty to watch.

Hudson, finally recognising the futility of the conflict and embattled daily by waves of outrage from the public, had called the troops back.

Barely weeks after Chinese soldiers set foot on Australian soil, Prime Minister Hudson addressed the Australian public from the SOF in Canberra, where he had been holed up since news of the attack. The government PR machine was now up to speed and trying to salvage some level of dignity in the face of such a horrific defeat. Hudson and his handlers spent hours honing the speech and the way he should deliver the address. Hudson felt prepared — he could easily have been an accomplished actor, had he the courage as a younger man to step into the spotlight.

Sitting in front of the camera, Hudson straightened his tie, though he desperately wanted to loosen it. The production crew fussed with cables and microphones around him. His make-up stylist walked up with her toolbox and started putting the finishing touches on Hudson, creating a flawless veneer impenetrable to the high definition cameras used.

'Thirty seconds, Mr Prime Minister,' said a young producer, clearly nervous.

Hudson nodded.

Matt approached him from where he'd been standing behind the cameras. 'Sir, Netrating data has estimated 27 million connections — that's an audience of pretty much everyone with a screen.'

'Thanks Matt,' replied Hudson, exhaling audibly.

'Ten seconds,' said the producer, 'clear the prime minister, please.' Matt gave Hudson a reassuring look, then turned to get behind the cameras, leaving Hudson alone.

'Five, four, three, two,' counted down the young producer.

Staring directly at the camera, Hudson blinked, felt his forehead prickle with sweat, swallowed once and breathed in. 'People of Australia. History has been written by a hand other than our own. Facing an enemy that greatly outnumbers our brave fighting men and women, we have stared into the abyss. On our present course, our future is bleak.

'The simple truth is that there is no physical way our troops can stop the Chinese from taking over the mines.' Hudson paused and intensified his look into the camera, which zoomed tightly in on his face. 'Which is why,' he continued, 'in consultation with the cabinet and our military leaders, I have made the difficult decision to remove our brave fighters from the path of the Chinese army.

'We know that history judges us by the decisions we make in harrowing times such as these. What we are yet to see is the sentence which history is to serve us.'

Hudson paused again and stared into the lens of the camera. 'I pray that you all understand the forces at work in the making of this decision. I can assure you that every attempt to establish diplomatic relations is being taken so that we can reach an acceptable outcome to this situation. Thank you, that is all.'

Finn was in his parents' living room with his dad, both of them staring at the screen.

'Thank God for that,' announced Tom.

Finn was trying to comprehend the implications of what the prime minister had just said. For the past two weeks he'd been holed up at his parents' place, doing little other than surfing with his dad and watching the news. He'd become strangely exhilarated by the events — watching the battles, he saw graphic evidence of how truly virtual his life up to that point had been. His job had been gaming numbers on a screen. This stuff, on the other hand, was reality. He was not prepared for Australia to just quit after all that.

'So that's it, we just roll over and let them take our land?' he said in disbelief.

'Finn, we hardly "rolled over" — ten thousand people are dead in just a few weeks of fighting. How do you call that "rolling over"?' asked Tom incredulously.

'Dad, what was the point? He just sent those people to their graves — and for what? So the prime minister is going back to diplomacy — why did he commit those soldiers to a fight in the first place if he wasn't going to fight to win?'

'He probably shouldn't have done that, either. Nothing's worth that many lives.'

'Oh, come on, Dad. You've been doing way too much yoga and meditation with Mum. You used to be a fighter — you were a CEO, for God's sake! If you were in the military you'd have wanted to put up more of a fight.'

'Maybe I'm older and wiser than I used to be, you ever think of that?' Tom scrutinised his son's face. He knew he'd been a hard man in his younger years, but he still had a hard time believing he could have ever been as ruthless and idealistic as his son was now being. 'Ten thousand people are dead. I think we should probably cut our losses.'

'Dad! What the fuck? That's my point. We can't dismiss what happened — what did those 10,000 die for, then?' said Finn, reaching the end of his tether. 'It can't have all been for nothing,' he muttered as he stood abruptly and walked to his room to get his things.

'See ya, Mum,' he yelled down the corridor.

'Finn, come here. Don't leave like that!' Tom called after him.

It was too late. Finn was too frustrated by his father's narrow-minded view. Throwing himself into his Jeep, he tore out the drive and through the deserted streets of the Northern Beaches, heading back to the city. It was a good thing the roads were empty as he wasn't in the mood to wait in traffic. The conversation with his dad, the prime minister's speech, and the events of the past few weeks — everything was flicking through his head and he couldn't control it.

Thirty minutes later he was coming down the freeway to cross the Harbour Bridge. Blue and red flashing lights accompanied by a small queue of cars greeted him before the bridge. The Jeep slowed to a stop and waited. A man in army fatigues walked up to his window and asked him to step out of the car.

'What's going on?' asked Finn.

'We're checking every vehicle that goes over the bridge or in the tunnel, as a precautionary measure. Can I please see your driver's licence?'

'Ah sure, yes, here you go,' Finn stuttered, a little surprised.

'Sir, please step out of your vehicle and stand here,' he pointed to a spot two metres from the car.

'Sure,' replied Finn, trying to regain his composure — all the fire he had from the conversation with his dad was now gone.

Two other men came alongside the car with long rectangular objects that they ran along the surfaces of Finn's Jeep.

'Sir, where are you heading tonight?' asked the soldier, formally.

'Home, to Bondi,' said Finn. He noticed the view across the harbour was different. Where normally the city and bridge were brightly lit, everything was now in darkness.

'What's with the lights?' asked Finn, feeling like an idiot the moment he asked the question. For some reason, he was intimidated by these guys. What did they see when they looked at him? A pussy, most likely.

'Security measures,' replied the soldier. 'Can't be too careful, what with all that's been happening.'

'All clear!' yelled one of the soldiers scanning the Jeep. With that, the soldier interrogating Finn handed him back his driver's licence. 'Move on please, sir,' beckoning Finn to his car.

Finn got back in the Jeep and made his way home in a daze.

Opening the door to the Bondi Beach apartment he rented from his parents, he noticed how stuffy the air was — probably because he hadn't been home since the invasion began almost two weeks ago. Opening all the windows and the sliding door to his balcony, he took in the moonlit view across Campbell Parade, onto Bondi Beach and out to the inky black Pacific. A warm breeze from the north carried the smell of salt and humidity. And at this time of year, with humidity came storms.

Later that night, while Finn was lying in bed trying to sleep, the storm broke. Normally Finn loved a good thunderstorm but tonight it just seemed to aggravate him even more. His whole room would light up with the lightning, and the booms of thunder felt like they were directly above him. Going out to the lounge, Finn opened the door to the balcony, the wind and rain immediately attacking him. He stood out there as the storm passed to the north, the rain soaking his t-shirt. Sydney sure knows how to put on a good storm, he thought to himself. He turned from the elemental beauty of the sky and ocean to the slick interior of his apartment. It didn't look real to him. It didn't look impressive, like the place of a successful and strong guy anymore. It looked hollow.

The next day he woke late in the morning. It was a Tuesday but it didn't matter, he wasn't going into work. The week before, his boss had given him and almost all of his colleagues their marching orders. He'd seen it coming. The city had basically ground to a halt and companies were shedding people left, right and centre. The ease with which he'd been fired from his prestigious job underscored to him that his job had not done anything that was actually useful to society. Financially, he was okay for the short term, having saved enough to see him through a year or so comfortably.

Not really knowing what to do, he took a walk down Campbell Parade, onto Hall Street, heading towards his favourite café. The storm had passed overnight and it was now a bright, glorious day on Bondi Beach. Yet it was a strange feeling walking through what was normally a bustling scene of cafés, restaurants, bars and shops. There were very few people about and, though it took a moment for Finn to notice, those who were around were silent.

No one was talking. And really, what was there to be said? thought Finn. Our country is being invaded and we lost the war in record time. What now? Are we supposed to just go back to our normal lives and get on with business like nothing had happened? Finn pondered.

Wandering up to the café, he was relieved to find it still open. He stepped inside, the coolness of the polished-concrete floor striking him immediately. 'Hey Sophie, can I get one of those egg rolls and a flat white?'

'Sure, Finn,' replied the tanned English girl behind the counter. She'd been working there for the last two months and had gotten on a first-name basis with Finn pretty quickly.

Finn watched her bending over to get the roll out of the display unit. Even with everything turning to shit, he was glad to see he could still appreciate a beautiful woman.

'Here you are. That'll be 16 dollars thanks,' she said with a smile.

'Thanks, have a great day,' replied Finn politely, walking out thinking how lovely she was. There was something about English girls that Finn found mesmerising.

At home he put on Bob Marley's *Kaya* and settled down on the balcony with his screen, going to the news sites immediately, out of force of habit. The news sites were entirely dedicated to the invasion and, not surprisingly, the withdrawal of the troops from the frontline. The headlines were pretty bleak — 'China Advancing', 'Army Morale at All-Time Low', and 'Mining Shares Fall to Historical Lows'. All of which was big news, obviously, but Finn was looking for someone to explain what would happen next.

Then, a call came through. It was Chris.

'Hey mate, what's up?' asked Chris, his voice lacklustre.

'I'm back in Bondi. Dad was driving me nuts.'

'Cool, I'll swing by.'

'Right, see you soon.'

Thirty minutes later Chris walked into Finn's kitchen, grabbed two beers from the fridge and went out onto the balcony. 'Crazy times, huh mate?' said Chris, handing Finn one of the beers.

'Yeah, don't really know what to do with myself,' Finn replied, tipping his bottle at Chris in thanks. 'Part of me wants to just go out, join the army and fight the bastards out there. The other part of me thinks, fuck it, let 'em have the shitty mines — we can do without them — might be tough for a while but, hey, life goes on right?'

'Yeah I'm hearing you,' said Chris, settling into a chair. 'I'd love to go out there and unleash on those fuckers. I just can't believe they think they can just steam in here and take over our land and mines.'

'Well it looks like they're right, from what's happening,' said Finn.

'Fuckers.'

'Hey, did you see Hudson on last night? What a pussy,' said Finn, settling back into his chair.

'Yeah, I saw him. He looked like he was shitting himself,' Chris grinned.

'He must have had a pretty rough few weeks, I guess,' Finn laughed.

'Well,' Chris said, getting serious, 'he should have seen this coming. It's been all over the news the last few years that China was building its military presence.'

'Sure, but to be fair, everyone thought they had India in the cross-hairs, not us,' replied Finn, staring out across Bondi Beach to the Pacific Ocean.

'Yeah well, I still think they should have seen this coming.'

That afternoon the boys drank and talked and were joined by a few others. They stayed at Finn's apartment until around 7 pm, when Finn kicked them all out. There were no bars open and besides, he didn't feel like going out — he wanted to be alone.

After they left, Finn ambitiously opened a bottle of red wine. He still couldn't help thinking about fighting the Chinese. Even though the government had just rolled over, he still felt a jolt of ambition to join the forces. He wandered around his lounge room, at a loose end. Suddenly, he went to his cupboard and got out an old disc. Putting it in his screen, he sat back with a glass of wine. A young Finn appeared on the screen, in army uniform, with a group of other reservists. They were hauling gear through the bush, joking and laughing. He remembered that weekend — they'd done a mock mission and his team had destroyed the opposing team, taking them all prisoner without a single casualty on their end. He sat there, the images from the screen flickering over his face, absorbed in his memories. He watched his younger self jubilantly high-fiving and back-slapping his teammates at the end of the mission, just before the screen went black.

He remembered why he hadn't stuck with it. The commitments became too much; he was missing out on valuable party time with his friends and, as his father had repeatedly said, you didn't win friends and influence people by playing army guys on the weekend. Eventually, missing out on all the fun with his mates while he was staring down the barrel of a weekend spent with smelly young guys, most of whom Finn considered to be dicks, lost its appeal.

He walked away from the reserves, in the end, listening to his dad's advice that his career should be his main focus. Finn had never before regretted leaving that phase behind. He went on to focus on other things — a high-income lifestyle that gave him plenty to keep busy and stimulated, even if he'd considered his job a joke. But now, seeing how easily the life he'd built had all been dismantled, he almost wished he'd stayed in the army. He remembered how truly challenged he'd felt by it. The feeling was akin to being sidelined in a game of footy, seeing your side miss tackles and get thumped while you're powerless to do anything about it. Finn wanted to get in there and do something, be challenged. Anything was better than this, doing nothing, feeling useless. After sitting there, dreaming of distinguishing himself with heroics in the field of battle, Finn told himself to quit being an idiot and went to bed, drunk, hollow and depressed.

Chapter 4

The night before, Ambassador Xian had watched Hudson's address to the nation from the heavily guarded consulate. All the news streams had broadcast the message. Xian felt an immense relief that Hudson had the sense to call it off. Given the withdrawal of troops and retreat, total surrender was now Hudson's only option.

So far Hudson had played right into China's hands. It was essential to the Chinese operation that Australia put up a strong defence early, so that the Chinese forces could destroy the bulk of the Australian military before taking over the mines and starting the transportation of resources. It was better to lose lives early than to lose valuable resources later. Had Australia waited for China to move down to South Australia and begin the transportation of iron ore and other materials, the Australian military could have proved far more costly, drastically affecting China's ability to export the resources.

The second thing China needed was for Australia to capitulate early in its defence. Chairman Yun knew that the Australian public could be the greatest threat or greatest asset to his plans. If the public lost enough heart in the war and could see that it was futile to try and defend the mines, the Australian public would ensure China's victory. However, Yun was very aware that if the initial defence dragged on, the public would become resolute in its belief that the mines had to be defended at all costs. This would have led to a disastrous campaign for China, costing trillions more and delaying the distribution of the valuable resources they needed so badly. As it was, the media played its role perfectly, beaming the bloody warfare into every Australian home. The prime minister, who was even more predictable, also played his role perfectly, putting up a defence without properly thinking it through and then, when it seemed all was lost, capitulating. Xian did marvel at Chairman Yun's ability to calculate the future.

A call came through from Hudson. 'Xian, I believe at this time it would be prudent of me to discuss the terms of our surrender.'

'Of course, Prime Minister,' replied Xian, wiping all emotion from his voice. Though he did genuinely believe that what China was doing was right for their people, he felt for Hudson.

'Can we please meet first thing in the morning at my office?' requested Hudson.

'Yes, of course. I will be ready and waiting from 7 am,' replied Xian.

'Thank you.' And with that, Hudson hung up.

Xian immediately called his secretary and instructed her to get Chairman Yun on a secure line. Thirty seconds later his secretary called, 'I have Chairman Yun on line one, sir.'

'Thank you,' replied Xian.

Pressing the button to connect, Xian began, 'Mr Chairman, I have just received a call from Hudson requesting a meeting to discuss the terms of surrender tomorrow morning.'

'Very good, Xian. The terms stay as they were — China wants only to control the mines of South Australia. As we have discussed, we will also require unobstructed access to Karumba where we will be building a port from which to export the resources back to China. If he is willing to agree to these terms, there will be no need for further bloodshed.'

'Of course, Mr Chairman. I will advise you of the outcome tomorrow, as soon as the meeting is concluded.'

'Things are going as planned are they not, Xian?'

'Sir, you have predicted these events with unfathomable accuracy,' replied Xian.

'The mind of a man is easily understood Xian. It is the mind of *men* that concerns me,' declared Chairman Yun in a reflective tone, and with that, he hung up.

Xian frowned to himself, thinking about what Chairman Yun had said. Slowly he realised that although everything had gone to plan and the prime minister was playing perfectly into their hands, there was much that could still go wrong. Australia's allies had not had a chance to help, which could change in the medium term. Australia's public might wake like a sleeping giant and resolve to purge the Chinese invaders. There were still so many variables. Still, tomorrow would be a historical day. Never before had a western country been so convincingly invaded and brought to its knees so quickly.

Back in the SOF, James Hudson was talking to US President Eric Allen on the Virtucon.

'Mr President, with all due respect, we appreciate the men you've sent over from the Darwin base, but even another 5,000 troops isn't going to slow the Chinese down. They are too strong and well equipped. If you can add another zero onto that number, plus air and sea support, then we might be talking,' said Hudson to the president's holographic image, which loomed large over the darkened room from a wide screen on the wall.

'I understand James, I wish there was more we could do,' replied President Allen.

'Yes, I wish there was too but it seems there is nothing that can be done. So here we are, being invaded for our resources because of the Chinese export quota scheme we established,' Hudson leaned forward, ensuring his words were not missing their target, 'based on your lobbying.'

'James, please, the quota system was suggested as a way to control the growth of the Chinese economy, something the entire western world was, and still is, concerned about,' replied President Allen. He was responding to Hudson like an indulgent parent reaching the end of his patience. 'Far be it for a US President to admit wrongdoing.'

'Well the so-called "western world" sure seems happy to feed us to the dogs,' said Hudson, who was suddenly tired, realising the futility of his argument but being unable to stop himself.

'I don't know what more to say, James. You know we are plugging holes all around the world, not to mention the situation we have in Canada, which could explode into a military nightmare any moment now. Our military is not what it used to be, James.'

'And what about ANZUS, our alliance? That obviously means nothing now.'

'Now just hang on a minute there, James. You've had it pretty easy with that alliance. What has Australia had to commit for us? A few troops to the Middle East and a cap on how much dirt you can send to China. Alliances work both ways James, and your country over the last fifty-odd years has been asked to do very little.'

'Well, in times like these you really learn who your true friends are, don't you Eric? Thanks for nothing,' snapped Hudson as he reached forward and shut off the Virtucon.

The screen went blank and soft, yellow-toned lights around the perimeter of the ceiling slowly illuminated the darkened room. The few aides that were standing on the periphery of the room looked at one another. No one had ever seen someone hang up on the President of the United States, let alone talk to him the way Hudson just did. Hudson was motionless, staring blankly at the empty space in the centre of the room. Shoulders slumped, he looked decades older than he had only two weeks before.

Moving slowly to the prime minister, one of the young aides leaned in. 'General Draven is waiting for you in your office, sir.'

Hudson simply nodded, still staring into the centre of the room. Slowly he pushed back his chair and, using his hands on the table to propel himself, stood up. Buttoning his jacket, he breathed deeply into his chest, sucking in his stomach and straightening his back. Composed, he swivelled on his heels and strode out of the Virtucon room, leaving the chair he had been sitting in pushed away from the desk. Behind him at least four people emerged, as if from nowhere, and hurried themselves around the room, prepping it for the next meeting.

As he strode down the hall, he returned to the same thoughts that had been occupying all his waking moments. From the outset of the defensive plans he'd known that their military was doomed. General Stephens was right — of course he was right. Australia could never go head-to-head with China in a military battle. What had he been thinking? He'd been played from the start. He felt like a fool — worse — he felt like the fool who had just handed China the keys to Australia's back door.

Striding into his office, Hudson saw General Draven sitting in the guest chair at the desk and, with his peripheral vision, noted the general's aide seated on the couch behind him.

He immediately went on the offense, using his most officious voice. 'General, your plan was a disaster; our forces have been destroyed. The Chinese have an open highway to our key mines and the public wants answers — what do you think I should tell them?' He walked around the side of his desk and lowered himself into his chair, fixing Draven with a level stare.

Draven wasn't thrown by Hudson's candour in the slightest. Returning Hudson's gaze he responded, 'Tell them what they want to hear, sir. That the man responsible for the defence plan has resigned. That diplomatic relations have been established with China to negotiate an acceptable compromise. I understand you are seeing Ambassador Xian first thing in the morning to discuss terms of surrender and I have here my letter of resignation.'

Hudson didn't break his stare at Draven. 'Lieutenant Jackson, you're excused, please leave,' he said to Draven's aide, the whole time staring Draven in the eye.

When the aide had left, Hudson's eyes narrowed. 'You think you can simply wash your hands of this mess now? Go and retire in Noosa and live out the rest of your life in the sun? No. It's not that easy, Draven. I will not accept your resignation.'

'Sir, you need a scapegoat. I am offering myself. Let me take the blame.' Draven lowered his eyes to the desk. Hudson wasn't the only one who'd been ravaged by the past few weeks. Draven had clearly been suffering, too, his skin greyish and slack. 'It was my idea. It failed. I'm no longer fit to serve.'

Hudson felt no compassion for the man sitting across from him. 'Paul, you don't get out of this so easily. The public will be happy to hear that we have pulled our boys back from the killing zone and are taking a diplomatic approach. They don't need a scapegoat. You're here to see this through.'

'Sir, as you wish.' Draven knew there was no point pushing the issue further. And, as much as the events of the past few weeks had made him question his own judgement, he knew Australia would be better off with him there to advise Hudson.

'Get out,' said Hudson, finally averting his eyes from Draven, looking down at his desk as though he couldn't stand to look at Draven anymore.

Draven left the room, shutting the door softly behind him. So things could get worse, thought Hudson. If Draven was ready to jump ship, what must the rest of them be thinking? What must the public be thinking?

'Jesus,' he muttered to himself, fumbling with his pen. He felt the onset of vertigo, familiar to him now, the dizziness taking over his mind. He tried to shut his eyes — not that it ever helped — opening them again to try to focus on one spot in the room.

After what must have been five minutes the feeling passed and he felt more anchored in his seat. But he still didn't know what to do.

Thinking more clearly now, he asked himself aloud: 'How did it get to this point?'

He pulled one of the hundreds of reports that had been sent to him since the invasion up on his screen. Entitled 'Historic Causes of the Chinese Invasion', he'd seen it before but decided to go through it again, if only to occupy his mind. Pressing play, he sat back and watched the screen as a calm female voice began to speak. Images started flickering across the screen, illustrating the points as she spoke.

'We can trace the causes of the invasion back to the start of the century. Australia was benefiting from the skyrocketing resource prices due in large part to China's massive economic growth. Chinese state-owned companies were snapping up resources faster than most countries around the world could dig them up. These same companies were on a worldwide shopping spree, not just buying from Australia. The Congo, Sudan, Myanmar — they were all countries rich in minerals, but in desperate poverty. They were also countries that the West had taken advantage of and then turned its back on. Where the US and the now-defunct EU would lecture and chastise the governments of these countries, China would simply come in and offer them what they needed so desperately: infrastructure. China simply traded infrastructure for resources. This, combined with the resources China could afford on the worldwide market, made the 2010s a relatively stable and peaceful decade, with the exception of America's ongoing and tedious struggle with the Middle East. It was also a peaceful period because China was able to control its growth. For much of the decade the Australian Government capped China's growth.

'The intention was to ensure that growth was evenly spread across the country and that the very poorest people were able to grow in prosperity with the country.

'This all changed in 2024 when China, on the back of unheralded growth in technology and export since 2020, invaded and successfully took control of Taiwan. For decades the small island off mainland China had been a manufacturing and exporting hub that had long frustrated the Chinese Government. After a wave of nationalistic pride had built up in China, the military went on a recruitment drive that saw hundreds of thousands of young Chinese join the armed forces. Their military had the might and the will to flex its muscle. All it needed was a target. The Chinese Government did not hesitate — the newly appointed Chairman Yun was eager to demonstrate his power and strength.' Hudson narrowed his eyes as an image of Chairman Yun, standing on a balcony and coolly observing a precise military drill, flickered across the screen.

'Taiwan bore the brunt of a grossly over-zealous Chinese military. Still, it sent a strong message to the world — China was not pulling any punches. This naturally sent the Asia-Pacific region into a tailspin. Alliances were formed, peace agreements were signed, and promises were made — and broken. Shortly after the invasion of Taiwan, the US President at the time, David Reynolds, made a visit to Canberra. This was likely the beginning of the end for Australia. Reynolds declared that China's growth needed to be controlled, as the invasion of Taiwan highlighted how great a threat they had become. He explained that it would take a worldwide effort to slow China's growth and that Australia could play its part. Then-Prime Minister Alexander Hastings, a Liberal, agreed that something had to be done to address China. He instigated heavy quotas on the exportation of iron, copper, uranium and coal to China. This was met with fury from China and the mining companies who enjoyed exporting to China, but Australia stayed firm, trusting in the wisdom of its alliance with the US. Every year the quotas changed and China was forced to make do with what it could get. The mining companies managed to find new customers without any difficulty and at the same time continued to push the prices up. So Australia's economy was booming while it did its part to slow down the tyrant of the East. Relations with the US were strong — and life in the "lucky country" continued to be blessed. The government put all the money it was making into the coffers and into upgrading infrastructure — such as schools, hospitals, and transportation. Lucrative construction contracts went to American firms, further building the alliance with the US. And because the relationship with the US was strong and their military might was still all-powerful, very little money went towards Australia's own defence force. The navy's duties were reduced to the policing of fisheries and illegal immigration. The air force became a relic and the army was reduced substantially, training more for operations in the Middle East to support the American force.

'And so Australia was deeply unprepared for what has happened. We can only speculate how long China has been planning this. We do know that their timing was sublime; America does have its hands full with Canada and the Middle East. England, even if it wanted to send over troops, is tied up in Africa and the Middle East. They would have known that the help Australia would get from New Zealand, which has amounted to 5000 troops, would be nominal.'

Hudson shut off the screen before the report had finished. He'd seen enough for today. China had, admittedly, played its cards extremely well. Again, Hudson had the feeling that he had been played — royally played — right from the start. Still, what were his options? Tomorrow he would meet with Ambassador Xian and accept the terms China had specified at the outset — that is, if the Chinese hadn't changed their minds and their terms.

Exhaustion now took over Hudson as he left his office and made his way through the labyrinthine complex to his bedroom, not engaging in any of his usual chitchat with the staff manning the security checkpoints he passed through. Once alone in his room, he undressed with his eyes already closed and, for the sixth night in a row, went to bed without brushing his teeth or washing. Sliding into the cool sheets, his head throbbing, Hudson had a heavy and dreamless sleep, his conscious, unconscious and subconscious minds all at the point of exhaustion.

Before dawn Matt woke him — not that James knew whether it was dawn or dusk underground, or whether that mattered these days. Getting ready quickly he made his way to his office. He wanted to be thoroughly prepared for his meeting with Xian. Following a breakfast briefing with his team of advisors, his briefing with the Governor-General, General Draven, his deputy and another raft of military advisors, he went to his office to process alone. He wanted to practise the words he would say to Xian, knowing that this was a moment in history that, no matter how terrible and how much he wished it wasn't him, would be recorded for eternity. He wanted to get this right.

At 7:52 am Hudson received the call from his secretary, telling him that Ambassador Xian had arrived and was entering through the security corridor. Asking her to send in the Governor-General, Draven and his deputy, he felt ready to follow through with the surrender. They filed in silently, which Hudson found unnerving.

'Bloody hell! Anyone would think we just lost a war around here!' said Hudson, trying to muster his once-heralded charisma as he moved to a chair that was flanked by comfortable couches. He gestured for Draven to sit to his left, and for Draven's deputy and the Governor-General to sit on his right.

'We all know we are making the right decision here. We are putting an end to the slaughter of our men and women out there in the desert,' Hudson declared as he settled himself into his seat. 'Once this is over, we'll see how the dust settles, and I am sure we can continue to push for a more profitable and diplomatic outcome.'

The Governor-General looked at a loss. He was an older man, a statesman from a very different generation to Hudson. If it were up to him he would have sacrificed every last man and woman to defend Australia rather than let it be occupied by another country. However, even he recognised the impossible situation they found themselves in: he just couldn't bring himself to lighten the situation with jokes.

A knock at the door secured everyone's attention — they all turned to see a smartly dressed infantry guard open the door, salute and announce the arrival of Ambassador Xian, who entered accompanied by three other Chinese diplomats.

'Come in, Ambassador,' said Hudson, rising.

'Thank you, Prime Minister. I believe you have met Xi Phu of our embassy, Wen Pan, our specialist counsel on Australian law, and Bai Cheung, my Executive Assistant.' Xian gestured to each person in turn as he introduced them.

After the pleasantries and introductions from both sides, the meeting went as predicted. Hudson accepted, in principle, the terms of the surrender as the Chinese detailed. All that was required was for the paperwork to be drafted and signed. It was all stunningly straightforward.

After the meeting, once everyone had filed out of Hudson's office, leaving him alone, it felt as though a weight of insurmountable density was lifted from his shoulders. He didn't normally drink alcohol, but he decided a scotch was what the moment required. Walking over to the liquor cabinet that he had never seen opened, he reached for a bottle of twenty-one-year-old Glenfiddich — the best of the best, according to a Scottish lord he'd once met. Pouring a large tumbler, he muttered 'What the hell'. Putting the same amount of water in the tumbler, he picked it up and took it all in one swallow. His mouth burning, the warm feeling made its way down his throat and belly. It made him feel more alive than he had been in what seemed like an eternity. Pouring himself another, he took the glass back to his desk where he sat, reclining in the leather chair that had first been used by Bob Hawke in the 1980s. Swivelling left and right, James Hudson arched his head back and closed his eyes, feeling the scotch take effect.

Suddenly he felt sure Australia would thank him — no, *praise* him — for his leadership and sense in its darkest hour. He would be forever known as the man that steered Australia through these troubled times with gravitas and decorum. Yes, he alone had saved Australia from further bloodshed and death.

Chapter 5

Six weeks since the invasion, and Australia was in turmoil. China's operation had gone to plan and it had already constructed a transportation link from the mines in the south to the makeshift harbour in the Gulf of Carpentaria. Chinese engineers had created a rail line linking the mines with the Gulf, utilising existing rail lines and new technology that allowed them to quickly lay down the tracks. The Chinese had resisted obvious option of taking over ports in South and West Australia. Their rationale was simple, minimal intervention will result in minimal conflict. By keeping their operations out of sight of the vast majority of Australian's they could reduce the chances of a protracted resistance.

Iron ore and uranium were now being transported north at an alarming rate. The train line split the country in two, dividing east and west Australia. The Chinese were already working on a second track that would run beside the existing line so that they could double the number of trains heading north to the Gulf.

In stark contrast with the efficiency of China, Australia had become paralysed by fear, disorganisation and racial hatred. Second- and third-generation Asian-Australians were frequently attacked and most were too scared to leave their homes. The government had, of course, tried to quell the racial problems but achieved nothing. The economy had been devastated by the Chinese invasion and with unemployment rising, many young people were out of work and out of patience, venting their anger and frustration at the people who looked like their enemy.

In Canberra, James Hudson was at his wit's end. His confidence in his leadership abilities had taken a rapid nosedive since his post-surrender celebratory scotch. 'Well, I don't know what else to do, Matt,' he said to his aide.

'Sir, the Committee for Chinese-Australian Rights has a number of proposed initiatives that could help minimise the violence,' replied Matt, trying hard to coax a decisive response from the despondent prime minister.

Hudson leaned forward, head in his hands. 'Initiatives, programs, proposals … it's all a waste of time. The problem is too many young people are angry and frustrated and they can't vent it in the right direction. I'm at a loss, Matt. Everything we've tried has failed — the economy has flatlined, unemployment is at an all-time high, our international relations are disintegrating and the Chinese are burrowing deeper into central Australia and we're powerless to do anything about it.' Hudson looked up at Matt, his face flushed. 'And on top of all that, I've got Premier Bright screaming at me that Western Australia will be next and what are we going to do about it? Well, what can we do? Nothing.'

Over the last few weeks, Matt had seen Hudson deteriorate into a husk of a man, his eyes hollow, skin ashen, stretched and hanging from his now shrunken features.

'Sir, please, you can't do this to yourself. Parliament is meeting tomorrow. We need to take the recommendations from the heads of department, make some sound decisions and get them actioned.' Matt immediately regretted speaking with such fervour. He hadn't meant to speak so directly to the prime minister, and he waited for a severe chastising.

'You're right. Can you talk to the heads and come up with some proposals?' replied Hudson, waving his hand vaguely in Matt's direction.

'What? Sir, you need to do this. You need to lead the heads. I can't do this for you!' demanded Matt, shocked into responding bluntly.

Standing up and walking to the fireplace, Hudson stared blankly into the flames. 'Just get on with it Matt,' he said in a feeble voice. 'Now please leave.'

Matt opened his mouth, about to say something, then stopped himself. With his brow set in a determined expression, he walked out of the room.

Finding a quiet corner down the hall, he pulled out a coded mobile phone from his suit jacket. Looking around to see if anyone was watching, he dialled and, without waiting for a greeting, spoke into it in a low voice.

'Hey, it's me. Okay, I'm with you tomorrow.' Matt paused. 'So, can I see you tonight? Good, see you then. Bye.' With that he ended the call, still looking around to see if he was being watched. Once sure that he wasn't, he strode off to his next meeting, heart pounding.

Early that evening, General Stephens assembled Sarah Dempsey, General Fletcher, Colonel Main and Connor Adams at his house. The gathering had the distinct feeling of dejavu, with everyone sitting on the same couches as the last time they met.

General Stephens stood, staring out the window. 'So the prime minister has surrendered. He finally realised what a futile exercise it was to try to stop the Chinese. Our troops should never have been in the firing line like that. We should have been smarter — we *have* to be smarter if we're to get China out. And now, Hudson's failing to even deal with the basic elements of running this country.'

Adams looked surprised. 'Martin, it's over. The Chinese have won, there is no getting them out now. They've already steamrolled South Australia and taken over the mines. The mining companies evacuated the mines and destroyed their equipment weeks ago.'

General Stephens turned to look at him. 'Nothing is over. Nothing has even begun. It's time for a new strategy to address the Chinese.'

'What the hell are you talking about Marty?' said Adams, irritated.

'I'm talking about the adoption of a new military strategy, an approach that will eventually send the Chinese invaders back to their motherland,' replied General Stephens.

Adams spoke levelly. 'Martin, we spoke of this a few weeks ago. You know what you're suggesting is madness, and it's certainly not in the best interest of the country.'

'Best interest of the country? Tell that to the thousands of people who live out in rural Australia — right in the path of the Chinese! Hudson has abandoned them — he's done exactly what the Chinese were expecting the whole time, and then he happily surrendered to them. The "best interest of the country" was never taken into account from the start of this nightmare. My only interest is Australia — and regaining our land.'

'And staging a coup is going to help the country?' asked Adams. 'Damn it, Martin. You may be right about the military strategy but have you considered what the people of Australia want? After what they've seen on BBCNN, do you really think they want more bloodshed in their own backyard? They've watched their kids being slaughtered in the desert — over what? A few lousy mines ...' Pausing for a moment, Adams composed himself and continued more calmly. 'The Australian people need some stability right now — and they're happy with the certainty that the killing has ended.'

'You speak of the "Australian people" like they're a bunch of scared children cowering in their homes, praying that it will all be over soon,' replied Stephens. 'I think you're underestimating their resolve, their strength, their will to remain a free nation. Connor, you should give them more credit. I believe that the public is appalled at the surrender. It is my intention to fight the Chinese and to continue to fight until they have been driven from our land. A coup may not be necessary. I am going public with my views and then we will see if the Australian people have lost their will to fight.'

'I'm with you Marty, I can't stand that we've simply lain down arms and let the Chinese stroll in,' said Fletcher.

Turning to Fletcher, General Stephens gave him a nod and glanced back at Adams. 'Look, you don't need to say anything more. I understand — but I think you're wrong. To do this I need your help — so please at least think about what I am saying.'

'All right, Martin, I will. I have to go now. Jane is cooking dinner for the family. Since all this started she's been insisting on the entire family being together for meals.' With a wry smile Connor picked up his briefcase and turned to leave. 'I'll see myself out. And I'll be in touch tomorrow morning.'

When the front door had closed, Stephens turned to Fletcher. 'Well, that went better than expected.'

'Jesus! What were you expecting Marty?'

General Stephens replied with a half-smile, 'Well, he could have called the military police and had me locked up.'

'He still might,' piped up Sarah, from her spot by the fire.

Laughing now, Fletcher added, 'He's more likely to call the local asylum'.

The tension of their earlier conversation was immediately eased by the laughter. They were all desperately looking for an excuse to laugh.

Once they pulled themselves together General Stephens looked to Sarah. 'So, Sarah, you've arranged the press conference for tomorrow afternoon?'

She sat upright, her dark brown hair falling over her shoulders as she leaned forward. 'Yes. *The Australasian*, *The Canberra Times* and all the major metropolitan news hubs will be there. Through the online polling system the news sites use we will be able to get a pretty good indication of the public's opinion of what you're suggesting.'

'Very good. Now Fletch, how did you go approaching possible collaborators?' Stephens asked, turning to his friend.

'Better than we could have hoped, Marty. All the people on your list have said they'd support us.' He grinned. 'Hudson must be even more of a mess behind closed doors than he seems in his press conferences.'

'Okay. The next step is your resignation. I've already tendered mine, but you'll need to do the same. You too, Main. Keep me updated on your progress, but not by phone. You know where to find me.'

With that, Fletcher and Main left Sarah and General Stephens.

Sarah sat back on the couch with an exhausted sigh. 'Well, General, there's no going back now. Adams was the last piece and he looks like he'll be onside when things get going.'

Stephens sat down beside Sarah and looked her directly in the eyes with absolute steadfastness. Her blue eyes returned his gaze unflinchingly. 'Sarah, you and I have worked together for a long time now. But what we're doing here is well beyond the call of duty. I just want to reiterate that you don't need to come on this part of the journey with me. What we're doing here is extremely serious and, well, illegal. We will go to prison for a very long time if it doesn't work.'

'I know, but I've given this a lot of thought and I believe in what *we* are doing. And I'd like to make it very clear that I am doing this for the country, not for you or any other individual. So please don't think that I'm doing this out of sycophantic loyalty,' she teased, folding her arms across her chest. 'Don't let your ego get the better of your judgement.'

'I … no, no, I never thought that you were only doing this for me. I just want to be sure that … you know what you're getting into, that's all.' Stephens stammered, flushing involuntarily. Despite the fact that they usually had the easy intimacy of two people who worked closely in a demanding job, it was rare for them to speak so personally.

'General Stephens, I am not dumb. I know what's at stake here and I've evaluated the risk and the importance of what we are doing. I won't blame you if we are arrested and sent to prison for life.' More serious now, she continued, 'When the opportunity to work for you came up, I leapt at the chance. I've learned more working for you than I got from my Masters and my time in DC combined. Don't forget I'm a strategist, too — and I believe in what we're doing.'

'Okay, well I'm sorry if I sounded patronising,' he replied, his composure regained. 'I know you are an independent person and I know you're smart enough to comprehend the implications of what we're doing. I just, well … I just wouldn't forgive myself if I got you into something you weren't 100 per cent behind.'

Sarah, cocking her head, looked deep into General Stephens' eyes. 'Thank you for caring, but please don't give it another thought.' With that she stood, ran her hands down the front of her sensible skirt and picked up her leather case. 'I have to go, I need to make some contingency plans in case things do turn sour,' she said, turning and heading for the door.

'There's no doubt about you,' said Stephens, with a wry smile. 'I'll see you here tomorrow morning, bright and early then,' he called to her as she left the room.

'Yes, you will. There's a lot to plan. See you tomorrow.' Sarah walked out, closing the door behind her.

Left on his own, General Stephens sat down and reflected on Sarah's ability to constantly surprise him. Ever since she'd joined his team with a stellar CV — a Masters degree from Australian National University in Strategic and Defence Studies, winner of the Thawley Scholarship from the Lowy Institute which saw her spending time at the Center for Strategic and International Studies in Washington DC — she'd been a great asset. She was still young, though, and sometimes he was shocked by her ignorance of what seemed to him to be fairly recent history. Her acutely honed knowledge of military theory more than made up for that, making her indispensable to his team. But, more than that, he'd come to trust her implicitly, and, yes, he cared for her very much. The way lifelong friends care for each other. Her personal life was a bit of a mystery because she never spoke of her lovers, which didn't surprise him. She was a consummate professional and never broached personal subjects.

The fact that she was making contingency plans said it all. For General Stephens there was little point in contingencies. For him, if things didn't go well he would be the first taken and the first sentenced. Treason. A terrible word — it sounded terrible, the implications were terrible, the act of committing it was terrible. But this was the path he was following. Though the death penalty for treason had been abolished back in 1985, the punishment was still very harsh — life imprisonment.

General Stephens knew his history. He knew that Australia had only ever been subject to one military coup, and that was in 1808. The Rum Rebellion, as it was known, had nothing to do with rum and everything to do with property — waterfront property, to be precise. The governor, William Bligh, went up against powerful property developers over the land around The Rocks in Sydney, which he believed was not being managed in the best interests of the people. Bligh was arrested by six officers — all with interests in property — and deposed. For two years an illegitimate government was in control of Australia, until a new governor, Lachlan Macquarie, was sent out from England. When Macquarie arrived he saw that the appointments made by the illegitimate government were reversed, all decisions made by the previous government reviewed, and the coup leaders expunged from the government. Law and order were restored.

While the two cases were very different — he was hardly overthrowing the government for his own financial gain — General Stephens couldn't help wondering how history would remember his group, and what they were about to do. What would the historians call it? A coup, an act of terrorism, or an act of great bravery? Stephens knew all too well that he would be judged depending on who was writing the history — him or Hudson. Hero or villain, crusader or terrorist — it was entirely dependent on the hand that wrote the history.

After leaving General Stephens' house, Sarah drove straight home to her apartment in the Canberra suburb of Kingston. The sun was already going down and she had a lot to do. While she had a deep respect and admiration for the general and she was absolutely convinced that what they were doing was best for the country, she didn't savour the thought of spending the rest of her life in gaol. She knew that once their plans were put in motion there could be no going back. She also knew that if the federal police took action they would come down on the general and Fletcher first. She might have a small window of opportunity to make her escape. In order for her to take advantage of that window, she had to be ready to jump the instant the Feds made a move.

Being nimble was something Sarah prided herself on. She had never had a problem with emotional attachment, and she could up and move easily with zero fuss. What she needed was an exit strategy, a detailed plan in her head of her exact actions if the moment came. Money was an obvious issue — she would need cash, which would have to wait until tomorrow now. No one ever used cash, so it would be an unusual errand for her. All her transactions were taken care of by the highly traceable personal Nokia Mobile Life Activator (MiLA), a device that handled her communications, diary, data and payments, among many other things. Its biosecurity system, which ensured only the owner could operate it, was a blessing in everyday life but a nightmare when it came to doing anything illicit. Any time it was used, it would put a definite lock on her physical location. She would also need documents, transport, at least two safe houses, and a route to get her out of the city that avoided major arterial roads and potential roadblocks. The trouble with Canberra was that its design allowed for the city to be effectively locked down by police, which ordinarily Sarah thought was brilliant. Not so much now …

She entered her darkened flat, turned on all the lights and strode past her well-worn treadmill to her desk. After three hours at work at her desk, thinking of the angles and detailing a plan, she decided to run a bath. Her head was pounding and she wasn't thinking clearly — this was when mistakes happened and she couldn't afford that now.

With the bath running, she walked through the bright white space of her flat to the warmly-lit kitchen and poured a large glass of Petaluma Shiraz 2027, a wine that had aged beautifully. Now seemed as good a time as any to open it. After all, she might not get another chance at it. Lighting some incense, then taking the glass back to the bathroom, she used her remote control to select some music for her bath. She picked out her favourite track at the moment, a haunting piano piece called *Glassworks*, by the Philip Glass Ensemble. Whenever she listened to it she wished that it would never end, that it would just keep playing. But she knew that, like anything wonderful, it had to come to an end.

Stretched out in her bath, Sarah allowed her thoughts to drift. Really, she couldn't blame the Chinese for what they were doing. Perhaps it was her ruthless side that helped her to see it from their perspective. If she were in their position, and a soft, lazy Australia was sitting on the key to her future, she would do the same thing. Stifling a laugh, she suddenly found it darkly funny that Australians were so surprised and upset by the actions of the Chinese.

How stupid had we been? she wondered. So blissfully unaware of China's intentions, we went about our business, raising the prices of resources, controlling the volume, choosing with whom we did business, and, in doing so, fooled ourselves into thinking Australia *controlled* the market. It really was brilliant. Feigning willingness to pay the prices and accept the crippling restrictions for years, all the while watching as Australia grew fat, lazy and stupid. We basked in our wealth and glory, relaxed by the notion that America would protect us from the bullies in the playground. Then, when China decides the time is right, they invade with such force that the possibility of defence is ridiculous. And then, the genius of it, they tell us they're not interested in our culture, our cities or our way of life.

After another 10 minutes soaking in the hot water and sipping the wine that, luckily, lived up to its reputation, Sarah stood, slowly letting the water slide off her long, toned body. Feeling momentarily dizzy, she waited for the blood to go back to her head then reached for the towel and stepped out of the bath. Her mind feeling refreshed and her body relaxed, it was time for work.

She knew that once she had satisfied her need for self-preservation by getting herself an exit strategy, she could dedicate herself to the job of overthrowing the government and taking back Australia. Doubt, until now, hadn't entered her mind — but she was beginning to realise the scale of General Stephens' plan and the difficulties they would face ...

A few hours later, she was just finishing up her work when she was startled by a knock at the door. Was it that time already? she thought to herself. She trotted to the door and opened it with a grin of anticipation.

Matt took the sight of her in, wearing only a white work shirt and knickers. Her skin looked radiant and the smell of incense lightly hit Matt's nose.

'Come in,' she said seductively, tilting her head and beckoning him inside.

Matt took just two steps into the hall and waited for her to close the door. Turning her, he pulled her in close and kissed her hard, forcing her against the wall. She moaned involuntarily and grabbed at his back.

Matt had one hand on the back of her head, the other inside her shirt, moving slowly down. Lifting her, wrapping her legs around his waist, Matt walked her into the bedroom and threw her on the bed. Taking off his shirt, he looked down at her.

She returned his gaze, her hair creating a tousled halo around her head on the mattress. Two months ago, she'd had made a play for Matt at a local bar. He was cute, and he had a demanding job that would keep this thing from getting too personal — he was the perfect candidate. It had been a passionate affair from day one. But then, when the invasion occurred and General Stephens signalled his intention to take over the leadership, the relationship took on a whole new meaning — for Sarah anyway. She'd been using their time together to carefully test Matt's allegiance and his loyalty to Hudson. It hadn't taken much to realise that Matt saw Hudson and his failings all too clearly. Sarah knew that if General Stephens was to succeed, they would need the support of the people closest to Hudson. And today, finally, Matt had given his. He was clearly eager to accept his reward for it.

Afterwards, lying on the bed exhausted, Sarah felt Matt's heart rate slowly come back to a normal pace.

'So tomorrow's going to be a big day,' said Matt.

'The biggest day in politics this country has ever seen,' replied Sarah, brushing her hair away from her face.

'It really is amazing. You're convinced you have majority support?' asked Matt.

'We won't know for sure until tomorrow, but yes, it looks like we will have most of parliament's support.'

There was a long silence as they both stared at the ceiling. Matt stroked her hair tenderly.

'You know Matt, after tomorrow we won't be able to see each other again for a long time. For one, I might be going to prison, but secondly, we can't be seen to have collaborated on this, for your own career.'

'Yeah, I figured that would be the case. And I imagine I'll be kept pretty busy, being the liaison between the military and the government. But if you go to gaol, it'll be a shame, really. You're a great shag,' he said, grinning down at her.

'Ha, you're not so bad yourself,' said Sarah, lifting her head to look him in the eyes.

'Who knows what might happen?' said Matt more seriously now. 'I mean, who would have predicted the last few months?'

'True, you never know what will happen,' said Sarah, reaching for MiLA to scan the latest emails.

DAWN OF THE TIGER

Chapter 6

Parliament was in progress, with the Minister of Chinese-Australian Affairs making a speech about the need for greater security in Asian-dominated suburbs. The sound of a door opening at the back of the large hall went unnoticed, until the sight of 20 men and women, some armed, marching down the steps to the floor turned all heads. Most of the people in the gallery knew what this was, but it was still an incredible sight to behold. Leading the group was General Martin Stephens, looking focussed and determined, flanked by General Fletcher, Colonel Main, Connor Adams and Sarah Dempsey. The Minister of Chinese-Australian Affairs looked confused.

'What is ...?' he started to ask, but his question trailed off as he moved to sit down. Hudson, who had been sitting, staring at his note pad, his mind a thousand miles away, looked up, confused and alarmed.

'Wh ... What's this all about? General Stephens, what are you doing? What's going on?' cried Hudson, panicked, looking around frantically for answers.

Standing and searching the faces of his own ministers, he stared in disbelief as every one of them averted their gaze. But Hudson's face did not twist in anger or flush with shock — it relaxed with a look of pure relief.

He didn't want this job anymore, he didn't want the responsibility, the guilt, or the pain. He suddenly realised that this was the perfect solution: let someone else take over. His expression was almost serene.

It was all over and General Stephens hadn't even opened his mouth. He didn't need to. He just stood there in front of Hudson, resolute. A silent coup.

Hudson was the first to speak. Standing to face General Stephens he gripped the collar of his suit jacket, pressing it down. 'So you want the job, do you?' he said, staring him directly in the eyes. Turning to his own ministers, holding out his arms, he asked, 'You want him to lead the country now, too?'

Again, his response was averted gazes.

Looking back at the general, Hudson took a step closer and stood just millimetres from the general's face. 'It's yours,' he hissed. And with that, Hudson turned and walked out of the building alone. A stunned silence pervaded the entire cabinet.

After the door had closed behind Hudson, the general took a deep breath and exhaled, slowly looking around at each of the faces in the room. He felt a rush of adrenalin like nothing he had experienced on the battlefield. But it was controlled, his mind free and lucid.

When he spoke his voice was clear, his tone deep, pace steady and even. 'You all know me and, for most of you, what has just happened is no surprise.' Pausing for effect, he continued. 'Today we start a new day in Australia's history, with one single-minded objective. There is only one strategy and only one tactic that will lead to just one result. We are getting China out of Australia, no matter what the cost. Since the invasion, we have done everything the Chinese wanted us to do, whether we knew it or not. Well, that's about to change. They're banking on our fear and weakness to keep us at bay, to keep us in our cities and on our coastline. But today we're not afraid. Today we fight back. And we will continue to fight back, whatever the cost.'

Raising his voice, General Stephens continued. 'We need a new strategy to fight the Chinese! We need to give our citizens the chance to defend their land, and we need to give our people hope that we can once again be a sovereign nation, free of this infection that splits our nation in two!' Rapturous applause broke out and the general felt the waves of applause break over him. He looked back at Fletcher and Sarah, both smiling and clapping.

'Ladies and gentlemen, we will be taking the fight to the Chinese, but not in the conventional way. We need a new strategy: our intention is to frustrate and sabotage their transportation lines so that the cost of excavating our land becomes so great that they realise it makes no economic sense to continue. We will strike at their Achilles heel — their efficiency. Make no mistake, though, this strategy will come at a cost. The Chinese will not take our actions lightly and they will make reprisals. We must all be prepared to accept this, or there is no point continuing.'

Pausing, General Stephens looked around the room. He needed everyone in that room to understand the path Australia was headed down and, importantly, he needed them to *want* to travel it.

'Such is the cost of freedom,' he continued. 'Australia must stand up and fight. On this we cannot compromise. We cannot back down and we cannot make the same mistakes again. Ladies and gentlemen, from today, we fight back on our own terms.'

Members from all parties stood and clapped, yelling their support. No speech in the Australian Parliament had ever elicited such a response. With that, General Stephens moved to exit the room, shaking hands with the parliamentarians as they swarmed in to surround him.

Once Stephens had managed to get out the door with Fletcher, Sarah and a security detail, Connor Adams took the floor. 'Ladies and gentlemen,' he called above the chaos, 'please be assured, we see no reason to change the ministerial operations that are currently in place, except, of course, the Department of Defence. General Stephens' office will take control of this department immediately, but everyone else will stay in their respective roles. The general wishes to meet with each and every one of you in the coming days to discuss outstanding issues. Now, I'd be happy to take any questions.' For the next two hours, Adams fielded questions from the ministers.

Hudson, meanwhile, walked back to his office to collect his things. Suddenly feeling light-headed, he stopped and put his elbow against the wall to steady himself. Overcome with emotion and shock, alone in the hallway, Hudson sobbed. Wiping the tears away quickly before anyone could see, he straightened himself, breathed deeply and focussed on getting to his office.

Once there, he slumped into his chair. He'd known from the moment the general stood on the floor in parliament that he had the backing of the cabinet. Stephens must have been lobbying for this for some time. His stomach twisted with a mixture of shame, humiliation and relief.

What would he do now? The only thing he could think of was to get out of Canberra, for good. Where would he go? Coastal Queensland? New Zealand? It was ironic, thought Hudson, how Australia, for the past 50 years had complained about the number of New Zealanders who migrated to Australia, 'sapping the welfare system' and 'taking advantage of Australia's superior economy'. The tables had well and truly been turned in the last few months, with hordes of wealthy Australians jumping ship and relocating there.

By the time Hudson reached his office he'd resolved to give himself some time to work out his next move. What was the rush? He was feeling strangely good, considering the embarrassment of what had just occurred. For the first time in months, James Hudson felt a glimmer of hope for himself. Free at last.

Later that day the news broke in the national media. *The Australasian* was first to get it online and the digital headlines were astonishing. Across every connected digital device, the news was entirely dedicated to the 'Silent Coup', as the media had dubbed it — describing how General Stephens had simply stood in front of Hudson and took control without uttering a word. *The Australasian* had a stock photo of General Stephens looking dignified and resolute. They called it the 'stare that won a nation'. *The Sydney Morning Herald* was running with the 'Silent Coup' headline and had managed to get photos of Hudson walking back to his office looking lost in a world of his own.

The news headlines were instantly spread across the world. The ramifications of the general's actions would be felt the world over. China, too, had the headlines on the front page of every news site in the country — much to their government's dislike. In the old days there was no way this news would have been declared in such an honest and immediate way. The government newsroom would have put a positive spin on it and hailed it as a further victory to China.

Finn was at his parents', sitting at the kitchen bench when the news came through of General Stephens' coup. Listening intently to the report on the screen in the kitchen, Finn was immediately galvanised, his mind racing at the possibilities now that Australia was being led by the military. Finally, he thought, looking around the room in elation, we can start to actually do something.

Tom entered the room, obviously having heard the news in the other room. He looked worried.

'How good is this? Finally we can start taking it to the Chinese,' Finn said animatedly, oblivious to his dad's state.

'Son, you seem pretty damn keen to see more young Australians getting blown to bits out there in the desert. I don't think this is good news at all. This is just a commitment to more dead Australians,' replied Tom, leaning on the kitchen bench.

'Come on, Dad. Are you serious? At some point we need to do something, otherwise do you really think they'll stop at our mines in South Australia? Western Australia will be next, and then who knows? Maybe they'll move in on the farmers so that they can feed their growing population. Then we're all screwed. There'll be no resources and no food!' Finn felt the all-too-familiar sense of rising irritation at his father.

'Look, all I'm saying is, hasn't there been enough bloodshed? Do you really think that military tactics can beat an army like the Chinese?'

'Well, Dad, if England had that attitude back in the 1930s imagine what the world would be like now.'

'You can't compare wars, Finn. This is a very different scenario—'

'Is it?' interrupted Finn, 'Is it really, Dad? I don't think it's that different at all.' He'd risen from his seat and was leaning tensely against the kitchen cupboards, arms folded defensively across his chest.

'Finn, war was very different back then and the Nazis were a very different enemy, with different motivations. The Chinese are in Australia for one thing. Let them have it and let us get on with rebuilding Australia the right way. It's pointless wasting energy and lives on fighting the Chinese.' Tom was becoming more agitated by Finn's naivety and ignorance.

'Maybe, Dad, but at least we'll be trying to do something, and it may even force the Chinese to take a diplomatic route to resolve the conflict,' said Finn, desperately trying to convince his father.

Tom paused, confused over why Finn was getting so heated. Something wasn't right.

'What do you mean by "we" son?' he asked in a strained tone.

'Well, nothing … Australia I guess,' replied Finn, hesitantly.

Tom started to crack. 'Son, you better not be thinking about doing anything stupid. There is no way in hell that you'll be going out there to fight.'

'Why not? At least I'll be doing something with my life that actually means something instead of thinking about how much money I've made or lost. And besides, it's not like I've got anything going on right now. The financial markets won't start up again for months, if not years.'

Tom finally had evidence of what he'd been dreading. He'd pushed his son away from military service once, getting him to funnel his energies into something constructive, like his education and building a career, rather than playing army on the weekends. Now he was going to have to do it again, it seemed — but this time the stakes were so much higher.

'Nonsense,' he said brusquely, trying to conceal his sudden panic, 'you'll find something soon enough.'

'Dad, financial companies are like submarines — they go up and they go down. When they go down they blow their ballast and people like me get spat out.'

'You don't know that. You might find that if Australia just knuckles down and gets on with rebuilding, the economy will bounce back.'

'Are you going senile? Our economy has always been predicated on easy access to valuable resources. Without them, we've got nothing. And besides, as soon as we do create a new economy, what's to stop China from taking that too?'

Both men stared hard at the kitchen bench, refusing to look the other in the eye. Finn recognised the conversation had become an exercise in futility. 'Anyway, gotta go Dad.'

Tom said nothing, frozen in his position braced against the kitchen bench. Finn left, angrily grabbing MiLA on the way out.

This is bullshit, he thought, climbing into his Jeep.

Later that evening Chris came around to Finn's apartment. After a few beers and debate over if and when the footy season would start again, Finn tipped up the last of his beer, set the bottle down and looked over at Chris. 'Mate, I'm thinking of joining the army.'

Chris stared at him, mouth partly open, beer bottle frozen in mid-air on its trajectory to his lips. 'You fucking serious?'

'Yeah, I am. I can't stand sitting around anymore. Plus, I really believe in what General Stephens is saying. I think we can still get the Chinese out of here, or at least make life bloody difficult for them.'

'Fuck off! You're serious?' Chris had a nervous grin on his face. 'You'll be killed out there mate. You're fucking insane.'

'Well that's a change of tune. What happened to "Oh I'm going to get out there and smash 'em back to Beijing"?' said Finn in a mocking tone.

'Fuck you, I wasn't serious. You saw what happened to our boys in the initial invasion — it was a bloodbath. Why would you go out there to be more meat in the grinder, you stupid fuck?' Chris was upset, tensely leaning forward at Finn. 'Tell me you haven't gone and signed up already, please tell me you're not that fucked in the head?'

'No I haven't — yet.' Finn replied, sitting back in his chair, as calm and quiet as Chris was now agitated.

'Good, well pull your head in. In case you haven't noticed, you're a money boy — not a fucking commando.' Chris raised his bottle to his lips and had a long drink.

'Another?' asked Finn as he stood waving his empty beer bottle, feeling a little light-headed. He didn't normally drink this much during the week, but he knew tomorrow would be another day with nothing much to do, so carrying a hangover didn't worry him.

'Yep, why not? I got nothing on tomorrow.'

'How is being back at home?' asked Finn, returning with two beers in hand, happy to change the subject.

'You know, pretty dull. But I'm not alone; most of us are in the same boat. You're the only guy I know who is still in their own place.'

'At least your parents live in a great spot, it's not like you're moving out to the mountains.'

'True. Still, can't wait to get out of there. You know if I could get a mortgage right now, I could probably buy somewhere!'

'Buy? Why the fuck would you want to do that?' said Finn.

'I don't know. My dad keeps carrying on about it,' said Chris, shrugging his shoulders.

'Fuck that. Spend your life paying off a mortgage? For what? Mate, there are easier ways to make money,' said Finn, handing Chris another beer.

'Yeah, well, whatever, first things first — I need a job,' said Chris, clearly bored with the way the conversation was going.

Reanimating, Chris sat up and asked, 'So, sorry, you never gave me an answer … are you fucking insane?'

'No, look, I'm just saying I think I want to do my bit for Australia. Actually challenge myself,' replied Finn, with a more serious look now.

Chris, sitting forward, mirrored Finn's expression. 'I get that, but mate, you saw the news coverage. Why would you ever go there? The things that happened to people out there, it was fucked up.'

'Mate, I know, but I trust General Stephens. He won't be ordering troops to fight like that on a frontline, up against the largest army in the world. He's smarter than that and, from what I've read, he's got the right idea for getting the Chinese out.'

Chris, flinging himself back on the couch, said in disbelief, 'Fucking dreaming. You really are a cock.'

'Whatever. I haven't decided yet, so let's just leave it. Besides you're a twat if you don't think we need to do something about the shit this country's in,' retaliated Finn, growing tired of trying to explain his motivations.

'Whatever,' said Chris, getting the last word in.

The boys turned their attention back to the screen and the reality show, *Australia's Most Open Personality*, which recorded contestants' most embarrassing moments for a year. This was Australia's top-rating show. Finn stared morosely at the screen, dejected by the banality of it all.

The next day the integrated ambient alarm system woke Finn, the room slowly brightening, mimicking a sunrise. Feeling the haziness of a hangover, he swung his legs over the edge of the bed, slowly rising to a seated position with his head hung low. He took a deep breath before heaving himself to his feet.

Stuffing his swimmers and towel into his sports bag, he was almost out the door before he realised he'd forgotten MiLA. I would've been screwed without that, he thought to himself, turning back to grab MiLA from the bench. Then he was in the lift and down to the carpark. He walked up to his Jeep, MiLA unlocking it automatically as he approached, and he climbed in. 'Morning car, destination pool, please,' he said clearly once inside. The car repeated the destination, started up and reversed out of the parking space. Finn sat back and watched the morning news as he travelled. Once again, the 'Silent Coup' and its ramifications dominated the coverage. Overall, the sentiment was positive, the feeling being that most Australians were tired of inertia and were looking for a more aggressive stance. Well, that was how Finn was taking it anyway, but maybe he was just projecting his feelings onto the public sentiment.

Getting to the pool at 6:45 am, he couldn't see any of the other guys' cars in the lot yet. Though the pool was heated, the water temperature was still brisk. Diving in, Finn swam the first hundred metres too fast, trying to warm his body up but only tiring his arms — not ideal when you have another 900 metres to do. And that was just the warm-up. Slowing to a more controlled pace, the water began to feel comfortable and his arms felt stronger and smoother through the water. By the 600 mark he was feeling really good, his stroke was long and powerful, his breathing controlled and regular. There weren't too many people at the pool this morning and his lane was empty until Jack joined him. Good, thought Finn, you can catch up this morning.

Finishing his kilometre, Finn stood at the shallow end of the pool, stretching his arms and looking out for the others, who had arrived while he was swimming.

After their sprints the boys lingered for the customary chat at the end of the pool before finishing off the routine with the 'Anzac', which was a 50-metre butterfly sprint. No small task after swimming two kilometres.

The sun was now up and the heat felt good on Finn's skin, the air fresh and crisp, void of the normal humidity at that time of year.

'Hey guys, so what do you think of this "Silent Coup" business?' asked Sam.

'Fan-bloody-tastic, about time someone stood up and took charge,' said Jack.

'Yeah, I think it's the best thing to happen to Australia since it all went to shit,' said Finn.

'Damn right,' continued Jack. 'I wish I could join up and go fight now.' This was nothing new. Jack had announced this many times over the last few weeks.

'You can, mate. The army is accepting people up to the age of 50 now,' said Sam with a smirk.

'Nah, it's not that. I got two kids to think about. I can't just run off and leave them,' said Jack, shrugging resignedly.

'Good point,' said Finn. 'You got to think of the family.'

'Still, you could get a non-combat job in the forces,' said Sam, not letting him off the hook.

'Yeah, I suppose, but what would I do? I'm not working in a kitchen or running around after some officer. If I joined the forces, I'd need to fight,' replied Jack.

'I'm thinking of joining,' said Finn matter-of-factly.

The others stopped and stared. Although they had talked about joining up many times before, not one of them had said it so seriously.

'You for real?' asked Jacob, looking amazed.

'Yeah, I am. I've been thinking about it for a while now and I think it's time to do something. I think General Stephens has the right idea and I believe in what he's trying to do,' said Finn.

'Good on you mate,' said Jack, sounding a little awed. 'I think that's bloody great.'

'Are you sure about this? You saw how many people died in the invasion. What makes you think it'll be any different going out into the desert now?' asked Sam.

'To be honest, I'm not sure. I'm not sure of anything, but I do know I've got to do something worthwhile with my life.'

'Well, I think you're insane going out there,' said Sam. 'What's the point in losing your life? There's no way we're ever going to take down the Chinese army, it's just not going to happen.'

'You may be right, but you may be wrong too. There's no way to know without trying,' said Finn.

'Mate, Australia needs more young guys with that attitude. Good on you,' said Jack.

'Well, like I said, I'm only thinking about it. I haven't signed up yet,' said Finn. 'Anyway, we going to do this Anzac or what?' He launched off before anyone could reply, getting a head start on them all.

As he swam he realised the truth was that the more he spoke about joining up, the more convinced he was of doing it. He knew though that if he didn't act on his decision quickly, he might pussy out and convince himself to do something completely different. Like he did when he quit the reserves.

Getting back home that morning, Finn went straight to the Australian Army website and filled out the registration form. Once he submitted it, he immediately got an email informing him that he had to go to the recruitment division in Pitt Street to sign up. 'Doesn't look like they're overrun with traffic to their site,' he observed to himself.

That afternoon he went in and signed the required papers. He knew he shouldn't be surprised at how easy it was to sign up, but it was still a little shocking to waltz into the nearly empty recruitment centre, put his name on a few forms and find himself a member of the army. He was immediately shuffled through a few physical and aptitude tests. He knew he was reasonably fit and didn't find any of the testing too difficult, but they refused to tell him how he did, so he wasn't quite sure.

After the battery of tests, he was sent to a waiting room to receive further information. A woman entered the room and handed him an information pack, then sent him on his way. As he strode back to his Jeep, he flipped open the pack and read the cover letter. It said he was to do his basic training for three months at a base in the Blue Mountains. From there, he would be selected for further training or be placed in a suitable role within the army. Finn had no intention of failing or even just passing his training — he knew he had to excel. He didn't necessarily want to be an officer, but he wanted to be in the top tier of soldiers — special ops or something like that. Given his training in the army reserve, the recruitment officer had said that he would be fast-tracked through his training and placed quickly with a combat-ready squad. The Australian army often did this, mixing the highly experienced with young soldiers with the best potential. It was a proven way to expedite the training of elite soldiers.

That weekend, Finn went to his parents' home for lunch. Midway through the meal, Finn decided to announce his news. 'I've joined the army. I'm going to fight the Chinese,' he said, deadpan.

Sonia dropped her cutlery and put her hand to her open mouth, eyes wide, her hands beginning to tremble almost immediately.

Tom, who was sitting directly across from him, placed his knife and fork carefully on the table, head bowed down towards his plate of food as his eyes slowly moved up to level on Finn. The room was silent. Finn was transfixed by the stare from his dad. It seemed to last an eternity. Finn gripped his cutlery hard and shifted in his seat.

Tom finished chewing, still not making a sound. Finally, he sat back in the chair. 'Not a fucking chance, son,' he said slowly, in a tone Finn couldn't remember hearing before.

Sonia, hands still over her mouth, turned to look at her husband with equal shock.

'Dad, it's too late. I've already joined. I'm going to training camp week after next.'

'You stupid, selfish little shit,' said his dad, face now flushed with anger.

'Tom, please, there's no need …' started Sonia.

'There is a *need* to give our son a reality check. There's a *need* for our son to get his head out of his own arse and realise what he's about to do!'

'Dad, I know what I'm doing. I've never been more sure of anything,' said Finn.

'I don't give a flying fuck what you think you know. I'm calling my lawyer, he'll know a way to get you out of this mess.'

'Dad! For once, can you just listen to me? I want to do this. I am going to do this, so get used to it.' Finn's control was slipping, his voice wavering.

'Get used to my son going out to get killed for some dirt? Finn, I will never support what you are doing. You're a smart kid with way too much going for you than to go and join the army. That's what stupid people do, stupid people who have no other option in life.'

'Listen to yourself, Dad. That's fucking pathetic. Because of people like you, Australia became an easy target for China. I don't blame them for attacking us. We're gutless.'

Pushing his chair back, Tom stood. 'There is no way I will condone this. No way!' With that he turned and left the room.

Sonia, regaining her composure, reached over and took her son's hand. Giving him a long, searching look, she seemed to come to a decision. 'Finn, your dad loves you. That's why he's upset. You can understand that can't you?'

'Yeah, I can, but he must be able to understand that I need to do this. I need to try to do something worthwhile with my life. I've never once been challenged — nothing I've ever done has felt real. This feels real.'

'I'm glad you feel like you're doing something important. Your dad and I just want you to have a long and beautiful life. I don't agree with what you're doing, but I respect your decision.'

'You do?' asked Finn, relieved to hear her say it.

'Yes. You're your own man, Finn, and if this is something you need to do, then do it. Just don't go getting killed or hurt. I want my son back alive and well.' Tears welling up in her eyes, she squeezed Finn's hand.

'Thanks, Mum, I really appreciate it,' Finn said softly, leaning in to give her a hug. For the first time, Finn actually felt scared. All the people who had tried to convince him not to go had bolstered his confidence and made him focus on creating more reasons to do it. Now that his mother was condoning it and supporting him, it suddenly felt more real.

Oh God, what have I done? he thought, hugging his mum.

Sunday morning in Bondi, and the sun streamed through the windows of Finn's lounge. Getting out of bed, he pulled on his board shorts and a shirt. Wandering down to the café barefoot he felt totally free, savouring the feeling, knowing that in a week's time he'd be starting a whole new chapter in his life.

Walking in he immediately spotted Sophie, the English girl, behind the counter. 'Hey, Sophie,' he greeted her with a broad grin, 'How are you? Been surfing lately?'

'Hey Finn. No, I've been focussing on my yoga. Loving it actually.'

'Ah, yoga, huh? Nice one.' He nodded, hands in his pockets.

'So, what can I get you?'

'Err, regular flat white, egg roll …' Finn paused and then decided to go for it. 'And your number?' he finished, emboldened by the fact that he had just a week to make this happen, if it was ever going to happen.

Sophie looked squarely at Finn without hesitating. 'Coming right up,' she said, turning with a smile.

Two minutes later, she handed Finn his coffee and roll. Written on the bag in black texta was her MiLA number. That's what I'm talking about, Finn thought to himself. 'Thanks, talk soon' he said. And with that Finn strolled out trying to look as casual and cool as possible, feeling a million dollars.

Later that afternoon, Finn sent Sophie an Instantext (IT). 'Hey, Sophie, it's Finn,' he said into MiLA, 'was wondering if you'd like to go out for a drink sometime?' He watched as the screen registered his words, converted them to text, and sent the message to Sophie.

Sophie's response was right on time — not too quick, not too slow — suggesting they meet at 8 pm the next day.

'Game on baby, game on,' he said to himself. Now that his time in Sydney was on the clock, he had a sense of urgency about him.

The following evening they met at Lewis's, on Curlewis Street, a cool old wine bar that spilled out onto the pavement. She looked incredible — long dark hair, tanned skin, and a beautifully yoga-toned body. She knew how to dress too, pulling off the bohemian chic look perfectly, totally natural but elegant at the same time. The confident smile she gave Finn when she greeted him showed him she was fully aware of how good she looked.

'So, how long have you been over here for then?' asked Finn once they'd settled down with their wine.

'Oh, about two years now,' she responded.

'No going back?'

'To England? No way, I can't stand being back there. My parents keep trying to convince me to come back home, given what's going on here, but I just love it here.'

'Wow, don't blame you. I lived in London a few years ago after finishing uni. I mean I had an amazing time, but it was never a place I could live.'

'So you're a Sydney boy then. Would you ever live somewhere else?' she asked.

'Well, I don't know where I'll end up. I've actually just joined the army,' Finn said, staring right into Sophie's eyes to see what sort of reaction he got.

'Are you serious? You're going to fight the Chinese?' she said, huge brown eyes holding his gaze but clearly astounded.

'Well, after training, depending on how I go, I'll be posted for combat, or I'll be assigned to some other duty.'

'That's amazing, Finn. Although I think you're mad,' she laughed, white teeth contrasting against her tanned skin. 'I think it's great that you're actually prepared to go and fight,' she said, serious now.

'Yeah, well, it's something I really believe in.'

'So did you just suddenly decide to do this? I thought you were a suit!'

'It was pretty sudden. Well, I was in the army reserve when I was a kid, so I kinda know what the training's all about.'

'Still, you're really going out there to fight for your country. I respect that.'

Feeling a little embarrassed by the attention, Finn tried to play it down. 'Well chances are I'll get posted to the mailroom or something lame like that. Anyone who has come from finance is probably earmarked for office duties, and I'm definitely not skilled enough for something cool like the Militech,' he said in a self-deprecating tone. The Special Military Technology division of the army, known as 'Militech', had been getting a lot of publicity lately, with their aggressive recruiting campaign to get all of the best hackers in the country on their staff. It seemed like it was working, as the buzz was they were getting close to being able to work out Chinese coding.

Smiling, Sophie straightened and looked directly into his eyes, 'I think you'll be able to get to exactly where you want to go. I think you'll be awesome.'

'Anyway, so what else has been going on in the life of Sophie?' Finn asked, wanting to put the conversation back on her.

The rest of the night went by quickly as they chatted and laughed. Finn couldn't believe it had taken him this long to ask her out for a drink. They even laughed about it. By the end of the night they were both mildly drunk. Finn walked her home, which was an apartment she shared on Roscoe Street with two girlfriends from the UK. At the door, she started to rummage through her bag to find MiLA. 'Oh my God, I can never find MiLA,' she said. 'Half the time I have to throw pebbles at the window to get my flatmates to let me in.' She finally dug it out, raising it with a smile of triumph. She turned and passed MiLA over the door sensor, unlocking it. She held the door slightly open and turned back to Finn.

'Hey, I really enjoyed tonight,' said Finn.

'Me too. So are you around this week, before you go to training?'

'Yeah, I am, but I got a load of things to sort out with the flat and everything. I'll give you a call later though. Yeah?'

'Yeah, that would be cool,' she said.

Finn moved closer to her. He had been on enough first dates to know when to go in for a kiss. As Finn stepped in, so did Sophie and they came together and gently kissed. Parting, Finn walked away with a wave and a goodnight.

Sophie occupied his thoughts for the short walk back to his apartment.

Two days later he sent her an IT to see what she was up to on Thursday night, and if she fancied dinner. To his disappointment she was out already with some friends, but they arranged to meet on Friday. He would have to reschedule Chris, but he would understand … he would totally understand.

They had arranged to meet at Ravesi's in Bondi at 8 pm to start the night and see where it went from there. Finn arrived early and grabbed a seat at the bar. Ordering a beer, he pulled a small white pill from his pocket. Throwing it in his mouth, he washed it down with the beer. It was a Harmony pill, completely legal and commonly used as an anti-depressant to calm the mind and create a sense of bliss. Mixed with alcohol, though, the Harmony created a far more exciting effect on the user.

Sophie arrived, turning heads in her wake. Even in a room full of beautiful people, she stood out. Finn stood and smiled, greeting her with a kiss. He felt a flush of pride being seen with her in public — much like how he'd used to feel when going on a shopping spree in his trader days. Like a master of the universe.

'Harmony?' he asked, once they'd settled down.

'Sure,' she replied with a casual smile, taking the pill he'd offered and washing it down. She gazed at Finn pensively. 'You know, I get a bit nostalgic when I see really old movies where people offer each other cigarettes ... it seems so classy and cool. Sometimes I feel like we're missing out. But I guess with the Harmony it's like the same kind of thing, huh?' she asked Finn.

That kicked off hours at the bar drinking, laughing, flirting, progressing to more drinking, more flirting and kissing at the bar. Finn would cringe if he saw another bloke behaving this way in a public space. But tonight it was like there was no one else around, just Finn and Sophie.

Neither of them wanted the night to end, so when the bar shut they hopped into Finn's Jeep and requested it take them to Kings Cross. It pulled up out the front of Resonate, one of the newest clubs in Sydney. Sophie walked up to the front of the queue, taking Finn along behind her by the hand. She approached one of the bouncers.

'Hey, Greg, how've you been?'

'Not bad, Soph. Looking good!' he replied, opening the door for them. They walked in and entered a long dark hall. The deep vibrations from the club rumbled. The walls along the hallway were like speakers. As the name suggested, they properly resonated. It created a strange feeling of disorientation — the sound so powerful it was more of a feeling in the whole body.

'Hey, want a patch?' asked Sophie.

Finn stopped. 'You got some?' he asked, surprised.

'Yeah, have you had one before?'

'No, I've heard too many stories about people being paralysed and shit.'

'That's all rubbish, come on, turn around.'

Finn turned and Sophie took the small patch from her clutch. It was a rectangular sticker the size of a 50-cent coin, which contained a sophisticated multi-layered optoelectronic circuit board.

Finn felt Sophie's hands on his neck, feeling for the C1 vertebra on his spine. She rubbed the area softly, increasing the blood flow. He felt her stick the patch on just above the vertebra. There was a momentary sting — and then a surge through his whole body. It took his breath away as his body convulsed once involuntarily. It passed quickly and he felt like never before. It was as if he had shed his old skin like a snake or cicada. His new skin felt everything — the air, the noise, the temperature. Then Sophie touched his hand gently. It sent a pulse all the way up his arm. It was incredible.

'Oh my fucking god, what … what's happening?'

'It'll settle in a second. Pretty incredible huh?'

'Everything is new, everything feels like, a million times more!' He stared at her, eyes wide.

Sophie smiled. 'Told you not to worry. Now you do me.' She handed him the patch.

Finn took it, again feeling a pulse up his arm and into his chest.

'Just make sure you get it above the last vertebra or else it won't get the neuro connection.'

Sophie turned around and lifted her hair. Finn touched her neck. The skin was soft and the hairs tickled his fingers. He slowly rubbed her neck the same way she had done to him. Putting the patch just above the vertebra he saw it glow light blue as soon as it was on the skin.

'Oh fuck,' groaned Sophie as she convulsed forward, steadying herself with one arm on the wall.

'You okay?' asked Finn, concerned.

'Never better,' she replied, turning, breathing heavily and smiling. 'Are you ready for the most amazing experience of your life?' she asked, taking Finn's hand and leading him to the door at the end of the hall.

Opening the door to the club, the music washed over them as physically as a wave on the shore break. Finn was swimming in the white wash of sound, the current pulling at his body. At first he thought he was choking, unable to breathe, then the sensation settled and he relaxed, letting the sounds flow over, around and through his body.

They brushed past people, each contact sending tingles and pulses through his body. Finding some space, they danced, moving their bodies together, touching, swaying, enveloping themselves in the music, the strobing lights and the sensation of their bodies. It was almost spiritual, Finn felt, as if he was transcending his body, feeling everything more cleanly and deeply than ever before.

They danced for hours, just the two of them, transfixed on one another, greedily consuming every heightened sensation.

Finn was losing himself. He was now swimming on his own, deep in an empty ocean. Darkness and water all around, he didn't feel scared. He felt at peace. His body was numb and warm and comfortable, he was alone, floating in the dark watching the stars, bright and vibrant. He was aware of the music, of Sophie, of the world, but they were all beneath him, under the water, deep down, so that only slight vibrations disturbed the otherwise slick and tranquil water.

He felt a hand on his neck, stroking him gently. And then it was over. Abruptly he came back to reality … the dark loud club, the pounding bass, the crowded dance floor and Sophie in front of him looking into his eyes. It all looked dirty and seedy now, the people in the club were swaying and dancing, but alone and in their own world.

'Come on, let's go!' she yelled above the music.

Once outside Finn's senses slowly re-calibrated to the real world.

'Sorry, I had to pull your patch off so quickly in there.'

'That's okay. That was incredible.'

'It is, but it's easy to lose yourself with a patch. You can see them in there,' she gestured towards the club with her thumb, 'it gives a whole new meaning to the term "losers". They just go too deep with the patch. It's not until closing time that the bouncers come around and tear them off. Talk about a crash.'

'I can imagine.'

'Well, you were on your way, back in there.'

'Sorry about that.'

'Don't worry about it, takes a bit of practise to get the hang of them. It's like you need to let yourself go to the point where you are still aware of what's happening, but as soon as you realise you're the only person in your space then you need to come back. Hard to control though.'

'Ever tried one with sex?'

'Yeah, it starts out incredible, but it's not that good. You just end up going into your own place — kind of makes it boring.'

'Sounds average.'

'Completely. It takes the beauty out of it.' She suddenly looked shy, tucking her hair behind her ear and looking up at him.

'So, do you want to come back to mine?' he asked, entwining his fingers with hers. Finns heart thumping as the question hung in the air momentarily.

'Only if you have water. I'm so thirsty,' replied Sophie, smiling.

'Whoa, it's 4 am,' Finn commented as he glanced at MiLA's screen before summoning his car through the device. They waited on the corner for the Jeep to arrive, happy to be leaving together. Back in Bondi they fell out of the Jeep in front of Finn's place. Walking arm-in-arm into the apartment building they were laughing, making far too much noise. In the lift going up Finn warned, 'You'll have to excuse my place, it's in a state'.

'Whatever,' said Sophie as she pressed herself against him and started to kiss him greedily.

Out of the lift, they ran along the hall to Finn's apartment. Once inside, he offered Sophie water, which she accepted as she walked off to find the bathroom. Three minutes later she came out to find Finn asleep on the couch.

Taking his hands, she tried to heave him to his feet. But he was way too heavy and too far gone to be woken. Giving up, she went to the bedroom, undressed and got into bed, the room spinning slightly but not enough to stop her from slipping into a deep alcohol-induced sleep.

The light from the uncovered windows woke Finn in the morning. Feeling like death, fully clothed, head pounding, and mouth dry and acidic, he felt the come-down from the night before acutely. Slowly, he pulled himself off the couch and stumbled into the bathroom to shower and brush his teeth. Walking out of the bathroom and into his bedroom he saw a shape under the covers of his duvet and unfamiliar clothes on the floor.

'Oh shit,' he whispered, as shards of memories from last night came back.

Dropping his towel, he slid into bed beside her. The bed was warm, her tangled dark hair a mess on the pillow. She was lying on her side facing away from him and he moved in to envelop her warm, beautiful body. Putting an arm around her, he felt her shuffle slightly.

'Good morning, soldier,' she said in a huskier tone than Finn remembered.

'Good morning, sexy,' he replied, with a smile on his face.

'I don't mean to be rude,' said Sophie, turning to face him, 'but I feel terrible'. She put a hand to her temple.

'Oh God, same, I can't believe you made us drink those tequilas. It's definitely your fault.' Finn said, squeezing her playfully.

'My fault?' replied Sophie. 'You got me drunk with military precision,' she said, rolling over and giving Finn a playful whack on the arm. 'Besides, you're the one who passed out on your couch.'

They lay in bed all morning, lazily and sensually discovering each other's bodies. After the second round, they finally got up to face the day at about 1 pm. Finn walked her to the lift. 'Thanks for an amazing night, and even more amazing morning,' he said with an easy grin.

'Thank you, soldier,' replied Sophie. 'So will I see you before you head off?'

'I'm not sure. I have to get out of here today and I'll be up at my parents' until I go to the training camp.'

'Okay, I understand,' she smiled, squeezing his hand. 'Well send me an IT to let me know how you're getting on.'

'You bet,' he replied as the lift doors opened. Bringing her in closer he gave her a last kiss. 'See you gorgeous,' he called after her as she got into the lift.

'Bye,' was all she said, smoothing down her hair as the doors closed.

Finn walked back to the apartment to finish packing before his parents arrived. 'Why is it that these things only happen when you're about to go away?' he asked himself. Maybe his dad was right. Maybe he had way too much to lose here. But there was no going back now.

Sonia arrived just after 4 pm to help him with his things. The apartment looked bare and depressing now that all his belongings were removed. Finn took one last look and closed the door on his way out. Driving down Hall Street, leaving Bondi behind, Finn passed the café where Sophie worked. What the hell am I doing? he thought to himself as he watched the life he had built recede in the rear-view mirror.

Chapter 7

The following Monday, Sonia and Finn packed up his basic kit and readied themselves for the drive to the Woodford Army Base. Standing in his room, Sonia gripped Finn's arm and gently said, 'You should go say goodbye to your dad.'

The previous night, as with every night lately, they'd had a fight. Tom had said he refused to come with them to drop Finn off, saying he couldn't drive his own son to his death. Finn had no doubt that the old man was still furious with him. He hesitantly walked into his dad's home office. He studied the room, walls lined with plaques, awards and photos from Tom's CEO years. Finn had always admired that office, had thought that was the kind of success he'd wanted to aim for. Tom had encouraged that in him as well. Now Finn was saying goodbye to all that. Tom was sitting at his desk, flicking through news feeds on his screen. He clearly wasn't reading anything, though, just flicking to occupy his mind.

'Dad? We're leaving,' Finn said, as gently as he could.

Tom didn't look up or at his son. He pretended he hadn't heard him. Finn, eyes stinging with tears, backed out of the room.

The moment the door clicked shut, sobs started to rack Tom's body. He bent his head down and wept, alone.

Finn was silent virtually the whole way to the training base. He felt scared.

'Fuck, fuck, fuck. Get your head straight you tosser, time to man up, time to do something real with your worthless life,' he repeated to himself.

Pulling up to the gate, they were met by a sign proclaiming: 'No cars beyond this point'. This suited Finn: he didn't want to be the one who gets dropped off on day one by his tearful mum. Kissing and hugging each other, they exchanged the ritual I-love-yous. Finn couldn't wait to get away — it was hard enough without his mother getting all emotional on him. He was trying desperately to keep his cool, and keep the tears at bay. Again he chastised himself. 'Toughen the fuck up,' he willed himself as he walked to the guard post.

'Finn Hunt. I'm reporting for training,' he said to the soldier behind the counter.

The corporal searched down his sheet of paper. 'Hunt, Hunt, Hunt. Ah yes, here you are. You've done time with the reserve it says here.'

'Yes, two years.'

'All right then. You're to report to bunker 12 to get processed. There you will be issued your instructions. Check the map on the wall to locate bunker 12.'

'Thank you,' said Finn, already feeling out of his depth.

Walking over to the map he was confronted with what seemed like a city, mapped out with hundreds of buildings.

'Fuck me,' he muttered to himself, not noticing the two others who had moved up behind him to read the map as well.

'Where you supposed to be?' asked one of them, surprising Finn.

'Ah, bunker 12, wherever the hell that is,' replied Finn, turning to look at his companions. They looked young, and rough as guts. They looked exactly like Tom's idea of a soldier, dumb shits who had no other options.

'Hey, same. I guess all the newbies are sent to bunker 12,' said the other guy, staring blankly at the map.

'Yeah, guess so,' said Finn. Without waiting to find bunker 12 on the map, Finn picked up his bag and walked out of the guardhouse. Looking around the camp, it didn't seem as big as what the map had made it look like — but then again, he could only see the first few rows of buildings before the ground sloped off down a hill. Starting to walk, he noticed signs pointing out directions for the different numbered bunkers and buildings. Following the signs, he walked along trying to take it all in. There was a great deal of activity along the tar-sealed roads and grassed areas. Groups of soldiers running in formation, some doing push-ups, other groups just standing at attention. It felt like something out of a movie.

Walking up to bunker 12, Finn pulled open the flimsy plywood door. The whole camp had a pop-up feel to it, as if it could be disassembled in less than a day. Stepping into the bunker, Finn was greeted by a burly-looking corporal seated at a small desk that only accentuated his size.

'Soldier! Over here,' said the corporal, gesturing for Finn to approach him.

Finn walked over to the desk, not really knowing what to say. 'Finn Hunt reporting for service, err ... sir.'

'Hunt,' he grunted, looking down at his papers. 'Right. You've been assigned to Tiger Battalion, report to tent 456, which is on the southeast corner of the base. Once processed, you will report to your tent and make yourself known to Sergeant Higgins who is in charge of your squad.'

When the corporal had finished his long list of instructions, most of which Finn barely took in, he directed Finn to a door on the right of the bunker. Here Finn was issued with his uniform and equipment, given a medical examination, a haircut and an information pack regarding the camp. After four hours of being processed, Finn emerged back into the sun and heat of the late afternoon, rubbing his freshly buzzed head. It had been years since he last shaved his head, and he couldn't stop rubbing it.

Finn was stunned by the level of activity in the camp. It was as if everyone had a specific job they were focussed on. They all seemed to have a purpose here, everyone except him. What the hell was he doing here? He was a trader, a city boy who used face creams and wore designer clothes. His whole image had been carefully constructed from magazines and movies. Finn had to will himself on, telling himself the panic he was feeling was good, it meant he was out of his comfort zone — actually challenging himself.

Finding tent 456, Finn walked in to find it empty of people. There was plenty of gear lying around in a tidy fashion. He spotted a bunk bed that looked empty, threw his bag and gear on the end and sat with his head in his hands. The self-doubt was now really kicking in and the voice in his head continued to tell him he didn't belong. He lay on the bed and tried to get himself under control.

It was dark by the time the others got back to the tent. In they streamed, all six of them. Dirty, smelly and exhausted. No one paid any attention to Finn. They were silent, perhaps too exhausted to talk.

'My name is Finn Hunt. Is Sergeant Higgins here?' Finn said to no one in particular.

No one in particular answered him. They all just carried on silently shedding their dusty equipment and stripping off clothes that were heavy from sweat and grime. It was as if they were all deaf and blind — or was it that Finn was mute and invisible?

Coming up behind a large man who wore the stripes of a sergeant, he said, 'Excuse me, sir. My name is Finn Hunt and I've been ordered to report to Sergeant Higgins.'

The man, who was bent over his rucksack, raised his torso slowly but did not turn to face Finn. 'Private Hunt, welcome to the war. Welcome to the Tigers. Are you sure you're in the right place though? I heard that the admin corps is looking for secretaries. You look like you'd fit right in over there.' A stifled snigger resonated throughout the tent.

Finn had to smile at that. He knew he looked out of place. 'Ah, no sir, I'm in the right place. I was injured in the field of typing — paper laceration to the middle finger meant I could never type again, sir, so they transferred me to the infantry to see out my time.' He looked solemnly at the sergeant's back.

Still facing his bunk, Sergeant Higgins asked the rest of the men, 'What do you reckon, boys? Sounds like we've got another wannabe action hero in our midst.'

'No room for heroes around here,' came a voice behind Finn.

'No room for pussies either,' said another.

Higgins turned now to face Finn. He was a big man with big features. His face had handsome proportions and structure, but he was battle-scarred and creased — he looked like an old campaigner from way back, but he was probably only in his thirties.

'So, Hunt, sounds like you don't fit in around here. We don't want pansies and we don't need any more heroes,' said Higgins. 'You've got some work to do to prove yourself around here.'

Finn's face was serious. 'Yessir, I'll do my best.'

Moving closer to Finn now, Higgins leaned in. '"Your best?" Your best won't do, Hunt. Not at all. You're going to need to tap into your worst.' Higgins' face was so close to Finn's that he could smell the stench of his breath and see the red veins in his eyes. 'You'll need to bring out the worst in yourself, the part of you that you haven't met. But you will, and when you do, you may not like who you are.'

Finn just stood, staring straight ahead.

Higgins continued staring him right in the eye, not moving but breathing heavily. 'Tomorrow you start learning about who you really are, Hunt. Dismissed!' And with that Higgins turned and got back to his unpacking.

Finn turned and went back to his bunk. The tent was silent and the rest of the men went back to busying themselves with their gear.

Following the initial battle for Australia, Higgins, like most of the surviving soldiers, had been promoted and posted to training camps. The theory being that Australia needed to train a small elite group of soldiers that could disrupt and cause as much havoc for the Chinese as possible. Higgins' extensive experience and training as a US soldier made him a valuable asset for the military. He wasn't exactly thrilled about the idea of training young men and women to go out and fight, to see the things he had seen, but he followed his orders to the letter like the professional soldier that he was.

The next day Finn was woken by the sound of the alarm, which was a piercing siren broadcast across the camp. In a repeat of last night, everyone silently busied themselves, getting their equipment together with a minimum of fuss. Finn had no idea what to do. He just started stuffing his kit into his rucksack. Leaning over to his right, Finn tried to get the attention of a young guy who looked remotely approachable. 'Hey mate, what do I need? I've got no idea what to pack. What the hell am I supposed to do?'

The soldier looked over at him and resigned himself to help Finn. Without saying a word he grabbed bits of kit from Finn's bed and stuffed it into his rucksack, stuffing it as full as possible. Finn noticed that he put all the heavy items into the bag and that the other rucksacks looked half-empty, while his was brimming over the top.

What an arsehole, Finn thought.

The men were now bantering between themselves and filing out of the tent, leaving it looking tidy and orderly. Finn followed them out and joined the line. All the way down the row of at least 100 tents, men were standing at attention.

Higgins was at the front taking orders from a lieutenant. Afterwards, he turned and faced the men of Finn's squad and relayed the orders, which consisted of the day's training program.

At first, Finn thought it strange that he had been placed in a squad of men who seemed to already be well into their training. It didn't make any sense to Finn, but there didn't seem any sense in complaining — he was simply expected to learn it quicker and make up for what he had missed. It was in fact a tactic used by the army in order to fast-track the training of new recruits who had previous military training and demonstrated the right qualities and abilities. Finn ticked all these boxes. His reserve training and the fact he had aced his aptitude and physical entry tests made him the perfect recruit to the new Australian army.

So began three months of hell. The training from day one was gruelling, a mixture of barbaric exercises and training runs, weapons training, hand-to-hand combat, communications, IT warfare, bush survival, and basic interrogation.

It took several days for the other men to let Finn into their group. He made the breakthrough during a particularly tough training run along a muddy trail. Higgins was leading the men and Finn was behind him. Finn had always been a naturally good distance runner and didn't mind the long runs they were subjected to every day. At one point on the trail a fallen tree had to be used to cross a shallow, muddy gully. Higgins leapt onto the fallen tree trunk, with his arms stretched wide to help keep his balance. He started to move quickly across the trunk. Finn was only a second or two behind, looking down at the trunk about two metres ahead to help him stay focussed.

Dead in the middle of the trunk a movement in front of him caught Finn's eye. Higgins had spun around to face Finn and was looking menacingly back at him. Finn watched as Higgins unhooked his rucksack and threw it back on the opposite bank, not once taking his eyes off Finn. The others in the squad knew what was coming and stayed off the trunk, grinning and nudging each other with glee.

Finn followed suit and unclipped his rucksack, fumbling with the clips and nearly losing his balance. His nerves suddenly raw, he felt certain his heart would burst through his chest at any moment.

'Come on then, Hunt. Remember your reserves training? Speed and aggression,' snarled Higgins.

Speed and aggression — how many times had that been drilled into him as a young reservist? he wondered. They were the two things every soldier is taught first and it sums up how a soldier should react to every situation in the field — though Finn wasn't convinced it was always the best response.

Not saying a word, Finn concentrated on Higgins. Getting his left foot forward he pointed it at Higgins, his right foot back, his body crouching low, centred and ready.

Higgins was quick for a big man. He shuffled his feet quickly forward, jabbing his right fist at Finn, who instinctively moved back fast and into the arms of the other men, who pushed him back out on the trunk.

The yelling and cheering intensified. The others were like a pack of wild dogs with a blood lust. Taking a quick look down at the gully below, Finn decided that landing down there was not going to be a good outcome.

Finn knew he didn't have a chance if he let Higgins come at him like that again, so he decided to employ the age-old wisdom that the best defence is a good offence. Moving out slowly, Finn waited until the exact split-second before he thought Higgins would attack. Rather than launching his upper body at him — which would undoubtedly have landed them both on the gully floor — Finn dropped his torso down and backwards while kicking out his leg, swiping at Higgins' shin. It was enough to surprise Higgins, catching him off guard and sending him off the trunk and into the muddy gully.

Finn ended up straddling the trunk, having lost his balance with his kick. The others were laughing themselves stupid. In the mud, Higgins was trying to catch his breath, the fall having knocked the wind out of his lungs. Covered in mud, he finally got to his feet and was forced to smile and congratulate Finn. 'You got lucky, Hunt. Don't let it go to your head. That won't happen again.'

'No, sir,' replied Finn, forcing himself to control his face and get the smirk off it.

McCaw, a huge guy nearly as scary and experienced as Higgins, and so taciturn Finn had never even heard him speak, helped Finn up. 'Good job, recruit,' he said, slapping Finn on the back.

About halfway through their training, Finn and the other squadies were opening large metal weapons cases in one of the vast munitions tents. The tents were enormous, covering four football fields' worth of space. They were air-conditioned, had solid flooring and bright lighting.

Pulling out a black assault rifle, Finn admired the feel of the weapon. It was big and solid in his hands, but incredibly light.

'What are these all about?' he asked the others.

'Dude, these are Archer RG-25s, outrageous killing machines,' said Carver, a young recruit who had been in training when the Chinese invaded but had not been sent out to fight.

'RG stands for Rail Gun. These guys are electromagnetic. They fire a kinetic 4.5 mm ball bearing munition at a muzzle velocity of 3500 metres per second, and all this with no recoil,' said Marks, a veteran with 10 years of military experience. He'd been injured in the initial fight with the Chinese, but was back to full fighting strength now, after his training with the squad. Finn got the sense that, while Marks was not exactly a genius, he was strong, observant and focussed — the kind of guy you'd be glad to have watching your back.

'And when things get really hairy, you can lob a grenade in over the line with this.' Jessop flipped his RG-25 on its side to show Finn the launcher. Jessop had only been in training a few weeks longer than Finn, but he was a farm boy who'd grown up with a gun by his side — he had an uncanny sense for them.

'Do we get these?' asked Finn.

At that moment Higgins walked into the room. 'Are you pussies still unloading this lot? Get a fucking move on. Hunt, quit masturbating that RG and get it unloaded.'

'Yessir,' snapped Finn, quickly focussing on unloading the case.

Higgins went back outside and started barking orders at some other poor bastards.

'So how the hell do we get these things? I figured we'd be firing some old M-21s,' said Finn.

'Hunt, you are so green it's not funny. Who do you think has lost the most here? And who has the most to gain by getting the Chinese out?' asked Carver.

'Everyone in Australia,' replied Finn.

'Bullshit. The people who have lost the most are the mining companies. They also have the most to gain by kicking the Chinks out,' Jessop piped up, enjoying not being the greenest guy around anymore.

'What, so the mining companies are bankrolling us?' asked Finn.

'Damn right. Right down to the army-issue boxer shorts you're wearing there.'

'Fuck me,' said Finn to himself.

It hadn't occurred to Finn that the huge mining companies, like IXR and BHR, were funding all of this. Many of the smaller Australian mining companies had gone bankrupt as soon as China stepped foot in Australia. Most of the other larger companies had come very close, but had managed to hold on, relying on their diversified overseas holdings to see them through.

The big mining companies also had their own private armies. It was a trend that started early in the century, in the Middle East. The companies knew all too well the volatile nature of mining in countries that have so much poverty. Though they couldn't afford to pull their corporate armies out of the Middle East and North America, they could afford to fund and arm Australia's new army. It was so obviously in their interests that Finn felt stupid for not realising it sooner.

The days became a blur of intense physical training, mental discipline, eating and sleeping. While Finn knew that technically he would be in for training for three months, it felt like he had no idea how long he had been in training for — it could have been a month, it could have been six. The training was designed to educate them on specific skills required for the sorts of missions they were likely to conduct. They were effectively being trained to be the best terrorists in the world, to learn and apply the principles of terrorism and guerrilla warfare for the most devastating effect.

Through the training process Finn's mind was rewired by the drill instructors, by Higgins, by the constant haranguing and abuse. Mindlessly repeating drill after drill after drill, exercise after exercise. There was no defined point at which he noticed a change in himself — it was a far more organic process that evolved over the three months of training. It wasn't until the end of their training that he realised how much he had changed. Physically, he was fitter and stronger than he had ever been.

His training had been extensive and beyond what was normally asked of new recruits. The war that would be fought over Australia would be like none the world had seen. The soldiers that fought the war would be like none the world had seen. Finn now had a confidence that he had never had before, a feeling that no matter what situation he was presented with, he could deal with it. He had always been an outwardly confident person but he now realised that it had been based on very little substance. He could see it now — he could see what a boy he had been before the training, how naive he had been.

The confidence he had now made him feel invincible and it felt good, but there was also a level of aggression he'd never had before. He wanted to test himself, to put what he had learnt into practice. He didn't really care about who they were or where, he just wanted to do what he had been trained to do — to be aggressive, to act quickly, to use his body and his senses more than his head. He wanted to fight.

Chapter 8

Sitting on the train back to Sydney felt good; the rhythmic motion, the forward movement and the warmth from the sun lulled Finn. With the initial training over, he and the others had two weeks' leave. Finn felt apprehensive but excited to see his mates again and to let go for a while. He realised after he walked out of the camp that the entire time he had been in training he was on edge, constantly alert and never really able to relax.

Arriving at Central Station, it was warm, the cloudless blue sky felt immense and open, and the air smelled of rainwater being evaporated off the ground by the hot sun. It was strange to have so many people around him, all going about their usual activities. It all seemed so foreign to him now — wearing a suit, walking to an office, sitting at a desk — he couldn't imagine ever doing any of that again.

Finn decided that he wasn't ready to see his parents yet. After the way his father had reacted to him joining the army, he couldn't face repeating that argument. He also knew that on a certain, immature level, he wanted to punish his dad for not saying goodbye.

Chris's parents were welcoming and had told Finn he could stay with them for as long as he wanted. With that organised, all Finn could think about was seeing Sophie again. It had been three months and, although they emailed constantly in the first few weeks, it had eventually whittled away to nothing.

Finn took a taxi to Chris's parents' home in the exclusive Sydney suburb of Rose Bay. Paying the cabbie, Finn heaved his army-issue rucksack over his shoulder and headed through the gate to the front door.

'Come here, boy,' yelled Chris with a big goofy grin as he pulled Finn in for a hug. 'Not too tough for a hug now, fella?'

'Yeah, yeah …' said Finn, returning the hug with a resigned grin.

'Mate, three months with a bunch of soldier boys. I bet you got a lot of practice hugging blokes, didn't ya?' Chris laughed at his own joke, as he was prone to do.

'Seriously mate, I'm a weapon now, so don't test me,' Finn said in the most serious tone he could muster.

'Yeah right, you just look like a meat-head to me,' replied Chris, laughing and pointing at his buzzed head. 'C'mon, drop your gear and let's head up to the Lord Dudley for a few beers. I've arranged to meet some of the guys at the Grand National later. Everyone wants to hear about your toy guns.'

That night, Finn felt relaxed, physically, but his friends noticed something different about him. He'd always had a bit of a scowl on his face when it was in repose, but they knew it didn't have anything to do with his personality. Now, though, the scowl seemed more meaningful. He was definitely more watchful, more alert than he used to be — and somehow much more physically imposing, even though he hadn't bulked up all that much. But they didn't let this new Finn get in the way of a good time — every time they got together they ripped shreds off each other and laughed themselves stupid in the process. Finn enjoyed the night out, but as they talked shit about their mortgages and their cars, Finn couldn't help but feel like his friends' lives were easy and trivial. He himself had been doing the same thing not three months before, but now he felt unimaginably distant from that world.

The one part of that world that seemed to have the same effect on him as before was Sophie. The whole time, Finn couldn't stop thinking about Sophie and wondering if she was out that night. Afterwards, walking back to Chris's parents' place he considered sending her an IT. How uncool though, firing off a drunken message at two in the morning. No way, he thought to himself. Have some class.

The next day he got up early and left before Chris and his parents were up. Finn wanted to get down to Bondi and surprise Sophie. He couldn't wait to see the look on her face.

Taking the packed 389 bus from Bondi Junction down to the beach and getting off on Hall Street, he started walking down towards the café. If there was one place in Australia that was oblivious to the Chinese invasion, it was Bondi. Same mix of bohemian cruisers getting by on the fumes of money, side-by-side with the mega-wealthy. Often it was hard to tell them apart, the rich dressed to look urban and rough to blend in, the rest dressed to stand out and be seen. Somehow, they all ended up looking the same. Finn wondered if any of them even realised that the Chinese had invaded, let alone cared. Unlikely, he thought.

He thought again about how he would walk in — with a cool, calm, collected look, he'd just stand and say nothing until she saw him. Or perhaps he would burst in and yell her name, Rocky Balboa–style; or maybe a witty one-liner?

'Shit,' he cursed. What's something witty? Witty, witty, witty … fuck — nothing came to mind. No, it wouldn't be the witty line approach. Ten metres to go. Fuck it, just walk in and see what happens, he figured.

Stepping in, the café was busy. He looked behind the counter and saw three girls serving, but no sign of Sophie.

'Excuse me, is Sophie working today?' he politely asked one of the girls.

'Soph? No, sorry mate, she's gone back to England, I think,' replied the girl. 'Hey, Georgie. Soph went back to England, didn't she?' the girl yelled to another out the back.

'Yep, she would have flown out about a month ago,' came the reply.

Finn was immediately and obviously deflated.

'Sorry, mate. I think she had some family problems. Can I get you anything?'

'Um, yeah, guess I'll have a flat white, thanks,' replied Finn glumly.

When he left, he turned towards the beach and started walking. Fuck it, he thought, resigning himself to the coastal track to Bronte Beach. It had lost a few millimetres of width with the rising water levels as the polar ice caps melted, but it was still a stunning walk and, with a spot of people-watching, he figured Sophie would be off his mind in no time. Finn told himself to apply some of the mental discipline he'd acquired and harden the fuck up.

The following day Finn called his mother.

'Hello,' came the familiar voice.

'Hi, Mum. It's me,' said Finn.

'Oh darling, how are you?' her voice lilted, immediately animated. 'It's so good to hear from you. Where are you?'

'I've got a few weeks' leave and I'm in Sydney, staying at Chris's place.'

'You must come home, we have to see you —'

'Mum,' Finn interrupted, 'I don't want to come home if Dad is still upset.'

'Don't you worry about your dad, Finn. I've properly sorted him out after his little performance when you left.' She sounded satisfied with her work — when it came to her and Tom, she usually won when she decided to take a stand on something.

'Are you sure, Mum? I don't want to fight with him anymore and I haven't changed my mind about what I'm doing.'

'I know darling, and your dad is okay with it now.'

'Cool. Well I'll come up this afternoon. Think I'll stay at Chris's tonight though if that's okay. Just want to see how Dad and I get along first. Is that cool?'

'Of course, Finn. You just get up here straight away.'

'Okay, I'll see you soon. Bye.'

'All right, darling. See you soon,' said Sonia. And with that Finn hung up.

That afternoon, Chris lent Finn his car so he could get up to his parents' home. Pulling into the driveway he felt nervousness combined with a sudden pang of homesickness.

As he was parking in the driveway, Sonia came out the front door followed by Tom. 'Finn!' she yelled. 'Come here, my boy.' With her arms stretched wide, her caftan making her look almost as though she had bat wings, she pulled him in for a hug, squeezing him tightly.

'I've missed you so much, young man. Look at you! You look so fit and healthy — except for that haircut.' She wrinkled her nose with distaste.

'Thanks, Mum,' Finn replied, smiling like a teenager.

'Come here, son', said Tom, pulling him in for an even bigger bear-hug. 'Missed you, mate. Glad to see you made it through training in one piece.'

'Thanks, Dad. It's great to see you guys, too.'

'Come on then, let's go inside. I want to hear all about it,' said Sonia.

They had so many questions for him. He did his best to answer them. Tom seemed genuinely interested in what Finn had to say. Gone was the anger and bitterness when he had left for training. He seemed to have done a 180 and was supporting Finn in what he was doing. Finn had to congratulate his mum — she sure knew how to play his father.

Later that afternoon while Sonia was out of the room, Tom leaned over to Finn. 'Look mate,' he said, his forehead creasing with regret, 'I'm really sorry about the way I behaved when you left … '

'Dad, stop, you really don't need to apologise, I … '

'No, son. Just listen for a moment. I'm sorry for what I said and how I reacted. You're a man now and you can make your own decisions. And I honestly do admire you for what you are doing. You feel like you need to do this, and you're doing it. It takes courage to make a decision like that. I see that now, mate. I didn't before. I just saw you going off to be cannon fodder out in the bush.'

Finn had listened intently, touched by the words of his dad. He'd never heard him talk about anything with so much emotion. It felt awkward.

'Dad, I could still wind up cannon fodder,' said Finn with a smirk. 'Seriously though, I think the new strategy is going to be much better. General Stephens knows what he's doing. We're being trained in tactical, guerrilla warfare. We won't be doing the all-out, head-on assault that we saw in the beginning. It'll be different from now on, trust me.'

'I hope so, Finn — for your sake and the sake of the country, because no one else seems to care if it goes down the drain.'

'Dad, don't think for a minute that there aren't people ready to fight. There are thousands of soldiers being trained just on the other side of the Blue Mountains. God knows how many more camps there are scattered around the rest of the country.'

Tom stared at Finn blankly before forcing an imitation of a smile and slapped his big hand on his son's knee.

'Son, I just want you to know that I support what you're doing and I'm sorry for the way I reacted. Now, we're out of beer, so I'm going to pop down to the bottle-o.'

Finn watched his father stand up and walk towards the door. 'Okay, Dad. Thanks.'

The two weeks of leave flew by. Finn split his time between his parents' house on the Northern Beaches and Chris's parents' place in the Eastern Suburbs. Life was good. The weather was cooler but the sharp, clear days were a welcome relief from the hot, sweltering training of the last few months.

Finn and Chris had numerous nights out, and had quickly discovered that telling the girls that Finn was heading out to fight the Chinese worked a treat.

But Finn also noticed a new tension between him and Chris. Late one afternoon the pair stepped into the Golden Sheaf in Double Bay. The bar was quiet and it was cold outside as the sun dropped, so the warm, inviting bar was a welcome sanctuary. As usual, Finn had positioned himself at a spot on the bar where he had a good view of the room, with an eye on the entrance. He did it without thinking — it had become his second nature. He'd also found himself scanning every new space he entered, as though assessing it for possible threats. When they were on their third beer, Chris, out of nowhere and in total seriousness, said, 'Mate, you've changed. I can't explain exactly how, but you seem different, don't you think?'

'I don't know. You're telling the story, not me,' replied Finn.

'Don't be a twat, mate. You have changed — you're more serious. It's like a control thing. You're not letting go of yourself like you used to.'

'Dude, of course I've fucking changed. I've just had three months of bollockings and physical and mental torture. I've learnt how to kill a person 20 different ways for chrissakes,' snapped Finn — more aggressively than he had intended.

'Yeah, I get that mate. I was just making an observation,' said Chris.

Sitting there at the bar it dawned on Finn that he had changed — and a lot more than he was showing Chris or anyone else. He was now a trained killer and, in all likelihood, that's exactly what he would be doing. There was an edge, or hardness, to Finn now that he never knew he had.

'I'm going to have to go out there soon,' Finn said, pointing to the west, 'and in all likelihood kill someone, or be killed myself. I'm not looking for anyone to be impressed, but mate, you gotta understand that I'm scared and I'm a little, well, angry too.'

'Angry about what, dude?' quizzed Chris.

'Angry that I'm going out there to fight while so many others sit around doing fuck-all. That's what I'm angry about,' replied Finn, staring into his half-full beer bottle.

'I see, so it's "fuck you Chris, stay at home with your mum and dad and masturbate yourself to sleep every night while I, Finn Hunt, go save Australia," is that what you're saying? Fuck you, mate.'

'I didn't mean it like that, and you know it.'

'Yeah, right. But that's what you're thinking, isn't it?' said Chris, now getting fired up.

Finn had gone too far to back down now. 'Dude, why don't you join up and fight then? How can you be happy letting people lose their lives for you while you do literally nothing?'

'"Fight"? You call what the army did up north "fighting"? In case you missed it on BBCNN, they were fucking slaughtered. Dude, what's the point of fighting against a force like that? You're just going to be target practice for the enemy.'

Feeling suddenly sober, Finn looked at Chris. 'What's the point of living if you never put anything on the line? Your life is as safe as a toddler's. How does that feel?'

'That's not the point,' Chris responded, visibly stung, 'You're fighting for nothing. We don't need the mines to carry on with a good life. What we need is to focus on rebuilding Australia's economy. Instead of you tossers running around playing with your guns, we should be putting our minds to the task of getting things back on track.'

'You're a fucking idiot, Chris. Do you really think that the Chinese will stop at a few mines in the outback? Think about it: we're now their bitches. Whatever we create in the future will be taken away from us as soon as the Chinese want it, because that's what bullies do. Me? I don't want to live my life as somebody's bitch and I don't want my future children growing up like that either.'

Fuming, the two sat facing each other at the bar. The bartender, overhearing them as their voices became louder, had quietly gone out the back. The rest of the bar was empty and quiet.

'You're the fucking idiot if you think that going out there to fight is going to make any difference,' Chris growled through clenched teeth. 'You'll be killed — and for what? Some shitty red earth and a load of iron ore — I mean, who gives a fuck?'

'You got it wrong, mate. This isn't about iron ore, it's about standing up and fighting for our independence — controlling our own destiny.'

'Ah, fuck you, mate. Since when did you become such a nationalistic fuck?'

'About the same time you turned into a coward,' said Finn, turning to raise his bottle to his lips.

Expecting to feel the cold glass of the bottle, Finn instead felt a force smash the side of his cheek. The blow from Chris's fist snapped Finn's head around unnaturally and he had to steady himself from falling off the barstool.

Turning, Finn launched himself at Chris, tackling him to the ground and then sinking his fists into Chris's ribs.

The two of them were blindly punching at each other in pure rage. Finn wrestled himself on top of Chris and planted a glancing punch to the side of Chris's nose. Blood spurted out of his friend's face.

Finn had him pinned down and his arm cocked above him, ready to deliver a final punishing blow. He suddenly looked at Chris's face: smeared in blood, eyes barely open, nose broken and angled to the side. He couldn't do it.

'Fuck!' he yelled, standing up, rubbing his rapidly swelling jaw.

Finn snatched MiLA off the bar as others came in to help Chris.

'Damn it,' Finn whispered to himself, spitting blood from his cut cheek, furious with himself and Chris.

As he walked downstairs, bouncers ran past him into the bar, oblivious that they had missed all the action. Stepping onto the street, Finn buckled himself into a ball, burying his head in his hands.

'Fuck, fuck, fuck,' he muttered to himself.

People walking past gave him a wide berth, staring at him, but mindful not to make eye contact with this crazy man.

He kept running it through in his head. All the opportunities he'd had to change the subject, to crack a joke, to lighten the conversation. But he hadn't. He just kept on going, had to make his point, had to make it clear he thought Chris was a coward, a pussy, a fucking pathetic piece of shit.

Finn could think of only one thing to do — drink. So, off to the one place where he felt comfortable sitting and drinking on his own — Trinity Bar in Surry Hills, an old Irish bar that had endured the changing trends in bars for the last hundred-odd years. Hailing a taxi, he threw himself in the backseat and told the cabbie where to go. Pulling up on Crown Street outside the Trinity, Finn paid the cabbie and walked into the bar. Pushing open the door, without looking around at any of the other patrons, he went straight for the furthest end of the bar and mounted a stool. Ordering two double Jack Daniels and Cokes he set about the task of numbing his mind. This was work. He was not drinking for pleasure now.

Two hours later the bar was heaving and Finn had achieved his mission: the rawness of his fight with Chris had been blunted. His mind dulled, he was working on autopilot now. Have to get home, he thought. Have to get out of here. Too many people now.

Pushing past patrons, he stumbled out onto Crown Street. Finn had no problem hailing a cab. By the time he had got to his parents' place, he was tired and at the height of his drunkenness. Fumbling with MiLA, he tried to unlock the door by passing the device over the doorbell a few times, missing the security pad by a large margin. Sonia, who heard the scraping at the door, came downstairs and opened the door to find a person resembling her son. Calling for help from Tom, they took him straight to his bed where he collapsed in a drunken stupor.

Sonia stood over him, her frizzy silver-shot bedhead casting a strange shadow over his ravaged face. She looked at him, concerned. Tom led her out by the hand. He knew the only thing they could do for Finn now was to let him sleep.

The next day Finn slept until 11 am, and even then he could barely move without wanting to vomit. Head pounding, mouth dry, eyes puffy and aching, his whole body felt broken, especially his aching jaw. Thinking a shower might miraculously cure him, he stumbled into the bathroom. While in the shower he had painful flashbacks from the night. He remembered bits about the argument with Chris, about being angry, and he remembered hitting the JDs hard. The rest was a blur. A wave of nausea hit him in the gut. Out of the shower, he dressed and went downstairs to face his mum, who had made him a cup of tea and some toast. She could see her son was suffering, and not just from the hangover.

The day was pretty much a write-off. He couldn't face talking to Chris yet, and physically he felt incapacitated — not how he wanted to spend his last full day in Sydney.

The following day, Finn woke feeling much better. The only good thing about a hangover, thought Finn, is the next day when normal feels amazing. He had to report back to base by 1600 hours, which meant leaving his parents by 2 pm. He considered dropping in to see Chris, but still couldn't face dealing with it.

He decided to call and apologise. The call went straight to voicemail so Finn, a little unprepared, left a stuttering message. 'Hey, mate. Look, I — ah, I'm really sorry about the other night. Don't know what got into me. I don't remember exactly what I said but I'm, err, you know, sorry. Anyway, I'm heading back to base this afternoon. If you get this message, gimme a yell. Cheers, mate. Talk soon.'

This time, Tom drove him to the base. Chris had still not called back and Finn was relieved that he didn't need to have an awkward conversation. After giving his dad a hug and saying goodbye, Finn headed through the gates. Immediately, he could feel the atmosphere. There was far more activity around the camp than he had ever seen. He headed straight to his barracks, where he found Sergeant Higgins. 'Sarge, what's going on?'

'We've been put on alert. Our division is being mobilised. Not sure where yet, but we'll be on the road tomorrow.'

Finn was animated now. 'All right! What do you want me to do?'

'Report to the armoury. They'll need some help with the gear. This is it, Hunt. Training is over — time to start learning.'

'Yessir,' Finn saluted, turning and briskly walking out of the barracks. On his way to the armoury he replayed what Higgins had said: 'Training's over, time to start learning'. What the hell had they been doing for the last few months if not learning?

Higgins watched Finn walking away. He knew all too well that training prepared the soldier, but only combat created the warrior. There was no substitute for battle, no proxy for being faced with death, no words to truly describe what it was like to be faced with the basest of human scenarios — fight or flight. Or, as Higgins believed, fight or die. He hoped Hunt was up to it.

The next day the convoy of trucks started leaving the camp. There was no point leaving under the cover of darkness. The Chinese had satellites with thermal imaging that could spot movements at night just as easily as in broad daylight. The air was cool and a light wind was blowing from the east, carrying with it the faintest scent of the ocean. With the breeze Finn felt a wave of melancholy, knowing he had to leave all his feelings from home behind. The other men were also quiet and introspective. They were leaving the safety of the camp that they had all grown fond of, despite its basic conditions. They were heading out into the unknown.

The convoy was enormous. The first truck headed out the gates at 0500 hours. An hour later the truck Finn and his squad were travelling in lurched forward and joined the long line snaking its way towards the west. The men on the truck remained silent. The noise of the engine meant they all had to wear earplugs, so there was no conversation. It was an uncomfortable ride and after two hours everyone was in need of a break, but that was not going to happen. The convoy had planned stops for fuel roughly every four hours. When they did stop the men were tired and sore, ears ringing from the roar of the engine despite the earplugs.

For two days the convoy rumbled west with very little respite. As they moved further inland, the heat became more and more unbearable. With no air-conditioning and a canvas roof, the back of the truck became an oven by 0900 each morning.

In each town the convoy passed through, crowds gathered. The welcome wasn't always that of heroes going off to do battle. Some towns seemed to consider the convoy with disdain, as though it was a rude interruption to their daily lives. But most of the time, the townspeople were receptive and excited to see the huge trucks rumbling through their streets.

Once the convoy reached Broken Hill, it headed north and the roads deteriorated rapidly, making the journey even more strained. Another two days on the road and they hit the dry, barren Sturt National Park, at the juncture of New South Wales, Queensland and South Australia. Finn and the other soldiers didn't see much of it, given there were no windows in the truck and the flap at the back had to be kept down to limit the relentless dust being blown in.

Their efforts at minimizing the dust were futile. The topic of dust seemed to fill the conversational void and quickly became their sole focus. Every time they stopped, the conversation always came back to the dust. They were constantly breaking down their weapons to clean them out. In the anticipation of going to battle, the dust became their obsession, their enemy — at least until they came face-to-face with the invaders.

From Sturt they headed northwest, which is when things got really interesting for the convoy. They were no longer on roads. They were travelling on dried-up riverbeds, unmarked trails and pure, untravelled country that only the sturdiest of 4WDs could handle.

The convoy slowed to a snail's pace due to numerous gear failures and vehicles getting stuck. It took them another week to travel the 700 kilometres to the eastern corner of the Simpson Desert. Along the way, it was hard not to comment on the Mars-like landscape. There was no denying it: the barren, red earth looked alien and unholy. It amazed Finn that Aborigines had survived out here in the desert for so long. What hard and resourceful people they must have been. The army was here, and even with all the technology and equipment, they were struggling.

At around midday on what Finn guessed was the fifth day of travel, their truck stopped. The men, who had been travelling for four hours, were already covered in red dust. Finn climbed down from the truck carefully. They weren't allowed to jump off, for fear of a rolled ankle or some other lame injury. Finn looked about the expanse. 'Where the fuck are we?' he muttered to himself.

'Hell,' said Higgins from behind him.

'Some say this is one of Australia's greatest marvels, Sarge,' said Dave, one of the older guys from the squad. He was scrawny to the point of emaciation, but tough as nails and a devastating sniper.

'Bullshit, Dave,' said Higgins. 'Anyone who says that has only travelled through here in an air-conditioned, air-sprung 4WD mobile palace. Trust me, boys. This ain't no place to relax in. The human body is not designed to last outside in these conditions for too long.'

'Well the Aborigines managed pretty well, didn't they?' said Dave, unwilling to let it go.

'Mate, the Aborigines survived off the land through generations of learning. How many generations of your family have been out here, living off the land? Fucking idiot.' Higgins, as he had a tendency to do, finished the conversation by walking away.

'Fuck me, I was just making a point that people can survive out here,' Dave said quietly to Finn.

'Don't worry about it. I think Sarge probably has some pretty shit holiday memories from his last visit to the desert, don't you think?' said Finn tactfully.

'Mhh,' grunted Dave. 'Whatever.'

Finn walked over to where Higgins was standing with some of the others, who were staring down the column of trucks in the direction they were headed. The column trailed off into the distance, evaporating into the heat haze. Beyond the trucks, though, was a break in the landscape's uniform flatness. Out of the sand and dirt rose a long mound. From this distance it looked smooth and lazy — an easy obstacle for their 4WD trucks. 'What's going on, Sarge?' he asked.

'According to the map, we're at the eastern point of the Simpson Desert, and this little lump of dirt is called Big Red. It's actually a fuck-off massive sand dune that'll slow the arse of the convoy down another day, at least. We might as well hunker down and find some shade because it's unlikely we'll be moving too far today,' said Higgins. Big Red stood about 35 metres above the rest of the plain. But the height wasn't the problem — the difficulty was in the gradient, and sand, which made it an extremely difficult obstacle to negotiate.

The heat was getting unbearable by 1400 hours. The squad had sought refuge in any piece of shade they could find, but the sun was high in the sky now, which meant the only shade was under the truck — so under they went. By 1500 they were on the move again, but not for long. A few hundred metres down the line and they stopped again. Higgins was right, thought Finn; it would take a damn long time to get every vehicle over Big Red.

That night they camped near the base of Big Red. The night was cold — in stark contrast to the heat of the day. Sitting around in a huddle, they were wearing their thick desert jackets to keep warm. The conversation had been the usual debates over which AFL team was the best in history, who was the greatest cricketer to ever swing a bat, whether General Stephens had any idea what he was doing. The usual stuff. One by one the men trickled off until it was Higgins and Finn alone.

'So, Sarge. You were in the initial battle for Australia, weren't you?' asked Finn directly.

'Yeah, I was,' Higgins replied, squinting into the distance.

'What was it like, if you don't mind me asking?' replied Finn.

'It was a fucking massacre — you probably got a better view of it than me on the evening news. From what I hear the coverage was extensive.'

'True, but that can't really explain what it was like.'

'Hunt,' Higgins turned to face Finn directly. 'It was a fucking nightmare. Let's leave it at that.'

Finn stared back at Higgins in silence, regretting asking him now. Higgins held his gaze, staring him in the eye.

'Err, yeah. Sorry, Sarge, didn't mean to pry.'

Higgins broke his gaze quickly. 'Yeah, don't worry about it.'

With that, Higgins stood, hesitated, and walked toward his bivvy.

For the first time, Finn felt scared and lonely. He sat there in the cold desert night, leaning against his pack, knees pulled up to his chest, chin tucked into the collar of his jacket, feeling the warmth of his breath on his neck.

Pull yourself together, he thought to himself. This was the only way he knew to fight the panic that accompanied self-doubt and fear. He had never experienced pure, raw fear, but he could feel it creeping up on him now, and he knew it was inevitable. Right now, he just wanted it over: all the training, this horrendous convoy. It was all delaying the ultimate reality of the total fear Finn would soon experience. He had to know what it would be like: whether he would cope, how long it would last. Would it cripple him? Or would he master it, let it go and perform his job? Of course, he had no idea. He only prayed that he would deal with it and live to reflect on the feeling. He'd asked for a real challenge; now he'd gotten it.

Next morning after breakfast, Higgins called the men in around the back of their truck. 'Right, I've got some info on where the hell we're going and what we're doing.'

Instantly, the men pricked up. ''bout bloody time,' said Marks.

'Shut your pie-holes for five minutes and I'll give you the good news. General Stephens and his crew have come up with a plan that I reckon could work. Now, we're here.' Higgins pointed to a spot on the map displayed on his roll-out plastic computer screen. The spot was about a hundred kilometres southeast of Alice Springs.

'The convoy is now going to hang a sharp right and head due north from here, running parallel to the Ghan railway line, which the enemy is using to transport resources to the ports in the north. As you well know, the Chinese have been watching us pretty closely with their satellites. Right about now they are probably flapping about wondering what a convoy this size is doing so far from home. And flap they fucking well should!' The men sniggered and laughed at this, but it was tainted with the tone of uncertainty. There were too many unknowns for them to be totally confident just yet.

'And here's where it gets fun. Each morning starting today, the convoy will head off as it normally does, but now, four squads will be left behind at each camp. Each squad's truck will leave with the convoy as normal so as not to arouse suspicion. Before daybreak, the assigned squads being deployed will get under a thermal tent that will hide the heat signature until the convoy is long gone and the satellite has passed. Each squad will then head by foot to its assigned base camp where rations, ammo and other supplies have been arranged. From this base, we will be conducting tactical strikes on the Chinese transportation and military infrastructure. This is it, boys.'

There were back-slaps and shouts from the squad. This was the best news they had received since setting out. Finally, it all seemed worthwhile. There was a plan, they were heading into action and they were the ones on the offensive. The atmosphere crackled and Finn could taste the adrenalin. 'Game on, boys!' he yelled, to more backslapping and cheering.

Chapter 9

In Canberra, the control centre of the SOF was a hive of activity. Gathered in the conference room were the heads of military operations. Entering the conference room, Fletcher, Adams and the general sat down with little fanfare. Sarah Dempsey walked to the lectern.

'Good morning, everyone,' she began, looking around the room, 'today I'll be taking you through our strategy for obstructing and ultimately defeating the Chinese and their illegal mining and exportation of Australia's mineral deposits.'

The briefing went for over two hours, with many questions. Sarah was unflappable and had a response for every question. Drawing the briefing to an end, she summarised the strategy. 'There will be a series of ongoing, coordinated guerrilla attacks on the Chinese transport infrastructure from South Australia to the Gulf of Carpentaria. The aim of these attacks is to destabilise their transport to the point where it becomes economically unviable for China to continue.' She closed her briefing notes, signifying the end of the presentation.

The room was quiet, which unnerved General Stephens slightly. But looking around, he could see the faces of people who were satisfied, nodding in agreement.

General Stephens leaned forward on the table. 'Thank you, Sarah. Essentially, people, our view is that our goals can only be attained through a carefully orchestrated, ongoing guerrilla operation. Make no mistake; this will be a war of attrition.'

Standing now, supporting his weight against the table on clenched fists, eyes boring into everyone in the room, General Stephens continued. 'The end goal is simple — get the Chinese out, reclaim our land, regain control of our mines and take back this country's freedom!'

The room erupted in applause, there were fists banging on the table, heads nodding, shouts of approval — the testosterone in the room was palpable. The air felt heavy and stale, but charged and energised at the same time. The meeting dissolved into motions of congratulations and backslapping. Small groups broke away to discuss the plans. The general was relieved. Sarah had done a brilliant job of presenting the strategy — and it looked like everyone was onboard.

Alone in his office after the briefing, Stephens felt tired. The adrenalin kick never seemed to last long nowadays. He slumped back on his leather couch putting a hand to his head, rubbing his brow, the light from the fireplace throwing the crags in his face into sharp relief. All he could do right now was breathe and just try to relax his exhausted mind and body. He really wished he could just go to sleep for 24 hours, but right now that was not an option. This was the point where all the planning of the past few months would be put into action. This was the point that mattered. All the planning in the world meant nothing if the execution of the plan failed.

There was a knock at the door and Fletcher opened it enough to poke his head through. 'You all right?' he asked.

'Come in,' Stephens said, raising his head just enough to look at Fletcher, 'I'm just starting to understand how Hudson must have felt.'

'Come on, Marty — you're not incompetent. How could you possibly feel like Hudson?' replied Fletcher with a short laugh.

General Stephens was too tired to reply with anything more than a wry smile. 'Give it a few more days and we'll see.'

'You'll be fine. And just remember — without you, Hudson would have had us all digging the mines for the bloody Chinese by now.'

'Yeah, well,' Stephens replied, face serious again, 'we're a long way from getting the Chinese out of here yet. This is going to be a long campaign, one that we may never win.'

Fletcher sat down opposite the general. 'Maybe, but we can't underestimate the resolve of the Australian people.'

Stephens leaned forward, elbows on his knees. 'I know what we're doing is right, but I can't help thinking that perhaps it's all futile, and that perhaps we should just be playing the diplomatic card and negotiating our way out of this mess.'

'Bullshit. This is the right approach — the *only* approach. We're doing the right thing here, Marty,' Fletcher said, trying hard to make Stephens look him in the eye.

Silence. General Stephens was in no mood for debating the rights or wrongs of their actions. Besides, it was too late now. The plan had been set in motion, the cogs were turning and there was no going back.

'Why don't you go and rest for a couple of hours?' Fletcher suggested. 'You haven't slept in over 24 hours. Sarah and I have got this covered. There's not a lot more you can do right now.'

'Yeah, maybe you're right,' General Stephens stood slowly, rubbing his head, which started pounding as soon as he stood. 'Wake me in two hours?'

Fletch stood as well. 'Sure thing.'

'I mean it, Fletch. Two hours,' Stephens said, looking sternly at Fletcher.

'I got it. Now bugger off and get some sleep,' replied Fletcher.

'Oh, and remind me when I wake up,' Stephens said, turning at the door, 'we need to arrange a meeting with Draven. He's been pestering me for documentation about our leadership. He wants it in writing that we'll cede leadership and return to a democracy as soon as a certain set of conditions, to be agreed upon, are met.'

Fletcher chuckled. 'He is a stickler, isn't he? I'll see what I can do.'

After General Stephens had left, Fletcher went over to the liquor cabinet and poured himself a large Glenfiddich with a splash of water, no ice, sighing heavily as he walked back to the couch. At least Hudson had the decency to leave his liquor cabinet fully stocked, he thought to himself.

Sarah knocked once on the door and walked in, smiling broadly. 'That seemed to go well, don't you think, Fletch? Where's the general?'

'In there, having a sleep,' replied Fletcher, head tilting to the adjacent room.

'Oh ...' whispered Sarah, 'finally. He hasn't slept in a long time.' She crept across the room and sat on the couch across from Fletcher.

'He'll be fine in a couple of hours. He's one of the toughest blokes I've ever met,' Fletcher replied, taking a sip.

'Sure, but he must be feeling the pressure. Anyone in his shoes would,' Sarah said, looking pensively into the fire.

'Sarah, I've seen this man take a round in combat and still manage to drag my sorry arse out of a red hot terrorist zone. He'll be fine.'

Sarah didn't reply, but nodded — staring at the door to the room where Stephens was resting.

'I need to return Ambassador Xian's calls,' said Fletcher, heaving himself up from the couch. 'He's left a dozen messages since this morning. No doubt he'll be upset over the convoy's presence near their transport lines. I bet his superiors in Beijing have been squealing away about the satellite imagery.'

Walking back to his office, Fletcher thought about the situation at hand. The Chinese extraction of iron ore and other resources was estimated to be nearing capacity. It had quickly become clear that the planning of the Chinese invasion had started long before it was executed. All their mining equipment had been manufactured and ready to use as soon as they had control of the mines. The whole operation had gone like clockwork for the Chinese — until now, that is. He wondered what approach Xian would take to their discussion.

Dialling his secretary, Fletcher asked to be put through to Ambassador Xian. Xian immediately picked up.

'Ah, General Fletcher, thank you for returning my numerous calls,' he said with an air of sarcasm. 'I am sure you have guessed why we so urgently needed to speak with you. We have seen the satellite imagery and we know you have mobilised a rather large convoy, which has been slowly moving toward our transportation lines. My superiors in Beijing wish to know why.'

'Well, Xian, it's very simple,' Fletcher replied cheerfully. 'We are creating a military base in the Northern Territory along the border of Queensland. As your government pointed out, it is our mines that you are after, not our cities and towns. However, we wish to assure our people that the Chinese forces are being watched and that the regional towns are being protected.'

'But General Fletcher, we have given you our word — we are not interested in coming near your urban areas.'

Fletcher was on a roll. He had practised this conversation many times today in his head. 'Xian, we have accepted what has happened to our mining industry. We are merely trying to move forward. To do that, the Australian people must feel safe.'

'Well, yes, I can see that, but I will need to discuss it with my superiors in Beijing.'

'I understand, Xian. Please let me know if there is anything more we can do to allay your concerns. Our interests are only concerned with the rebuilding of Australia.'

'Yes, of course. Well we shall talk again soon,' said Xian hesitantly, not sure what to make of the conversation — believing what Fletcher had told him, but at the same time … not entirely sold.

'Okay, then. Thank you, Ambassador. Goodbye,' said Fletcher, hanging up. He couldn't help smiling. It was good to hear Xian so unsure of himself. Fletcher knew that the Chinese wanted to disrupt the Australian way of life as little as possible; the sooner the country let go of the South Australian mines and set about rebuilding its economy, the more efficiently China could extract and export the resources. But Fletcher and the others also knew that once they were beholden to China, that was it. They would forever be at the whim of the Chinese. How long before another resource became of great interest to China?

After Fletcher had gone to call Ambassador Xian, Sarah left the SOF on a high. Her adrenalin was bursting and she could think of only one way to release it.

In her car, Sarah voice-activated Matt's number.

Matt answered from his office. 'Hey, what's happening?'

'Just driving back from work. We had a win today. Fancy celebrating with me?' she said in a suggestive tone, as her car turned onto her street.

'Sure, what did you have in mind?' asked Matt, tilting his chair back, already having a pretty good idea.

'I don't know. Perhaps you could come by and surprise me with a bottle of something sparkling?' she said seductively as her car pulled into its space.

'Hmm. Not much of a surprise now, is it?' replied Matt, grinning.

'That depends on what you do to me after the champagne,' she said, still sitting in the car.

'I'm on my way,' Matt said quickly, immediately hanging up.

Sarah smiled to herself — she did enjoy their repartee and Matt was certainly eager to please, which was always a bonus. She enjoyed his company, and sexually they were extremely compatible. She didn't have time for a complicated relationship, and neither did he, especially now as he was acting as the head liaison between the military and the government. They were both very clear on emotional boundaries and it suited them — although sometimes, for example when she was smiling like she was now, she wondered if that was as easy said as done.

General Stephens opened the door to his office and walked in, rubbing his face. Fletcher was sitting on a couch, screen in hand, reading through a report.

'Morning,' Stephens grumbled, his voice deep and coarse, face rough and unshaven.

'Morning? It's nearly 2100 hours,' replied Fletcher.

'Urgh, I feel terrible … What happened to two hours?' he glared at his friend. Not waiting for a reply, General Stephens continued. 'Give me some good news.'

'This should cheer you up. I spoke to Ambassador Xian earlier. You should have heard him squirming away about the convoy.'

'He bought the story though?' asked Stephens, yawning.

'I think so. Hard to tell. I think he took it like a shit sandwich — didn't like the taste, but ate it anyway.'

'Hmmf. Regardless, we don't have long. A few more days and the tactical strikes begin. That's when things will get interesting with the Chinese,' said Stephens, rubbing his face again. 'Where's Sarah? You seen her?'

'No, she might have gone to get some sleep. Or celebrate her presentation to the chiefs. She did a pretty damn good job — presenting to that audience is no easy task, especially if you're a woman.'

'Yes, she did do well. You don't think I've thrown her in too deep with all this?' Stephens asked.

'Well, she seems to be treading water pretty well right now — head decidedly above water.'

Back in the convoy, Finn's team was breaking camp at 0400 hours. The sky was black but the stars were bright and the nearly full moon cast obscure shadows on the faces of the men around him. No one spoke. Everyone knew what to do — the only voice was that of Higgins, who was quietly and efficiently giving orders. The men were sombre but focussed. Their time had come, and they were well practiced in what had to be done.

'Bull! You and Hunt keep putting the thermal tents up over there so that we can unload the rest of the supplies,' ordered Higgins.

'Yessir,' said Bull stoically. 'Come on, gimme a hand,' said Bull to Finn, tilting his head towards the truck containing the remaining thermal tents. His real name was Simon Kelly, but the squad nicknamed him 'Bull' due to his bull-like figure. The man was huge and his dimensions cartoon-like, with little or no neck, shoulders like cannonballs, a barrel chest and, to top it off, skinny legs which further accentuated his taurine physique.

The tents were designed to camouflage the heat and X-ray signatures of the men and their equipment. The Chinese satellites were regularly over this area, and the barren landscape made it difficult to conceal anything from the 'eye in the sky', as the satellites were nicknamed. The tents were just large sheets of a carbon-fibre material that dispersed the heat source and reflected the X-rays, so that to the satellites' imaging software it looked like nothing but more desert.

They knew the times the satellites passed over the top. The Chinese had at least two that were in orbit over Australia, which meant every day and night, for about three hours, they had to ensure that everything was under a tent, otherwise they would be spotted.

'You reckon these things can fool the satellites, Bull?' asked Finn as they were erecting one of the large square sheets.

'Mate, we'll know before lunch. If you hear a San' coming low over the desert, you know we're fucked,' replied Bull.

The San', or rather, Sankaku-104, was a three-man attack helicopter that was both revered and feared. The Sankaku had been devastating on the ground troops, they were fast, heavily armed, and the crews that flew them were merciless.

'Yeah, great. But these things must have been tested, right?' said Finn, somewhat concerned.

'They would have been tested on our satellites and the Yank ones, but who really knows what the Chinese have up their crafty little sleeves?'

'Ah well, too late to worry about it now, I guess,' replied Finn.

Once the tents were set up they helped the rest of the grunts unload the truck. The black sky was now turning into a dark, inky blue. Not long now, and the sun would be up. Not long now, and a Chinese satellite would be overhead, concentrating on their position with an array of imaging devices.

'Right. Come on, boys. We've got just under half an hour to get this area under cover before the satellite comes over. Let's move it!' yelled Higgins.

The men sped up their actions, and five minutes later everything was off the trucks. With 20 minutes to go, Higgins was doing last-minute checks with the platoon commander, Lieutenant Taylor. Hovering over the laptop perched on the back of the truck, they were checking the inventory list. Once everything was accounted for, they ordered the men under the thermal tents. They got comfortable with 10 minutes to spare. It was surreal because the other squads in the convoy, who were packed and loading their gear onto the truck, were leaving today.

Finn watched as a couple of guys he knew from another squad were climbing into their truck. Finn waved but they did not wave back. Nobody knew the extent of the Chinese imagery technology and the last thing anyone wanted to do was give away the fact that there were soldiers staying behind. The success of the mission depended on stealth and the ability to stay concealed for as long as possible.

The trucks, including their own, moved off at 0530 that morning. The plan was that, hopefully, the Chinese would stay focussed on the number of vehicles in the convoy. It would travel north for many more days, dropping teams off every morning but continuing on with the same number of vehicles as though it was still one large convoy. Finally, the convoy would turn east and away from the Chinese transportation lines. After two days of driving east, they would stop and set up an outpost with the remaining men and women.

The eight-man squads, subsets of their platoon, were independent and self-sufficient. They would have scattered and disappeared into the desert by the time the Chinese figured out that the outpost had less than half the personnel that started on the convoy.

Sitting under the tent, the sun was already up and the heat felt good after the cold desert night. As more and more trucks left, the dust cloud became thick, making it difficult to breathe.

They had to stay under the tents for at least another two hours after the last truck had rumbled past before it would be safe to come out. Looking around, Finn saw three other squads huddled under their tents. 'Sarge, are we going to be operating with the other squads out there?' asked Finn, squinting at the bright sunlight as he pointed to the other groups.

'No, Hunt. We'll be working independently, as will they. None of us will know the other squads' positions, so that if we are captured we can't give away any useful information,' replied Higgins, addressing the whole squad.

'So, Sarge. What if they need back-up in a firefight — or if we're in trouble, will we be able to locate one another?' asked Jessop.

'No. What part of *independent* don't you understand?' said Higgins, somewhat irritated. 'We'll have zero contact with other squads — if we get into trouble, we get ourselves out of it. We're on our own now, boys. This is what we trained for, this is what our mummies raised us to do, and this is what we've been ordered to do by our supreme leader, General Stephens. Now, the lieutenant is going to brief us on our specific orders. So listen the hell up,' said Higgins, now in operation mode.

Taylor stood from the crates he was leaning on. He was a slender man, and seemed to Finn like an oddly gentle type to have chosen a career in the military. Most of the squads had only a sergeant to lead them but, by the luck of the draw, their team had

Higgins and had also pulled the lieutenant, bringing their total to nine men. 'Thank you, Sergeant. Right men, our orders are very simple — simple, but not easy. We are to break camp and move 11 clicks northwest of here, to a point that is elevated and within strike distance of our objective. This will be our base for operations. There is an abandoned mineshaft there that we will be appropriating. Supplies and equipment have already been deposited there for us. We must reach this point by sundown. The next satellite fly-over is scheduled for 2034, and although these thermal tents seem to do the job, I would prefer to have 30,000 tonnes of rock between us and their satellites, wouldn't you agree?'

The men nodded, listening intently.

'So, in 90 minutes we can come out from under our tents and get moving. Until then, get your gear in order. We have a long hike and a lot of gear to lug through the desert. Keep your fluids up, hats on and sunblock reapplied regularly. It's going to be toasty out there today and we can't afford to be slowed down by illness.'

Higgins, who was standing next to the lieutenant with his muscular arms crossed, dropped his hands to his hips. 'Right, you've heard the platoon commander — get your kit together. In a little while we'll be hiking through the desert.'

The men loaded the crates onto the US-made Mule, which, unlike most Yank equipment, was not an acronym. It was called a mule because it had the ability to carry phenomenal loads over rough terrain. The Mule was essentially a small but powerful golf-cart-sized all-terrain cargo carrier. It was controlled remotely by a man on foot but, cleverly, the Mule did not need to be driven by anyone. It could determine the best path to take over any obstacle through its onboard cameras. The Mule made operations like this achievable, as there was no way the men could carry their own supplies into this unforgiving territory. Higgins wasn't sorry that they were using the Mule rather than PALs — most of the PALs had been destroyed in the initial conflict, and he had some bad memories of those. Besides, he doubted they'd be used in such a remote location — they were finicky and needed routine maintenance, so couldn't be used on such specialised missions like this one.

By 0915 the squad had moved out. At first the going was relatively easy, with hard-packed sand and rock. But after a few hours it got much harder. The sand became softer and deeper, the rocks bigger. The Mule was handling it better than the men, which prompted some to ask why the military hadn't bought Mules for the soldiers, too.

Eventually the landscape transformed from a desert wasteland to a craggy, stony, valley-riven terrain. After nearly nine hours of agonising slog, the squad found its base. It looked like just a crack in a rock face, high enough for a man to walk through, and about two metres wide. It was extremely well hidden, the opening to the mine being a natural cave, which made it perfect for concealment. There was no evidence outside the cave that it had been used as a mine. Any equipment that was left had eroded or been buried by the desert. With red rock around them, only a few scattered bushes broke up the landscape. Finn imagined that it may have once been a hideaway for outlaws, it had that sort of feel to it. In reality, he knew that not even an outlaw would come this far out.

As Finn walked into the mine, his torch automatically activated in response to the sudden dimness. His jaw dropped. 'What the fuck?' he whispered in amazement.

Higgins walked in right behind him. 'Fuck me,' he said in an impressed tone.

Though the entrance was relatively narrow, inside, the cave widened out, clearly carved out by man. The ceiling vaulted up and along the walls of the mine were stacked boxes of weapons, explosives, ammunition, rations and communications equipment. There were eight motocross bikes painted in desert camouflage lined up just inside the entry.

'It's like bloody Aladdin's cave in here, Sarge,' said Finn.

'You're not wrong, Hunt. Not wrong at all,' said Higgins as he went over and opened one of the crates, revealing a shoulder-mounted missile launcher.

'One of these things can take down a San' from over a kilometre away. Bloody brilliant!' said Higgins. Noticing a piece of paper lying on top of the missile launcher, he muttered 'What's this?' to himself and unfolded it.

He read aloud from the sheet: 'Happy hunting. We hope you find a good use for the hardware contained in these crates. With compliments, Karl Jost, chairman, IXR'.

'So IXR is funding us?' asked Finn.

'IXR has security forces more impressive than most nations' armies,' Higgins explained. 'For the last decade they've been fighting wars around the world to keep control of their mines. I know a lot of guys who left miserable army pay to work as contractors for IXR or one of the other mining companies.'

'Makes sense, I s'pose. Still, seems a bit odd that a publicly-listed company is more a front for a private army,' said Finn.

'Hunt, you're a soldier now. Leave the business and the politics to those who give a rat's arse.' Higgins was in no mood for an ethical discussion over the rights or wrongs of how wars were fought in the 2030s.

Finn took the hint and started examining the crates of gear.

'All right, you lot. No time to piss about ogling the kit,' Higgins said, gathering the men. 'We need the supplies on the Mule loaded into the mine and a perimeter secured. Hunt, you and Carver grab the two Centurions down there and come with me. The rest of you get moving,' ordered Higgins.

Heaving two large, rectangular metal boxes between them, Finn and Carver awkwardly carried them out of the mine, following Higgins.

'Okay. Drop one here and bring the other one,' said Higgins, setting off up the narrow valley.

About a hundred metres from the mine entrance Higgins stopped and waited for Finn and Carver, who were struggling with the weight of the Centurion.

'Deploy it here, lads,' ordered Higgins.

Three short metal legs dropped down from the box and the Centurion was placed, facing up the valley. Higgins opened a panel on the back and started punching in settings on a small keyboard.

'Okay. We're live,' said Higgins, more to himself. Tapping his earpiece, he muttered, 'Lieutenant, do you copy? North Centurion is in place. Can you confirm comms link?' he paused, listening. 'Okay, very good, moving out to set up Centurion South.'

Turning to look at Finn and Carver, he explained. 'We can all sleep easier tonight knowing these guys,' he patted the Centurion, 'are on watch. Any unwanteds come down here tonight and this guy will be one mean welcoming party.'

Higgins arranged a thermal camouflage net over the Centurion, and gestured to Finn and Carver to move on. 'Right. Let's get the southern one done.'

That night spirits were high, though they had to keep the noise low. The men were clearly pleased with themselves. They had pushed hard to get to the base before the next satellite passed over. They had endured days on the convoy and were now doing what they had joined the army to do — to soldier.

Higgins stood in the mine entrance, facing inwards to the men who were sitting eating their food. 'All right, men. I know you're all pretty happy with yourselves after today. It was a big hike and we achieved our objective. But let me remind you, our work hasn't even begun yet. Tomorrow we will begin preparations for our first operation, so finish up your grub and take a shit if you need to because the satellite will be coming over in 30 minutes and we don't want some young Chinese technician seeing an image of one of you lot with your white arses hanging out.'

Finn slept soundly that night. Thankfully, he was not on watch duty until the following day.

The next morning they were awoken by Higgins. Again, there was no fuss, very little noise. The men got out of their sleeping bags, rolled them up and put them away. Dressed, they went to the assigned latrine area, came back, brushed their teeth and ate breakfast, all in relative silence. There was apprehension in the team. It was coming home to them that they were in unfamiliar surroundings, and for three of the eight soldiers, Carver, Jessop and Finn, this was their first time in combat. Normally, a soldier straight out of training would not be expected to go on a mission like this, but in the current circumstances there was little option. Australia had to send who it could, not who it should.

The squad gathered at 0700 hours for a briefing on the day's activities. The equipment that had been left needed to be inspected and a complete inventory of all their gear completed. Solar panels were to be set up outside to recharge the numerous batteries they used. Small satellite dishes and aerials were to be placed outside the mine entrance. A mass of cables, which were all covered in dirt, led back into the mine. An Atmofier was set up outside which, in outback conditions, could produce up to 40 litres of water a day from two sources: sucking water vapour out of the air and condensing it, and filtering the urine of the men. Finn preferred not to think too much about the second source of the water. By mid-morning the area had transformed into a buzz of activity. From the air, however, their camouflaging would ensure their operations base looked like the rest of the barren landscape.

Higgins and Taylor were musing over the unfurled, clear plastic screens that were hung on the walls of the dark, damp mine. They had their computer-generated maps of the area. Normally, the mapscreens would display the positions of their own ordnance and people. However, given the secrecy of the operation, their mapscreen showed only the area and the known enemy positions.

'So, if we're to attack here, there's a good chance that they won't be able to divert a patrol quickly enough to engage,' said Taylor.

'We would be incredibly lucky, sir — that's based on week-old intel. There's no reason to believe the Chinese patrols are holding the same rotation and patrol grid,' replied Higgins in a hushed tone, conscious of the other men listening in on their discussion.

'Well, I don't see much choice, Higgins. We need to execute our attack tomorrow at 1200 hours. If we don't hit them here,' Taylor said, jamming his finger to the point on the mapscreen and speaking a little too loudly for Higgins' liking, 'then there's no way we can get our guys back before the satellite moves overhead.'

'Yes, I agree,' said Higgins calmly, trying to lower the lieutenant's voice, 'I just think we're leaving a lot to chance on this, sir.'

'Fine,' said Taylor, taking Higgins' hint and lowering his voice, but clearly indicating that the decision had already been made, 'so who do we send? My pick is Carver, Hunt, Bull and yourself. Good mix of experience, and I think the sooner we blood Hunt and Carver the better.'

Higgins looked at Taylor. He respected him but he also found his cavalier attitude a little hard to swallow sometimes. 'Well, sir. I was thinking McCaw, Bull, Marks and myself. Hunt and Carver are too green for an op like this.'

'No, I want those two blooded early. The sooner they see action, the sooner they become useful to the squad, and to this war,' replied Taylor without hesitation.

Higgins could see his point, but he didn't like it. He'd seen enough young men slaughtered in the first battle. 'All right, sir. I'll round up the men. We better brief them and start going over the plans.'

Higgins assembled the men and stood before them, beside the electronic mapscreen on the wall. 'Tomorrow, at noon, we will be engaging the Chinese. We will be part of a coordinated series of attacks on the Chinese transportation lines and logistics centres. The first attack will start in the south. A further three attacks will occur, each moving north before ours at 1200 hours.

'The plan is this: a four-man team on motocross bikes will travel at high speed to this point and lay an explosive charge, a rail-splitter, on the railway line. This bomb is designed specifically for inflicting maximum damage on railway infrastructure. I will be leading the team accompanied by Hunt, Bull and Carver. The rest of you will remain here and assist the lieutenant in communications and base defence.

'We will be relying on our comms team back here to give us advanced warning of any enemy activity. We don't know how they will react after this series of attacks, but I think we can safely assume that they will be upset.'

Finn was still reeling from hearing his name called out. His mind was so scrambled he hadn't heard a word Higgins had said. Finn forced himself to listen and concentrate on what Higgins was saying.

Higgins continued. 'I'm going to be briefing my team outside. The commander is going to take the rest of you through the comms protocols. That is all.'

General Stephens was sitting at his desk in the SOF finishing his dinner. With a single knock on the door, Fletcher came bursting in without waiting to be asked. 'Marty, you're going to love this — the first squads are all stationed at the assigned ops bases. The first deployments have all gone to plan. Tomorrow morning the first attack wave begins. There will be a series of successive operations, which will start in the south and move north. We'll be hitting them where it hurts — their transportation and logistics centres.'

'Fantastic!' said General Stephens, dropping his fork to his plate and wiping his mouth with a napkin.

'It's finally happening, Marty. Can you believe how big a shit Xian is going to have when he hears? That skinny little fucker is going to get his ear chewed off by someone back in Beijing.'

General Stephens suddenly looked contemplative. 'It's not Xian that concerns me, it's the possibility of Chinese reprisal attacks. Beijing may well go back on their word and put civilians at risk.'

'God knows,' replied Fletcher, 'I mean, they've been true to their word so far, but I guess we've never tested their word like this, have we?'

'No, we haven't. I guess we'll have to cross that bridge when we come to it,' said Stephens. What he meant, really, was there was nothing they could do about it now. If the Chinese decided to lash out at a civilian population because of their attacks, then that was a price that had to be paid. Though the general would do everything in his power to avoid civilian casualties, there would be one positive to a Chinese strike on civilians. It might jolt the public into realising that they were all being held hostage in the greatest act of geo-terrorism the world had ever seen. Alternatively, the public might turn on Stephens and demand a return to diplomacy. These were such extreme times that there really was no way of predicting how the media, and therefore the masses, would react. There was no way of telling how the Chinese would react, either.

'Well, by this time tomorrow, we should know how the Chinese are going to take it — one way or another,' said Fletcher.

Chapter 10

As the men milled about after the briefing, Finn noticed that the mine had taken on a darker, more sinister look with the weaponry unpacked. His chest had tightened the moment he'd heard his name called and he realised his breathing was shallow, a sheen of nervous sweat accumulating on his brow. Was he ready? How would he react under pressure? How would he react to being shot at?

Higgins walked past. 'Hunt, Carver. Outside please,' he said, without stopping to make sure they heard.

In the scorching afternoon heat outside, Higgins faced them both. 'Well, you two have landed yourselves right in it, haven't you?' he said with a faint smile.

'We're ready, Sergeant,' said Carver, not at all convincingly.

'Shut it, Carver. You're barely ready to wipe your own arse,' Higgins retorted.

His gaze now alternated between the two of them. 'Now, you two have done well in training. In fact, I think it's fair to say you've excelled. However, that does not make you real soldiers in my book. Out there is a very different story. I have faith that you will both do well out there tomorrow, but slow down. Remember your training, listen to my orders and keep your eyes open — always looking, always thinking.'

Finn and Carver nodded, staring at Higgins' face as though hypnotised.

'You stay alert and you stay alive,' said Higgins, so fiercely that it frightened Finn.

'So what's the objective, Sarge?' asked Carver.

'Right, Hunt. Get the other monkey over here, will you,' said Higgins, gesturing at Bull.

The team gathered. They went over the plans time and time again until late into the night. The operation was choreographed down to the smallest detail and they went through the specific actions as a team. Everyone had to know their role in the operation and the role of the other men, in case something went wrong. The plan itself was very simple: tear in on the bikes, secure the area where they would be laying the explosives, place the device, retreat, detonate and then get back to the ops base as quickly as possible. The rail-splitter explosive they'd be using worked by creating an extremely low-frequency shockwave that travelled through the railway line. The shockwave would go for over a kilometre, literally tearing the rail from the sleepers, lifting the rail into the air. Once the explosion happened, the Chinese would be left with over a kilometre of busted, twisted and buckled metal instead of a railway. The Chinese could build railways so quickly and efficiently that the Aussies had to try to damage as much rail line as was devastatingly possible to have any effect on their operations.

By midnight the men were all exhausted and thoroughly versed in the operation. 'That's enough for tonight, boys. Let's get some shut-eye,' said Higgins, wearily rubbing his eyes.

The men grunted as they shuffled off to their sleeping area.

'I suggest you take a Nightcap to help you sleep better. You'll need to look lively tomorrow,' called Higgins after them. The Nightcap was a pill used by athletes that moderated the body's heart rate, temperature and deep brainwaves to ensure the optimum night's sleep, with no drowsiness the next day. In the field it was every soldier's best friend. Finn took the pill and slept soundly all night.

For an instant, upon waking, Finn forgot where he was and what he was about to do. Unfortunately the blissful ignorance didn't last long, as he quickly remembered what was happening. The squad gathered in the cave where Higgins and Taylor were giving the day's briefing. The attack group needed to leave by 1000 hours to make the target on time.

'All right, men,' said Higgins. 'You all know the plan. Attack team, we need to be on the bikes and out of here at 1000 hours on the dot. Check your gear and the bikes; we can't afford any mechanicals out there. That is all, unless you have anything to add, Lieutenant?'

'No, thank you, Sergeant. Except that this is a momentous day, gentlemen. This is the day Australia fights back against our adversary. It's up to us to make sure they get what's coming to them.'

At 0951 Higgins was standing with Finn, Carver and Bull. 'Boys, you can bet the Chinese are going to be upset about what we're up to, so stay frosty and keep your eyes to the skies. Our primary threat is the San's. Any sign of one and you know what to do. Now, let's get moving.'

They mounted the electric-powered bikes and started them up. When idle, the bikes emitted a crackling, low-pitched hum. The sound, though not loud, seemed to electrify the whole canyon. Finn's heart was racing, the adrenalin was pumping around his body.

At first, they just coasted along the canyon floor, weaving around obstacles. The canyon then dipped down and after a few minutes they came out of it and into an expanse of desert. The going was rough but the bikes were more than up to the task. Finn felt strangely relaxed riding with the others. He knew he had a job to do, he knew how to do it and he trusted the guys around him.

'Okay, boys. Stay focussed. Let's pick up the speed now,' Higgins said over the comms. Leading the men, Higgins twisted the throttle and leant into the bars, lowering his body. They all accelerated their bikes and their powerful motors crackled, the noise becoming a higher-pitched whine. They were tearing across the vast, flat desert plain in a tight formation. Each rider hunched down low, with elbows flared out to the sides so their arms could absorb the bumps that their suspension couldn't handle.

What a rush, thought Finn, if only Chris could see me now. Fuck, stay focussed dickhead, he reminded himself as he hit a rock that caused him to release the throttle momentarily. His body armour lifted and jagged him painfully in the throat.

'Keep it tight, boys. This speed is good. Eyes on the ground, no stacks,' said Higgins through their comms units, loud in their ears. None of the others spoke. They were too busy concentrating on the tricky terrain.

After an hour's riding Higgins ordered the men to stop.

'Hunt, let's see the map.'

Pulling the mapscreen out from a holster on the side of the bike, Finn unfurled the tough A3-sized digital sheet. Pressing a button on the side, the mapscreen flickered into life.

'Here you go, Sarge.'

Looking at the map for a few seconds, Higgins furled it back up and handed it to Finn. 'Okay. We've got another 10 clicks to the target. We pull up a click short, secure the area, ensure it's clear, then Bull and I go in, place the device and rejoin you before detonating.'

The guys knew the plan inside out and backwards, so there was no confusion, no questions. 'Right. Let's hit it!' said Higgins, revving the bike hard. His rear wheel tore up the red dirt and he sped off with the others following.

At the one-kilometre mark they stopped. Finn, Carver and Bull dismounted their bikes and unpacked their weapons. Higgins turned off his bike but stayed straddling it. 'Hunt, Carver. Set up the tactical surveillance gear. I want a sweep of the area to make sure there are no patrols in the vicinity.'

Carver pulled out a computer tablet from his pack and sparked it up. The screen gave an aerial view of the surrounds. If it detected human biometric readings apart from their own, they would have shown up as red dots.

'No bio readings, Sarge,' said Carver.

'Electronic?' replied Higgins.

'Just checking … nope. We're clear,' said Carver, still pressing buttons on his tablet. 'No patrols, no drones, no other airborne objects.'

'Okay then. Bull. You've got the device there. One last check, please.'

Bull pulled the small explosive package out of his pack and checked its digital screen. 'Green light, Sarge. We're good to go.'

Higgins looked at Finn and Carver. 'Eyes in the skies, understood. I want you to talk to me the whole time — regular updates. I want to know that you two are watching for any sign of the enemy.'

'All over it, Sarge,' said Finn.

Higgins called into their ops base. 'Lieutenant, we're in position. Ready to place device now.'

'Roger that Sergeant. Proceed,' came the reply.

'C'mon, Bull. Let's do it,' said Higgins before starting his bike and tearing off towards the target, Bull right behind him.

Higgins pulled up five metres from the rail track, got off his bike and left it to be kept upright by its proprioceptors, engine still running. Bull did the same.

Both men looked around, somewhat surprised by how eerily quiet and empty it seemed.

'Place the device, and let's get out of here,' said Higgins.

Bull walked up to the railway track and placed the device. It was small, but he knew how much damage a rail-splitter could inflict.

Higgins felt that at any moment a chopper or a drone would drop out of the sky to wipe them out. Memories of the first battle for Australia surged back — the Pinyins that flew in formation and annihilated so many of them. Nothing like that here, though. It seemed surreal, being so quiet and empty. As if on cue, Hunt's voice came over the comms unit saying all was clear.

Within three minutes Higgins and Bull were back with Finn and Carver, all of them lying chest-down on the ground, facing the target.

'Still no sign of patrols or aircraft, Sarge' said Carver.

'Very good. Detonate the device,' said Higgins, calmly.

Bull took the small remote detonator, tapped in the activation code and pressed the button. A second later they saw the massive dust-and-fire-ball erupt from the tracks. A split-second later, the shockwave hit, causing them all to drop their heads into the dirt.

Once the dust had settled, Higgins contacted Taylor to advise him that the operation had been executed.

'I can see it from here, Sergeant, on our sat imaging. I think half the bloody world can see it. Now, get your arses back here immediately,' replied the lieutenant.

'Right, boys. Job done. Let's get a hustle-on back to base,' said Higgins to the men as they picked themselves up off the ground.

The ride back to the base was as fast and exciting for Finn as the ride out. They were constantly being updated of enemy positions or aircraft by the ops base. Even though the bikes left minimal tracks, there was still a risk the Chinese surveillance technology could identify their signature so they had to ensure they spread out to minimise the risk.

After more than an hour of flat desert the gradient began to increase, as they rode up to the entrance of the canyon. At the entrance Higgins ordered them to stop. Looking back, there was still an enormous dust cloud where the device had been detonated. And still no sign of Chinese patrols — Higgins couldn't believe their luck.

'Sarge, look over there.' Finn pointed to the south of their target where a plume of dark black smoke was rising into the air.

'Gimme the binos,' demanded Higgins.

Looking through the powerful binoculars, Higgins could make out three Pinyins circling an area near the source of the smoke plume. The dust cloud below them made it impossible to see what was happening on the ground.

'C'mon. If we can see them, they can see us,' said Higgins grimly.

He knew that the San's didn't circle like that unless they had targets on the ground, and the likelihood was that it was one of the other squads down there getting a hammering. There was nothing they could do for them. They were too far away and, besides, four more men wouldn't make a bit of difference against three San's and whatever Chinese patrols were on the ground. But the knowledge of the distant bloodbath still left a sick feeling in Higgins' gut.

They slowed down in the canyon with the relative safety that it provided — not that they had much choice. It was far more technical riding than on the open desert plain.

They pulled into the base camp just after 1400 hours, covered in dust and sweat, exhausted from the ride and the waning adrenalin kick. Stumbling off their bikes they stretched their aching backs and joints.

A few of the men came out to greet them, though there were no high-fives or backslapping. Finn immediately sensed an air of sobriety.

'What's going on, boys? Thought you'd be glad to see us!' Finn asked the group.

'Sorry, mate. But we just heard that Delta squad has been hit hard. Reports are that they got mowed down by a couple of San's and a Chinese patrol,' replied Jessop, worriedly rubbing his straw-coloured buzz cut.

'Fuck me. I think we saw them on our way back, poor bastards,' said Finn, his stomach suddenly clenching.

At that moment Taylor came out of the mine. 'Well done, men. Mission accomplished. Clean yourselves up, have some food, then let's debrief at 1530. Oh, and make sure the bikes and all the gear come inside. The Chinese are likely to be sending out recon drones after what happened today.'

The men dispersed, deflated by the news of Delta squad. Finn shuddered at the thought that it could be them next.

That night Finn couldn't sleep. He was too wound up after the day's activities. He was replaying the mission in his head, trying to memorise every moment, how he felt, what he was thinking, the sensations. He was trying to distract himself from a nagging thought … how easily it could have been their team that was taken out by the Chinese helicopters. How it really just boiled down to luck. Yes, he was finally getting what he'd set out to get: a real challenge. But was it worth it?

He popped a Nightcap to help him relax. It seemed to do the trick and he managed to get half a night's sleep.

General Stephens, Sarah and Fletcher were in the conference room with the military leaders and advisors, going through the reports on the day's attacks. After the final presentation by Fletcher, who was in charge of the overall operation, the room was silent.

'Well, ladies and gentlemen, I must congratulate you on a successful first wave of attacks,' said General Stephens, leaning back in his chair. 'There can be no doubt that we have inflicted serious damage to the Chinese transportation lines and it will prove costly to them.'

'With the exception of Delta squad, we sustained minimal losses in the five attacks. But you can bet we won't have it so easy next time. Tomorrow we strike again with the squads in the north. This will be a different story, I expect,' said Fletcher.

Stephens nodded grimly.

'It will be interesting to see the Chinese response to these attacks. The reality is we caught them well off-guard today — and it meant low casualties for us. I wonder how quickly they sharpen up to our guerrilla tactics,' pondered Fletcher.

'Unfortunately, as we all know, there's only one way to find out — keep attacking,' replied General Stephens.

There was a knock at the door, and a young assistant strode over to General Stephens, bending at the waist to whisper something into his ear as he handed the general a note.

Stephens quickly read the note, then looked up to the assembled group. 'Well, people. You will have to excuse me.

Ambassador Xian is threatening all sorts of things to my assistants if I don't return his call immediately,' he said with a wry smile.

The general was already walking to the door. 'Fletch, Sarah. Come with me to my office. I want you to hear what he has to say.'

'Sure thing, Marty,' responded Fletch.

Sarah did not reply. She just gathered her things and moved over to the door, a picture of emotionless efficiency.

Once the three had entered his office, Stephens called his secretary, putting it on speaker setting, and asking to be put through to Ambassador Xian.

Xian picked up immediately. 'What is the meaning of these attacks on our infrastructure?' shouted Xian through the speaker.

'Well, hello Mr Ambassador. You seem to have forgotten who you are talking to. I suggest you conduct yourself more professionally or this call is finished,' replied Stephens, coldly. Both Fletcher and Sarah were in awe of the general's ability to remain cool and calm.

Xian paused. 'I … please excuse me, General, but you must understand. Beijing has learnt of these attacks and my superiors are asking many questions. They are also threatening reprisals. Please, explain these attacks.'

'Well, Xian,' said the general, his voice emotionless, 'let me explain something to you. You are on our land. We don't want you here anymore, so we're going to get you out. We will not stop this line of aggression until you and your army are swimming back to Guangzhou. Mark my words, this is only the beginning.'

It was Xian's turn to drop the temperature. After a few seconds of silence, his voice came through the speaker. 'Well, General, I can only conclude that you have lost your mind and I pity your fellow-Australians. I am very sorry but your actions will result in serious reprisals against your nation that are outside of my control.'

'So be it, Ambassador. The Australian people are ready for whatever you decide to throw at us,' replied General Stephens.

'Goodbye, General,' said Xian, hanging up without waiting for a reply.

General Stephens looked up at Fletcher and Sarah with a wan smile. 'That could have gone better, don't you think?'

They both stared back speechless, stunned by the threat Xian had made, but also still in awe of General Stephens' composure when confronted by such aggression.

'Yes, well, I think we've hurt their feelings,' said Fletcher dryly.

'They're certainly not happy about us crashing their little party, are they?' said Sarah, desperately trying to refrain from smiling.

General Stephens picked up on the guilt they felt, having a laugh when it could mean that soon innocent Australians would probably be in danger.

'You know, Winston Churchill once said, "War is a game that is played with a smile. If you can't smile, grin. If you can't grin, keep out of the way till you can." I think he was absolutely right. If we are to win this game we can't paralyse ourselves with fear and self-doubt. We are doing the right thing here, guys.'

Chapter 11

'Drone! Drone! Drone!' yelled Carver from inside the mine.

'Fuck. Inside now!' yelled Higgins.

Finn sprinted towards the mine entrance as the others were running into the opening. Higgins was right behind him, but stopped. 'Hunt, wait! Help me with this lot.'

Finn skidded to a halt, turned and ran back to help Higgins with the weaponry and tools that had been left behind by one of the others. It looked like only a day after their first mission, someone was already getting sloppy.

'C'mon, Hunt. Take the rifle. I've got the rest. Move! Come on!'

Finn grabbed the rifle and together they legged it back to the mine.

Gasping for air, both men collapsed on the ground, dropping their loads.

'Quiet! It'll be overhead in a second — it may have audio sensors,' hissed Taylor.

Higgins had recovered enough to start glaring at the men huddled in the mineshaft. As soon as the drone was out of range, he was going to let someone have it for leaving his weapon outside.

Half a minute passed, and the sound of the jet-propelled drone went directly overhead. 'Sounds high,' said Taylor, once the sound faded. 'Must be doing a broad aerial surveillance. That's good. They obviously have no clue where we're holed up.'

Higgins didn't waste a second once they were clear. 'Okay. Which one of you cocksuckers left your rifle and cleaning kit out there?'

The men all stared back, no one owning up. 'Oh, I'm sorry. Maybe I'm mistaken. Perhaps it was left out there by a fucking roo. Or maybe Father-fucking-Christmas left it there as an early present! Who left the weapon outside? I won't ask again.'

'Sarge. Where's Jessop?' asked Bull.

Higgins' face dropped, when he realised, looking around, that Jessop was not in the mine. 'Little cunt,' he muttered through gritted teeth.

Striding outside, Higgins saw Jessop walking back to the mine, looking sheepish. The other men trickled out of the cave to see what would happen.

'What the fuck are you doing walking around like you're sniffing the roses, Jessop?' yelled Higgins. 'Tell me you weren't out in the open when that drone came over.'

'I was taking a crap, Sarge, and I heard the call. Figured I wouldn't make it back to the mine in time so I hid in a crevasse over there.'

'You dopey little cunt. The latrine has been positioned so that even a retard like you could get back in time,' said Higgins, so close to Jessop's face that it was showered by Higgins' spit. 'If our position has been given away by your white ass hanging out your pants, I will personally tear you a new asshole. Understood?'

'Yes, Sarge. Sorry, Sarge. I thought I was doing the right thing,' stuttered Jessop.

'Don't think again. Your brain has not developed enough for you to think. You just do as I say, and when I say "into the mine", I mean get in the fucking mine!'

Jessop was clearly shaken by the verbal hammering dispensed by Higgins. The rest of the squad was also shocked by Higgins' reaction. Finn felt bad for Jessop, mainly because he would have done the same thing if it had been him out there when the alarm came in. Jessop was only 18, and Finn often felt protective of him, even though they'd been in training for around the same amount of time.

Higgins now turned to the rest of the men. 'That goes for all of you! We cannot risk being spotted. Our number one offence is our ability to operate covertly, which is also our number one defence.

'Right. Back to work. Hunt, you and Carver get onto those bikes. They need to be cleaned and checked by the end of the day.'

The rest of the day was uneventful, but everyone was now on edge, just waiting for another drone or chopper to buzz the camp. The game had just stepped up a notch.

For two days the squad had done little else but clean their gear and rest, the boredom relieved only by the numerous aerial reconnaissance drones and false alarms. This was more agonising than their nine-hour hike across the desert. Their routine was determined largely by the satellite sweeps, which also meant much of their time was spent in the mine. Nine men, on edge, inside a confined space, will generally result in frustration, anxiety and occasional aggression. Still, they were well trained and well led by Higgins, so discipline was generally good.

Carver and Finn had somehow become the bike maintenance go-to guys and spent hours every day shooting the shit as they went through the routine checks.

On the evening of day two, sitting outside alone, wondering what the next 24 hours would bring, Finn reflected on how he managed to get himself involved in this war. Though it almost made him dizzy thinking about how quickly his life had changed, he knew he'd never felt stronger or more purposeful and he loved the sense of camaraderie in the squad.

The light was going now. Soon it would be time to go in, before the satellite came over. Finn gathered his gear, stood slowly, stretched, then picked up his kit and moved gingerly back inside the mine. He was hoping for another mission to come up soon. The tedium of checking and rechecking gear was now getting unbearable, no matter how much of a pisser Carver was.

Most of the squad was doing the same, making their way inside, dropping their gear, finding a spot to park-up until it was time for dinner. The only thing that kept the men sane in times like this was humour. It may have been war that brought them together, but it was humour that created their bond. It was typical Australian humour, not for the faint-hearted. Some cultures might've called it bullying or cruelty, but for them, it was the greatest form of bonding that could be done. That night, unexpectedly, they were given emails from their family, loved ones and friends. It had been over three weeks with no mail, so it was a welcome surprise.

Each man's email was downloaded onto his personal tactical unit, the military equivalent of the civilian's MiLA. Sitting around the mine in the low light, the men talked about news from home.

'Oh shit, guys. I'm a dad! Bella had a baby boy! I'm a dad!' yelled Dave.

Calls of congratulations went around the mine.

'Hey, Dave,' called out Bull. 'You better call the Guinness World Record people. This could be the first time ever that a newborn baby weighed more than its dad!'

The mine erupted in laughter.

'Fuck you, Bull. I'm not a sniper for nothing. I'm such a crack shot, even my sperm never miss their mark,' responded Dave smugly, to more wails of laughter.

Higgins, who had been laughing, was standing now. 'All right. Cut it out, guys. The satellite will be overhead soon, and I don't intend to find out how good their hearing is, so let's keep it quiet.'

The men calmed down, and Finn went back to his emails. As well as emails from his mum and dad, there was one from Chris. Finn opened it and started reading with trepidation.

From: Chris08@me.com
To: Finn.Hunt@austinf.gov.au
SUBJECT: You're a Knob
AUTHORISATION: CENSORSHIP APPROVED

Dude, hope you're ██ ██ and have all your ██ attached. I've been meaning to write for a while now. To be honest, until recently, I was still pretty pissed off with you, fella. Anyway, let bygones be bygones and all that. I just wanted to say you're an arsehole for breaking my nose, but I

168

know I had it coming. Anyhow, apparently we gotta keep these short for some ███ ███ reason. Call me when you're back in ███.
Chris.
PS You still owe me $50 and I want it back, dickhead.

Typical Chris, thought Finn: simple and to the point, no faffing about. Even though the overzealous military censorship spiders had automatically gone through and edited it, hearing from Chris still made him smile, and he felt relieved that there would be no drawn-out apologies required.

Another email caught his eye — it was from Sophie. With a little shock, he realised he'd completely forgotten about her. It felt like a lifetime ago he had last seen her. When he had found out that she had gone back to the UK, he'd tried to put her out of his mind — he had no idea how effectively he'd managed to do that.

He started reading, curious to see how he'd feel.

From: Sophie.Marks@gmail.co.uk
To: Finn.Hunt@austinf.gov.au
SUBJECT: Apologies
AUTHORISATION: CENSORSHIP APPROVED

Dear Finn
    I hope this finds you well. I'm so sorry I didn't write sooner. I had to leave Australia quicker than I had hoped. My father wasn't well and the rest of the family was pressuring me to come back. They thought it safer to be back in the UK, but given what's going on around Europe, I tend to disagree. Anyway, all is generally well here. My father made a miraculous recovery once I returned — think I was tricked into coming home!
MESSAGE LENGTH EDIT [MILITARY CENSOR]
    I miss you, and I hope that we can meet up again. It was a shame we couldn't spend longer together.
    Big kisses + hugs, Soph

Well, at least he knew she was safe and that everything was okay, despite the army deciding her email was too long. He briefly considered writing back to her, but after trying to think of what he could tell her and coming up with nothing, she slipped from his mind again.

The rest of the emails were from friends, all wishing him well and looking forward to seeing him again. Looking around the dim, orange-lit cave, he could see that everyone's spirits were lifted, hearing from home. It made why they were fighting so much more real. It also reminded them of their reasons to survive and not die out there in the desert.

The next day their orders were received. Their next mission was much bigger than the last. This mission was classified as 'extremely dangerous', and would involve enemy contact. Higgins called the men into the mine for the briefing. It was immediately clear that this operation would be different, as both Higgins and Taylor were far more on edge. This set the tone of the briefing from the outset. All the men listened intently as Higgins spoke.

'The target is a Chinese outpost south of our position,' said Higgins, pointing to the mapscreen. 'This outpost houses around three platoons and support personnel. They conduct regular patrols of the transportation lines, both road and rail. Tomorrow night there will be a coordinated attack by our forces on a fuel depot to the north of us being used by the Chinese iron ore trains. Our role is to link up with Bravo squad, here,' he pointed to a spot on the mapscreen, 'and hit the garrison before the attack on the depot. This way, the Chinese response to the fuel depot attack will be minimised. If we fail, the Chinese will be able to react to the attack on the depot and probably wipe out our guys up in the north.'

The men looked up at Higgins, each of them visibly shifting with the new weight of responsibility.

'There can be no mistakes on this mission. I don't want to live with the fact that our failure directly caused other men's deaths.

But that's exactly what will happen if we fuck this up.' Higgins let this linger for a moment before continuing.

'Tomorrow, at 1600 hours, we will get on our bikes and travel to the target. We will deploy two clicks east of the target, link with Bravo, and together engage the target. The attack will be full-frontal — the element of surprise on this mission is critical to our success.

'So, gentlemen, I think it is safe to assume that we will be getting our hands dirty tomorrow. The stakes are high and, if we are to pull this off, we need to be on our game,' said Higgins, wrapping up the briefing. 'Questions, anyone?'

'Sarge, even if we're successful, this operation could take a while to fully secure the area. We could be riding back to our base when the satellite is doing its evening sweep. Isn't there a risk that we'll compromise our position?' asked Finn.

'Good point, Hunt,' responded Taylor. 'I will remain here at base camp and monitor all Chinese surveillance. If it's looking too hot, you'll be camping out under a thermal tent until it's safe to come back in.' Silence filled the mine. 'All right. We'll be doing incursion drills this afternoon and assigning roles and responsibilities,' said Higgins.

'Dismissed,' said Taylor.

The men stood and shuffled their way out of the mine into the sunlight.

'Fuck me! No pressure, huh?' said Carver.

Finn, squinting in the bright sun, replied, 'Mate, I guess this is what it's all about.'

'S'pose so … ' said Carver, trailing off as he walked away.

The next day final preparations were made, gear checked and rechecked, the plan discussed and talked through in the finest detail. Everyone had to know all the details in case a man went down and someone else had to step in and do his job. Lieutenant

Taylor had been in communication with Bravo squad to ensure they were all clear on the rendezvous point.

At 1550, the men assembled with their motorbikes. They were to travel in formation. Finn, Carver and Jessop, as the least experienced, had to sit in the middle at the back. If they encountered a Chinese patrol, having the most experienced men at the sides meant they could react quicker to a situation.

The ride down the narrow canyon was slow and they again had to carefully negotiate around all the larger rocks and boulders.

Once out of the canyon, things became slightly better. They had enough space to get their speed up. After two-and-a-half hours of exhausting travel along the plain, Higgins, who had been monitoring a GPS the whole time, spoke into his comms unit, ordering the men to stop.

Higgins got off his bike. 'Stay on your bikes, men,' he said to the others. Checking his GPS again, Higgins dialled in a frequency on his wrist-mounted communications unit. This was the rendezvous point, but there was no sign of Bravo squad. Higgins spoke while pressing a button on the small microphone attached to his neck that picked up the sound of his voice.

The sun was low now. They needed to dock with Bravo and get moving to the target. There was still another hour of riding, possibly two depending on the conditions.

'Bravo, this is Alpha, do you read?' Higgins said again into the comms unit.

'Alpha, this is Bravo, we read you. Coming up to the rendezvous point in 15 minutes,' came the reply.

Higgins breathed a sigh of relief — at least they weren't far off.

The desert was silent but for the slight sounds of the men shifting their weight on their bikes. Higgins imagined it would have been a nice time to be in the desert, if there wasn't a war on.

'All right, men. Dismount, stretch the legs, take a piss, but stay close to the vehicles,' barked Higgins.

Fifteen minutes later Bravo team rolled up on their motorbikes. They discussed the plan as a group. It was pretty simple, in theory. But of course nothing is that simple in the mayhem of battle. They would travel separately to the target, taking divergent routes. Once at the target zone they would employ a pincer movement that would have Alpha team attack from the west and Bravo from the south. This way they would minimise the possibility of being hit by friendly fire. It would also confuse the Chinese troops and split their defence.

There were two key elements to the plan. The first and most important element was surprise, and the second one was speed. Once they engaged the target they had to move quickly and with maximum aggression. If one team was pinned down by return fire, there was little chance of the other being able to breach the fence and take control of the compound. Both teams had to make it into the compound for them to have a chance of achieving their objective.

With the final arrangements discussed, they mounted up and rode off into the still, quiet desert.

They rode now using night-vision goggles, so that they could keep their headlights off. It was slow going, not because of the night-vision goggles — they projected an almost perfect full-colour image of the landscape ahead — but the harsh terrain made it impossible to travel any faster. Higgins regularly checked the GPS map, ticking off the distance to the target, directing the men every 50 metres to keep them on course.

After two hours of rough and uncomfortable riding, they were close. Higgins addressed them over the comms unit. 'All right, boys. Fifteen minutes. Remember your training, remember your job. When we stop, stay on your bikes until I tell you to dismount. No noise. I want absolute silence. The moment we stop, check your weapons quietly. I don't want to hear anything metallic alerting the Chinese of the shitstorm we're about to fuck them with.'

The tension in the group was mounting. The last two hours had been spent with only the hum of the bikes breaking their thoughts. The anticipation was stifling.

Finn's gut was churning. He really needed to go to the toilet but there was no way he could do anything about it now. His mouth was dry and his heart was pounding. He had been visualising himself for the last two hours, running the attack through in his head. The trouble was he had only been able to visualise himself getting off the bike and dropping to the ground, waiting for orders. He just kept visualising the same action over and over. He couldn't imagine anything past the point of dropping on the ground.

'Ten minutes, boys,' said Higgins' voice calmly came over the comms unit. 'When we're on the ground and I give the order, we will be running to the fence line. We need speed and silence. Speed and silence,' Higgins repeated.

No one said a word. Finn nodded to himself. His eyes were wide under his goggles, his body stiff. Higgins switched his comms unit so it would only transmit to Finn, Carver and Jessop. 'Breathe, guys. Think about your training.' Finn concentrated on taking a few deep breaths — immediately feeling better.

A couple of silent minutes passed. 'Okay, boys. Five minutes. Let's get frosty.' Five more tense minutes passed before Higgins' voice again came over the comms unit: 'Right here, men,' as Higgins rolled to a stop.

Finn concentrated on his breathing, trying to stay focussed and slow his mind down, repeating the mantras that had been drilled into them during training.

The bikes all rolled to quiet stops. Finn could see the lights of the camp, searing in the night-vision goggles. It looked big, like more than 30 troops might be sitting there waiting for them, thought Finn.

Higgins jumped off his bike, double-checked his GPS, and then called Bravo team who responded immediately. They were in position and ready to move.

'Dismount,' said Higgins quietly. 'Bravo team, move in. I repeat, move in,' said Higgins into his helmet comms.

'Copy that. Bravo moving in,' replied the leader of Bravo team, which came through everyone's integrated headsets.

Turning to the rest of the men who had now gathered near the lead bike, Higgins waved his arm. 'Let's move out.'

Finn's legs felt heavy and useless. Running across the desert towards the lights, he felt out of control, as if someone with a remote was controlling his leaden legs. He forced himself to slow down, to regain control; the last thing he could risk now was a rolled ankle. As he ran he kept an eye on Bull, who was ahead and to the left of him.

After a few minutes of running, they were 50 metres from the fence. Higgins raised his hand, ordering them to stop and get down. Dave dropped down and took up position with the silenced sniper rifle. Lifting the protective cap on the high-powered sight, a very faint green glow was emitted. Dave, who was a crack shot, would stay here until they breached the fence. His job was to take out the guards and he was already scoping out his targets, mentally assigning an order in which he would take them out as efficiently as possible.

Higgins spoke into his comms. 'Bravo, this is Alpha. Final position achieved. Are you ready to breach?'

'Affirmative. In position, ready and waiting,' came the reply.

Higgins had one last look around at his men to ensure everyone was in position and ready. 'Go for breach. I repeat, go for breach,' waving to his men, ordering them to move up to the fence.

Finn saw Bull get up and run. This was it, he thought as he hauled himself off the ground, running toward the fence line.

The 50 metres to the fence line seemed to take forever. Finn felt utterly vulnerable, just waiting for the first bullet to lodge itself in his head. Every step closer to the fence felt like another step closer to death. Finally, after an agonising run, Finn quietly crouched down at the fence. He couldn't believe that they'd made it this close to the camp without being spotted. Looking to his left, he saw Bull crouching down, going to work with his wire cutters. Finn fumbled with the cutters in his belt. Finally getting them out, he began shakily cutting at the fence. His hands got worse, to the point where he had to use two hands to keep the cutters steady. The tension was agonising; with every snip of wire Finn was convinced a guard would hear. But still nothing.

Looking over, Bull was sliding through the fence. 'Fuck,' Finn whispered to himself, concentrating even harder on cutting the wire.

Finally done, he pushed his rifle under the fence and then slid under himself. Looking down the fence line, Finn signalled Bull the all-clear. Bull looked back and gestured to his eyes. Finn, confused, took a second to realise that Bull was referring to his night-vision goggles. Finn hadn't noticed how bright the display was. Lifting the unit from his head, he could see the camp was illuminated like daytime.

Dave, who was watching their progress through his scope, now trained the rifle on the first of his targets standing on a tower at the northern end of the camp. Squeezing the trigger gently, the rifle dispatched a high-velocity round straight into the chest of the unsuspecting guard. The only sound from the rifle was a faint, dull thump of high-pressure air being released, which, from his distance, was virtually silent.

Quickly, Dave moved on to his next targets, professionally and economically taking out guard after guard in the pre-assigned order he had established earlier in his head.

Higgins gave the order to engage. Finn stood and, like the others, put his rifle to his shoulder, knees bent, both eyes open, sweeping his weapon and his gaze to find targets, just as he had been trained. The first shot came from Higgins, who spotted a soldier coming out of the latrine. The noise destroyed the quiet of the camp. Seconds later came a piercing siren and a flood of lights around the compound.

Deafening noise erupted.

Movement everywhere.

The air alive with bullets.
Fear.
Screams of panic.
Screams of pain.

The fighting raged for 20 minutes. For Finn it felt like an eternity. But then the Chinese were surrendering, throwing down their weapons, kneeling and putting their hands behind their heads. Finn registered this with a shock of disbelief. They were surrendering.

Bravo and Alpha teams converged on the centre of the compound to organise a clean-up. They had to go through the entire camp and lay their explosive charges and get out before the Sankaku attack helicopters responded. Luckily for them, it seemed that their action in the north was keeping the San's occupied.

Higgins and Mac, the highly-experienced soldier who led Bravo team, went in search of intelligence, while Bravo team set up the explosives and Alpha team processed the prisoners. There was no way they could take the captured soldiers with them, so they had to be marched out into the desert.

Higgins and Mac went into the communications building and found what they were after — Solid State Computers (SSCs), innocuous-looking small black rectangular boxes, small enough to fit comfortably in the palm of a hand. The SSCs had no moving parts, no wires, no heat signature, no inputs and no outputs, nothing that could be damaged or broken, yet they were capable of holding up to a petabyte of data. The only way to access the information inside them was through coded wireless technology, which the Australian Militech teams were just starting to learn how to break.

'Take the office next door, Mac. I'll clean this lot up,' said Higgins.

'On it,' replied Mac. 'I wonder if there's any Chinese porn on these things,' said Mac with a chuckle, examining an SSC.

'Only the highly classified stuff I would imagine,' said Higgins, in no mood to joke. 'Make it quick, Mac. We've probably got 15 minutes to be the hell away from this place.'

'Understood,' said Mac, walking into the office.

A single shot rang out in the small room. Higgins dropped the SSCs he was carrying onto a desk and unholstered his side-arm, bringing it up to take aim at the dark doorway. He leapt forward and threw himself against the thin wall beside the door.

'Mac, you there?' yelled Higgins.

Nothing, no response. 'Shit,' whispered Higgins to himself. Looking slowly and carefully around the corner, he saw Mac's lifeless body on the ground.

Bull and Finn, hearing the shot from where they were processing the captives, ran to the building and burst through the door from the outside, weapons at the ready. Higgins gestured to them to keep quiet, to take the SSCs they had secured and to retreat back out the door. He showed them the grenade he had in his hand. They got the message and backed out the door without closing it. Higgins knew there was no time to flush this resistant fucker out — he could only neutralise him. Silently and slowly he pulled the San on the grenade, let go of the catch and waited two seconds. Rolling the grenade into the room, he ran for the door. When he was just out the front door, the grenade did what it was meant to do — the shockwave from the blast sent Higgins flying to the ground. The flimsy building did not hold up well. The outside wall, where the office was, virtually disintegrated leaving a gaping hole in the side of the building.

Picking himself up off the ground, Higgins walked purposefully back to the destroyed building. Finn followed him, not really sure why.

'Sarge, what are you doing? We gotta get out of here,' yelled Finn.

'Just checking something,' replied Higgins coldly.

Finn followed him into the smoking shell of the building. Higgins walked into the room where he'd thrown the grenade. Looking around, he found what he was after.

The Chinese soldier lay on the ground, his face badly burnt and his body wrecked but, amazingly, still alive.

'Jesus, he's alive,' stuttered Finn, unable to pull his eyes away from the ruined face of the soldier.

Higgins looked at Finn and put his boot on the soldier's chest, causing him to cough blood. Finn was shocked and confused.

'What are you doing, Sarge?'

Higgins kept looking at Finn as he unholstered his side-arm. Drawing the weapon down to the dying soldier's head, he fired once.

Finn recoiled from the sight of the man's head exploding, spraying Higgins' boot with blood.

'Now we can go,' said Higgins, striding past Finn who was still staring at the soldier, his mouth open, shocked.

Outside, Higgins walked up to the others. 'All right. Are the charges set?'

'Yessir,' came the reply from the next-in-command of Bravo team.

'Good.' Higgins turned to Finn, McCaw and Jessop and gestured at the line of kneeling, blindfolded prisoners that their team had restrained. 'March these fuckers out into the desert and meet us at the bikes.'

'Yessir,' said McCaw, as he kicked one of the prisoners seated on the ground.

'Let's get the fuck out of here,' said Higgins, picking up the SSCs and walking off towards the main gates on his own.

A short march and they made it back to the bikes. The prisoners were forced to kneel, blindfolded and bound, berated and beaten by McCaw and Jessop. They seemed to be taking too much pleasure in it, and Finn felt disgusted by the way they were treating the prisoners — which was strange, given he had just shot and killed some of their compatriots. He was now cold and exhausted

— the adrenalin had worn off. Higgins arrived not long after, with Bull, Carver, Dave and Marks. It looked like they'd all made it out, which was a miracle. Heaving his pack onto his bike, Higgins didn't say a word. He was still in operation mode and clearly very focussed. Rummaging through the pack, he pulled out a large pair of wire cutters. Holding them in his right hand he walked directly to the prisoners.

Finn, who had been slouching against a rock, straightened as he wondered what Higgins was about to do with the cutters. Higgins looked like a man possessed. He marched up to the first prisoner and bent down behind the man. Finn suddenly felt the jolt of his senses becoming hyper-aware again. A loud snap and the prisoner's arms were released. The man lurched forward. Higgins moved on to the next. Finn felt relief at first, and then confusion.

'Sarge, what are you doing?' asked Finn incredulously.

'Releasing the prisoners. What does it look like?'

'But shouldn't we take them back for questioning?'

'Can't risk it. Easier just to let them go. If they found our base we'd be compromised,' said Higgins in a matter-of-fact tone. 'And don't worry about them starving in the desert, they'll get picked up once their drones find them.'

Higgins ordered the prisoners to start walking and to keep their blindfolds on. He signalled his men to get back on their motorbikes.

The journey back was uneventful. The mission had been an enormous success but as they retreated, so too did the energy and high of the attack. Finn felt weak, his arms were heavy and his legs felt like lead.

Reaching the base, the men pulled up outside the cave where Lieutenant Taylor greeted them. The men unloaded their motorbikes quietly and efficiently while Higgins walked off with Taylor to discuss the mission.

Chapter 12

Both prongs of the attack had been successful — the fuel depot had been neutralised with minimal Australian casualties, and the outpost had been completely destroyed. Soon after the news of the Australian army's success was widely publicised, however, reports followed about the inevitable reprisals on townships near where the attacks took place. The Chinese had levelled some tiny townships and caused at least 150 civilian casualties and an unconfirmed 30 fatalities.

General Stephens and Fletcher were in Stephens' office in the SOF, reviewing reports on the damage that had been inflicted in the attacks. Images flickered on the screen before them, detailing the carnage.

'Goddammit,' sighed General Stephens wearily, 'we knew this was on the cards, but did they have to go so far?'

'I know, Marty. They've gone too far now, especially after all their promises of not targeting civilians,' replied Fletcher.

'That's it. I've had enough of this. Time to put some more heat on China. I'm not going to sit by and let them get away with attacking our people,' said Stephens, visibly upset. Calling his secretary, he asked to be put through to Ambassador Xian.

General Stephens sat in silence for the minute that it took to get the Ambassador on the line.

'General Stephens, how can I help you?' said Xian, in a calm and unctuous tone.

'How dare you … how dare you take action against Australian civilians, Xian,' said Stephens hoarsely.

'You give us no choice, General. You continue to wage war against us, damaging our property and killing our soldiers.'

'That does not give you the right to injure and kill civilians!'

'Perhaps not, but it gives us the right to defend our infrastructure, General Stephens.'

'Your infrastructure?' Stephens repeated incredulously. 'What are you talking about, Xian? It is in fact largely our infrastructure, our land, and our people. You invaded us. Remember?'

'General, please, you must remember the agreement we made, that we would not involve your people — so long as you did not interfere with our mining.'

'That was not an agreement, that was a command from your country — something the Australian people never agreed to,' said the general, his rage building to a fever pitch.

Xian was now feeding off General Stephens' anger. 'Cease with these puny guerrilla attacks on our facilities and we will have no need to retaliate, General. You have the power to stop it immediately.'

'I want you out of the country, Xian — you and all your cronies. China has crossed a line that the Australian people will not tolerate.'

This threat seemed to sober Xian. 'General, please. It is imperative that we maintain diplomatic communications. If I am not here I fear that our leaders in China may not be so amenable,' Xian said in a pleading tone. 'I have had to persuade them many times to minimise their military action against Australia.'

'I, and the Australian people, have now seen how you "minimise" military action, Xian. Get out. Now.' With that, Stephens cut the connection. He looked up at Fletcher in disbelief.

'My god, Fletch. What have I done?'

'You've done the right thing, Marty. I think we have crossed a line — a line that we needed to cross if we are to get the Chinese off our land.' Fletcher's tone was calm and firm.

'Make sure Xian and all his staff are on a plane tonight, Fletch. I want to make sure the Chinese get the message that we're no longer playing by their rules.'

'Of course, Marty. I'll see to it myself,' replied Fletcher, turning to walk out.

Alone in his office, the light from his screen, showing graphic image after graphic image of civilian suffering, flickered across Stephens' face.

The day after the mission, the squad rested, sleeping for most of the day. It was now dark at base camp. Finn had just finished preparing the evening's meal of chicken, pasta and vegetables. They took turns to prepare the meals. It was a ridiculously easy chore. The SFR, or squad field ration, was a ready-made, long-life meal for nine. The simple, rectangular box contained everything needed for a meal — just rip the tab off at the bottom and a chemical reaction immediately heated it up. Ten minutes later, open the top and the piping-hot meal was ready to be served. It actually tasted good, too. The US army had spent millions on the technology, as they recognised how important a good hot meal was for morale when out in the field. The only trouble was it had very low nutritional value, due to the long-life nature of the contents. So, to supplement their diet, they all had to take 'nutrient-rich paste' — or NuRiP, as they called it. Technically, they could live off NuRiP and water alone for months, but no one wanted to test that theory.

Finn couldn't sleep that night. He kept running through the mission in his head, analysing everything he'd done and seen. He tried to recount everything, every detail, but his mind wasn't being so forthcoming. Flashes came to him, recollections of smells, light, movement, blood and, most of all, the sense of crippling fear. He remembered watching as the others stood and ran forward as he lay on his stomach. He remembered finally getting up and running forward. It was like his legs were made of hardwood, they were so slow and clumsy. He remembered shooting at people, shapes, shadows and muzzle flashes. He remembered Higgins and the way he put his boot on the dying soldier's chest and shot him in the head. But one image was more vivid than the others. One image kept replaying in his mind over and over. He couldn't get it out of his head, and he didn't think a Nightcap would be the healthiest way to sort out how he was feeling.

He stepped outside into the cool night air and was surprised to find Higgins out there, sitting on a rock and staring out into the distance.

Finn approached him hesitantly. 'Sir ...?'

'Hunt, what are you doing up at this hour?' Higgins said, turning to Finn. Finn was worried he'd get a bollocking from the sergeant for interrupting him, but it seemed like he didn't mind. He seemed more mellow than usual.

Finn decided to try to get what he was thinking about off his chest. 'Sir, how do you feel about ... killing people?' he asked, cringing at how idiotic the question sounded before it was even fully out of his mouth. Hoping to save a bit of face, he rushed on. 'I mean, you've obviously been through a lot, seen a lot. I can't even imagine how many kills you've had.'

The silence continued so absolutely that Finn momentarily questioned if he'd spoken at all. But then Higgins sharply took in a breath, and began to speak.

'You strike me as the kind of guy who's used to being successful, Hunt,' he said. It was such a non sequitur that Finn jerked his head around involuntarily to stare at Higgins. He could only see Higgins' profile in the moonlight — his voice sounded almost disembodied. The voice continued, 'Killing a certain number of people is not a great way to define success for yourself. Having a certain number of kills under your belt is not all it's cracked up to be.' There was a long pause. Finally, Higgins turned his head, staring directly at Finn. His eyes glinted in the moonlight. 'I don't have any regrets. I don't look backwards, and I don't know any different. But I wouldn't recommend this life to someone who had other options.'

Another long pause rang out in the silence. Finally Higgins nodded once, sharply, and got up from the rock and went back into the cave.

Finn stood out there in the darkness for a long time. Finally, he decided to email Chris.

From: Finn.Hunt@austinf.gov.au
To: chris08@me.com
SUBJECT: You're the knob
AUTHORISATION: CENSORSHIP PENDING

Hey mate,

Thanks for the note and I'm sorry about what happened at the Sheaf. And, yes, I know I owe you fifty but you'll have to wait. Actually, it'll be a miracle if I ever get to pay you back ... the way things are going here. I was in a proper firefight the other day. It was crazy and, to be honest, I was scared shitless. As soon as the shots started firing everything around me went into high speed but I was still moving and thinking in slow motion. It's the strangest thing.

I did get a kill though. Probably more than one, but I only remember one. It was crazy, mate. I can still see this guy's face. He was running away from me and as he turned to see me I saw his eyes. I lined him up and shot him in the back, landed a couple of rounds in him. He went down real quick in a spray of blood. He twitched for a bit and I just stood there staring. Can't believe I wasn't shot myself. Anyway, it was fucking crazy and I'm glad it's over now.

I feel a bit bad about killing. But I mostly feel bad about not doing more. Like I let the others down. They were awesome mate. You should have seen them, they moved like animals hunting, especially our Sarge, he's a real warrior. Next mission I'm going to be more switched on, more like him. I really feel like I let them down, though they all reckon I did well for my first mission.

Well mate, I can't wait to get back and go for a steak and a beer at Woolloomooloo (and give you your fifty back)! We've been out here for ages now and it's really starting to get to me. The heat, the dust and the constant worry about being attacked. It's so mad, you're either bored senseless or completely crapping yourself. There's nothing really in between. Anyway, enough of my babbling...

Take it easy,
Finn

Chapter 13

The squad had been in the cave for nearly two months now, having completed six gruelling missions and losing McCaw to enemy fire in the process. They were tired, frayed and despondent. Every day, the conversation returned again and again to the futility of their attacks. They saw time and again just how efficiently the Chinese forces could rebuild any damage they might inflict.

'Gather round men, we have new orders,' Higgins called.

The men gathered, standing and crouching in a circle outside the cave in the morning sunlight, the air still, cool and crisp.

'All right, guys. We're going to break camp today and move out to the north,' started Higgins, interrupted by cheers from some of them. 'Okay, quiet down,' Higgins said, his hands motioning for everyone to calm down. 'I know you're all happy to be moving out. Our orders are to move north-west, a 150 clicks east of a town called Duchess. The Chinese rail line goes through Duchess, Mount Isa and then on to Karumba where they're exporting the minerals. We will create a base camp and from there we will be given our objective. Transportation will be arriving tonight, so we will need to break camp immediately. Questions?'

Finn put up his hand. 'Sarge, what's the transportation?'

'We will be extracted tonight by chopper and flown to a rendezvous point to the west. From there we will be issued with three light-armed vehicles, which we will use to locate a base camp. Anything else?'

'What are we doing with all the gear here?' asked Carver.

'We leave everything except your personal kit. Everything goes in the cave and we do a thorough electronic wipe-down of the whole valley — I want no trace of our being here. Understood?' replied Higgins.

A chorus of 'Yessirs' came from the men.

'Right, get to work then,' said Higgins, clapping his hands once.

That night the sound of the beating rotors was like music to Finn's ears. They had been disconnected from the world for so long that the chopper seemed like an outstretched hand pulling them back to civilisation.

Finn stood beside Carver as the huge, modified Blackhawk troop carrier came in slowly to land. Nothing could be heard above the roar of the engines. Higgins waved his arm, signalling the men to board. Finn noticed that overhead there were at least two other choppers, probably Apaches, to cover the Blackhawk. On board, they took their seats and buckled in, dust flying in the open sides in waves and covering them from head to toe. Finn lifted off his goggles to look back on where their camp had been, now devoid of any trace of their presence — the cave again just a crack in the rock face. He was suddenly stricken with the realisation that all they'd managed to do while there had been completely undone by the Chinese. All the fighting, the struggling, losing McCaw — they may as well have never been there. The powerful engines revved and they slowly lifted off the ground, rotors straining to gain height.

It felt good to be moving. Nobody bothered to talk over the noise. Finn looked around at the other men and saw tired but relieved faces. The vibrations and movement lulled him into a sleep despite the roar of wind and machine.

They landed just outside of Duchess. The town had been taken over by the military, but everyone wore civilian clothes and the vehicles were almost all civilian. It was a way of keeping the Chinese less suspicious about the tiny town. It was in fact a hub for a number of military operations in the region. The squad was given a two-day rest to clean up, eat well and bandage their frayed nerves. They were informed that Lieutenant Taylor was to stay in

Duchess and Higgins would take command of the team, which was fine by everyone.

After two days' rest, Finn felt stronger than ever and was already looking forward to some action. While he'd started to admit to himself that he had doubts about the effectiveness of what they were doing, that didn't stop him from wanting to help out his mates in action. Somewhere during his time in the cave, without him really realising it, he'd started fighting for his mates, not for himself.

They received a thorough briefing of the mission and how it would fit into the overall coordinated attack on the Chinese. They learned that General Stephens was planning an all-out attack on multiple targets, all designed to wreak havoc on the Chinese transportation lines. Simultaneous with their mission, there would be joint operations by what was left of the navy and air force. They were not told what the other missions were, only that they would be part of a coordinated joint attack.

A further three days of training in high explosives gave the men more time to physically recover from the previous few months. Finn found it therapeutic to have something to think about, to learn, even if it was learning how to blow up things — or people.

Three nights later they prepared the vehicles, loading up their supplies and equipment. They were issued with three Canadian-built Conquest Knight XX Light Tactical Vehicles. Despite having the word 'light' in their names, the 'Connies', as they called them, were hulking great trucks. Armoured and armed, they were an awesome vehicle for extreme landscapes like the outback.

The plan was not to stay at a remote camp for as long this time, but they had to be prepared for any eventuality. At 0100 hours they fired up the three Connies and headed out of the town. The driving was slow and rough and took a long time, as they were only able to travel at night and, when they were travelling, they had to stop every few hours while the satellites passed overhead. Two nights later they reached their operations base. Spirits were high and the men felt like a cohesive unit again — even Private Samuels, McCaw's replacement, now fitted in seamlessly. Finn always felt safe around his squad-mates, especially Higgins, who'd proven to his men over the past months that he was a warrior and a survivor.

With the base communications and defences set up, Higgins gathered the men around the bonnet of one of the Connies, under the shade of a thermo-tent pitched over the top. They had received their mission objective.

Higgins stood with hands on hips. 'Okay boys, you're gonna like this: as you know, we're part of an all-out offensive on the Chinese. Our target is of strategically high importance to the Chinese. So, we're going to blow it to bits.'

A few sniggers and wry looks were exchanged at this news.

Higgins continued. 'Our target is a bridge, 120 metres high, that crosses a river valley north-west of our position — about 30 clicks over hard terrain.'

'Will it be guarded, Sarge?' asked Bull.

'I'm getting there, Bull. Yes, it will be guarded. We will need to approach the target under darkness,' Higgins said, pointing now at the mapscreen on the bonnet of the Connie. 'The way I see it is we position snipers here and here to cover a smaller team that comes down either side of the bridge on the western bank.'

'What's the design of the bridge, Sarge?' asked Finn.

'Here are photos and schematics of the bridge.' Higgins turned on a projector that flashed the images in front of the men. 'It's an old truss bridge, single rail track, built back in 1963. All we need to do is correctly place and detonate charges on one end of the bridge. That will cause it to give way and slide into the valley and river below.'

There were nods all round as the men took in the plan.

'If it's such an important asset, what defence can we expect?' asked Finn.

'Our intel suggests we can expect medium resistance, probably a platoon, two at the most — and likely to be based on the eastern side of the bridge where there is easier access to the river below.'

Finn was surprised that such an important asset would only be defended by a single platoon. Surely, thought Finn, the Chinese must have increased their security in the last few months — what with all the attacks they had been conducting? Something about it didn't feel right.

Something else was on Finn's mind, too. His mouth opened before he had a chance to stop himself. 'Sarge, what's the point of these attacks? We've been blowing up their trains, roads and camps for months and every time they just build more,' he was egged on by nods from the other men. 'It all seems pointless.'

Higgins shifted, putting his hands back to his hips. 'Hunt, you're a soldier. You don't question "why?" you only question "how?". Am I clear?' he said gruffly.

'Yes, Sarge — crystal,' replied Finn, feeling like a schoolkid being scolded by a teacher.

Higgins looked around, daring anyone else to ask a question. 'All right, then. Get yourselves organised, we're moving out at 0100 hours tonight.'

Bull turned to walk away with Finn. 'Mate, it's all a bunch of bollocks. He's right, though: all you ask is how, how you're gonna stay alive, so that once it's all over you can ask someone in Canberra "why the fuck?"'

Finn smiled ruefully, nodding his head. ''Spose you're right, mate.'

That night they drove the Connies to within five kilometres of the bridge and then set out on foot. The air was cold and the lack of a moon made it dark as hell. Finn walked silently, bent at the knees, rifle held across his chest. He was sweating despite the cold, which created a clammy, shivery layer of moisture over his skin. His mind was unsettled and he couldn't stop thinking that something wasn't right about this mission. Creeping further away from the

Connies and closer to the bridge, Finn felt more nervous than on any of the previous missions. The eerie view through the night-vision goggles didn't help settle his nerves, either.

In front of him he could just make out the silhouette of Higgins, who was leading them through the thick scrub. Higgins had stopped, with his right arm raised, fist clenched in a ball, staring straight ahead.

Finn froze and stared at Higgins, who slowly crouched. Everyone followed Higgins' lead and crouched down. Straining his ears, Finn tried to hear beyond the sound of the rhythmic chorus of the frogs, which filled the night.

Still in a crouch, Higgins looked back and waved the others forward to his position. Without a word, Higgins used hand signals to send Dave and Jessop, the snipers, out to their positions, and the rest of the squad to follow him down the hill towards the bridge.

Through the scrub the lights of the bridge could be seen, bright and sparkling — the Chinese, thought Finn, were making no attempt to be covert about the bridge. It was so brightly lit it was almost challenging them, tempting them to come closer.

Moving more slowly now, they crept through the scrub to a point where the bush stopped and grass began. They could see the train track to their left, and directly ahead was the bridge.

The plan was for Higgins and Bull to go it alone from here, running forward and placing the explosive charges on the bridge. The others would cover them if they were spotted.

Finn watched as Higgins and Bull ran forward silently, crouching low to minimise their profiles. They disappeared into the darkness, beyond the power of Finn's night-vision. He crouched down and leaned against a tree for support, his rifle trained on the dark ground ahead.

The minutes seemed like hours. Higgins and Bull had attached the explosives and were on the return journey when suddenly Finn heard voices speaking in Chinese. They were coming from the left. He immediately realised it must be a patrol, walking along the train track towards the bridge. At the same time, Higgins and Bull ran right into them. Higgins stopped, looked up and without any hesitation lifted his RG and started firing, the plasma discharge lighting up the end of his barrel. The Chinese hit the ground, some dead, some alive.

'Blow it!' yelled Higgins at the top of his lungs, before launching into a sprint for the bushline.

All hell broke loose. The Chinese were yelling, returning fire on Bull and Higgins, who were both legging it to the cover of the scrub. Finn and the others began laying down suppression fire on the patrol.

Carver was fumbling with the remote detonator. After what seemed an eternity, he finally hit the button. The explosion was nothing spectacular, just a dull thud and massive shock wave that made everyone's ears pop. This was followed closely by the torturous scream of metal bending and warping and, finally, the crashing sound of the bridge collapsing.

Higgins and Bull were still running towards them under furious enemy fire. Finn and the others were returning it just as liberally. The two snipers were devastating but the Chinese outnumbered them at least three to one.

Higgins threw himself into the shrub near Finn, rolling over and into a crouch with lightning speed, immediately opening fire on the Chinese who were moving up on their position.

Bull crashed into the bush not far behind.

'Move back!' yelled Higgins above the gunfire.

Standing in a low crouch, Finn shuffled backwards, still firing on the Chinese. There were so many of them now, and they were moving up quickly.

A grenade went off near Finn, the force of the explosion punting him sideways and to the ground. Stunned but not hit, head fuzzy, ears ringing, he could still see the insanity that was raging around him. Pulling himself together, he shook his head and opened his mouth wide, trying to pop his ears.

He saw Higgins yelling, but he couldn't make out what he was saying. All Finn could think was to get as far away from there as possible. Turning to run, Finn held his rifle behind him, firing randomly.

Looking over to his right, he could see Carver running through the scrub, doing the same. He saw him stop to throw a grenade. As soon as Carver had thrown it, his left shoulder jerked wildly backwards. He had been hit.

Finn changed direction and ran over to Carver, who was unconscious on the ground, his shoulder at an unnatural angle and bleeding profusely.

Reaching for his good arm, Finn lifted him to a seated position. Heaving him desperately up to his shoulder, panic kicked in. He knew the Chinese were close.

Finn sensed something close to him, moving quickly. Turning too late, Finn felt a split second's pain … and then, blackness.

Chapter 14

Consciousness came slowly to Finn. The first thing he noticed was an intense pain in the front of his head, which shot through to the back as he opened his eyes. His mouth was bone dry, his vision blurry. A sound was slowly registering above the ringing in his ears. A distant scream, like nothing Finn had ever heard before. It was removed though, detached from reality, like it was happening far away. He tried to sit up but realised his hands and feet were bound. Rather than struggle, Finn looked around, taking in his surroundings — dirt floor, dim light, confined space, corrugated tin walls, a single wooden chair in the middle of the room, a workbench opposite.

Finn grunted, trying to get up again. Head pounding like mad, he squeezed his eyes shut to try and counter the feeling of his eyes popping out his skull. His vision was still blurry when he opened them again.

The sound of the man screaming was louder and clearer now — it made Finn's whole body feel raw. It also sobered him up and sharpened his awareness of his surroundings. He started to remember what had happened at the bridge. Though he couldn't be sure, he thought it was still dark, given the dim light in the room, so he had to assume that he had only been unconscious a few hours and that he was still somewhere near the bridge. Taking inventory of himself, he didn't think he was bleeding anywhere — but his comms unit and weapons had been stripped from him at some point.

The screaming stopped. Finn's body immediately relaxed, as though an electrical cord had been unplugged in him. A moment later, the door to the tiny shed was thrown open. A Chinese officer strode in first, followed by two men dragging in another by the shoulders. The man being dragged was unconscious. The officer pointed to the ground and barked an order. The two soldiers flung the man to the ground, wiping their bloodied hands on their jackets.

The officer looked over quizzically at Finn, who was lying face-down on the ground. He walked over and crouched beside Finn. 'Ah, you're awake,' he said, 'I'm glad. I hope your head does not hurt too much.'

Finn just stared groggily, his eyes straining to focus, his mind trying to make sense of the compassionate tone of his captor's stilted English.

The officer leaned in closer to Finn's ear. He could smell the officer's rancid warm breath. 'You're next,' was all he said. With that the officer stood and walked out, followed by the two soldiers.

Finn's mind was reeling. He looked over at the lump of human flesh beside him. It was Carver. What the hell had they done to him?

'Carver,' whispered Finn, as loudly as he could. 'Mate, wake up.'

There was no movement. Finn watched carefully. He was still breathing.

There was nothing Finn could do for him from where he was, with his hands and feet bound. All he knew was that they had to get out of there. Suddenly the prospect of an excruciatingly painful death sharpened his mind.

Looking around, Finn noticed a piece of the corrugated iron wall had bent back slightly, revealing an edge that just might cut through the rope that bound his hands. He shuffled over to the spot and went to work, slowly at first, making sure it did not create noise, then getting faster when he realised it was working. What noise he did create was drowned out by the sound of a nearby Fusor neutron generator that was powering the camp.

Furiously he rubbed the rope up and down the tin, not even noticing the pain each time the rope slipped and he ran his arm down the tin instead.

After about 20 minutes of rubbing, the rope finally gave way. Arms bleeding and sore from the effort, Finn wriggled out of the binds, then undid his feet.

Crawling silently over to Carver, he rolled him over onto his back. 'Jesus, what did they do to you?' he muttered to himself.

Carver's shoulder was bloodied from the gunshot wound, but his face was covered in blood, too. Finn shook him gently, trying to revive him. There was no way, even if they could get out of this shed, that he could carry the unconscious Carver too far.

'C'mon. Wake up, mate,' he whispered, shaking his body roughly.

Carver gradually came around, blood-crusted eyelids flickering up. Finn took his shirt off and rubbed Carver's face clean, starting with his eyes, then moving down to his mouth. When he rubbed Carver's chin, Carver's eyes suddenly widened in pain and he let out a high-pitched grunt of agony.

He opened his mouth slightly to reveal a gaping hole where his lower front teeth had been. They had ripped his front teeth out.

'Didn't ask nuthin,' spluttered Carver, his eyes wet from the tears of pain.

'I'm sorry, mate. Don't talk. Just keep your mouth shut, okay? I'm going to try and find a way out of here, so you have to stay conscious and be ready to move at any time,' whispered Finn, trying desperately to keep his mind focussed.

Carver nodded, looking like he may pass out at any time.

Finn went to the door to see if he could get a visual on the camp and the guard situation. From what he could see, there were no guards on the shed.

Satisfied that there was nobody immediately outside the shed, he set about inspecting the walls of their cell.

The walls of the old shed were flimsy, kept together by rotten wood and rust. Finding the spot where he had cut his bindings, he pulled the sheet of tin back even more, revealing the darkness of the outside world. As quietly as he could he bent it back even more, creating a hole that he could just squeeze through. Clawing at the dirt floor, he made the hole big enough for them both to slide through.

Finn's heart was racing. Panic and fear were starting to take over. If the Chinese came in now, it would be over and he could look forward to a visit from Carver's dentist.

He shuffled back over to Carver. 'C'mon, we're getting out of here. You gonna be able to run?' asked Finn.

Carver grabbed Finn's shirt with his right hand, hoisting his head and torso off the ground. With a wild look in his eyes, Carver grunted, spitting blood over Finn.

Finn interpreted this correctly. Carver would run. 'All right, let's go. Don't know where we are, but let's just get the fuck away from here.'

Sliding out the hole, it was a relief to feel the cool air of the night. The horizon was brightening to the east. It would be light soon. They needed to get moving — and fast.

Once they were both outside Finn looked around, lifted Carver by his right arm, then crouched and started slowly creeping away from the shed. He desperately wanted to sprint straight for the bush, but he knew that the noise would alert the Chinese.

With every step the anticipation grew. The need to reach the bushline was all-consuming, the sound of Finn's quickening pulse pounding through his ears.

Forty metres to the bushline — hold your nerve.

Thirty metres — nearly there. Stay calm.

Twenty metres — you're going to make it.

Ten metres from the safety of the bush, the silence was broken by yells in Chinese, followed quickly by automatic fire. Rounds were whistling past Finn and Carver, tearing apart the dirt and foliage around them. Finn gripped Carver by the sleeve, willing him to run faster.

In an instant, Finn heard a strange thump — something warm and wet was on his face. Carver's sleeve was ripped from his fist. Stunned, he stopped to see why Carver had fallen. Crouching low and turning around to reach for him, he realised in horror that his friend's head was split in half. The remaining half was splattered all over Finn — tiny bits of bone and brain, and a lot of blood. Finn reeled from the realisation, frantically wiping what he could off his face. A bullet whistling by his head snapped him out of it. No time to do anything about it now. Finn was up and running as fast as he could, the bullets landing all around him.

A powerful force wrenched his left shoulder forward, followed quickly by a searing pain in his arm. Finn looked down to see his shirtsleeve had been torn and darkened by blood. He kept running, the adrenalin keeping the pain manageable.

Into the scrub, bullets still flying all around him, Finn didn't slow down. He was on autopilot now, his legs moving, but he was no longer in control — his body was now in charge and doing its job to execute a flight response.

He was going downhill now, gathering pace. The gradient was steepening. At the same time, Finn's limbs were tiring, his legs were struggling to keep up with the momentum of his body. The shooting had stopped but Finn could still hear yelling — they were coming for him. The light was brightening now, enough to make out shapes and clear silhouettes, though not enough to distinguish colours.

Resting against the trunk of a tree Finn gasped for breath, chest rising and falling deeply and rapidly. His heart felt as though it would burst through his ribs at any moment. A mixture of his sweat and Carver's blood dripped down his face to his lips, connecting with his tongue — the metallic taste horrified him. Finn rubbed feverishly at his face using his shirtfront.

Ahead, the gradient dipped steeply and beyond that Finn thought he heard the sound of the river. Setting off again, he tried desperately to slow himself as he descended to the river. The last thing he could risk now was an injury that would really slow him down. The pain in his arm was beginning to intensify but he blocked it from his mind, focussing entirely on getting to the river safely.

The shouts and yells of the Chinese were fainter now — perhaps they had given up on him, thought Finn. Unlikely. They were probably just regrouping to conduct an organised search.

Crashing through the bush to the river's edge, Finn threw himself into the freezing water and scrubbed at his face, neck and shirt. Washing off the remains of his friend, he noticed the white bits float away and sink into the now bloodstained water. He knew he had to keep moving and get as far away from here as possible. Tearing off his shirtsleeve, he revealed an ugly, open wound where a bullet had ripped through the flesh of his left arm. Tying the sleeve around his arm, he pulled it tight to try and stem the flow of blood.

He stood in the river, water up to his knees, searching for something to help him float downstream. Spotting a log caught up in the trees and hanging over the river, he hauled it out and pushed it and himself into the river. Going with the gentle current, Finn slung his arms over the log and began kicking gently. He had a flashback of swimming at the Boy Charlton Pool with the swim squad. It seemed like someone else's memory, something that someone had told him about — not something that he used to do every other day.

Chastising himself for daydreaming, he started to think about his next move. It was now fully light, though the sun had not yet risen. If the Chinese saw him drifting down the river they could easily shoot him. Finn decided to angle across to the other side of the river. At least that way he could get to cover quickly if he was spotted.

After three hours of drifting down the river, Finn felt like he had put some distance between himself and the Chinese. His arm was throbbing now and his legs were beginning to cramp. Reaching the bank, Finn hauled himself out — exhausted, thirsty, hungry and completely lost. His legs shook weakly. He needed to get his bearings, work out a way of getting help. Finn knew if he headed east he'd have a better chance of finding help — he'd just have to be careful not to run into an enemy search party. The prospect of being captured again was not a thought Finn wanted to entertain, having seen what they were capable of. But what choice did he have? He could die out here, wandering around lost, or he could give himself an objective and see how far he could get.

He would head east, directly away from the river for as long as he had to. That had to get him back into the vicinity of a town or farm.

Finn drank as much as he could from the river, praying that it would not make him sick, and then set off up the hill. After six hours of beating his way through the bush and desert, Finn felt he could go no further. Exhausted and weakened by the loss of blood from his injury, he collapsed on the ground.

Heat, throbbing arm, nagging hunger and an all-consuming thirst conspired to create a fog of delirium. The sun was still high in the sky, with no clouds. There was no sign of respite. The terrain had changed markedly from the hillside near the river. He was now in semi-arid desert — no cover if a Sankaku flew over. He only hoped that, if their mission was part of a coordinated attack, the Chinese would be far too busy to run after a lone escapee who may or may not be alive.

Finn heaved himself up off the ground, telling himself to keep moving. One foot in front of the other, his head drooping, all he could look at was his feet, making sure that they landed securely on every step.

Darkness came quickly, as it does in the desert. He was so exhausted he collapsed beside a rock. The cool desert evening felt good after the heat of the day, but quickly Finn started to shiver as the temperature continued to drop. That night Finn slipped in and out of consciousness — fitful dreams and hallucinations played with his mind as he tried to deal with the shock of what he had been through.

Waking as the sun rose, Finn struggled to his feet and willed his legs to move forward. His head thumped from dehydration and his shoulder now ached mercilessly. He looked at the ugly mess of his shoulder wound. It was only a flesh wound, but it could be serious if it became infected. Finn tried to keep it from his mind. If he didn't get some help soon, his shoulder would be the least of his concerns.

Five hours of erratic stumbling and the horror of feeling his body shutting down began consuming his mind. The pain was now being eclipsed by the panic of realising the symptoms they talked about in training were actually happening to him — swollen tongue, cramping legs, headache and dizziness. Finn had to fight the rising panic — he knew that if he let the terror of what was happening to him take over, he would be dead.

The sun was dropping low again. Finn, exhausted like never in his life, cried a tearless cry at the thought of another night in the desert. Between sobs he tried to talk to himself, willing himself to harden up and just deal with it, telling himself that tomorrow he would find help and get out of this hell.

That night his body convulsed and shivered from the cold, hallucinations playing with him mercilessly, replaying images back to him: Carver's head being blown off, the Chinese commander with a pair of pliers, his mum being shot, his arm being amputated with a saw. On and on the dreams and visions came to him — it was like his mind was punishing him.

Finn woke feeling just as exhausted as when he went to sleep. His mouth was dry as sand. His tongue felt huge, but his gums had shrunk and his teeth felt loose.

'Get up, just get up,' he told himself.

As soon as he moved, his head started to pound again with a vengeance. His shoulder thumped as blood came back to the wound. Clutching his shoulder, he stumbled onwards. Walking towards the morning sun, he knew this would keep him heading east.

By the afternoon he was so delirious he did not notice the dust plume on the horizon. In fact, Finn didn't even register the sound of the truck as it got closer, not until it reared up over the steep ridgeline he was on and skidded to a standstill only a metre from him. Startled, Finn fell backwards as his balance gave way and he collapsed on his back. Closing his eyes, darkness engulfed his mind as consciousness slipped away.

Chapter 15

In the general's office in the SOF, General Stephens was with Sarah and Fletcher going over the post-attack evaluation reports.

'Looks like a good success rate, Fletch,' Stephens said with a satisfied look on his face.

'It certainly does, Marty,' replied Fletcher, grinning.

Sarah turned away from the screen she was reading from. 'Australian casualties are low and the key missions were all successfully executed.' Sitting forward, Sarah continued. 'Our strategists say these attacks will slow down their exports to a point where it is about four times more expensive to get a ton of iron ore out of Australia than it was for them to buy it from us two years ago.'

'That's an excellent result,' said Fletcher. 'At this stage our only game plan is to make it economically untenable for China to stay here.'

'I think we're succeeding,' said Stephens, 'however, the Chinese have massive resources — they may be able to take short-term losses, holding out for long-term gains. They know that we cannot continue with a guerrilla war for long. Whereas, for them, every day they're on Australian ground, they're expanding their roots, creating more infrastructure.' He rubbed his face with both hands, moving them to the back of his neck, squeezing his shoulders. 'I just don't know if we're being utterly futile with these guerrilla attacks.'

'Marty, this is like back in the early 2000s. Remember when the Howard government got us involved in Afghanistan and Iraq? We were the invaders then, along with the US coalition. Do you remember the terrorists who fought so hard to get us out? Well, remember how godawful they made it for us — remember how many lost their lives trying to fight the local terrorist cells?'

General Stephens nodded wearily.

'Well, we can keep making life hell for the Chinese, just like they did to us then,' Fletcher said. 'We just have to stay resolute. We will win in the end.'

'I know what you're saying, Fletch,' said Stephens. 'The trouble is that there's no halfway point in this strategy. We have to commit fully to this line of warfare if it is to succeed and, like it or not, we will be bringing the Australian people into the frontline — just like in Iraq and Namibia.'

After Sarah and Fletcher had left, General Stephens sat back in his chair reflecting on their options. Deep in thought, Stephens didn't register the phone ringing at first. On the third ring he came out of his reverie and answered languidly.

'This is General Stephens.'

'General, surveillance has identified three Chinese aircraft moving at hypersonic speed down the east coast towards Sydney.'

'Jesus.' General Stephens' eyes widened.

There was a knock at the door and two security officers walked in. 'Sir, you're required in the conference room immediately. Please come with us.'

'Yes, of course,' replied General Stephens.

The two security agents led the general down the corridor and into the lift, which dropped quickly. Once through the security protocols, General Stephens walked into the dimly-lit conference room. Looking up at the main screen showing real-time satellite images of the three jets, he found himself marvelling for a second that the image was so clear, given how fast the jets were travelling. The images were so detailed they could make out the pilots and see their arms reaching to press buttons in their cockpits.

'Time to reach Sydney?' asked General Stephens.

'Two minutes, sir,' said the young operations officer seated at the other end of the long table.

Sarah and Fletcher walked in, mouths dropping as they took in the image of the fighters on the screen.

'Have all the appropriate services been alerted — fire, ambulance, hospitals, police?' demanded the general.

'Yes, all services have been alerted according to protocols,' replied Sarah.

'Fletch. Likely targets?'

'We're really not sure. Could be the nuclear power facilities, could be Garden Island naval base, or Port Botany. They're our likely targets.'

'Have they been warned?'

'Yes, Marty. We've done everything we can. A fighter squadron has been launched from Picton, but at this rate they are still five minutes away.'

General Stephens looked up at the screen again. The image of the jets pulled back to show the coastline as they tore past a populated area.

'That was Newcastle, sir,' announced the imaging operator.

Then the jets slowed as Sydney came into view.

'Sir, they've reduced speed to Mach 0.9.'

General Stephens and the others sat, mesmerised by the image on the screen as the jets, still in formation, turned sharply down the harbour.

'It's got to be Garden Island,' said Fletcher, staring at the screen, horrified.

The recently installed Garden Island missile defence battery located on the waterfront at the naval base had struggled to achieve a radar-lock, given the low altitude of the jets. Inside their crowded control room, it was pandemonium. As the jets passed Palm Beach on the Northern Beaches, the Garden Island radars locked on, a shrill alarm was emitted in the control room and the head operator immediately slammed the fire button. Over 100 missiles erupted from the large square missile battery. Shooting out to meet the jets, they left a cloud of smoke lingering above the water. Individual guidance computers, constantly calculating the expected point of contact with the Chinese warplanes, controlled each missile. They worked both individually and as a network by splaying themselves to create the widest possible line of defence. With three seconds to calculated impact, the missiles disintegrated, firing thousands of pieces of shrapnel forward and creating a huge curtain of destruction through which the fighter planes could never fly unscathed.

The moment the missiles had launched, the state-of-the-art Chinese fighters detected the threat and automatically released counter-measures, taking evasive action. The computers took over the planes, as human reaction speeds could never compete — there were only microseconds to evade the missile defence. When the missiles exploded, creating their defence curtain, the Chinese jets were already well away and were stabilising and returning to their flight path.

The jets screamed through the heads of Sydney Harbour at low altitude — low enough to clip a mast if a yacht got in their way. The noise was deafening. It was 11 am in Sydney and people were going about their daily lives. The war in the desert was everywhere in the media, but still so far away. Most of the people who were quick enough to see the jets thought it was a display by the RAAF.

Three seconds after turning into the harbour, the jets had their target locked and they let loose a total of six TOM-TOMs (Tailored Ordinance Munitions). These missiles were individually programmed to provide precise detonation to deliver the maximum destruction to their target.

The missiles tore ahead of the jets with a trail of fire, smoke and a screaming roar. The three lead missiles, broke away from the formation, shooting high into the sky until they were directly above the bridge before angling down into the bridge. The TOM-TOMs were so accurately guided that they weaved in between the huge spans of the bridge so as to hit the preordained point of contact. All six TOM-TOMs ploughed into the Sydney Harbour Bridge in concert, erupting into a series of fireballs that engulfed the structure.

The jets screamed above the bridge, banking steeply before circling around and heading out the way they had come.

In the conference room of the SOF, they saw it all happen in high-definition.

'Christ, they've hit the bridge,' muttered Fletcher in shock.

General Stephens stood and stared, teeth bared.

'Can we estimate how many people were on the bridge?' he asked, not taking his eyes off the screen.

'Could be a few hundred,' said Sarah, stunned.

'They didn't even bother with the fucking military targets,' said Stephens, trying to make sense of it.

The entire centre section of Sydney's famous landmark and major transport link was engulfed in a cloud of thick black smoke, flames rolling out. The intense heat generated by the explosions quickly melted the steel. Then, with a sickening jolt, one side of the bridge dropped and broke away from the northern end. Vehicles and train carriages slid down into the boiling harbour waters. Then the southern side let go. With a horrifying groan, the entire mid-section of the bridge collapsed, crashing into the harbour, sending fountains of water and steam into the air.

The enormous smoke cloud hung around the bridge like a veil.

'Dear God, what have they done?' whispered General Stephens. He ordered Fletcher to get a chopper organised. 'I want to be there in 30 minutes.'

'Marty, that is not a good idea. They may … '

'I'm not asking. Do it,' said General Stephens, staring at Fletcher.

Fletcher got up and left to organise the helicopter and fighter escort.

Sarah, responded to her MiLA's ring, listened for a few seconds, then hung up. 'General, Chairman Yun wishes to speak to you.'

General Stephens was flustered. He needed to compose himself and he knew it. 'Okay, set up the link in here, but don't open the link until I say. Understood?'

'Yes, General,' said Sarah, immediately turning to the young operations officer and gesturing for him to leave the room with her.

General Stephens rested his elbows on the table and put his head in his hands. Sitting back in his seat, he took two deep breaths and leaned forward to open the up-link. Chairman Yun's image came up on the massive screen in crystal-clear high-definition.

Struggling to maintain his composure, General Stephens started. 'Yun, you have purposely attacked a major city, killing hundreds of civilians. What the hell do you think you're doing?'

'General Stephens, I am deeply sorry for your loss of civilian life,' the chairman said calmly. 'I am most regretful that it has come to this. However, it was necessary to demonstrate that you will not go unpunished for your continued actions against our supply lines and infrastructure. I learnt yesterday of your attack on a rail bridge near Mount Isa in Queensland. I decided that if you destroy one of my bridges, I will destroy one of yours.'

'Yun, that is absurd! There is no comparison between a rail bridge in the desert and the Sydney Harbour Bridge!' Stephens' eyes blazed with righteous fury.

'I have no intention of repaying like-for-like, General. If you continue to attack our infrastructure, we will continue to destroy yours,' the chairman responded, unflappable, 'and I assure you, General, our targets will be far more destructive to Australia than yours are to China.'

General Stephens leaned forward, thrusting a finger at the screen. 'I think you underestimate the Australian people, Yun. We're a bit tougher than to worry about a bridge or any other piece of property, for that matter.'

'Do I really underestimate, General? I guess we shall test public resolve then if you persist with your terrorist activities. From what I have seen, General, your public does not have the stomach for war. I am already looking forward to seeing the news headlines this week.'

'You will not get away with this, Yun,' spat General Stephens, reaching forward and ending the call.

Pushing back on his chair, General Stephens stood and paced with his arms crossed, cradling his jaw with his hand. Gnawing in the back of his mind, he couldn't help but think that perhaps Yun was right. Would the Australian public stand for this attack? And what about the many more attacks that they may suffer if he continued with this strategy? How long down this path before Sydney looked like Basra or, God forbid, Tehran?

There was a brisk knock at the door, and Fletcher appeared. 'Marty, the chopper is ready and we have diverted the fighters from Picton to escort us. Ready when you are.'

'All right. Thanks, Fletch,' said General Stephens in a softer tone.

'How was Yun?'

'Oh, he's very sorry for our civilian losses,' started General Stephens, sarcastically, 'but advised us to get used to these sorts of attacks if we continue with ours.'

'Christ, talk about a disproportionate response,' replied Fletcher.

'This is what scares me, Fletch. How far are we willing to go? How much are the Australian people willing to sacrifice in the face of this sort of enemy? It was fine to support a war that was being fought between soldiers in the desert — but this, this is too close to home,' Stephens said, pointing to the screen now showing aerial footage of the bridge with its twin plumes of smoke rising from the sandstone pylons at each end.

'You're right. The public may not have the stomach for this, Marty,' said Fletcher, awed by the footage.

'I may not have the stomach for this either,' replied the general, staring at the screen. How many people had been on the bridge? What were they doing — going to a meeting, going for a walk, sightseeing? The horror of all those people being obliterated sunk into his bones with sickening finality.

The helicopter landed at Kirribilli House. Stepping onto the lawn, General Stephens looked up at the twisted wreckage of what was once the famous Sydney Harbour Bridge — an engineering marvel of its time. The entire middle section had dropped into the harbour. Because the harbour was only 11 metres deep below the bridge, the top of the arch span was still above the surface. The two huge Australian flags on the east and west sides of the bridge lay burnt and limp on their white poles. Near the pylons on each side, two huge black plumes of smoke continued to pour up into the still sky. The harbour was already packed with boats being held back by police vessels with flashing lights. The fire-fighting tugs sat beneath the bridge spraying thousands of litres of water on the smouldering, warped remains.

The air was still and, from Kirribilli House, the harbour seemed silent and frozen, broken only by the sound of distant sirens and helicopters circling overhead.

Thousands of people lined the shores of the harbour to witness the sickening wreckage.

'Let's get down to the ops centre. I want to talk to whoever is in charge,' ordered General Stephens.

Fletcher talked into his lapel microphone and ordered the general's car to be brought around.

The motorcade left Kirribilli House for the ops centre at the park in Milsons Point. After a short drive, the traffic congestion near the bridge was too much and the general jumped out and walked to the array of mobile military buildings that had been set up. He was waved through security and directed to one of the buildings already on site.

'Who's in charge here?' asked General Stephens, stepping into the room.

'Attention! Officer,' yelled a young private, immediately standing from his chair. The rest of the soldiers did the same, saluting the general.

'Yes, yes. Now who is in charge?' demanded the general impatiently.

'That would be Colonel Bremner, sir,' replied the young private.

'Well, where is he, son?'

'Outside, sir. Down near the waterfront, I believe.'

General Stephens, wasting no time, turned and left. Walking down the hill to the waterfront he, like everyone else, was transfixed by the smoking remains. It defied belief to see the vast mid-section simply gone, the once-mighty Sydney Harbour Bridge replaced by chaos and destruction.

Spotting a group of officers standing with a large mapscreen opened between them, he walked over.

'Colonel Bremner?'

One of the men turned, letting go of the mapscreen when he realised who it was. 'General, pleasure to meet you. Wish it could be under different circumstances,' he said, saluting the general.

'Likewise,' replied Stephens. 'So where are you at?'

'Well, sir. The bridge was hit by six TOM-TOMs, laser-guided to hit the precise points that would cause a catastrophic failure of the design … '

'Yes, Colonel, I know all that. What about the people?'

'Based on the footage from the traffic cameras just before the attack, we estimate around 340 people were on the bridge at the time the missiles hit. We're estimating around 300 of those people will be fatalities, sir. It's going to take a while to accurately tally the deaths here. We need to recover all the vehicles and bodies down there, ASAP.'

General Stephens looked across the harbour at the wreckage and down to the water, where hundreds of civilian victims now laid. 'Thank you, Colonel. Here's my direct number,' he said, handing him a card. 'Anything you need, you call.'

Colonel Bremner saluted. 'Thank you, sir. Appreciate you coming here.'

Chapter 16

Slowly opening his eyes, the first thing Finn saw was a white ceiling with an intricate plaster of Paris design. He gradually began to come to his senses — he was in a bed, it was warm and he felt comfortable. The light in the room was dim, but the sun was cutting through the blinds in dusty motes, so it must have been daytime.

Sitting up too quickly, Finn felt a searing pain in his left shoulder, then his head started pounding and darkness squeezed in on his vision. Lying back down, he held his head, trying to make the pain go away. Gradually, the thumping eased and the pain turned into a dull ache. Slowly he looked around the room, trying not to move too much. It was a big room with old-fashioned furnishings. To his left was a large set of glass doors that seemed to open out to a veranda. The doors were flanked by large windows with curtains drawn across them. A light, warm breeze played with the curtains, lifting them in a hypnotic dance. There was no sound apart from the birds outside. Finn felt safe. He had no idea where he was, but it felt a lot better than the dirt floor of an old tin shed.

Feeling darkness tugging at him again, Finn let himself drift back into a deep, dreamless sleep, his body and mind still exhausted from the ordeal of the last few days.

He woke to the sound of people talking. Finn had no sense of time or place. He was just thankful to be alive and comfortable, despite the pain in his shoulder. Keeping still, opening his eyes only a crack, Finn wanted to listen and see the people first, before they knew he was awake. From what he could tell, there was a woman around his age and an older man on the other side of the room, talking in hushed tones.

Blinking, Finn focussed on their conversation. Slowly and quietly he pushed himself upright, careful not to make any sudden movements.

Though they were whispering, Finn could see they were in heated debate, still unaware that Finn was conscious.

Finn cleared his throat. The conversation stopped immediately. The couple turned their heads, staring at Finn.

'Ah, hello,' said the woman, smiling broadly at Finn while shooting the man a look that said 'this isn't over,' as she walked over to the bed. 'My name is Jess, and this is my father, John. I found you out in the desert two days ago. You were in a pretty bad state. You've been shot in the arm.'

Still feeling groggy and a little delirious, Finn started shakily. 'Thank you, thank you very much. My name is Finn Hunt. I'm in the army. I was captured by the Chinese but managed to escape. I need to get back to a town or city.'

Finn squinted into her face, noticing her dark brown hair and tanned olive skin. She was looking sympathetically at him with large, soft brown eyes, which contrasted almost incongruously with her strong, defined cheekbones.

The old man, John, came over to the bed. His voice was rough like gravel, with a strong Australian twang. 'You need to rest, young man. Besides, we can't go anywhere right now. The Chinese have got patrols out everywhere and if they find you, we're all in hot water.'

'Dad's right,' Jess said, leaning against the foot of the bed. 'Since the attacks you lot have been doing, the Chinese are out of control. They've been attacking towns and homesteads all over the place — we've been lucky so far.'

'Can I have water?' Finn whispered, his throat dry and parched.

'Oh, yes. Of course. Jess rushed out of the room and returned with a glass of water, lifting it to Finn's lips. 'Sorry — here.'

Finn gulped greedily. Water had never tasted so good.

'Are you hungry?' asked Jess.

Thinking about it for a second, Finn realised that he was famished. 'Yes, yes very.' He'd barely finished speaking before she was out of the room, going towards the kitchen, he assumed.

John walked closer to the bed and called out, 'Not too much, Jess. His body has been shut down for days.' Turning back to Finn, he added, 'and you go easy on the water to start with.'

Finn nodded, looking up at John. 'Thank you for helping me. I understand that this is dangerous for you both. I will be on my way as soon as possible.'

'That's all right, mate,' John said, sitting down gently on the edge of the bed. 'We're happy to help out anyone who's doing their bit to reclaim our land.'

'Have you heard anything of the attacks? We were part of a much larger operation to destroy their transportation lines. Has anything been reported?'

John looked down at the floor. 'Son, the only thing in the news at the moment is the attack on Sydney.'

'Sydney? They attacked Sydney? What happened?' stuttered Finn, unsure what he meant.

'The Chinese sent a couple of jets down the harbour and blew up the bloody bridge. Killed 300 people, the bastards,' John said, looking disgusted.

Finn stared up at the ceiling, mind reeling from what he had just heard. He couldn't help but consider it fitting — he had been part of the operation to blow up one of their bridges and they retaliated by destroying the Sydney Harbour Bridge. He couldn't help but feel responsible in some way.

'My parents,' he said, suddenly realising they could have been affected. 'I've got to call home. I've got to see if they're okay,' said Finn quickly.

'I'm sorry, the Chinese have shut down the phone and internet lines in these parts. We can only receive radio, but no transmission.'

Jess came back in carrying a tray. On it was a bowl of soup and two slices of toast, cut in half. 'I've got veggie soup and toast. How does that sound?'

Finn looked away, a feeling of sickness creeping in at the realisation that his actions may have been partly to blame for the attack on the bridge. His mind spiralled out, trying to work out everything that had happened. What about his mates in the squad, what happened to them? Christ, Carver! He'd left his body there in the bush. The Chinese wouldn't do anything with him, just leave him there to rot. His parents? Chris? His other friends? Innocent people being attacked in Sydney — what was happening? It wasn't meant to be like this. It was supposed to be a war fought in the desert, not like this.

'Finn, do you want to eat?' repeated Jess, gently, looking at him with concern. Finn just continued to stare in front of him, eyes wide, not seeing her.

'Leave him be Jessie,' said John gently. 'Come on.' he put his hand on her shoulder to lead her out.

Finn lay there contemplating what had happened, confused and uncertain of everything he had fought for, wondering how far it would go, how many more innocent people would die for this barren desert that had nearly killed him. What was the point in continuing the fight?

Forcing himself to eat, he played with the food Jess had left. Sleep eventually took over again, but this time it was filled with horrific visions and dark dreams. Images of what he had seen and done, Carver's head half blown-off, the river, the young Chinese bloke he'd shot in the back, his parents, people drowning under the bridge.

Finn slept fitfully the rest of the day and night, but the next day he woke feeling much better. Sitting up, he was able to ease his feet off the bed and onto the polished wooden floor. Slowly he stood, naked, looking around for his uniform. Noticing a pile of clothes on a chair, he dressed, gingerly guiding his wounded arm through the sleeve of the cotton shirt. Hunger was taking over now. He felt ravenous, his stomach hurting from the thought of food.

He shuffled out of the room, his right hand cradling his wounded arm against his stomach. Looking around the unfamiliar house, Finn could tell that it was big and old, but beautifully restored and maintained. He decided to go left. 'Hello, anyone there?' he called.

No answer. The house felt empty. Finn walked into a spacious lounge room, decorated comfortably with traditional furniture. The next room was clearly a bedroom. With a grin, Finn thought it must be Jess's, judging by the underwear lying about.

Heading back down the hall, back the way he came, he went to the back of the house and found what he was looking for — the kitchen.

Opening the pantry door, Finn reached for a loaf of bread and thrust slices of it in his mouth, barely chewing. His mouth was still dry and he nearly gagged on it. Coughing painfully, he headed for the sink. Filling his hands with water, Finn bent over the sink and drank. Standing upright, face flushed, eyes watering, he looked out the window above the sink and saw Jess near a shed. She was brushing a chestnut horse, which stood motionless while she worked on its hind legs.

Taking another piece of bread, Finn went out the door, onto the veranda. 'Hey there,' he called, coughing again.

Jess looked up and came over to meet Finn between the house and the shed, still carrying the brush. She had a smudge of dust on her nose — she'd clearly been outside for some time. 'You're up. How's the shoulder?'

'Doesn't exactly tickle, but it's okay.'

Jess smiled, looking at the piece of bread in his hand. 'Bit hungry, huh? Not surprised. Come on,' she said, cocking her head toward the house. She headed to the veranda. 'Think we can do better than that.'.

Finn looked at the piece of bread, shrugging his good shoulder. 'Sounds good to me,' he replied, following her back to the house.

For the rest of the day Finn caught up on the news on the radio and rested, feeling infinitely better for being up and eating and drinking. He felt alive again, like he had been waking up slowly from a bad dream.

That night, after the three had dinner, they sat in the lounge, sipping red wine and talking. Finn was slouched back in a large comfy chair. The room was dim and warm, a light breeze billowing the muslin cloth hanging over the open windows. Finn noticed old family pictures on the walls and in photo frames on the mantle of the big fireplace.

'So, I know you said we're a long way from town, but exactly how far?' asked Finn.

'We're not that far in distance from Winton. Probably 80 kilometres, but it's a hard road. It takes a good three hours each way, and that's when the road's in good nick,' replied John.

'Do you mind if I take your truck to town tomorrow?' Finn asked, feeling bad for imposing but unable to spend another day without knowing if his parents were all right. 'I need to make a few calls, tell people that I'm okay.'

'I'll take you in tomorrow,' John replied, without hesitation. 'The road in places isn't that obvious and you wouldn't want to run into a Chinese patrol. If I drive and we get pulled up, you can hide or make a run for it.'

'You really don't need to do that, John,' said Finn, suddenly worried. 'You have both taken a huge risk already, having me here. I don't want to be responsible for getting you into trouble,' he finished earnestly.

'Finn, it's fine. We're happy to help, and the risk is acceptable,' replied Jess with a smile. 'It's great just to have a new face around here — believe me.'

'Thanks, but I'd still rather go alone tomorrow, if it's all the same.'

'Well, we'll see in the morning,' said John, pushing himself out of the chair. 'I'm off to bed. I'll see you both in the morning.'

''Night, Dad,' said Jess.

'Good night, John. And thanks again,' said Finn.

'Yep, 'night, both. And you can stop saying thanks now, Finn,' John said reassuringly.

'Fair enough,' replied Finn with a smile as John left the room.

'Another glass?' asked Jess, lifting her wine glass in his direction.

'Sure, why not,' Finn said, settling back in his chair. 'I haven't had wine in months. Think it's already going to my head.'

'That's a point. You probably shouldn't have any more, given how dehydrated you were,' Jess said, looking over her shoulder from the table where she was pouring her wine.

'Yeah, but one more can't hurt,' Finn said, holding out his glass.

Jess poured him a glass and placed her own back on the side table as she curled her long legs up underneath her, sitting back down on the deep couch.

'So, how long have you lived here for?' asked Finn.

'I grew up here as a kid until I was about 12. Then Mum and Dad shipped me off to boarding school in Brisbane. I used to come back every holiday. My brother and I used to have a brilliant time playing around on the farm.' She looked a little sad and was silent for a few seconds, then resumed her story. 'After school I went to uni in Melbourne and I spent less and less time back here. I finished uni, went travelling, as you do, and then settled back in Melbourne, working in finance for Lampton Construction.'

'So when did you come back here, then?' Finn asked, wondering how she could reconcile a finance career with this outback Queensland location.

'A couple of years ago. My mum passed away and Dad was alone out here. I took extended leave and came back to help out. After a while I realised that I didn't want to leave, didn't want to go back to city living,' she looked around the comfortable room with clear affection. 'I love it out here, being on the farm.'

'Don't blame you. It's a stunning place,' said Finn, finding himself staring at Jess, noticing her long slim fingers wrapped around the wine glass. Her short but perfectly groomed fingernails seemed far too manicured for someone who lived on a farm.

'Yeah, it's a very special place,' she said softly, nodding.

'Still, must have been a hard transition from city life to being back on the farm, and in such a remote place?'

'No, not really. I never actually sat down and thought about it too much. It just felt like the right thing to do. In my heart I felt that this was where I belonged, not in some grimy city. It's funny. It was only after I'd left the city that I thought perhaps it wasn't for me. Guess I didn't really know any better,' she said, raising her glass and taking a sip. She turned to Finn, changing the subject. 'So how did you end up in the army? Got to say, you don't come across like a testosterone-fuelled army boy,' she said with a smile.

'Hmmm, no,' Finn said, laughing, 'I grew up in Sydney on the Northern Beaches. Lived a pretty charmed life, worked in finance, cruised along. Then, when all this happened, something kicked in and I decided I wanted to do something, to fight for something, rather than keep living what was really a pretty vacuous life.'

'A "vacuous life," huh?' Jess said, raising her eyebrows. 'That sounds pretty harsh. Was it really that bad?'

'Well no, it wasn't bad as such,' Finn said, trying to express his feelings. 'But it was devoid of meaning. Looking back, I think I was pretty lazy, selfish, and didn't really do anything useful. I mean, I was very good at my job, but I was never challenged by it, and that job did nothing to better people's lives. I just made rich people richer. It was like this war — as bad as it is — was my chance to prove to myself I wasn't a complete waste of space.'

'So you had an epiphany and just came out here to fight a war — that's a pretty extreme change. Why didn't you just go work for a charity or do something else in the city that gave you more of a sense of meaning?' said Jess, brow furrowed, looking curious.

'I can't explain it. I just knew, I didn't really decide, it just happened.' Finn trailed off and shrugged at Jess helplessly.

'Kind of like me staying here,' she said, nodding. 'I didn't decide to stay. It just happened.'

'Yeah, I think that's when you know you're on the right path, when it just happens,' said Finn thoughtfully.

'That's very poignant, I like it,' said Jess, lifting her head high with a slight smile. 'The warrior philosopher.'

'Well, I guess that's what red wine does when you haven't drunk in over six months,' Finn said, embarrassed.

'Ah, the miracle of red wine,' she said laughing, holding her glass up to the light.

'So, you mentioned your brother earlier — where's he based?' asked Finn, wanting to change the subject.

Jess shifted on the couch. 'He died a few years ago in a car crash,' she said matter-of-factly. 'It was pretty tough on the family, Mum especially. She didn't deal with it at all really. It was strange. Growing up, Mum always seemed so strong — she was the one who pushed us to challenge ourselves, to step outside of our comfort zones, to go with our hearts. Then when Aaron died, she became completely reclusive. Overnight, she just cut herself off from everyone, including Dad. It really broke Dad's heart. He ended up losing a son and a wife at the same time.'

'God, I'm so sorry. That must have been tough,' Finn said softly.

'It was. But you know,' she said, turning the wine glass in her hand, 'some good came of it all. I came back home and Dad and I have never been closer.'

'So did your mum pass away not long after Aaron?' asked Finn, surprised at his own question.

'Um, yes. Mum actually took her own life not long after Aaron died,' said Jess, staring into her wine glass.

Finn's mouth was open, but he was silent. He had no idea what more could be said.

'Jesus, red wine, huh?' said Jess, holding up the glass. 'Gets you to talk about the craziest things.' Flashing a forced smile, she took a deep breath and exhaled.

Finn was still, staring directly into Jess's eyes. He did not buy the fake smile or the obvious deflection to the wine. 'I'm so sorry for your family's losses. I can't imagine what you and your dad must have been through, even though I do understand what it is to be around death.'

The smile was gone from Jess's face. 'Thanks. It's strange: I've never actually spoken about it with anyone. I mean Dad and I have talked around it, but I've never actually told anyone what I just told you.'

A moment of silence descended. Finn didn't know where to take the conversation next.

'Um, it's late. Think I might go to bed now,' said Jess, putting her glass on the side table.

'Yeah, you're right,' said Finn, standing up.

'Okay. Well, I'll see you in the morning then before you and Dad head off to town,' said Jess standing to face Finn.

'Yeah, sure. Hey thanks for everything,' Finn said, twisting his wine glass in his hand. 'I really mean it. You saved my life. I'm beyond grateful for everything you guys have done for me.'

'Don't mention it — seriously, we're just glad to help,' said Jess with a smile.

'Okay, well goodnight then,' said Finn, watching her walk down the hall.

'Goodnight, see you in the morning,' she replied, glancing back at Finn as she walked down the hall.

The next morning after breakfast, John and Finn took the Nissan Patrol and headed towards town. Finn wore some of John's clothes, which were a bit big but would do the job. Finn's plan, when he got to town, was to call his parents first, find out if they were okay and let them know he was safe, then call the army to see if he could arrange an extraction.

The 'road' to town was barely a track in places. Finn was grateful that John had insisted on driving, sure he would have wound up lost again on his own.

There was no sign of Chinese patrols, which was good news. They had decided that, if stopped, there was no point in hiding Finn. Their only hope would be to convince them that he worked on the farm for John.

'So it must be good to have Jess out here with you,' said Finn, making small talk.

'Good and bad really — selfishly for me, it's great having her on the farm, but really I wish she had stayed in Melbourne. There's nothing here for her, no future,' replied John, watching the road ahead.

'Talking to her last night I didn't get the feeling that she's here just for you. I think she genuinely loves being on the farm,' Finn said, trying to reassure John.

'Finn,' John said, turning to look at his passenger, 'women have an ability to convince themselves of something that might not be true, purely in order to justify their decisions.'

Finn smiled, 'You might have something there, John.'

'Her life isn't going anywhere out here in the middle of nowhere,' resumed John.

'I don't know. She didn't give me that impression. Sounds to me like city life was going nowhere for her and that out here she could really live life her way.'

'What Jess says and what's really going on in that head of hers are two very different things — just like her mum,' said John, with a distinct edge to his voice.

Finn let a moment of silence grow, not wanting to push the conversation any further.

'So, when we get to town, can you drop me at the post office, or council building? I need to make some calls.'

'Yeah, of course. The post office should be open, otherwise the pub has a pay phone.'

'If it's okay with you,' Finn said, 'depending on what the army wants to do about getting me out of here, I might come back to the farm.'

'Of course, that's fine. You can stay as long as you like.' John said, looking Finn reassuringly in the eye.

'Great. Thanks, John.'

After a good three hours of rough driving, Finn spotted the township. Winton was a fair-sized town, considering where it was. Driving down the sealed main street was eerie. The town was deserted — no people, no cars, no signs of life whatsoever. John pulled into a car space outside the post office. 'Strange, it looks closed,' he remarked.

They stepped out of the Patrol. It was quiet, and even though it was only just after 10 am, it was hot and dry. Finn went up to the door of the post office, finding it locked.

'Yep, nothing going on here,' said Finn.

'Let's try The Australian, it's just down here,' said John, pointing to the pub down the road.

Walking down the empty footpath, Finn felt like he was in a movie where the town had been taken over by zombies. If all was going according to the script, the zombies would be waiting at the end of the main street to attack them.

John pushed on the main door of The Australian — it was open. Walking into the bar, it took a moment for Finn's eyes to adjust to the darkness. He couldn't see if there were people in there or not. It was a disconcerting feeling.

John had walked up to the bar and started talking to the bartender. Gradually Finn's eyes became used to the light. He walked up and joined John at the bar.

'Finn, Dave here was just saying how the Chinese have been destroying homesteads and property all around the town.'

'Is the army sending troops?' asked Finn.

Dave, the old barman, looked at Finn. 'Nah, mate. Apparently the army is too busy reorganising itself after the last big push — it's every man for himself.'

'Can I use your phone, please?' asked Finn.

'Sure, it's over there,' said Dave, pointing to a pay phone in a corner of the bar.

Finn walked over to the booth and picked up the heavy receiver. He started to gingerly push the sticky buttons, but nothing was happening. He felt a tap on his shoulder and turned around to see a grinning John proffering a fistful of coins.

'You'll need these, mate,' he said, chuckling and turning around to return to Dave, who was laughing so hard he was bent over the bar. Flushing bright red, Finn shoved some coins in the slot and dialled his parents' house. There was no answer, so he tried his mum's mobile. It went through to her voicemail, her message freshly recorded a few days ago. Finn listened in relief to her message. She couldn't have been injured in the attack on Sydney — she wouldn't attend to petty personal admin like updating her voicemail message if she or Tom were hurt. He took a deep breath and left his message.

'Mum, it's Finn. I'm okay. I'm somewhere in the desert up north. I'm staying with some good people until the army can get me out of here. There isn't a phone on the farm, so you can't call me. I hope you and Dad are okay. I love you guys and I'll see you soon.'

Finn hung up the receiver and immediately started dialling the army hotline number. As he lifted the receiver to his ear, John ripped it out of his hand.

Finn turned to John. 'What are you —'

'Come on, we have to get back to the farm,' John interrupted urgently. 'I just heard that the Chinese are headed that way. They've been destroying everything in their path — killing civilians, for Christ's sake!'

'Wh, what? You can't be serious!' Finn stuttered in disbelief.

John was pulling at Finn's right arm. 'Very. Come on. I need your help. Jess is out there all alone. If the Chinese find her God knows what'll happen.'

'Okay, let's go!' Finn broke from John's grip and ran for the door.

John drove the Patrol like a man possessed, not slowing at all for ruts or ditches. The Patrol took a hammering, as did Finn's injured arm. Every bump now intensified the ache from where the bullet had torn through his flesh.

Coming down the long straight road that led directly to the homestead, Finn was searching for signs — smoke, military vehicles, San's, any sign of destruction. The homestead was now visible — it all looked in order.

The Patrol came to an abrupt halt outside the homestead, John braking so hard the wheels locked. They leapt out.

'Jess! Jess!' yelled John.

Finn went inside the house to search. 'She's not in here,' he yelled to John, coming back outside.

'Dear God, where the hell is she? Please don't say they took her!' desperation saturated John's voice.

'The horses. Where are the horses?' Finn asked.

'Around there,' said John, gesturing to the stables, 'I've been over there, though.'

Running around to the stable, Finn looked around. There were only three horses. 'John, don't you have four horses?'

'Ye … Yes, yes four horses,' he nodded frantically. 'Think she's gone for a ride?' he asked, his face alight with hope.

'Pretty sure of it. Look, let's keep searching but I reckon that's what she's doing. There are no signs the Chinese have been here, nothing suspicious. I think we can assume she's okay,' Finn reassured John.

'Hang on. Normally she writes up on a board in here where she's headed and when she'll be back,' said John, pacing off into the stable.

A whiteboard on the wall just inside the door to the stable had a neatly written log of the day's date, where she was going and when she would be back.

Finn turned to John, his training taking charge. 'Okay, that settles it then. Let's load up the Patrol with everything we can take, and I mean food, water and essentials. We need to be out of here in one hour — tops. Jess should be back in half an hour but, if she isn't back in an hour, we head out in her direction until we find her. Then we make a beeline for the most remote area around here. I'll need your help with that, John.'

'Leave? No bloody way, mate,' John said, shaking his head. 'You take Jess and get her the hell out of here, but I'm stayin'.'

'John, I know what the Chinese are capable of — you won't be able to do anything to stop them. There's no point in trying.' Finn said forcefully.

'Bullshit,' John said, folding his arms, 'there's no way in hell I'm getting run off my property, son.'

Finn was getting frustrated. 'John, they'll destroy your homestead. It's just a building, no building is worth dying for — think of Jess, please.'

John wavered. Thinking about it now, he realised that Finn was right, but he was not quite able to let his pride settle. It seemed totally foreign to flee his own property, which he had worked so hard to create.

'Alright,' he said, finally relenting, 'come on then. We better get cracking.'

Half an hour later Jess rode up to the barn, smiling. Finn jogged out to meet her. Jess jumped off the horse, her smile broadening in surprise. She was glad to see Finn had come back. She'd thought that perhaps he would just leave straight from town.

Her smile was met by Finn's scowl. 'We have to get out of here right now,' he said, all business. 'Unsaddle your horse and let them all go. We're leaving in 30 minutes.'

Jess's smile immediately evaporated and her face twisted with confusion. 'What's going on? Where's Dad? Why are we leaving?'

'Your dad's in the house, we're loading up the Patrol. We've got to get out of here because the Chinese have been on a rampage, destroying properties around here. We've heard that they're killing civilians, too.'

'Jesus, how long do we have?' asked Jess.

Finn started back to the house. 'I don't know, but we're not taking any chances. We leave in 30.'

Jess stood stunned for a moment while it all registered, then immediately started unsaddling the horse.

Finn loaded the final boxes of food into the Patrol. They had enough to survive for a few days if necessary. They had sleeping bags, a tent, a cooker, everything they would need to get by out in the desert overnight. John had a .308 Tikka hunting rifle and a 12-gauge shotgun, which Finn packed along with extra ammo.

'Finn!' yelled John from the veranda. He was looking through a pair of binoculars at a dust cloud in the distance. 'That dust cloud means someone's coming, can't say who though.'

Finn didn't turn to look or question John. 'Jesus,' he muttered to himself before yelling, 'We leave in 30 seconds.'

Piling into the Patrol, John drove and Finn sat beside him in the front, with Jess in the back seat holding the rifle and shotgun across her lap. John tore out the rear gate and headed towards the low range of hills to the west.

It was a three-hour drive to the top of the hills, and the whole time Finn was constantly looking back to see if they were being followed. John brought the Patrol to a standstill, which was a relief after the hours of cross-country driving. They were at the top of a range of hills and had views in every direction. The afternoon sun was setting now and the light was quickly dimming. To the west was a magnificent sunset, a brilliant orange that looked like the world to the west was on fire. To the east was another orange glow, but this was a heavier, sinister glow. John and Jess got out of the car and looked across the desert plain as they watched their home in the distance burn. John put his arm around Jess as they stood there on the rock looking down.

Finn, too, was looking towards the homestead, but he was looking for signs of the Chinese. Nothing — perhaps the Chinese didn't notice their tyre tracks leaving the homestead, or, more likely, they couldn't be bothered chasing after people in the desert, particularly in the dark.

Finn wanted to get moving, to find somewhere to pitch their tent and get sorted before it was completely dark. Looking at John and Jess though, he didn't have the heart to hurry them up. They were mourning the loss of their home.

Finn turned and walked back to the Patrol, leaving them to grieve in peace. It wasn't ideal, but Finn scoped out a spot for the tent. He would have preferred more tree cover, in case a drone or San' was about in the morning, but there wasn't much point in driving around the desert in the dark looking for the perfect camping spot.

The next day the sun rose to greet a perfectly clear morning. Finn woke in the back seat of the Patrol. It had been an uncomfortable night and his legs and back now ached. The others were still sleeping and there was no sound coming from the tent. Finn shut the door of the Patrol loudly, hoping it might stir them. Walking over to the rock ledge, where last night they had stood watching the burning homestead, Finn squinted in the direction of the house. It was quiet and still with no wind, only the sound of the odd bird breaking the silence — even the animals seemed to be sleeping in this morning. Looking down onto the desert floor and over to the homestead, Finn noted the layer of smoke hanging low in the sky. Taking a deep breath of the crisp, clean air, Finn noticed a distinct note of smoke, a sharp but woody smell that, if it were not due to the fact that it was these people's ruined homestead, would have been pleasant.

Finn could now hear John and Jess talking in the tent. He sat down on the ledge, wanting to give them some privacy. Today would be a hard one, Finn knew, going back down to their ruined home — especially for John.

While Finn prepared breakfast, the other two packed up the tent and sleeping bags. When breakfast was over, they climbed back into the Patrol and headed slowly down the hill towards the homestead. They took their time now, and the journey was much more comfortable. Bar a few discussions on the best route and how to negotiate some of the trickier parts of the track, the drive was silent. Finn thought about how hard it would be to lose the house you grew up in, and with it your entire lifestyle.

Finn looked ahead and thought he recognised where they were. 'How far are we from the homestead, John?'

'About three kilometres, I reckon.'

'Okay, pull over here,' said Finn, unbuckling his seatbelt.

Jess leaned forward, holding on to the back of Finn's seat. 'Why are we stopping here, Finn?'

'I'm not stopping, but you two are,' replied Finn, as John brought the Patrol to a standstill.

Finn opened the door, twisting his neck around to look at John, with Jess in the corner of his eye.

'Guys, there is a remote chance that they've stuck around, or left a guard behind to alert them if we come back. It's unlikely, but there's still a chance. So I'm going to get up a bit closer, alone on foot. If there's someone there I'll come back and we'll just have to stay away until they clear out.'

'What will you do if they spot you?' asked Jess.

'If I'm alone, they shouldn't see me. But if I am spotted I can lead them away from you guys, lose them and then I'll come back. So whatever you do, stay here, don't move.'

'But Finn, you're injured. How are you going to get away from them if they see you?'

'Jess, seriously I'll be fine. I'll do a lot better if I'm alone, okay?'

'Finn's right,' said John, 'Let him go. We'd only slow him up if he had to make a run for it.'

Jess got out of the Patrol, slamming the door harder than necessary.

Finn turned to John and whispered. 'If I get into any trouble, you'll hear the gunfire. If you do, get away from here, as far as you can, for as long as you can.'

Not waiting for an answer from John, Finn set off toward the homestead with the .308 rifle across his good shoulder and spare ammunition bulging in his jeans pockets.

Around 30 minutes later, Finn came to a large rock. Clambering up awkwardly, he reached the top and crouched down to minimise his profile against the background. He checked that the safety switch was on and that the chamber of the .308 was empty. The last thing he wanted was to let off a round that would be heard for miles. Painfully, Finn wrapped the shoulder strap around his left hand and wrist then put the butt of the rifle to his good shoulder. Propping his elbow on his knee, Finn looked through the scope on the rifle, adjusting the zoom and focus. It gave him a good view of the homestead. Finn spent a long time in this position, scanning the homestead for movement. The sun was now high and the heat was getting stifling. He constantly had to wipe the sweat from his brow, which stung his eyes and prickled the skin on his face.

Remarkably, a large part of the house looked in reasonable condition, though the front was charred and ruined, with wisps of smoke still rising from it.

There was no sign of movement, at least nothing that Finn could see, which didn't mean there was no one there. He decided to walk up and take a closer look. Finn now crept slowly forward, staying low, in case someone was watching him. Now 200 metres from the homestead, he lay down on his chest and looked through the scope on the rifle — still no sign of movement. Not satisfied, Finn moved around to the right, circling the homestead to be absolutely certain there was no one waiting. He moved quickly from one point of cover to another, staying low. At each point he scanned the homestead and listened until his ears strained. All he could hear was the sound of wind over the chorus of blood pumping loudly in his head. He had now come around 180 degrees and there was still no sign of movement. Finn felt tense, uneasy with the situation. He had visions again of Carver's head, his mangled mouth, the dimly-lit shed and the Chinese officer who'd tortured Carver. The sweat was rolling off his forehead now and Finn felt a sickening feeling in the pit of his stomach. He squeezed his eyes shut and rubbed them with his dirty hand.

'Pull it together, dickhead,' he said to himself. 'Let's go take a look,' willing himself to move in towards the homestead.

Out in the open, Finn ran for the cover of the homestead. Reaching the corner at the back of the house, which was unscathed by the fire, he stood with his back flat against the wall and caught his breath, rifle across his chest. The sweat was trickling down his forehead and he wiped it away with the crook of his arm.

Looking around the corner, Finn could see where the back steps led up to the kitchen, and across to the shed and horse stables. He thought about where he would hide if he were ambushing someone. It wouldn't be the house, it would be the strongest structure, with the least vulnerability and an easy exit route, if required — which made the shed the most likely place. There was no cover near the shed, nowhere to run if bullets started to fly. Finn looked around, but there was nothing, no way of getting to the shed other than a 50-metre dash across the open driveway. It was a suicide run, no question. Realising that it would be better to flush out anyone with a weapon, Finn decided to make a run for the kitchen, which was closer. Anyone watching would see him and very likely respond with fire. He would be running across the line of fire and had only 10 metres to reach the steps to the kitchen. Taking two deep breaths, Finn turned and ran for the kitchen. His legs felt heavy and slow, like they weren't getting any traction in the dirt. It seemed to take an age to get even halfway to the steps. Finn felt panicked that he wasn't going faster. He felt exposed and vulnerable, just waiting for the shot or the feeling of pain, or worse — blackness.

A flash of movement caught his eye.

Someone was coming down the steps from the kitchen. In a split second his mind reacted and his torso pulled back viciously — instinctively. His legs were slow to react. It was as if the instinctive stop command from the receptors in his brain sent a pulse travelling down his body and, as it went down, each fibre of his body obeyed accordingly. He fell backwards, fumbling with the .308.

Finn's focus sharpened and the rifle went up. He held his breath, straining his neck to take aim. No soldier, not even a person. A blue heeler — a cattle dog! It stood on the steps panting cheerfully, turning its head to look at Finn lying on the ground. Then it walked down the remaining steps and wandered over to the stables, oblivious to any danger and ignorant of Finn's rifle.

Finn relaxed his muscles, letting his head fall back in the dirt, breathing heavily. If there was anyone around, they would have heard him and sent a volley of bullets his way. After a minute, Finn composed himself and sat up, smirking now at what had happened. He was glad no one had seen his reaction to the dog. Shaking his head, Finn stood and walked over to the steps and went up to the kitchen. He walked through the wreck of the house. The fire had destroyed most of it, and what was left was badly damaged by the smoke. Before heading back to the others, Finn did a thorough search of the shed and stables — just to be sure there was no sentry or sniper.

Getting out of the Patrol back at the house, John was unsteady on his feet, clearly upset at the sight of his home in this state. He and Jess walked around the burnt remains while Finn unloaded the Patrol in the shed. Finn figured it was best to give them time alone.

After walking around the house, John and Jess stood at the front. The sun was low now and the air was getting cooler.

'So many memories of this house,' murmured John, staring blankly at the charred ruins, 'so many beautiful memories.'

'I know, Dad. I have them, too. But isn't that the point? The fire can destroy our home but it can't destroy our memories,' replied Jess, a tear welling in her eye as she put her arm around her dad — her invincible father who had been a tower of strength her whole life.

John choked back the lump in his throat, determined not to let himself be consumed by emotions. 'Yep, I guess you're right, Jessie-girl,' he patted her back tenderly.

Jess wasn't going to choke anything back. The tears welled up and spilled down her cheek, the corners of her mouth quivering and pulling down. She tucked her head into the side of John's chest as he put his big arm around her shoulder.

'I remember you and your brother playing out here for hours. You two used to fight like cats and dogs, but if either one of you got hurt or was in trouble, you were always there for each other. Do you remember when your brother broke his ankle when you two were out tearing around down the drive?'

'Yeah, I remember,' Jess replied, her voice quivering through her tears. 'He was being an idiot, trying to climb that big old tree down the driveway.'

'That's right. But when he fell, you piggybacked him all the way back to the house. I remember standing on the veranda here and seeing you coming down the drive, carrying your brother.' John continued, tears in his eyes and a smile on his face. 'You were both crying like mad, but my God, I knew you two would always be there for one another. I knew that so long as you two were together out on the farm, or anywhere for that matter, you'd be fine.' John swallowed hard, resisting the urge to wipe his eyes, determined not to show any sign of weakness in front of his daughter, his only surviving child, his only family.

Jess smiled at the memory, her face damp with tears, eyes glazed and distant, looking over the ruined homestead that lay before them.

'It's funny,' said John, regaining control of his emotions, 'I actually thought of that moment the other day, when you brought Finn in from the desert, all shot-up and dying.'

'I think Aaron would have liked Finn. They have a similar way, don't you think, Dad?' Jess said, looking up at her father.

John smiled. 'Yes, Jessie. Yes, I do.'

They stood there until the light was squeezed from the sky by the sinking sun. They talked a bit more, but mostly they stood and simply remembered in silence.

Looking over the smouldering remains, Finn guessed that the Chinese had been in a hurry, as they had not bothered to stay and see that the building had fully caught alight. The sheds were relatively unscathed, while the homestead was partially gutted, but not completely.

That night they slept in the shed. Sleeping mats on the hard concrete floor took the edge off, but it was not the most comfortable of nights. In the morning they all woke feeling achy and cold. Finn felt like he had a hangover, his head pounding, mouth dry and feeling nauseous. It was dehydration again. His body had still not recovered from the ordeal with the Chinese, and yesterday he'd barely drunk anything.

The large shed they slept in had a fully-kitted kitchen that was used by the farm hands at times throughout the year, when the cattle were brought in.

Over breakfast, Finn was distant. Both John and Jess noticed it but didn't say anything. Something was clearly on his mind — Finn had never been good at masking when he was deep in thought.

After they had eaten, Finn went outside. He stared out to the mountain range in the distance. Finn reflected on how, if Jess had not found him in the desert and brought him back here, he would in all likelihood have died. If they had not attacked the Chinese transportation in the area, the Chinese would not have gone on reprisal attacks. He did not feel guilty for what he had done; he did not regret anything. But he did feel some sense of responsibility. Any which way he looked at it, he felt responsible for his actions.

Jess joined him outside on the veranda. 'Hey, you all right there, Finn? You seem pretty distant today,' she said with a worried smile.

'Oh hey,' he said, her presence pulling him out of his thoughts. 'Yeah. I've just been thinking about a few things.'

'I just want to thank you for what you did yesterday,' Jess said, her voice husky with emotion. 'You were really amazing out there. We really appreciate it. I, um … I really appreciate it.'

Finn looked at Jess, his face softening under her gaze. 'It's nothing, no problem at all — God, I owe you my life. It was really the least I could do.'

Jess smiled and blushed, breaking her gaze from Finn's eyes.

'I actually have something to ask, something that would mean a lot to me,' said Finn seriously. 'I want to stay and help you guys rebuild the homestead.'

'You don't need to do that. It's not your fault,' said Jess, genuinely shocked at his offer.

'No, I know, but I want to help. My parents know I'm safe, the army doesn't know where I am — in fact, they probably think I'm dead. Besides, once you guys are back in the house, I can go back to the fighting.'

'Finn, no. We really can't ask you to do that.'

'You're not asking me. I'm telling you that's what I want to do. Please, Jess … I want to help,' Finn said, looking at Jess pleadingly.

'I … well, I guess … I don't know Finn, are you sure?' she asked, her forehead crinkling with concern. 'Dad and I could really do with some help. He can't do it all on his own and I don't think there are many builders who will come all the way out here — especially with our current neighbours.'

'Jess, please. I want to help. It would be good to create something rather than running around destroying,' said Finn earnestly.

'Well, so long as it's okay with Dad,' said Jess.

'Okay, great. Well, I'll be over at the house then,' said Finn awkwardly.

Halfway to the house, the blue heeler from the day before ran over to greet him, tail wagging furiously. Finn bent down to pat him with a wry smile. 'Cheeky bugger. You scared the shit out of me, but don't tell the others. Okay?'

Chapter 17

After the horrific attack on the Sydney Harbour Bridge, General Stephens was inundated with calls from politicians and lobbyists insisting that Australia lay down its arms against the Chinese and to let them continue mining the land in peace.

He had spent the last five days staying at Kirribilli House, overseeing the clean-up of the Harbour Bridge with barely any sleep. Sitting now at his desk back in SOF, shirt collar undone, sleeves rolled up, he felt the familiar, nagging exhaustion that had been with him since the first day he took over the country. He looked like a very different man from the immaculately dressed, square-jawed commander of the Silent Coup.

Fletcher knocked and walked into the room.

General Stephens looked up immediately. 'Jesus Christ, Fletch! What the hell do we do?' he gestured at his screen, showing the clean-up of the wreckage of the bridge in real time. 'We can't win this war without plunging Australia into the Dark Ages. I've got every bloody lobbyist and pollie knocking down my door, demanding we immediately withdraw our forces.'

Fletcher sighed and sat down in the chair facing Stephens' desk. 'I hate to say it, Marty, but I don't think there's much more we can do.'

'It can't end like this though, Fletch — too many people have died, too many have sacrificed too much. We can't just throw in the towel when the going gets tough,' said Stephens, dropping his clenched fist on the desk.

'Marty, I know,' Fletcher replied. 'But a lot more innocent people will die if we continue with this strategy. It was always a gamble. We were always at the mercy of the Chinese, and them being true to their word.'

'Their *word*,' Stephens repeated bitterly, 'they didn't hesitate to break it as soon as we started to inflict real damage on their mining operations.'

'Well, if we want to regroup, we should at least scale back the operation, pull our forces back and create a lull in the fighting. The Chinese will think that we've succumbed and the public will feel like we're looking after them,' Fletcher offered. 'In a month or two we start up again, but this time we take it a bit easier. That way the Chinese may not retaliate in the same way.'

'Damn it! Listen to us — we sound like politicians!' Stephens cried. 'Worrying about what people will think of us. We need to stay focussed on what's best for this country, not worry about the polls. We're in the middle of a major operation right now, an operation that could make the Chinese seriously reconsider their strategy.'

'Right now,' said Fletcher calmly, 'what's best for the country is to eliminate the threat of reprisal attacks. The public won't stand for another attack like the bridge.'

Stephens stared at Fletcher, his face flushed, eyes tired and red. He was calm now, a powerful wave of exhaustion washing over him. 'What a nightmare, what a fucking nightmare,' he muttered to himself. 'You're right, Fletch. You're absolutely right. What were we thinking? Guerrilla tactics only work when there is nothing for the enemy to hit back at. Christ, that's what made it so damn impossible to deal with insurgents in Afghanistan and Namibia.'

'Why don't you get some sleep?' said Fletcher, standing. 'How can you make decisions when you're in this state?'

Pondering the suggestion, Stephens knew Fletcher was right. 'Perhaps just a couple of hours,' he said reluctantly.

Standing slowly, he felt like an old man, crippled by the weight of a nation in shock, the weight of the bridge, the weight of all those people who had died and their loved ones left behind. He shuffled over to the couch and lay down.

Walking out of the general's office, Fletcher went straight to Sarah's adjoining office, knocking once and walking straight in, as was his habit.

Sarah was at her desk, talking to someone on MiLA. She looked up at Fletcher and waved him in. 'Okay, well look, I have to run,' she said firmly. 'Perhaps you should put down your thoughts in an email and send it through to me. I'll make sure that the general understands your point of view.'

Hanging up the receiver, she let out a deep breath. 'That was our friend over at Foreign Affairs, wondering when the general is going to make a public acknowledgment of our defeat and pull back all the armed forces.'

'My God, what a nightmare. We really are stuck between a rock and a hard place, aren't we?' said Fletcher, leaning back in the leather chair opposite Sarah.

'Fletch, can I share something with you?' Sarah asked, looking nervous. 'Something I've been working on privately that I think might be a consideration right now.'

'Sure, what is it?' Fletcher asked, intrigued.

'Well, it's a last-resort strategy I've been thinking about for a while now. I'm not even sure if it's possible, but … well …' she trailed off.

'Shoot. Let's hear it, Sarah,' said Fletcher, sitting up in his chair.

'Okay, well,' Sarah said, putting on her no-nonsense presentation voice, 'we can't get the Chinese out of here using traditional force. They have the ability to easily kill civilians and destroy infrastructure, coupled with the fact that we don't have the ability to retaliate like-for-like, let alone adequately defend ourselves.'

'No question of that after the other day,' remarked Fletcher.

'So, we are somewhat powerless to get them out of our own accord. We don't want them to be here because, well, who's to say they'll stop with the mines? Plus, this nation will never grow and prosper while we have a foreign power in our borders, right?'

'Absolutely,' nodded Fletcher. 'Where are you going with this, Sarah?'

'Well, the question is, would we be prepared to live in an Australia that existed without the Chinese *and* without the mining industry?'

'Without question, yes. We have nothing to lose on that front — the mines are completely controlled by the Chinese and will continue to be as long as they occupy this country,' replied Fletcher, getting more animated.

Sarah looked hard at Fletcher and paused for a brief moment, continuing slowly for effect. 'Then would we be willing to detonate nuclear devices in our own country?'

'Nuclear bombs ...?' said Fletcher, gobsmacked.

'Yes, nukes,' said Sarah firmly, leaning forward. 'What if we detonated a series of tactical nuclear weapons, specifically at the key Chinese-held mines? Australia is one of the few countries in the world that can actually use nuclear weapons on its own soil to defend itself. We could minimise civilian casualties by evacuating the area under the guise of a complete submission to the Chinese occupation. When the conditions are right, we launch.' She sat back with a satisfied look on her face.

'The mines would be useless for hundreds, if not thousands of years — the Chinese would have no reason to occupy Australia,' said Fletcher, thinking it through.

'That's right. We're being held hostage by our own resource wealth. By taking out the ransom, China has no reason to stay and continue to fight what they know will be a pointless and drawn-out war.'

'So, we would be making the ultimate sacrifice to get them out.'

'It would be a good sacrifice,' replied Sarah, more introspectively.

'So, where do we get a nuke from?' Fletcher said, almost to himself. 'The Americans, I guess.'

'That's right. They've been sitting on those nukes for decades, just waiting for a good reason to use one,' said Sarah quickly, then pausing. 'I'm sure they will have some caveats, some requirements from us, but we shouldn't underestimate their willingness to cling on to what slender primacy they think they still have in Asia.'

'Oh, I don't doubt it,' said Fletcher, impressed at how much thought Sarah had obviously put into this. He suspected she'd fall at the next hurdle, though. 'How do we sell this to the Australian people, then?'

Sarah was ready with her answer. 'We don't.'

'Sarah,' said Fletcher, almost laughing now, 'we have to get approval from a number of people. It's likely to go to cabinet for a vote. We need to consider how it gets sold to the politicians.'

Sarah, sensing she was losing him, replied with urgency. 'Fletch, we can't afford the time or the possibility of it getting back to the Chinese. If they catch wind of an operation like this, they will no doubt threaten us with another strike on one of our cities. Probably much bigger than the last attack. Do you think the politicians will have the stomach for that? Not a chance.'

'Perhaps not, but doing something like this on our own is insane.'

'I don't think we have a choice, Fletch. There's too much at stake.'

'Are you sure it's even possible to execute this without endangering civilians?'

'I've spoken to a few people, and it is feasible,' Sarah said eagerly.

'People?' Fletcher said, suddenly suspicious. 'Who have you told about this, Sarah?'

'I asked Connor to look into it. I thought he'd be perfect — an ex-defence minister, he's got a lot of good contacts as you know. And he's not officially part of this administration, so it can't be linked back to General Stephens if it got out.'

'I'm pretty new to this politics game, but one thing I do know is that you can never be too careful,' Fletcher said sternly. 'You're positive nobody else knows?'

Sarah blinked, suddenly doubting herself. 'No, nobody else knows.'

'Good. Look, I'm not saying it's a bad idea,' Fletcher said, standing, 'but it is a politically dangerous one. Let's talk to Marty when he's up, see what his reaction is.'

Later that afternoon, in General Stephens' office, Sarah had just taken the general through the idea. The room was silent. Stephens' face was expressionless, his gaze rooted on the empty chair opposite him. Sarah and Fletcher, sitting on either side of the empty chair, watched him, waiting in anticipation for his response.

'Interesting,' said General Stephens finally, his gaze still on the chair, his face stoically resisting expression.

Sarah leaned forward and perched herself on the edge of her chair. 'General, I have to tell you. I've spoken to Connor about it. He understands that it is highly sensitive and is using the utmost discretion. But he is putting together a viability paper on it, which we will have by the end of next week. We've codenamed it Operation Fulcrum.'

'Good work, Sarah. I want to understand the scenario completely. Get me the report as soon as you can,' replied the general. Looking directly at Sarah, he continued, 'It's an interesting option you've raised Sarah, radical. But interesting.'

'Marty,' interjected Fletcher, 'we need to understand the legalities of this sort of action. You know cabinet will never allow us to nuke our own country. If we are going to do this, we'll be making the call and we'll be solely responsible.'

'I understand what you're saying, Fletch. I will be solely responsible. No one else. It would be unfair to ask the government. It cannot be held responsible for a decision like this. It needs to remain beyond reproach so it can run the country, once this is all over.'

'General, we will stand by you no matter what decision you make,' said Sarah, raising her head confidently.

General Stephens looked at her and gave her a grateful smile, hope lighting his face for the first time in months. 'I know you will, Sarah, I know you will. But let's see that paper from Connor first.'

That night Sarah lay in her bed with Matt. Most nights were ending up like this these days. They'd become a steady, regular thing without ever discussing it — cooking meals together, spending whatever free time they had with each other. It was nice. They both enjoyed how naturally it had evolved.

Rolling over to face Matt, Sarah propped herself up on her elbows. 'If you were General Stephens right now, what would you do?'

Matt, a little taken aback by the question, pondered it briefly. 'Well, I'd do a deal with Yun, get paid a fortune, buy an island in the Caribbean, take my Number One female advisor and disappear forever,' he grinned, idly playing with her hair.

Sarah let out a short laugh. 'Very funny. But seriously, what would you do?' she said, brushing her hair back behind her ear.

Matt sat up, trying to consider the question. 'I have no idea,' he said finally. 'It's a no-win situation we're in. I guess I would do what's best for the greatest number of Australians. This war will never be won. It will only ever result in the annihilation of our way of life. So, the first thing I would do is lay down our arms, then I would hand over the running of the country to people who can rebuild our nation under a new paradigm, with new borders and a new focal point of prosperity.'

'Aha! So you have thought about it,' she said with a smile.

'Of course I've thought about what's right for this country ...' he trailed off. It was bizarre talking about all this — they never talked shop, at Sarah's insistence. He was pleased with her sudden openness.

'So you don't think that what we're doing is right then?' Sarah interrogated.

Matt paused and continued slowly, deliberately. 'No, no I don't actually.' All of a sudden, he felt the conversation take a turn. *This* is why we don't talk shop, he thought to himself.

Sarah sat up, shocked by Matt's admission. 'That surprises me,' she said, folding her arms across her chest. 'I would've thought you could see that by surrendering to the Chinese, we are not benefiting the greatest number of Australians, because the greatest number of Australians are yet to be born, the greatest number of Australians are the future generations,' she felt her voice rising involuntarily. 'The sacrifices we must make now will benefit the greatest number of Australians. You just have to broaden your point of reference.'

Matt leaned back tensely. 'But Sarah, that assumes whatever sacrifice we make now will benefit future generations. There's a good chance our actions now are not good for them, are possibly even destroying them.'

'Come on, Matt,' cried Sarah, 'if we don't fight now, it will be impossible to get the Chinese out of here until they have sapped our land of every natural resource we have, and that will take hundreds of years, even at the rate they're going.'

'But what option do we have, Sarah?' asked Matt, his voice rising in volume to match hers. 'After the Sydney attack, we know our future if we continue to resist them.'

Sarah was flustered now, frustrated and surprised by the realisation that Matt's view was so different from hers. She'd thought they were on the same team, had been so confident that she'd never even thought to ask him what he thought. 'There is something we can do, rather than wait to be annihilated — we can annihilate the Chinese.'

'What are you talking about Sarah? That's impossible.'

'No, it's not impossible; it's actually entirely possible,' Sarah said, throwing out her trump card. 'We nuke them, we nuke the mines — wipe them and our mines out completely.'

Matt had heard enough. He got off the bed and started to dress. 'You're fucking insane. Is the general seriously considering that as an option? It would never get through parliament, you know that.'

Sarah knelt on the bed with a sheet wrapped around her shoulders. 'It's not insane, Matt — it's our only option, our only chance of saving ourselves.'

'What you're talking about,' said Matt, furiously buckling his belt, 'will result in civilian deaths, possibly thousands. And God knows what will happen to our environment! The ecology would be destroyed. You might get the Chinese out, but at what cost?' He paused, looking at her with disgust. 'My God, you talk about future generations of Australians, Sarah. What about the kids born into a nuclear-poisoned land?'

With that Matt walked out, slamming the bedroom door. Sarah stared at the door, stunned, listening as Matt slammed the main door on his way out.

'Fuck,' she said to herself, realising what she'd done.

The next day, Sarah sat on a bench at City Park on the banks of Lake Burley Griffin, looking across to Parliament House. The afternoon sun was hot. Sarah could feel the heat even in the shade. Out of the corner of her eye, she noticed Connor walking towards her. She did not turn or stand to greet him. She just waited for him to come and sit.

'Hello Sarah,' said Connor, with as little emotion as could be wrapped in a greeting.

'Connor,' replied Sarah without looking at him. 'So, do you have the report?'

'Yes, I do. I must say Sarah, I'm impressed. I didn't take you to be the sort who would consider, let alone come up with, an idea like this,' said Connor.

'Well, I can be full of surprises, Connor,' she said drily.

'Oh, I'm sure you are,' he chuckled.

Sarah was in no mood for repartee. 'So, may I have the report then?'

'Of course,' replied Connor, quietly pulling the report out of the briefcase on his lap, handing it over.

Sarah slid it into her attaché case. 'So, can Operation Fulcrum work then?'

Connor's demeanour changed. He was all business again. 'Provided the right measures are taken to evacuate the area, then we should be able to minimise the initial civilian death toll. Assuming the weather conditions are forecast accurately, then we should be able to contain the fallout. Environmental and ecological ramifications are more difficult to estimate. No one has ever detonated these devices in such an environment. There are concerns about poisoning the farming land to the south and east. There is the possibility of the water table being poisoned, affecting crops and water supplies. There is a question mark over Adelaide and the possibility of long-term fallout. And of course, there is the question over the Chinese. If they were to find out about this plan, who knows what they might do to protect the mines? Equally of concern is what they might do in retaliation, given what they did in Sydney.'

'But do you think it's feasible?' prodded Sarah.

Connor paused. 'Yes, it is a plausible plan that may very well result in the Chinese extricating themselves from Australia.'

'Good. That's all I need to know,' said Sarah, standing up.

Connor looked up at her. 'Sarah, I don't need to remind you that if anyone finds out about Fulcrum, the general will be in seriously hot water, as will you and the rest of the administration. Frankly, I want nothing more to do with this.'

'I understand. Thank you for your help,' replied Sarah before walking back towards the road, leaving Connor on the park bench.

She decided to walk back to the general's office. When she arrived she went straight to see Fletcher and show him the report.

Sarah knocked and walked immediately into his office. 'It'll work, Fletch. There are some calculated risks, but Connor agrees — Fulcrum can work.'

Fletch looked up from his screen. 'Come in Sarah, tell me what's on your mind,' he said sarcastically, referring to the way she had stormed into his office.

'Like you don't do that all the time to me!' she exclaimed. 'But look, the feasibility report is back and he agrees it could work.'

'Let me see it,' Fletcher held out his hand. 'A paper report. Haven't seen one of these in a long time,' he mused.

'I naturally didn't want to risk transmitting it or saving it on a portable device.'

He was already reading the executive summary. 'Very smart. See, paper still has its uses.'

Sarah didn't respond — she just watched Fletcher reading the report. They sat in silence for a few minutes while he flipped the pages.

'Well? It's all there, Fletch — and it could work,' said Sarah after a few more minutes.

Fletcher continued to read in silence, nodding occasionally, rubbing his lower lip with his index finger. Sarah looked around the room impatiently, noticing the photos on the wall, which she had seen before, but never actually looked at. One was of Fletcher and General Stephens in a desert somewhere, arms around one another's shoulders. They were young and, despite their dirty combats, they looked strong and happy. Sarah thought about what they must have been through together over the years.

'Well Sarah, it seems you have come up with a viable plan — can't say I like it, but I think we need to consider it,' Fletcher said finally, putting the report down.

'I don't like it either, Fletch, but I dislike the alternative even more.'

'Yes, that's a good way to look at it. Let's get it to Marty as soon as he's out of the transport meeting this afternoon.'

Sarah stood to leave. Fletcher leaned back in his chair, looking at Sarah, who stood and gently brushed down her fitted suit jacket. 'Sarah, put that report in your safe at the office. There can be no leaks of this at all.'

'Of course, Fletch. I'll take it straight there now,' replied Sarah, heading for the door.

'Sarah,' he said suddenly, 'have you seen the effects of a nuclear explosion?'

Sarah froze, staring at her hand on the door handle. 'No, no I haven't,' she said quietly.

'I suggest you take a look in the archives at the Iranian attack of 2021. Take a look at what happened after the attack — the years of fallout the Iranian people had to endure. The land at ground zero is still uninhabitable. Generations of children were born disfigured and sick. Marty and I were serving in the region at the time of the attack. What I saw there scared the hell out of me. The level of destruction was on a scale like you could never imagine.'

Sarah turned back to Fletcher, who was leaning forward on his desk. 'I will Fletch … I'll take a look.'

'Good. You need to know before you start pushing this to Marty with any zeal.'

Locking the feasibility report in her safe, Sarah went to her screen and opened up the Iranian archive. The Iranian bomb, as they called it, was actually an American bomb — it was just dropped in Iran. The first report she opened was a text-based Wikireport to give her a quick and easy-to-understand perspective on the event.

She remembered vaguely learning about this episode in her studies, but since her education had been mainly in strategy and had focussed on the polar regions, she hadn't considered it important. Slightly embarrassed that she had to research such an important and relatively recent event, she started to read.

... By 2018, the tensions in the Middle East had reached a fever pitch. The entire region was in turmoil and inter- and intra- country wars were raging. In all the unrest, the US was losing its hold on the oil in the region and realised that there could be no peace settlement and no decisive victory for a conventional army. Resistance in the region was so strong that the US decided that something devastating would have to be done to put an end to it and again make the region cooperative. So, to protect their dwindling leverage on energy resources, they decided to put an end to the fighting by dropping a 20-Megaton nuclear bomb. Iran was chosen as the target, as it had risen up against the US after once being its closest ally in the region. The Iranian Government had sanctioned what the US considered to be terrorist attacks on their military bases in the region. This was used as justification for the nuclear attack.

The bomb was dropped on Teheran on the 12th of August 2019 with catastrophic effect. More than two million people were killed in the initial blast. A further million died soon after the blast, and the long-term damage to those who survived was monstrous.

The attack did not have the effect the US had projected. The theory was that the neighbouring countries would see what would happen to them if they kept fighting and would lay down their arms. Then they would set about producing more oil for the US energy market.

However, shortly after the bomb was dropped, the neighbouring Middle Eastern countries, realising they could be next, took a united stand against the US, forming the United Middle East Coalition (UMEC). Under this agreement, they severed all exports of oil to the US. The US threatened more nuclear destruction, but was severely chastised by the international community.

Since the Iranian bomb, the US has restrained from further nuclear strategies, opting for the more conventional approach of ground troops combined with air and sea supremacy. The US still had to secure energy resources from other parts of the world, so they turned their attention firstly to Canada and then to drilling for oil in the geo-political minefield that is the Arctic Circle.

As a result of the polar ice melts, a new shipping laneway between Europe and Asia had opened up. It also opened up vast sub-sea oil reserves. No one country has a clear ownership of the region and so at the time of writing the conflict in this region is still unresolved ...

Sarah realised that this event had helped conspire against Australia. A severely stretched US military and a highly unstable global political environment all worked to China's advantage, leaving the door wide open for them to invade Australia.

There were thousands of reports and videos about the incident in the archive, so Sarah refined the search to 'fallout'. There were still hundreds of reports and videos, so she decided to add another search term — 'graphic'.

She started to view the videos — reports by military scientists on the horrifying casualties from the explosion. Children burned, people walking around naked, clothes burned or torn from their bodies. Corpses, thousands of them — the fatalities were staggering, millions of people dead in seconds, millions more dead in the months following.

Sarah spent hours in the archive, unable to stop herself from watching. One report was created only two years before, and it gave a sobering assessment of the long-term effects of the nuclear explosion. The report painted a bleak picture of a land completely toxic — nothing lived there, nothing could be grown. The land was completely poisoned. Teheran was never rebuilt. It was deserted, left as a sickening reminder of the destructiveness of mankind.

Leaning back in her chair, Sarah realised she'd been clenching her jaw and fists for the last few hours watching the videos. She felt drained. What was she thinking? Could they really do this to their own land? She questioned her own sanity, confused about how she could go to General Stephens now. Before, she had been evangelical about the plan — she thought it was a stroke of strategic genius to remove the ransom that was holding Australia hostage. Now, however, she realised the gravity of this decision, the terrible consequences that it could have on the people of Australia — on the future generations.

MiLA rang. It was General Stephens. 'Can you please come in here, Sarah?'

'Of course, I'll be right there,' she replied, rubbing her face and standing up.

Sarah knocked on his door and went in. Fletcher was already there, seated opposite the general.

'Come in, Sarah. Take a seat. Fletch tells me that the feasibility report is looking good for your idea.'

Sarah felt unsteady. *Your idea.* She didn't want this to be her idea anymore. She wanted distance from it. In truth, she wanted nothing more to do with it after what she had seen in the archives.

'Yes, sir. Connor and his team have reviewed the plan and believe that Operation Fulcrum has potential, though there are significant risks and side effects.'

'Yes, I'm sure there are,' replied General Stephens. 'I'll read the report later, but I have a pretty good idea of what it will say — and Fletch has briefed me. What I want to know is: are we doing the right thing? Are we thinking of Australia's best interests, for now and in the future?'

Fletcher started. 'I've considered all of our military options. We don't have any moves left. We're hamstrung because this country is effectively under siege. Our resources are too valuable and we're gambling with the lives of innocent people. Conventional tactics are not going to win this war, and neither have guerrilla tactics. There is no way around it.'

General Stephens nodded. 'I agree. There is nothing more we can do from a conventional military perspective. Sarah — your thoughts?'

'Well sir,' Sarah began, 'I agree that we cannot progress with our current military strategy. We have the diplomatic option, which we know will achieve nothing for us. We can independently set about getting on with rebuilding our nation by redrawing our borders — effectively walking away from the mining industry. But then, whatever wealth we create in the future will be at the mercy of the Chinese. Our third and final option is the nuclear one, Operation Fulcrum,' she took a deep breath and looked down at the desk. 'An option that I am increasingly uncertain about.'

'Uncertain?' repeated General Stephens in disbelief. 'This was your idea, Sarah. Are you having doubts?'

Sarah raised her head to meet General Stephens' eye. 'Yes, as a matter of fact, I am. This may have been my idea initially, but I do not wish to own or champion this strategy. I realise now that the nuclear option is one that will change this country forever. I can't carry the burden of that responsibility — this cannot be "my idea", sir.'

General Stephens stared right back at Sarah, his grey eyes cold. 'No one is saying that you will carry the responsibility of this decision, Sarah. I alone will labour with that load. However, if you want a seat at the grown-ups' table, you need to make — and live with — some hard decisions.'

Sarah blinked. Her mouth dropped open. The general had never spoken to her like that before. 'Sir, I just … I realise now what it means to take the nuclear option.'

'Why, because you've watched a few videos? Read a few reports? Seen some statistics? You have no idea, Sarah, until you see it first-hand,' Stephens said, glaring at the young woman across from him. 'You cannot comprehend the destruction. Like Fletch, I've seen the horror of nuclear weapons and, since taking control of this country, I dared not consider the possibility of a nuclear scenario. I couldn't let myself think it, even for a second, in case the thought took hold and then, God forbid, became a reality.'

General Stephens stood up, feeling too constrained by his chair. He had to move. 'Sarah, unfortunately, the evil we face with

China scares me more than the evil of a controlled nuclear explosion — which is why we need to make a decision and act on it in total secrecy. There can be no debate, no discussion, outside of this room. I alone will make the decision and I will live with the consequences.'

The room fell silent. Fletcher and Sarah remained motionless. They all felt the decision had been made.

'So, what next?' asked Fletcher. 'If we're going to do this, we need to start evacuating people as soon as we can.'

Sarah sat forward. 'We do it under the guise of relenting to Chinese dominance — have the military start moving people out of the area so that there is as little questioning as possible. If the Chinese ask what's going on we just say that we're redrawing our sovereign borders — that the mining region is all theirs.'

General Stephens nodded. 'Yes, I agree. Fletch, can you please instruct the military to suspend all operations? We need the Chinese to think that we're submitting.'

Fletcher nodded.

'Sarah,' continued General Stephens, 'handle the evacuation — I don't want one Australian citizen to be anywhere near the area.'

'Yes, of course, General' she replied.

'All right, then. Get to work. And remember, not a word to anyone. I'm going to make a call to President Allen and see if he would be willing to help.'

Chapter 18

Days of planning all merged into one. Sarah was exhausted. Getting home after midnight, she checked MiLA and noticed four missed calls from Matt — she had been screening calls all day. Too tired to call him now, she threw MiLA on the couch and stumbled into bed, falling asleep half-dressed.

In the morning, her ambient alarm system brightened the room at 6 am. Waking groggily, Sarah felt like she had been asleep for all of five minutes. After a quick shower and getting dressed, she headed out the door, calling Matt.

He answered immediately. 'Morning. I was trying to get hold of you all day yesterday. I even came by the house, but you weren't there.'

'No, sorry. Yesterday was a manic day like you wouldn't believe,' she said, getting into her car.

On the other end of the line, Matt paused. 'You're doing it, aren't you? You're planning to detonate a nuke in South Australia.'

'Matt, don't be ridiculous,' Sarah replied immediately. 'We were talking hypothetically the other day.'

'Bullshit. I know when you're lying, Sarah. Something big is going down and I know you're involved,' Matt's voice was harder than Sarah had ever heard it.

'Matt, please. Just leave it alone. I have to go, I'm at work.' With that, Sarah hung up, cursing to herself. Matt was on to her and she knew he wouldn't stop until he found out what was going on. He knew what she was capable of after the coup went ahead. He wouldn't underestimate her.

Later that day at the office, Matt called again. Sarah saw his name on MiLA's screen. She wanted badly to avoid him, but not answering would only make him more suspicious.

'Hey, what's up?' Sarah answered as casually as she could.

'I don't know — you tell me Sarah,' Matt spat. 'I want some answers — or I go to the press.'

'Matt, please,' Sarah tried her best to sound like she thought he was being silly. 'Let's talk about it tonight, at mine.'

'Fine. Nine o'clock at yours — and make sure you're there.'

'I'll be there. See you tonight.'

'Okay, see you then.'

Sarah wondered how she could have been so stupid to have mentioned it to Matt. It would have been so much simpler had she just kept her mouth shut.

Staring at her screen, Sarah thought about what they were about to do — and the possibility of it all going wrong.

A knock at the door startled her. Fletcher peered around the door.

'Hey, Marty wants to see us.'

'Okay, yes,' said Sarah looking up, her face flushed.

'You all right?' asked Fletcher, concerned.

'I'm fine, just haven't slept much lately,' Sarah replied, standing up and walking briskly around her desk.

'Know the feeling. Hang in there,' Fletcher said, putting a reassuring hand on her shoulder, 'not long to go now.'

'Yeah, I think that's what I'm worried about.'

Fletcher just gave her a half-smile and turned to walk down the hall with her.

Sarah stopped suddenly and said in a whisper, 'Are you convinced we're doing the right thing?' She looked at Fletcher with pleading eyes.

'I am,' he replied reassuringly. 'We don't have another option. It's definitely a gamble but it's worth the risk.'

A young aide walked past them. They both smiled innocently until he'd passed.

'I just,' Sarah said softly, suddenly struggling with tears, 'I pray no civilians get hurt.'

'You need to steel yourself for the possibility that there may be fatalities,' Fletcher replied in a no-nonsense tone, continuing down the hall, 'but it is for the greater good. And remember, we're doing everything we can to remove people from harm's way. The army is being extremely thorough with the evacuation.'

'I know,' said Sarah, following after him, 'and telling people that the Chinese are planning reprisal attacks seems to be working as a motivation to clear out of the region.'

Stopping outside General Stephens' office, Fletcher again put his hand on Sarah's shoulder. 'We're doing the right thing, Sarah. Hang in there.'

'Thanks, Fletch,' she said as she knocked firmly on the door.

'Come in, come in.' General Stephens beckoned them to sit down.

Fletcher and Sarah sat opposite the general at his desk in their usual spots.

Stephens looked grave. 'President Allen has agreed to help. He was somewhat excited about it. Not at all surprising, really. So, in less than a week, the plan will be executed.'

Fletcher and Sarah nodded slowly. 'What's the date, General?' asked Sarah.

Stephens leaned back in his chair. 'On 3rd October, two US B-5 stealth bombers, with the capability of flying well above the Chinese zone of defence, will take off from Christchurch airbase in New Zealand. They will fly due-west, passing the southern tip of Tasmania. Shortly after that they will turn north and commence their run over Adelaide. Then they will split up, one heading towards Western Australia, and the other through central Australia at the border with Queensland. They will be dropping a series of tactical nuclear devices, the biggest of which is a 50-kiloton bomb. Operation Fulcrum will effectively render the major mines useless and inaccessible for decades.'

Fletcher finished the scenario. 'The Chinese will have no further use for us and be forced to go elsewhere to find their resources.'

'There's always the risk of them moving further into WA, creating new mines,' said Sarah.

'Yes, but they will know what we're capable of — what we're prepared to do to keep them out of our country,' replied Fletcher quickly.

'Besides, this was an economilitary invasion,' said Stephens firmly, 'they were here to secure cheap resources from our existing mines. If they have to build new mines, they would sooner build mines in their own country. God knows they've got enough iron ore and precious metals over there.'

Stephens suddenly pushed his chair back. 'That reminds me — Western Australia. That idiot, Ian Bright — the premier who cut a deal with the Chinese — will be left out in the cold after this. I want him removed from office and charged with treason as soon as this is over. I want some company when they lock me up for bombing our own country,' he finished, wryly.

'Sir, you will not be going to gaol. You will be a hero,' replied Sarah earnestly.

General Stephens kept his smile. 'I hope you're right, Sarah, but I can't see it happening. Anyway, how are we going with relocating the civilians living in the region?'

Sarah opened her leather folder, pulling out a screen and handing it to Stephens. 'The relocation is going as planned and we have already cleared 70 per cent of the townships and properties there. We've encountered minimal resistance from the locals, and nothing from the Chinese.'

'Very good!' Stephens said, flicking through the screen. 'My not going to prison after this is completely dependent on two things: the Chinese not finding out about our operation, and not one Australian getting so much as a suntan from the blast. Fletch, have the Chinese been in touch? Are they asking questions yet?'

'Nothing, Marty. I assume they just think we're capitulating and clearing out.'

'Good. If Xian or Yun tries to contact us, I'll feed them the same story. All right,' Stephens said, gesturing to the door, 'if you could please excuse me I have some calls to make. The Minister of

Agriculture wants to talk about why farmers are being asked to leave their properties.'

That night Sarah made sure she got home early. She needed to figure out how to talk Matt out of going public with what little he knew. She was pacing with a glass of wine in hand, cursing herself for not having her strategy already planned. She'd been stretched so thin with the relocation of the civilians that she hadn't had time to come up with contingency plans.

The buzzer sounded. Sarah opened the door and Matt walked in, his tie loosened, his shirt creased. He looked dishevelled and flustered.

'So Sarah, you want to tell me what's going on?' asked Matt with an air of forced calm.

'Come in, Matt. Nice to see you, too,' replied Sarah sarcastically.

'Whatever. Tell me what's going on.'

'Nothing!' she cried teasingly. She playfully tugged on his lapels, pulling him in for a kiss. 'You have to let it go, Matt.'

'No chance,' he said, pulling away. 'I know you're up to something. Either you tell me everything, or I go to the press with what I think is going down. You can't be allowed to do this. I couldn't live with myself if this happened and I didn't do whatever I could to stop it.'

Sarah could feel the situation slipping away from her. 'Matt, please,' she pleaded. 'You have got to let it go. There is no plan, but if you go to the press talking about nukes you could start wholesale panic and people could get hurt.'

Matt, exasperated, grabbed Sarah by both shoulders and shook her. 'Just tell me, for God's sake!'

Sarah wrestled free of his grip and slapped him hard across the face. 'Get the fuck out of here!' she shouted. 'You're out of your mind.'

Matt recoiled from the slap and for a split second considered hitting her back. 'You fucking power-mad bitch,' he spat, putting a finger to his swelling lip. 'I'm going to the press!'

He started for the door. Sarah panicked. She couldn't let this spiral out of control anymore. She needed more time to think of a way to deal with Matt.

Picking up the heavy glass vase that stood on a small, ornate hall table, she ran for Matt, her footsteps silent on the carpet. Lifting the vase high above her head, she swung it down just as Matt reached for the door handle. The vase connected with Matt's skull with a loud crack, and he collapsed to the ground.

'Fuck!' she swore, breathing hard and holding her hair back from her face.

Fumbling for MiLA, she decided to call Fletcher. Staring down at Matt's inert body, she didn't bother with pleasantries. 'Hey, I've got a serious problem and need your help. Can you come over now? Great thanks.' She hung up.

Twenty minutes later, Fletcher arrived. Sarah opened the door to let him in. Confused, he stepped over the broken glass on the floor, trying to work out what was going on. Walking into the lounge, Fletcher saw Matt lying face-down on the floor — gagged, his hands and feet expertly bound in a submission hold, still unconscious.

'What the hell is going on, Sarah?' asked Fletcher, turning to Sarah with a confused look.

'He found out that we were up to something,' Sarah explained. 'He threatened to go public.'

'What's he even doing here?' Fletcher asked, genuinely baffled.

'We've been seeing each other, Fletch — but that's none of your business,' Sarah replied defensively.

This agitated Fletcher. 'Jesus. Well I think it's my business now, Sarah. How did he find out about our plans?'

'He didn't know anything,' said Sarah, still defensive. 'He was speculating but he was on the right track. If he had gone public and mentioned the word "nuclear" our plan would have been destroyed.'

'Again, how did he even "speculate" that we were working on a plan?' Fletcher insisted, sceptical.

'Look, Fletch. I might have mentioned something to him early on, before we were really going to do this, okay?' said Sarah, exasperated.

'You stupid ...' Fletcher cut himself off before saying something he might regret. 'Your pillow talk has seriously jeopardised this operation. What the hell are we going to do with him now?'

'Look, we just have to keep him quiet for a few days. Until this is all over.'

'You want to kidnap a political aide, formerly the prime minister's advisor?' Fletcher laughed. 'Are you fucking insane?'

'Damn it, Fletch. What choice did I have?' Sarah cried. 'He was going public. The operation would have been finished. I had to do something — and now we need to sort this out.'

Fletcher held up his hands in resignation. 'All right, okay. We need to get some people we trust to not ask questions to guard him somewhere safe — and well out of contact.' Fletcher sat down on the couch and stared at Matt's prone figure.

'We need to get him out of Canberra,' said Sarah. 'They'll be looking for him after 24 hours and we can't risk him being discovered.'

'Okay,' said Fletcher, sighing. 'I know some men who can be trusted. We can get him out of Canberra — I think I know the safest place for him.'

'Where?'

'On a boat. A fishing boat to be precise. We can have him taken out on a cruise up and down the east coast for a week. The weather is lovely at this time of year,' added Fletcher, deadpan.

Sarah smiled and nodded her head slowly. 'Oh, you're good, Fletch. You're very good!'

He made some calls. By 1 am, two men came around to Sarah's. Matt had come to and was wrestling with his ties, to little effect.

Both men were clearly ex-military, casually dressed in jeans and shirts, their hair closely cropped. They were muscular, but not big men, and had an air of professionalism — they moved calmly and efficiently towards Matt. One of the men took a small leather pouch from his rucksack and unzipped it to reveal a patch.

Matt, who could see what the man had, started to panic and wrestle furiously with his bonds, screaming through his gag.

Sarah watched, horrified. 'What are you doing, what are you giving him?'

The man said nothing, not breaking his stride for a second.

Fletcher put an arm around Sarah. 'It's okay — it's just a patch that'll put him into a deep sleep for about 12 hours. When he comes around he'll be on a fishing boat somewhere off the coast with a bit of a comedown, but otherwise fine.'

The man crouched down and attached the patch. Almost instantly Matt's thrashing stopped and his groans drifted off as he passed out.

'Jesus,' said Sarah. 'For a moment there I thought   well, I didn't know what he was doing.'

The two men picked Matt up between them. 'Sir,' one of them said to Fletcher in a clear, respectful voice, 'if you could please lead the way and check that the hallway is clear to the lift and the parking lot.'

'Of course,' said Fletcher. Turning to Sarah, he said 'I'll leave now, too. Does anyone know that Matt was here?'

'Not that I'm aware of,' she replied.

'All right. Get this place cleaned up and work on your story in case he told someone that he was coming here. Keep it simple.'

Sarah walked them to the door. 'Thank you so much, Fletch.'

'Don't mention it. Literally. Don't mention this to anyone, even Marty. He cannot be made aware of this. If it all turns to custard he needs to be able to swear that he knew nothing.'

Sarah nodded, looking down, suddenly ashamed.

'Hey,' said Fletcher, grabbing her by the shoulders. 'Look at me. You did the right thing tonight. Get some sleep and let's not talk about it again.'

'Okay. Thanks, Fletch. I'll see you tomorrow.' Sarah closed the door and stared down at the mess in her hallway.

Chapter 19

It was yet another perfect blue-sky morning as Finn walked from the shed to the house. Over the past week, John, Jess and Finn had removed the charred rubble from the homestead and had begun rebuilding. Luckily for them, John's cousin ran the hardware store in town so he was able to quickly get the deliveries to them.

Finn's shoulder was healing well, even though it still ached most of the time. He had mobility and the pain was manageable. Despite the injury, Finn had worked hard over the last few weeks. The heat made it tough work though, and often all they could do was rest in the hottest part of the day.

'Morning,' Finn called out to John, who was already working on the roof.

'Morning, mate. How are you?'

'Never better. Want a hand there?' Finn asked, squinting upwards.

'Get yourself some breakfast and then we can get stuck into it,' John replied, returning to his work.

Finn headed around to the kitchen where Jess was preparing eggs and bacon.

'Morning,' said Finn cheerfully.

'Good morning. Finally decided to join us?' teased Jess, flipping the bacon over.

'Yeah. This resort ain't all it's cracked up to be. I was expecting breakfast in bed and it never arrived,' Finn complained, leaning against the kitchen bench beside her.

'Oh really? Well, I'll have a word with the staff,' said Jess smiling, sliding the food onto a plate for Finn.

'Thank you. That would be good,' Finn said formally, carrying on the game as he took his plate to the table.

After breakfast he headed out to see John and help with the construction. John was an excellent builder and already Finn had learned a lot from him. The fire had stopped at a brick wall in the middle of the house. John had explained to Finn how the wall had been part of the original homestead and that, when he had married Jess's mother, he had built the kitchen and extra rooms that had luckily remained relatively unscathed by the fire.

After a morning of hard work on the roof, they stopped for a long break at lunchtime. Finn lay in the shade of a big tree, contemplating how much he relished the feeling of hard work. He couldn't help but ponder the purity of building — using his hands and energy to create shelter, doing what men had done since moving out of the cave. He also couldn't help but make the comparison between what he did in the army and what he was doing here. In the army he congratulated himself on doing something that benefited the Australian people, but really he'd been congratulating himself for being such a legend, and all he'd done was destroy things. He felt embarrassed at how he had thought himself so much better than everyone who wasn't fighting in the war. Remembering the fight he'd had with Chris back in Sydney, he physically cringed at what he'd said, and how superior he'd clearly felt to Chris. How could he have blamed Chris for reacting like that? He realised now that he'd been wrong, deluded by self-importance.

Working here on the farm for two people he barely knew — who had saved his life and been so generous and welcoming — was a much better way of proving his worth, being useful. He recognised that this was the essence of being a man.

'Finn, can you pass me that drill down there?' called John from the top of a ladder.

'Sure,' called Finn, getting up from his spot under the tree. He strode over to pick up the drill. 'So John, have you always been a farmer?'

'Thanks,' said John taking the drill. 'No, not always. After growing up out here on the farm I went off to school in the city, just like Jess and Aaron did. I had a whale of a time once I settled into boarding-school life and all that. I studied art history, would you believe?' he looked down at Finn, grinning. 'I figured that if I ended up back out on the farm, at least I'd be a cultured bloody farmer!'

'I'm beginning to not let anything surprise me about you and your family, John,' Finn laughed. 'So what made you come back?'

'Well, I guess I never really left in a way,' John paused to drill a hole in the wall in front of him, 'or should I say the land never left me. I enjoyed the city life but in the end I just found it lacked the soul and substance of the bush. Out here I feel like I'm part of the world, part of nature. In the city I just felt part of the bloody rat race.'

'Yeah, I know what you mean,' said Finn, nodding. 'Trouble is it took a war for me to get out and find myself.'

'It's funny how things work out, isn't it? I remember when I first left the city and came back here, I was in pieces — hated the place! Ended up having to go travelling for a year to find myself. Then when I came back for the second time I realised it was right, and that this land was part of my creed.'

'Your creed?' asked Finn.

'Yeah,' said John, handing the drill back down to Finn. 'Every man has a creed by which he lives his life. Mine involves living out on the land. You have a creed — it's inside you.'

'That's pretty philosophical, mate,' said Finn genuinely surprised.

'It's the art history, mate. Can't help myself!'

'So what's your creed, then?' Finn probed.

'I'm not telling you,' John chuckled. 'But like I said, it involves living out here, on the land, communing with nature every day.'

For the rest of the day, Finn pondered the idea of his creed while he worked on the house.

That night he went for a walk with Jess to the river that lay to the north of the homestead. The sun had already set, but the sky was still light. The air was cooler and smelled crisp, clean and alive — every breath was like a drug. He wanted more. The birds were noisy, as they always were at that time. The riverbank was a remarkable spot, a true oasis in the desert where trees grew green and lush. The current was not strong at this time of year, but Jess had told him that in the wet season the river would swell, with millions of litres rushing through.

Sitting on a fallen tree trunk, Finn and Jess stared out at the river.

'I need to go into town tomorrow,' Finn said, breaking the long comfortable silence. 'I have to find out what happened to the rest of my squad. I need to know they got out okay.'

'Is it safe for you to go into town, though?' Jess asked, looking at him with concern.

'I think so. The Chinese patrols seem to have eased up again.'

'Are you going back to the war?' asked Jess hesitantly.

'I'm not sure,' Finn replied honestly.

'Finn, what's the point?' Jess burst out. 'You said it yourself. There's no way Australia can win. The Chinese are here now. We need to adapt, not fight.'

'I know Jess, but it doesn't matter. I realise now that I gave up fighting for Australia a long time ago. I've been fighting for my mates, and there is no way I can live with myself knowing that they are out there dying while I'm here.'

Jess turned away and looked at the river, the water gently drifting past.

'Your call, Finn. We can't stop you leaving and we're really grateful for everything you've done,' she said, her voice sad.

Finn looked at her as she stared out at the river.

'Come on. We should get back before it gets too dark,' said Finn, standing and offering Jess his hand.

The next morning Finn took the Patrol into town on his own. He knew the way now, from the trips he had made with John. There was more life and buzz in the town today — people were starting to come out after the recent reprisals. Finn sensed the feeling of apprehension among the people of the town, though. It wouldn't take much to make these people go running for the hills again, he thought.

He found it odd that there was still no military presence in the town, given the recent attacks. Going to The Australian, Finn went straight for the pay phone with a little salute to Dave the barman. He called his parents first, managing to speak to them both. The relief in their voices was palpable, and Finn felt a lump in his throat when he spoke to Sonia.

He then dialled the army hotline and asked to be put through to his base command in the Blue Mountains. They would be able to tell him about the others and where he should report.

A young corporal answered and put him through to a lieutenant in the camp. Finn gave the man his details and explained what had happened to him. The lieutenant listened intently and brought up the operational files.

'Says here that only four men made it out of that operation alive. You are listed here as MIA, along with Carver,' said the lieutenant.

'Carver is dead,' Finn said immediately, holding his voice steady. 'I saw him with my own eyes. Who made it out, sir?'

'Ahh, looks like Sergeant Higgins, Private Samuels, Private Jessop and Corporal Kelly. Although Kelly was injured pretty badly and appears to still be in hospital.'

'Jesus, Bull. Is he going to be alright?'

'I can't tell that from this file, I'm afraid.'

'So where are the others then? I'd like to rejoin them as soon as I can,' Finn said.

'Like most divisions, they've been sent down to South Australia to help in the relocation of civilians.'

'Relocation? What's going on?'

'The government has decided that we should leave the Chinese to it and clear out all civilians from the area to avoid any further conflict. We're letting them have it, mate.'

Immediately Finn wondered whether John and Jess's farm would be affected. He didn't think they could take it if they had to abandon their home a second time. 'Is the Winton area going to be evacuated?' Finn asked.

'If the place was going to be evacuated, it'd be evacuated already,' the lieutenant replied.

Finn was relieved to hear that John and Jess would be unaffected by the relocations. Knowing they'd be fine, he felt the pull of responsibility to get back with his squad.

'So where's the nearest base to me? I'll go there tomorrow,' said Finn.

'You'll need to get yourself to Rockhampton. From there we can arrange transport for you.'

'Rockhampton. Okay. It'll take me a day or two, but I'll leave tomorrow.'

'I'll let them know to expect you.'

'Thank you, sir.'

'No problem. And well done on your escape. Sounds like we'll need a thorough debrief when you're back.'

Finn walked out of the pub and into the warm morning sun and buzzing street. He felt conflicted. The last thing he wanted to do was leave Jess. He savoured every moment with her, but at the same time he wanted to stand beside his mates again. Christ, my mates, he thought to himself. Only four of them had made it out.

Climbing into the Patrol, he started the engine and headed back to the homestead. The drive back seemed even longer than usual, as he mulled over his predicament. He wanted to stay and finish helping John and Jess. It was the least he could do for them. But at the same time he felt like he should be with his mates, even if it was just herding civilians around. The really hard, heavy work on the homestead was almost done. John and Jess could finish the rest themselves. Soon his conscience would be able to let him go and he could get back to his mates.

Chapter 20

It was 0500 hours, pitch-black and drizzling steadily at Christchurch airport. The two B-5 stealth bombers taxied into a huge hangar, engines deafening to unprotected ears. The planes looked like huge angular boomerangs, the wings melding into the fuselage seamlessly. The powerful lights of the hangar reflected off the black, wet surface of the planes as they came to a standstill, ushered in by the ground crew.

The US Air Force normally used the enormous hangar for covert survey missions to map out the enormous oil reserves in the Antarctic region, as well as for scientific flights down there. Now the only other aircraft in the hangar was an enormous C-8 Galaxy transport, which had arrived before the B-5s. The Galaxy carried the logistical support equipment for the bombers. The Americans had brought a crew of 20 technicians and scientists, who would ready the plane and its nuclear cargo for the mission. As soon as the B-5s began to wind down their engines, technicians busied themselves, attaching power cords, fuel lines and numerous other cables to their fuselages.

After 20 minutes of shutting down, the pilots climbed out from beneath the planes. They were led immediately to an area where they were checked for radiation and helped out of their flight suits which, due to the altitude the planes were to fly at to avoid detection from Chinese surveillance, were more like astronaut suits. For the rest of the day the planes would be prepared for the mission. Every millimetre would be thoroughly checked by the technicians and pilots. While the aircrews were doing this, the scientists would be testing the circuitry and diagnostics of the nuclear devices.

Later that morning, General Stephens was in his office with Sarah, Fletcher and General Draven. Draven was brought in to update them on the relocation of the civilians. He, like the vast majority of military officials, was unaware of Operation Fulcrum, believing that the mission was to remove civilians from the region and to accept defeat.

Stephens looked across his desk at Draven. 'So, Paul. You're 100 per cent sure that the areas now deemed to be Chinese territory have been cleared of all civilians? I want your personal assurance that there is not a single Australian in that region.'

'Our boys have been through that region with a fine-toothed comb. We have cleared out everyone within the demarcation lines,' replied Draven punctiliously.

Stephens nodded. 'Good. Have all your men remain outside the demarcation line and guard all routes into the area. I don't want any civilians deciding to nip back home, is that understood?'

'I'll make sure that it's locked down tight.'

'Thank you, General. That will be all.'

Draven stayed put. 'Stephens, I hope you are seriously working on the terms of your leadership agreement. I know we are in the middle of a crisis, but I believe the Australian people would sleep better at night knowing there will be an end to military rule at some point in the near future.'

Stephens gave Draven a level stare. 'I assure you, Draven, I have no interest in appointing myself leader for life. I'll deal with the documentation next week. That will be all.'

With that, General Draven stood and turned to leave the office. On his way out, he bumped into Anne McKinnon, the government's senior meteorologist, on her way in. Draven paused and looked back. Why is Stephens seeing a meteorologist? he wondered to himself.

McKinnon finished her briefing and left the room. Sarah and Fletcher stared at General Stephens.

'Well, it looks like we're all set to do this then,' said General Stephens, leaning back in his chair.

Fletcher looked anxious. 'Draven noticed the meteorologist when he left. He even did a double-take. Do you think he suspects something?'

'Nothing surer,' said General Stephens. 'He's a suspicious bugger, Draven. His mind will be working overtime trying to figure out what we're up to. But by the time he does, it'll be too late.'

'I suppose so, Marty. But all the same, too much is at stake to have him blow the lid on us now,' said Fletcher, unwilling to brush it off.

'Draven is not a concern,' Stephens said firmly. 'Now, more importantly, the stealth bombers have landed at Christchurch and are being prepped for the mission. Tonight we will observe the mission from the American Embassy. They have full satellite telemetry and operational control and we will be able to communicate directly with the pilots from there.'

Sarah was silent. She felt dizzy. She couldn't believe Fulcrum had come this far. What began as a wild conjecture was now about to become a reality, with very real consequences. After the previous night's incident with Matt, she was very much on edge. What they had done was clearly illegal and she could only pray that the situation would be resolved quietly. The repercussions would have to be dealt with once this was over.

'Sarah,' said General Stephens. 'You okay? I don't want you losing your nerve at this stage of the game.'

Sarah blinked quickly. 'I'm fine, General. Sorry. I was just thinking about any possible way General Draven might have to find out what's going on.'

'He won't. Don't worry about Draven,' Stephens said, exasperated. 'Let's keep our eyes on the prize here, guys. Don't let him break your focus. I can handle him.'

'Yes, sir,' replied Sarah sheepishly.

'All right. I want you both at the embassy by 1800 hours. The B-5s will take off at 2000 hours. Sarah, can you ensure that fire, ambulance and hospital services are all put on alert this afternoon? No need to give an explanation — just have them on alert.'

General Draven walked to his office, not feeling right. Something was going on that he wasn't being let in on. He was well aware of the excesses that rulers who were not accountable to their people were capable of, and this situation was setting off alarms in his head. Despite the fact that he was not part of the Stephens' inner sanctum, he was still a high-ranking official with extensive access to records and intel. He decided to put this to use. Pulling MiLA out of his briefcase, he called his personal assistant.

'Jackson,' said Draven. 'I want you to do some sniffing around. Something is going down and I need to find out what. Whatever it is — it's big. Get back to me when you have something.'

Matt regained consciousness about 30 kilometres off the south coast of New South Wales. He felt sick and disoriented, and his neck was stiff. It took a moment for the feeling of nausea to pass. He raised his hand to his neck, trying to rub the soreness from it — his fingers felt the roughness of synthetic material on his skin there. With a grimace, he picked the thing off his neck and looked at it. A patch! He realised slowly that he was on a boat — the room he was in was rocking rhythmically, with the occasional larger wave making the vessel reverberate. Matt looked around — he was in a tiny cabin with nothing but a bunk bed, mattress, pillow and a plastic jug of water. The sound of the engine was a constant monotonous drone. There was no light coming in, as the tiny porthole had been welded shut and the glass painted black on the outside. He had no idea of the time or how long he had been unconscious.

Matt scanned the room, taking in every detail, his head clearing by the minute. He noticed a tiny camera in the corner of the cabin — he was being watched.

The cabin door opened and Matt lurched back on the bunk bed as a large man wearing a black suit and balaclava came into the room and stood by the open door. Another man in identical clothing walked in with a tray of food, placing it on the side table. Without saying a word, they shuffled their large frames out of the room, closing and locking the door behind them.

Matt leapt off the bed when he realised he wasn't going to be hurt. Launching himself at the door, he started banging with both fists. 'Let me out! Let me out of here!'

He knew it was pointless, so he stopped quickly and, suddenly ravenous, turned his attention to the food. There were no utensils on the tray, so Matt used his hands, shovelling the food into his mouth.

His mind was still cloudy. What was going on? Why was he here? He tried to retrace his last memories. He remembered being at work, going to Sarah's, having a fight and then — that was it, nothing. He remembered what the fight had been over — the nuclear bomb. He remembered confronting her about the bomb. He must have been right — Matt remembered threatening to go to the press — this must be why he was being held captive.

After finishing the food, Matt sat back on the bunk bed with his knees tucked up to his chest, both hands to his forehead. He had to get off this boat to warn people, stop this madness ... But how? He was being held captive on a boat — God knows where or how far from shore. By the feel of the boat's motion, they were in deep water.

Come on, think! There has to be a way out of here, Matt thought to himself.

General Draven was at his desk drumming his fingers when MiLA rang.

Draven got straight to the point: 'Jackson, what have you got?'

'Nothing much, sir. The only things out of the ordinary are a missing political advisor — Matthew Lang, who did not come into work this morning and is not contactable. Though not suspicious, his disappearance is uncharacteristic and does not fit his psych profile. The only other anomaly is in New Zealand — Christchurch airport was closed last night for "unscheduled runway repairs."'

'What's unusual about that?' responded Draven.

'Normally nothing, except it was raining all night there. We thought it strange to conduct repairs at night — in the rain, sir.'

'That's it? Nothing else?' he barked.

'Well, yes. The only other thing, which is not unusual,' said Jackson, 'is that we're picking up a lot of coded chatter from the US Embassy. They do this now and then, so we don't think it's particularly unusual.'

General Draven was silent. He was trying to piece it all together, to understand the link. What it all meant.

'Anything else, sir?'

'No, Jackson. But keep me updated on anything else that happens.'

'Yes, sir.'

Draven knew there was a link — clearing the population in regional South Australia, a meteorologist, a missing political advisor, increased US communications and the closing down of a New Zealand airport. How did it fit together?

'Matthew Lang,' muttered Draven — the name was familiar.

Picking up MiLA he hit redial. 'Jackson, this Lang bloke — he was Hudson's aide, then helped General Stephens to power. And now he's missing. He's involved somehow in whatever is going on. Find Lang — I need to talk to him. He's the key.'

'The key to what, sir?'

'Just find him, Jackson. I want a report in an hour,' said Draven impatiently.

'Yes, sir,' replied Jackson.

An hour later and General Draven was on MiLA again to Jackson.

'Where are you at?' Draven demanded.

'We've located his abandoned car at Bermagui, the small fishing village on the south coast of New South Wales. There is no sign of Mr Lang.'

'Bermagui?' repeated Draven. 'Jesus, I know Bermagui. The Secret Service has a fishing boat there that they use to disappear people that need removing — temporarily or permanently.'

'I don't know anything about that, sir,' said Jackson. 'But we did learn something else, sir. All government cars are fitted with tracking devices. Even though his device was deactivated last night, I was still able to track where it had been.'

'Yes, yes. Where has Lang been in the last 24 hours?' demanded Draven, impatience getting the better of him.

'You're going to like this, sir: the last place he visited was Sarah Dempsey's home.'

'Dempsey?'

'Yes, sir. He arrived at Ms Dempsey's apartment at 2100 hours last night — and that's it. The tracker was switched off at 2230. Federal police located the car first thing this morning.'

'Why would he go from Dempsey's to Bermagui? And why would he switch off his tracking device? I'm surprised he'd even know how to. It doesn't add up,' Draven mused.

'I don't know, sir,' said Jackson, knowing full well that it wasn't a question.

'I need to get satellite imagery from last night at that time. Go back over the imagery and see if you can get anything on Sarah Dempsey's place between 2100 hours and 0300 hours. Send it through to me as soon as you find something.'

'Yes, sir. It might take a while though.'

'Then get busy,' said Draven, hanging up. Pressing MiLA absently into his chin, General Draven contemplated his next move. He needed to get to the bottom of this — and fast.

Sarah Dempsey was in her office staring blankly at the BBCNN 4 pm newsfeed on her screen. In her mind she was convincing herself that what they were doing was the right thing for the country, despite the risks and the consequences.

A knock at the door startled her from deep contemplation.

'Come in,' she said shakily, turning off the screen.

'Ms Dempsey,' said General Draven, stepping into the room. 'May I have a moment?'

'Yes, General Draven, of course. Come in,' Sarah said, her stomach clenching.

'Thank you,' said Draven, taking a chair.

'What is it General?'

'Well Ms Dempsey —'

'Sarah, please,' she interrupted, trying her hardest to seem warm.

'Of course, Sarah,' Draven said, slightly irritated with her interruption. 'See, the problem is Matthew Lang.'

Sarah blinked quickly, her spine tensing. 'Matthew Lang is a political advisor. Why would he be a problem?' she said with what she hoped was a nonchalant smile.

Draven allowed a thin smile to form on his lips. 'Well, he's missing and no one can get hold of him, which, Sarah, as I'm sure you know, is completely out of character.'

Sarah looked composed. 'Well, maybe he has gone to see his mother? Or his friends in Sydney, perhaps? I really don't see how this concerns me, General.' She glanced back at her screen as though she had other important work to get to.

'So, when did you last see Matthew Lang?' Draven asked directly.

Sarah realised that somehow Draven knew Matt had been at hers last night and changed tact. 'He came over last night, actually.'

'Really, and where did he go after he left yours?' asked Draven quickly.

'I don't know. We'd had a fight,' Sarah allowed an upset look to flit across her face. 'Look, we've been seeing each other and I broke it off last night. He didn't take it very well, and when he left, he was in a terrible state.'

Draven froze. This was entirely plausible. Perhaps he had just taken a break-up badly and gone off the rails. That instant, his MiLA beeped. He pulled it out, all the while holding his gaze on Sarah, scanning her face for the slightest nuance of a lie.

Draven looked at MiLA's screen. Jackson had sent him a message with an attached video file. Opening it quickly, Draven saw a black-and-white image of two men bundling a body into the boot of a car. Jackson's message read:

> Location: Sarah Dempsey's apartment
> Vehicle: Matthew Lang's
> Body in car: Unknown but alive at the time
> Suspects: Unknown
> Time: 0118

Sarah was frozen. She desperately wanted to see what was on his MiLA. Draven's face was giving nothing away. Outwardly she remained a picture of calm; inwardly, her mind was racing at full speed.

Draven, without showing any emotion or the slightest change of expression, put MiLA back in his pocket. Taking a deep breath, he leaned back in his chair. 'Shall we start again, Sarah?'

Sarah was fuming. She was being played here and she didn't like it one bit. 'What do you mean? I've told you everything. Now I'm very busy, so if you don't mind, General Draven, please either leave or get to the point.'

Draven, unflustered, leaned forward. 'What have you done with Lang?'

Sarah was speechless, trying to form words 'I … I told you …'

'You told me lies!' yelled General Draven, thumping his fist on the table.

'No, I told you the truth,' she insisted, regaining her voice. 'I don't know where he is, General.'

Draven was losing his patience. 'We have satellite footage of Matthew Lang's body being put in the boot of his own car outside your apartment last night. We have found his car at a small fishing village on the south coast of New South Wales. Now, I want to know what happened to him last night — and you're going to tell me.'

Sarah glared at Draven. 'I'm not telling you anything. If the police want to talk to me, then they can come and do so. Until then, I have nothing more to say.'

Draven was fuming — he would have to get the police involved now, which would take up time that he didn't have. Standing up, Draven headed for the door. 'We'll talk again soon, Ms Dempsey.'

Sarah remained seated. 'I look forward to it, General.'

As soon as Draven had closed the door, Sarah collapsed forward onto her desk — head in hands, her whole body shaking.

Draven stormed down the hall and called Jackson.

'Jackson, good work. But this angle isn't going to work. I need to find Lang another way.'

'Sir, I've made some calls. At 0400 hours a navy-registered fishing vessel left Bermagui. I tracked it on satellite and it appears to be in a holding pattern, steaming up and down the coast about 10 kilometres offshore.'

'That's it — they're holding him out there on the boat. Jackson, I want a full tactical Navy Special Forces team on that boat in one hour to secure Lang. Make it happen.'

'Yessir — I'm onto it.'

Chapter 21

From the *HMAS Creswell* on the south coast of New South Wales, two MRH95 helicopters lifted off simultaneously. The lead chopper was heavily armed with air-to-sea torpedoes, missiles and a forward-mounted cannon. The other was carrying a nine-man Special Forces team, charged with boarding the fishing vessel and securing the target — Matthew Lang. They flew low and fast over the sea to avoid radar.

Within 10 minutes they were upon the fishing boat. The lead helicopter fired a missile across the bow of the fishing boat then took its position, hovering above and in front of the boat. The co-pilot switched on the loud-hailer, ordering the boat to cut its engines, for all crew to come out on deck and lay down any weapons they were carrying.

The second helicopter circled above and waited to see the crew out on the deck. On the boat, the skipper killed the engines, then he and the crew came onto the deck with their hands in the air. Seeing five men out on the deck with their hands in the air, the second helicopter swooped down in a steep left-hand turn, pulling to a hover 10 metres above the fishing boat. Six men, three on each side, threw black ropes down onto the deck of the boat and abseiled down — the whole movement taking less than 30 seconds. As soon as all six were on the boat and unclipped from their ropes, the helicopter pulled up and took position to the starboard side of the vessel. The Special Forces team secured the crew with zip-lock thumb ties and, after a brief interrogation of the skipper, the team moved below.

The skipper had informed them of the whereabouts of the target and also that there were two Secret Service operatives somewhere on the boat. The Special Forces team moved through the upper cabins and bridge, swiftly but carefully — ensuring all the rooms were clear before proceeding below decks. The boat was old and had a heady smell of salt and dead fish. The light was dim down below and the space confined and claustrophobic. It was a terrible access route for the team. They were effectively boxed in and, even though they outnumbered the two agents, in this tiny corridor, numbers meant nothing.

Inside Matt's cabin, the agents had barricaded the door. One of them was on MiLA to Fletcher advising him of the situation.

'We've been boarded by Navy Special Forces — we're outnumbered and barricaded in the cabin.'

'All right,' said Fletcher calmly, 'Do not engage, understood? Just surrender when they get to the cabin. But before they do, inject Mr Lang with a shot of the tranquilliser. That should keep him quiet for long enough.'

'Yes, sir.'

'Oh, and naturally, not a word of this to anyone — at least until tomorrow. Is that clear?' said Fletcher.

'Of course, sir.' And with that he hung up.

He handed the MiLA to the other agent. 'Here, destroy this.' While the other agent crushed the device under his boot, he reached for a small black rucksack, pulling out a rectangular box containing the tranquilliser. Expertly he measured out the right dosage into the syringe and turned towards Matt. Fearing the worst, Matt lurched back on the bed as far as he could, curling himself into a ball. He was scared and frantically trying to think of a way out. A loud bang on the door, followed by an order to open the door, made the agent pause for a second. Matt, seeing his attention diverted, seized the opportunity. He threw himself at the agent, screaming for help at the top of his lungs.

The agent was stunned as Matt wrestled him to the ground. The second agent launched at Matt, trying to pull him off. The Special Forces were now smashing down the door, using the butts of their automatic weapons. They had smashed enough of a hole in the door to poke a rifle through and see what was going on. Matt was still screaming but the agents had regained control and had him in a submission hold on the ground. Matt was grunting in pain, still struggling against the two agents.

'Stop, don't move!' yelled a Special Forces operative.

The agent holding the syringe had just punctured Matt's skin with the needle. He looked at the other agent briefly — both men were flushed and sweating from the exertion of controlling their charge. In a microsecond's look, the agent holding the syringe pushed the button at the top, releasing the tranquilliser into Matt's bloodstream.

Seeing this, the Special Forces operative squeezed the trigger of his automatic rifle, delivering a round directly into the agent's head. His brains exploded in the small confines of the cabin, painting everything red and white. Matt was already slipping into unconsciousness. He had a vague sense of noise and the feeling of something warm and wet on his skin. Then it all quickly turned black.

The second agent froze, putting his hands in the air, not saying a word.

The Special Forces team smashed through the rest of the door and entered, pulling the dead agent's body off Matt and hauling the other agent out of the room.

The Special Forces medic knelt beside Matt, checking for his pulse. 'He's still alive, but unconscious. We need to get him and the syringe to a hospital immediately to find out what they gave him,' he said urgently.

Within 10 minutes, Matt was aboard the helicopter, heading towards Creswell base.

General Draven took the call from Jackson in his office. 'Well? Is Lang secured?' he demanded.

'Sir, we have secured the target, neutralised one agent and taken another prisoner, along with the crew of the fishing boat.'

'Get me on the line with Mr Lang. I need to talk to him immediately.'

'That's not possible, sir. He was administered a drug that has rendered him unconscious.'

'God damn it! Well how long before we can talk to him?' said Draven furiously.

'Sir, he is on his way to Creswell base as we speak. Special Forces have recovered the syringe that was used, so that the sick bay people can work out what drug was used. And hopefully give him an antidote.'

'Call me when he's conscious,' demanded Draven. He hung up and tossed MiLA on the desk. Standing with hands on his hips, he took a deep breath and stared at the wall, unclear on his next move.

Reaching for MiLA again, Draven called Jackson. 'And get a security detail on Sarah Dempsey and General Simon Fletcher. I want to know where they are going, who they are seeing and what they're doing every minute. Is that understood?'

'Sir, that will take some time for clearance to sanction a tail for both of them, particularly General Fletcher,' said Jackson.

Draven was fuming. He spoke slowly. 'Listen, Jackson! If you value your job, your life and your balls then I suggest you hang up right now and make it happen — immediately.'

Draven hung up again and resumed his furious gaze at the wall.

Sarah left her office at 5.30 pm. It was a short drive to the US Embassy, but she did not want to be late. She knew what had to be done. She also knew that it was not her responsibility to make the call. This was one decision she was relieved not to be making. Parking outside the embassy, on a wide, tree-lined street, Sarah got out of her car and noticed a dark blue Ford pulling in a hundred metres behind her. She knew this had to be a tail — and that Draven had arranged it.

The man in the passenger seat spoke into a discreet headset. 'Sir, Dempsey is parking outside of the US Embassy and is getting out of her car.'

In his office, Draven was patched in to the live feeds between the agents, listening to every word.

'Jesus! Don't let her into the embassy — do you understand? Do not let her get inside the embassy!' he yelled.

The two agents in the car looked at each other, stunned. For a brief second they froze, then realised how close to the embassy Sarah was — and how far from her they were.

Both agents leapt out of the car and sprinted towards Sarah, who was already walking towards the embassy gates. She sensed the commotion behind her. Turning, she saw the two men bearing down on her. She began to run. The embassy gates were close, but she could now hear the agents' footsteps close behind her. Breathlessly, she ran to the security gate at the embassy, fumbling briefly with her bag to get out her security ID for the sentry. Glancing to her left, she saw that the two agents were less than 10 metres away now — they'd be upon her in seconds.

'Thank you, ma'am. Please come in,' said the smiling sentry, oblivious to the commotion.

Sarah lurched through the gate as the two agents skidded to a stop just outside it. She sprinted to the main door of the old stone building, brushing down her suit jacket and smoothing her hair back, trying to compose herself and catch her breath. Glancing back, she saw the two agents — bent over, red-faced and out of breath, looking up at her.

Inside the embassy, Fletcher and General Stephens were already talking to the ambassador and Colonel Gregory, a high-ranking US Air Force officer. Walking into the opulent office, Sarah was still catching her breath. The men stopped their conversation and looked around.

'Ah, Sarah. Please come and join us,' said General Stephens, the picture of composure. 'Colonel Gregory here, from USAF, was just taking us through the flight plan.'

'Thank you, General,' said Sarah, walking over to the table where they were huddled.

She positioned herself beside Fletcher, leaning over to whisper in his ear. 'Draven is onto us. I just had some agents try to stop me from getting in here.'

Fletcher nodded slowly before turning his head, whispering to Sarah with a wink, 'Nothing they can do now.'

'Well, Matt could go to the press, let the Chinese know of our plan and allow them to make some threat. Once that happens our plan's over,' said Sarah, trying desperately to whisper, but her voice breaking from the stress.

Fletcher took Sarah by the arm and led her away from the table. General Stephens didn't notice, engrossed as he was in conversation with the ambassador and Colonel Gregory. Once out of earshot, Fletcher gently turned Sarah to face him, with both hands on her shoulders. 'Listen, Sarah. Pull yourself together. You've come this far — don't blow it now by losing your bottle. Perhaps we need to have a chat with General Draven and explain things. I'm sure he, of all people, will understand what we're trying to do here.'

Sarah nodded, taking a deep breath, trying to restore her composure.

Chapter 22

A medical team was waiting on the helipad as the navy helicopter swooped in. The pilot jerked the helicopter back suddenly while landing, the motion like a rider reining in an out-of-control horse. The whole machine shuddered under the stress of the rapid deceleration. Matt was lying unconscious on a stretcher in the back of the dimly-lit cabin, crowded in by the medic and some members of the Special Forces team. Before the chopper had landed, the side door slid open. As soon as the landing struts hit the tarmac the medical team was upon Matt, moving him onto a gurney.

The Special Forces medic ran alongside the gurney, yelling to the doctor above the roar of the helicopter's rotors.

After analysing what was left of the drug in the syringe that had been injected into Matt, the doctors ascertained the type of tranquilliser, and an antidote was administered. Matt slowly came around. He was still very groggy, talking gibberish. It took a few long minutes for him to shake off the drug-induced cloud fogging his mind.

'Where am I?' he asked the doctor.

'You're safe. You're at Creswell naval base in New South Wales,' replied the doctor.

'What happened? How did I get here?' he asked, trying to sit up.

The captain of the Special Forces team stepped forward, motioning for the medical staff to leave the room. 'Mr Lang, you were kidnapped and being kept on a boat off the coast. We rescued you, but as we did they knocked you unconscious with a tranquilliser.'

'Jesus,' said Matt, rubbing his head, noticing the drip that was hooked up to his hand.

'Sir, I need to ask you some questions — do you know why the Secret Service wanted you kidnapped?'

Matt sat there rubbing his face with both hands, trying to comprehend everything he had been told.

'Mr Lang, please can you tell us why someone wanted you kept quiet?' repeated the captain.

Matt suddenly remembered. He dropped his hands to the bed, his eyes red and swollen, skin pallid and unshaven. 'I remember, the nuke — they're going to bomb Australia, they're going to drop a nuclear bomb on Australia!'

'What do you mean? Who's dropping a bomb?' said the captain, stunned as much by the mad look on Matt's face as the words 'nuclear bomb'.

'Sarah … Sarah Dempsey and General Stephens — they're planning to drop a nuclear bomb on Australia.'

The captain didn't waste any time, immediately calling Jackson.

'What is it?' Draven demanded into MiLA.

Jackson was on the other end. 'Sir, Mr Lang has regained consciousness, although he's not making sense.'

'What's he babbling about then?'

'Well, sir, he's saying Ms Dempsey is going to drop a nuclear bomb on Australia.'

General Draven sat at his desk, frozen, staring at the wall opposite in silence.

'Sir? Did you hear me?'

'Christ! Of course, of course! That makes sense,' he said in a hushed tone, to himself more than Jackson.

'Sir, one other thing. We have reports of two US military planes taking off from Christchurch. They are, however, unconfirmed by the US or New Zealand military.'

'It's on its way already. They're actually going to do it. They're going to nuke the mines in South Australia,' said Draven incredulously. 'Thank you, Jackson. That will be all. Not a word of this to anyone, do you understand?'

'Of course, sir. Let me know if there is anything else.'

Throwing MiLA on his desk and sitting back in his chair, Draven considered his next move. What they were doing was illegal, unethical, bordering on insanity. But, at the same time, there was method to the madness — he could see that instantly.

MiLA rang. The room seemed excruciatingly quiet — between the rings was a tense silence that seemed to strain Draven's ears. Looking at the screen, Fletcher's name flashed up. Answering it, Draven brought the device slowly to his ear.

The words were out of his mouth before he was even aware of what he was saying. 'What the hell do you think you're doing, Fletcher?'

'Saving this country is what we're doing, and you know it.' Fletcher knew how to control his voice to suit the audience. He knew that a man like Draven responded to a firm hand.

'Seems to me like you're willing to destroy a very large chunk of it in doing so!' said Draven.

'Look, Draven!' Fletcher said impatiently, 'We don't have time to debate the ethics of what we're doing. The reality is the wheels are in motion. It's too late, it's happening. I need to know that you're on board. We cannot risk the Chinese finding out at the last minute through a leak. You know that if they make a threat, they're likely to follow through on it — if only to save face. Then we'll be hamstrung and forced to abort.'

'It's a little extreme, don't you think, Fletcher — nuking our own country?' Draven said dubiously.

'Cut the bullshit, Draven,' Fletcher retorted, getting heated now. 'You know the pointlessness of a conventional war against the Chinese — we'd be turning Australia into the Middle East of the South Pacific.'

Draven sat there, silently. He could see what they were doing was the right thing, in a perverse way. But his pride wasn't letting him see clearly. He felt belittled that he wasn't involved in the planning, that he had been lied to — and now he felt like a fool.

'Why didn't you bring me in on it sooner?' asked Draven, finally.

'Plausible deniability, Draven,' responded Fletcher, glad the conversation had turned. 'After this event, we will, in all likelihood, go to prison. The country will need you to rebuild our defences quickly — if the plan works, that is.'

Draven immediately felt ashamed. They were sacrificing their careers and lives for all Australians, including himself. He saw his resistance now as absurd. 'Yes, you have my word that I won't go to the press — or anyone else, for that matter.'

'Thank you. You're doing the right thing,' said Fletcher, trying to keep the relief out of his voice.

'No, you're doing the right thing — I'm just staying out of your way,' replied Draven.

'One other thing,' said Fletcher, with an air of sombreness. 'Tomorrow morning, provided everything goes to plan, you need to pick us up and take us into federal custody. I've already spoken to the general about it — you need to stay beyond reproach on this and the best way for you to do that is to arrest us. You'll need to act quickly to secure the defences — particularly in WA — despite that idiot of a premier doing a deal with the Chinese.'

'I understand,' said Draven.

'Very good. Well! I guess we'll be seeing you tomorrow, then?' Fletcher said, his tone cheerful.

'Yes, until tomorrow. And good luck.'

With that, the conversation ended.

Draven went back to staring at the wall, contemplating the enormity of what was about to happen.

In the ops room of the US embassy, Fletcher went back to the table to monitor the progress of the B-5s with a spring in his step.

In the dark cockpit of one of the stealth bombers, the two pilots had climbed to their cruising altitude and had just made their final turn into the approach path. The sky was clear, and at their altitude the stars were like searchlights, bathing the huge aircraft in light.

'Opening bomb-bay doors,' said the captain.

'Two minutes from Alpha drop-point,' followed the co-pilot.

'Received final confirmation code for arming of device,' said the captain.

'Requesting final verbal clearance from General Stephens,' said the co-pilot.

Over the satellite link, General Stephens' voice was crystal clear. 'This is General Stephens. You have my authority to proceed with Operation Fulcrum.'

'Voice recognition confirms General Stephens. Confirming order to proceed,' said the co-pilot.

'Confirmed,' returned the captain. 'Thirty seconds to drop-point.'

'Switching to computer-release mode,' said the co-pilot, reaching forward to engage the computer that would determine the exact moment of release from the B-5.

In the ops room, General Stephens was looking down at the satellite image of South Australia, staring intently. The tension was palpable.

Fletcher's hands were shaking mildly. He had to remind himself to breathe, his chest tight and shoulders clenched. Sarah was staring at General Stephens, unnerved by the real-time updates and hearing the calmness of the pilots.

Back in the B-5, a screen on the instrument panel flashed three times and a soft electronic beep sounded. 'Bomb is away. I repeat, Alpha bomb is released. Thirty seconds to detonation.'

General Stephens, who was stooped over the table staring at the image, looked up at Sarah.

Her heart missed a beat and she felt a punch in her chest. Leaning forward on the table to steady herself, she breathed deeply through her mouth.

The screen on the table went white — there was no sound, just bright white. The image on the screen zoomed out, providing a wider view of the area. The image now was of the entire continent. There was a large white bulge in the middle of South Australia, reflecting the intense heat generated by the explosion.

'Successful detonation of Alpha device,' said the captain. 'Continuing to drop point Bravo. ETA, two minutes.'

Finn stood outside the barn in the unusually mild, eucalyptus-scented air, staring out into the blackness. His bag was packed for the next morning. The idea of going back to the war made him feel anxious. But while in his heart he wanted to stay, he knew he couldn't.

'Hey,' said Jess, walking up behind him.

'Hey,' replied Finn, his voice sounding heavy.

'Wish you didn't have to go,' said Jess, smiling sadly. 'Who's going to do all the lifting around here now?'

'Oh, I'm so sorry! You might have to roll up your sleeves for a change,' said Finn, straight back at her.

'Nah, I'll just start a list of jobs you can do when you come back,' she said, bumping him playfully with her shoulder.

'You know this war could go on for years and years,' Finn said, serious now. 'I might be an old man by the time it's over.'

'Yeah, that's okay,' said Jess, quietly. 'I'll find a use for you, old man ...'

The flash of light on the horizon to the north-west was bright enough to silhouette the trees in the distance and make night into day. It flickered once, then softened into a sustained glow. Finn's immediate thought was lightning — but lightning didn't have a residual glow, or linger like this. It had dulled now into a menacing red glow.

'What the fuck was that?' exclaimed Finn, his body tensing and involuntarily straining upward.

'I don't know. It's not lightning,' said Jess, staring at the glow.

'It must be massive, whatever it is,' said Finn concerned. 'Where's your dad?'

'I'll go get him,' said Jess, turning to go back to the shed.

Finn stood staring at the glow, trying to work out where the light was coming from. A moment later he heard footsteps behind him as John and Jess joined him.

'I've never seen anything like it,' remarked John. 'Could be a bushfire, I suppose.'

'But it happened so quickly. It was a flash of light and then this glow — now it's fading quickly,' replied Finn.

A dull, sinister thud of a soundwave hit them — not so much a noise as a feeling in the chest, a vibration so deep it felt like a solid mass hitting them.

Panic swept over them all.

'Jesus, what the fuck,' Finn pulled Jess in tight to him.

John steadied himself by grabbing the wooden railing. 'Don't know what that was — but it ain't natural, that's for sure. Come on! Let's see if there's anything on the radio,' he said, turning hurriedly to go back into the shed.

John went to the radio while Finn shut the shed doors. John worked on the radio, hands trembling, trying to find a frequency.

Their minds were racing. Were they under attack? Were they going to die? What could they do?

Silence hung in the air.

'It's okay, guys,' said Finn, willing his heart to slow down. 'We're alive. It's going to be all right — just stay calm. Keep trying the radio. We have to get something.'

The static suddenly gave way to silence. After a pause that seemed to last forever, a newsreader's voice came through. 'This is breaking news. Nuclear bombs have been detonated in the northern area of South Australia, the Northern Territory, Western Australia and Far North Queensland. At this point, this is all the information we have. We will keep you updated as we learn more.' With that, the message repeated. John turned down the radio.

'Oh shit,' said Finn in an awed voice, 'they're nuking us.'

'Jesus, are we going to be all right?' asked Jess, moving closer.

'Dunno,' mumbled Finn.

'It makes sense, though,' said John. 'Doesn't it? The flash, the sound. None of it was caused by weather, that's for sure — it had to be from a bomb.'

'It does make sense, but what doesn't make sense is that they would do it in the first place,' said Finn, still staring at the radio, his mind working overtime.

Jess mused aloud. 'Why would the Chinese nuke this area? They've invested huge energy to secure the mines. Why nuke out here — where the mines are?'

Finn's mouth dropped open slightly, and he started blinking rapidly. 'I think we dropped them on ourselves. I think we nuked the mines and the Chinese port up in the gulf,' said Finn excitedly.

'What? There's no way the government would do that,' scoffed Jess, refusing to believe it.

'No,' Finn said, standing up, 'when I spoke to the army yesterday they said that most troops were involved in an operation to move people outside the demarcation lines that the government had established. I think they were moving people out of harm's way,' said Finn, more convinced of his theory with each word.

Both Jess and John contemplated the theory for a moment.

'Keep listening. They might say,' said John, looking back at the radio.

The three of them stayed up most of the night, debating and discussing the theory, checking the radio for news. But it just continually repeated the same news, shedding no new light.

The wick in the lantern cast only enough light to show their faces. Exhaustion soon took over and they all fell silent. Sleep came quickly to them. Even Finn couldn't hold off sleep, despite his mind doing its best to resist with thoughts of what would happen next. Perhaps, he hoped, this meant the war would be over. Or was a new, far worse war just beginning?

Chapter 23

In Beijing, Ambassador Xian received a call at 4 am, demanding his presence with Chairman Yun. Xian left his apartment in distress. To be summoned at this hour to see Yun could only mean bad news.

While he sat outside Chairman Yun's opulent, old-world-style office, waiting to be granted entry, his assistant briefed him on the news of what had happened in Australia.

'My God!' said Xian, genuinely stunned by the news, 'General Stephens must be insane to do that to his own country.'

At that moment one of the enormous, polished wooden doors opened smoothly. A young, impeccably suited woman silently ushered Xian into the room with only a very subtle gesture of her eyes and head.

Xian strode into the office. 'Chairman, I am aware of the actions of General Stephens and am shocked that he would make such an act of aggression on our mines. I assume there are to be retaliations,' started Xian, injecting enough anger into his voice to ensure Yun did not think him a coward.

'Yes, Xian,' said Yun from his richly upholstered chair. 'It is shocking, though it was always a risk. It seems we underestimated General Stephens. He has proven to be courageous to the point of insanity. A difficult breed of adversary.'

'Indeed. So what is our response?' Xian prompted respectfully. 'They cannot take nuclear action against China without consequences!'

Yun gave Xian a pitying look. 'Our response will be a pragmatic one, Xian. There will be no retribution, no further attacks on Australia — just a withdrawal of all remaining military forces.'

'But sir, are you not obliged to retaliate in kind?' Xian asked, shocked.

'I am not interested in wasting any more time or resources on what is now a nuclear wasteland. We must be smarter and use our heads, not our fists.'

Xian immediately relaxed. They were not going to retaliate. 'Of course, sir. You are wise in your decision.'

'Xian, you should well know that I am not interested in fighting wars,' Yun said wearily. 'I want only to grow our empire for the sake of our people. Australia no longer has anything that we need or desire. It is of no use to us.'

Xian's relief was obvious. He was fond of Australia, despite all that had happened, and would have been devastated if Yun had ordered nuclear retaliation.

'China needs you to re-establish diplomatic ties with Australia, Xian!' Yun said, smiling paternally at the ambassador.

'I will do my best,' Xian replied, 'but given the manner of my departure, I would be surprised if General Stephens would even accept my call.'

'Ensure he does, Xian — and ensure diplomacy is reinstated as soon as possible. Is that understood?' Yun asked, indicating their discussion was over.

'Yes, Chairman. I understand.' Xian turned and walked to the doors at the end of the vast office, sombre at the prospect of extending the hand of diplomacy.

In Canberra the morning after the bombings, there was full coverage of the events. The media sat in their rightful position, on the fence, providing arguments both for and against the actions taken by General Stephens. The journalists and media technicians at every major news provider quickly developed interactive maps and computer-generated re-enactments, detailing the extent of the destruction. Some pundits called for the general's immediate arrest. Some hailed him as a national hero, the saviour of Australia.

There were no reported civilian deaths in the attack, which helped General Stephens' cause immensely. Had just one Australian died in the attacks he would likely have been hung, drawn and quartered by the media and the public. Thankfully, the vast majority of the public supported the move. An overwhelming 89 per cent of Australians on the Social News feeds agreed with General Stephens' decision. The public very quickly decided that General Stephens was a hero — that he had acted selflessly, and with the nation's best interests at heart.

While the overwhelming majority supported the general, the victory over China came at such a cost that the mood of the country quickly came back to earth following the euphoria of defeating the invaders. An article in *The Australasian* captured the feeling perfectly:

> ... the deepest wounds throughout this terrible incident, by far, were inflicted on the environment. The repercussions of the bombs will be felt for a long time. Environmentalists are right to be furious that General Stephens took such extreme measures to rid Australia of the Chinese. Their argument that he rid us of one enemy but introduced another, far greater one to the environment, is in many ways right. But for most Australians it is the lesser of two insidious evils.
>
> The Aboriginal First Nation Coalition party leader, Sam Hislop, agreed that General Stephens' actions were, under the circumstances, warranted and he endorsed them. As he points out, the nuclear wasteland of the inland of South Australia, created in a microsecond by the bombs, is what the Chinese would have spent a decade creating.
>
> Many things changed when the Chinese invaded. The lucky country became the desperate country, and then, under the leadership of General Stephens, the courageous country. The nation has proven its resilience in the face of true adversity. What remains to be seen is how we will move forward, how we will prosper without the endowment of

natural resources and, most importantly, how we will adapt to ensure we are never again an occupied country.

General Stephens was also lauded internationally. In the succeeding months, the Americans performed the role of his personal global PR machine. They made General Stephens an honorary citizen of the United States and awarded him the Medal of Honour, their highest decoration. It was, of course, in America's interests to celebrate a leader who turned to them for help in his country's time of need. Clearly, the bombings had also cemented US primacy in the Asia-Pacific. Once again, the US felt like the dominant force in the region — a position it wanted to maintain for as long as possible, even though it was clear their projection of power was now limited to tactical nuclear methods. Their military resources were stretched too far, their domestic economy too fragile to be involved on any other level. No longer could Australia rely on the ANZUS agreement. The country had to take control of its own security.

This was just one of the things on General Stephens' mind as he sat at his desk in his new office outside the SOF, signing documents. The moment the Chinese withdrew, he vowed to spend as little time in the underground bunker as humanly possible, and moved his team above ground. The sun streamed through the window behind him, cutting a bright path as it illuminated small flecks of dust caught in the beam. It was mid-morning and he was in his productive zone, burning through the workload. In the three months since the Chinese withdrawal, he had regained his youthful energy. He even looked younger.

There was a knock on the door, but he didn't look up. 'Come in,' he called out, continuing signing papers.

'Morning, Marty. Mind if I come in?' asked Fletcher politely.

'You don't normally ask, Fletch,' replied General Stephens, now looking up from his documents.

'Well, I have some news.'

'What is it?' General Stephens took off his reading glasses, his curiosity piqued by his old friend's seriousness.

'Well, Marty. It's been a hell of a year …' Fletcher started.

'No denying that.'

'And well, to cut to it, I've had enough,' Fletcher finished. 'It's time, Marty.'

'Time for what?'

'Time to pull up stumps. I'm done. I'm retiring.'

General Stephens smiled. 'It's funny, I've been thinking of doing the same.'

'It feels like the right time.'

'I agree, and I graciously accept your resignation, Fletch,' Stephens said, smiling.

'Thanks. I hoped you'd understand,' said Fletcher, more relaxed.

'I won't be far behind you. I promised to step down once this mess was over, and I intend on doing just that.'

'Glad to hear it, Marty. When?'

'Soon. Just need to make sure this defence blueprint gets signed off so that Sarah and Draven can start to implement it,' Stephens said, gesturing at the image on his screen.

'How long do you think?'

'God knows,' said Stephens, sighing. 'The budget side of it won't be a problem, even though we're more than quadrupling it. The problem will be the social changes.'

'That's it, isn't it — the toughest thing will be getting people to recognise we need a defence culture, not just a defence budget,' said Fletcher.

'Precisely. I like that, mind if I use it?'

'My gift to you,' replied Fletcher with a smile. 'It's a big job, mate. Glad I don't have to deal with it!'

'This is our one chance to get it right and set in motion a change of culture,' said Stephens, mulling over the enormity of it.

'I agree, but I also think getting the compulsory military service bill passed will be harder than defeating the Chinese!' Fletcher laughed.

'Don't joke, mate. I reckon you could be right,' replied Stephens, smiling. 'Actually, the hardest thing is yet to come. Building this country back up without the wealth from resources — it's a whole new paradigm for our economy and it's going to be a long road back.'

'Too true.' Fletch stood and headed for the door. He paused with his hand on the doorknob and turned to face his friend. 'Thanks, Marty. Was a hell of a year.'

'See you around, Fletch,' said General Stephens, watching him leave the room.

Stephens sat playing with his glasses. Swivelling his chair, he turned his back on the screen practically bursting with paperwork and stared out the window, watching the leaves on the trees outside playing in the sunlight.

'One hell of a year …' he murmured to himself.

Chapter 24

The one o'clock sun was at its merciless worst, beating down on all those who stood under it. Finn and John had been out most of the morning mending fences — a bad enough job without 37-degree temperatures. Walking towards the kitchen, Finn took off his dusty Akubra and used his neck scarf to wipe the sweat and dirt from his brow. He squinted in the direct sunlight, creasing his deeply tanned face.

Up the steps and into the relative cool of the veranda, Finn could smell the aroma of lunch coming from the kitchen. The unmistakable aroma of pan-fried steak made his dry mouth water. Dropping his hat on the bench seat outside the door and taking off his neck scarf and boots, he opened the flyscreen. Stepping inside, it took a moment for Finn's eyes to adjust to the light.

'Hey, take a seat. I've got a steak and salad ready to go,' said Jess, greeting Finn with a smile.

'Thanks. What a morning! Once again your old man is working me to within an inch of my life,' said Finn, taking a seat and reaching for the glass of water on the table.

'You should both be taking it easy out in that heat today. One of you will pass out,' said Jess, tipping the steak onto a plate.

'Yeah, it'll be me that does it, too,' said Finn, rubbing his face.

'Here you go,' said Jess, putting the plate on the table. 'Where's Dad? Is he coming in?'

'He said he'll be in shortly. Think he was going down to check on the guys doing the fencing in the bottom paddock,' replied Finn around a mouthful of steak.

The distant sound of an engine made them both look up at one another. 'Not expecting anyone today, are we?' asked Finn.

'No. Might be the builders?' Jess suggested, shrugging.

Finn got up from the table and walked to the kitchen window to see who was visiting them unannounced. Looking out, he saw that it was a military 4x4 — the kind they used out in the desert. The vehicle drove past the fence and up the driveway, coming to a stop outside the house in a cloud of dust.

'Stay here,' said Finn, walking to the door. Jess took his place at the kitchen window.

Outside, Finn stood on the veranda, watching the vehicle suspiciously. No one got out and, from what Finn could make out, there was only one person in the truck. But the windows were so dusty he couldn't see who it was.

Though the engine was switched off, it was ticking as it began to cool, the metal contracting.

Finally, the driver's door opened. Slowly the driver stepped out, walking around the front of the vehicle, allowing Finn to see who it was.

'Sarge!' yelled Finn, starting down off the veranda.

'Hunt. Finally tracked you down,' replied Higgins, walking with a limp to greet Finn.

The two men embraced hard, slapping each other's backs.

'It's good to see you, Sarge,' said Finn, grinning broadly. 'I tried to find out what happened to you guys after the bridge mission, but it was impossible getting anything useful out of the army.'

'You know the army,' drawled Higgins, 'can't make anything too easy.'

Finn stared at Higgins. It was strange to see him again. His face was clean and no longer permanently sunburnt. He looked 10 years younger. He was dressed in a light blue shirt, tucked into dark grey combats. Almost normal.

'Come on inside, out of the heat,' Finn said, moving towards the house. 'I want you to meet Jess.'

Stepping into the cool of the kitchen, Finn introduced Jess.

'Hello, Jess,' Higgins said politely. 'Lovely to meet you.'

'You too. So you fought with Finn then?' asked Jess, somewhat suspiciously.

'Yes, I had the distinct pleasure of leading Hunt here into both his first and last battles,' Higgins said, smiling.

'Well, you two must have a lot to catch up on,' said Jess, moving away. 'Think I'll leave you to it.'

'Thanks, Jess,' said Finn, watching her leave. 'Take a seat, mate,' he gestured to Higgins. 'Can I get you anything?'

'Just a water, thanks. After the war I swore never to come back out to the desert again, so you should feel pretty bloody special that I would break my promise to come and see you.'

'Thanks, mate. You could have just called,' remarked Finn, chuckling.

'Smart ass.'

'So what's been happening?' asked Finn.

'Before I get into that, tell me what happened to you and Carver. The last I saw of you two, we were tearing through the bush being chased by a bunch of angry Chinks — pissed off that we'd blown up their bridge.'

Finn looked down at the table momentarily, his smile erased. He crossed his arms. 'Mate, what can I say? It was fucking crazy.'

'I know it was. I was there, remember? But what the hell happened to you two?' Higgins insisted.

Finn squirmed. He didn't want to talk about it. 'Okay. So when it all went to shit we began moving back, not far behind you lot. I saw Carver take a round in the shoulder, so I went back to get him. Everything was happening so quickly, by the time I had him up and moving we were cut off from you guys. I don't actually remember what happened but next thing I know I'm coming to in a shed, tied up and with a cracking headache. And I hear these screams, these fucking awful screams, you know,' he nodded to himself. 'And it wakes me up pretty quickly, yeah. So, I'm trying to figure out what the hell I'm going to do when the door opens and they drop Carver down. They'd been torturing him. Pulled his front fucking teeth out. They hadn't even asked him a single question, the sick bastards.'

Higgins was listening intently now. Nodding.

'I'm lying there and this officer comes up to me, right, and leans down and just says, "You're next". That scared me, mate, because I'm looking at Carver and thinking he's going to do that to me.'

'Fucking sick bastards. Did you get the officer's name?'

'No, nothing.'

'Damn,' said Higgins, looking away.

'So, anyway,' Finn resumed, 'I managed to cut the ropes and find an opening in the shed. I pulled back a corner of corrugated iron and dragged Carver out with me. He's able to walk, but then, about 50 metres from the shed, we're spotted and all hell breaks loose. We're going as fast as we can, but there's no way he's going to outrun them. Our only chance is to get into the bush and hide. Then Carver gets hit ...'Finn paused a moment and drank some water. He noticed that his hands were shaking. Breathing deeply, he tried to slow himself down.

'It's all right, mate. Take your time,' said Higgins encouragingly.

'Yep. I haven't told this to anyone,' Finn exhaled. 'Thought I was okay with it, but it's hard when you talk about it.'

'I know, but it helps in the long run — trust me.'

'So Carver's hit, I've got his blood and brains all over me. And I'm standing there in the dark, and these Chinese fuckers are coming down on me fast. So I run for it. I don't check Carver. I'm pretty sure he's dead, but I didn't check. I just leave him and I leg it as fast as I can ...' Finn choked back hard. The emotion had been rising in his chest and he felt a huge lump rising in his throat. 'I was so bloody scared. There was no way they were going to do that to me, no way, no fucking way,' Finn snorted, the snot running down his throat, and he wiped angrily at the tears in his eyes.

'It's all right,' Higgins extended his arm across the corner of the table and gripped Finn's shoulder. 'I'd have done exactly the same thing — you were acting on instinct. You didn't have time to stop and check his vital signs, you were operating in survival mode and your instincts took over — and they knew what to do. When you're acting on instincts you don't need to think, they do that for you way faster than your mind can. In that situation, your instincts are right on and, I know you, you've got good instincts. Carver was dead. Deep down you knew that, and you kept running to stay alive. That's why we've got instincts — they look after us. Y'know what I mean?'

Finn had calmed down now and was staring at Higgins with bloodshot eyes 'Yep, I know. It's just hard coming to terms with it, with the guilt.'

'You gotta let it go — it's the only way to survive.' Higgins looked Finn straight in the eye and held his gaze for a long time.

Finn nodded.

'I'll try, mate. Thanks. So what about you, then?' Finn asked, desperate to change the subject and take control of his emotions.

'Well, I resigned from the army after the Chinese pulled out — had enough. Didn't last long though, 'cos I'm back. But this time I'm private army — for IXR Mining. The pay's much better, travel is good and most of the time it's just glorified security work.' Higgins shrugged.

'Nice one,' said Finn, not surprised. It seemed like Higgins was made for that life. 'Sounds like a good move.'

'Yeah, which is part of the reason for finding you,' said Higgins, sizing Finn up. 'I'm recruiting some men for a job in Canada, up near the Arctic. I need good men: men who know how to get a job done. It's a bit different from here, as you can imagine, but I'm hoping you might be interested.'

Finn played with his glass, rolling it around in circles on its edge, staring at the old wooden table, avoiding Higgins' eyes.

'The money is really good. You'd be gone three months and that would be it. Canada's great at this time of year,' Higgins said hopefully.

But Finn wasn't thinking of the money or the country — he was thinking of the thrill of action, of being part of a team again. Turning his head to look out the window, he saw Jess walking back from the barn. As a gust of wind kicked up dust around her, she squinted and put her hand to her old Akubra to keep it from flying off.

He turned back to Higgins. 'Nah mate, not interested,' he said.

Higgins nodded slowly and followed his gaze. 'Fair enough. If I had a woman like Jess, don't think I'd go anywhere either,' he said with a wink.

Finn smiled. 'She's not my woman, mate.'

'Sure, sure. Well,' he said, standing, 'I better be on my way. Long drive back to town.'

Finn walked him out to the truck and held out his hand to shake.

Higgins looked at him again, squinting in the orange sunlight, now lower in the sky. 'You take it easy, soldier,' said Higgins, shaking his hand.

'You too, Sarge. Watch your back out there.'

Higgins nodded. 'Call me if you change your mind.'

'I will mate. Drive safe,' said Finn.

Higgins turned without another word, climbed into the truck, started the engine, saluted Finn and drove off down the driveway.

Finn returned the salute — then stood, hands on hips, his eyes squinting as he watched the truck bounce down the dirt road, red dust-cloud trailing behind. Turning back toward the homestead, he saw Jess leaning against the doorway. She smiled at him. Finn smiled and started walking back. As he did, he couldn't help twisting and looking back one more time at Higgins, disappearing down the road.

THANKS

Firstly, to my wife Kate, without your support, belief and advice, none of this would have been realised. My editor, Allison Hiew, for your enthusiasm and the clarity you brought to the story. Rochelle Ransom for your detail and finishing touches. Kamal Sarma, you were ground zero in terms of inspiring me to write, you are a true architect of life. Tabitha Fairbarn, Marie-Claire Sayers and Michael Gibb for your help and guidance in publicising the story. Georgie Spencer and Grant Henderson whose creativity and vision made for a cracking cover design. Sam Robertson, for the professional advice. Andrew Norris for the support and understanding. And last, but by no means least, Bill Athanassiou, Steve O'Connor, Chris Walton, Ed Harrison, Christiaan Van Vuuren and Tom Charles – thanks for following the black line with me all those mornings.